"Thank you."

Megan leaned to kiss his cheek in a heartfelt thank-you just as he turned to answer.

Their lips brushed. Just barely skimmed, but a crackle shot through her so tangibly she could have sworn the storm had returned with a bolt of lightning.

Gasping, she angled back, her eyes wide, his inscrutable.

"Um." She inched along the riser. "I need to get Evie, and um, thank you."

She shot to her feet, racing toward her daughter, away from the temptation to test the feeling and kiss him again.

That wasn't what she'd expected. At all. But then nothing about Whit had ever been predictable, damn his sexy body, hot kiss and hero's rescue.

* * *

Sheltered by the Millionaire
is a Texas Cattleman's Club: After the Storm
novel—As a Texas town rebuilds, love heals
all wounds...

SHELTERED BY
THE MILLIONAIRE

BY
CATHERINE MANN

Published in Great Britain 2014
by Mills & Boon, an imprint of Harlequin (UK) Limited,
Eton House, 18-24 Paradise Road, Richmond, Surrey, TW9 1SR

© 2014 Harlequin Books S.A.

Special thanks and acknowledgement are given to Catherine Mann for her contribution to the TEXAS CATTLEMAN'S CLUB: AFTER THE STORM series.

ISBN: 978-0-263-91483-2

51-1114

Harlequin (UK) Limited's policy is to use papers that are natural, renewable and recyclable products and made from wood grown in sustainable forests. The logging and manufacturing processes conform to the legal environmental regulations of the country of origin.

Printed and bound in Spain
by CPI, Barcelona

USA TODAY bestselling author **Catherine Mann** lives on a sunny Florida beach with her flyboy husband and their four children. With more than forty books in print in over twenty countries, she has also celebrated wins for both a RITA® Award and a Booksellers' Best Award. Catherine enjoys chatting with readers online—thanks to the wonders of the internet, which allows her to network with her laptop by the water! Contact Catherine through her website, www.catherinemann.com, find her on Facebook and Twitter (@CatherineMann1), or reach her by snail mail at PO Box 6065, Navarre, FL 32566, USA.

To my parents, Brice and Sandra Woods.
Thank you for the joyous gift of always having
pets in my life as a child.

One

The airbag inflated. Hard. Fast.

Pain exploded through Megan Maguire. From the bag hitting her in the face. From her body slamming against the seat. But it wasn't nearly as excruciating as the panic pumping through her as she faced the latest obstacle in reaching her daughter after a tornado.

A *tornado* for God's sake.

Her insides quivered with fear and her body ached from the impact. The wind howled outside her small compact car on the lonely street, eerily abandoned for 4:30 on a weekday afternoon. Apparently she was the only one stupid enough to keep driving in spite of the weather warnings of a tornado nearby. In fact, reports of the twister only made her more determined. She had to get to her daughter.

Megan punched her way clear of the deflating airbag to find a shattered windshield. The paw-shaped air freshener still swayed, dangling from her rearview mirror and releasing a hint of lavender. Files from work were scattered all over the floor from sliding off the seat along with the bag containing her daughter's Halloween costume. Then Megan looked outside and she damn near hyperventilated.

The hood of her sedan was covered by a downed tree. Steam puffed from the engine.

If the thick oak had fallen two seconds later, it would have landed on the roof of her car. She could have been crushed. She could have died.

Worst of all, her daughter would have become an orphan for all intents and purposes since Evie's father had never wanted anything to do with her. Panic pushed harder on Megan's chest like a cement slab.

Forcing oxygen back into her lungs one burning gasp at a time, she willed her racing heart to slow. Nothing would stop her from getting to her daughter. Not a totaled car. Not a downed tree. And definitely not…a…panic…attack.

Gasping for air, she flung open the door and stepped into the aftermath of the storm. Sheeting rain and storm winds battered her. Thank heaven she'd already left work to pick up her daughter for a special outing before they announced the tornado warning on her radio. If she'd been at the shelter when the warning sirens went off she wouldn't have been able to leave until given the okay.

But if she'd left at 1:00 to go to the movie as they'd originally planned, Evie would have been with her, safe and sound.

As a single mom, Megan needed her job as an animal shelter director. Evie's father had hit the road the minute Megan had told him about the unexpected pregnancy.

Any attempts at child support had been ignored until he faded from sight somewhere in the Florida Keys. She'd finally accepted he was gone from her life and Evie's. She could only count on herself.

Determination fueled her aching body. She was less than a mile from her daughter's Little Tots Daycare. She would walk every step of the way if she had to. Rain plastered her khakis and work shirt to her body. Thank goodness her job called for casual wear. She would have been hard pressed to climb over the downed tree in heels.

At least the tornado had passed, but others could finger down from the gathering clouds at any minute. With every fiber of her being she prayed the worst was over. She had to get to her daughter, to be sure she was safe.

The small cottage that housed Little Tots Daycare had appeared so cute and appealing when she'd chosen it for Evie. Now, she could only think how insubstantial the structure would be against the force of such a strong storm. What if Evie was trapped inside?

Sweeping back a clump of soggy red hair, Megan clambered over the tree trunk and back onto the road strewn with debris. She took in the devastation ahead, collapsed buildings and overturned cars. The town had been spun and churned, pieces of everyday life left lining the street. Glass from blown-out windows. Papers and furniture from businesses. Pictures and books. The tornado's path was clear, like a massive mower had cut through the land. Uprooting trees, slicing through lives, spewing a roof or a computer like it was nothing more than a blade of grass sliced and swept away.

She picked her way past half of a splintered door. Wind whistled through the trees, bending and creaking the towering oaks. But she didn't hear the telltale train sound that preceded a tornado.

Thoughts of Evie scared and waiting dumped acid on Megan's gut. Even knowing the Little Tots Daycare workers were equipped to handle the crisis didn't quell her fears. Evie was her daughter.

Her world.

She would trudge through this storm, tear her way through the wreckage, do anything to reach her four-year-old child. The roar of the wind was calling to her, urging her forward until she could have sworn she actually heard someone speaking to her. *Megan. Megan. Megan.* Had she sustained a concussion from the wreck?

She searched around her, pushing her shoulder-length hair from her face, and spotted a handful of people every bit as reckless as her venturing outside for one reason or another. None of them looked her way...except for a looming man, a familiar man, charging down the steps of one of the many buildings owned by Daltry Property Management. For three and a half years, Whit Daltry had been a major pain in the neck whenever they'd crossed paths, which she tried to make as infrequently as possible.

The fates were really ganging up on her today.

Whit shouted, "Megan? Megan! Come inside before you get hurt."

"No," she shouted. "I can't."

His curse rode the wind as he jogged toward her. Tall and muscular, a force to be reckoned with, he plowed ahead, his Stetson impervious to the wind. Raindrops sheeted off the brim of his hat, as his suit coat and tie whipped to and fro.

He stopped alongside her, his brown eyes snapping with anger, warm hand clasping her arm. "I couldn't .

believe it when I saw you through the window. What are you doing out in this weather?"

"Dancing in the rain," she snapped back, hysteria threatening to overwhelm her. "What do you think I'm doing? I'm trying to get to Evie. I had already left the shelter when the tornado hit. A tree fell on my car so I had to walk."

His jaw flexed, his eyes narrowing. "Where is your daughter?"

She tugged her arm free. "She's at Little Tots Day-care. I have to go to her."

And what a time to remember this man was the very reason she didn't work closer to her daughter's pre-school. When the shelter had decided to build a new fa-cility shortly after she'd signed on as director three and a half years ago, Whit had started off their acquaintance by blocking the purchase of land near his offices—which also happened to be near the day care. The Safe Haven's board of directors had been forced to choose an alternate location. Now the shelter was located in a more industrial area farther from her daughter. Every single work day, Megan lost time with Evie because of an arbitrary decision by this man.

And now, he could have cost her so much more if something had happened to Evie.

Whit grasped her arms again, more firmly this time, peering at her from under the brim of his hat. "I'll get your daughter. You need to take shelter until the weather clears. There could be more tornadoes."

"You don't know me very well if you think I'll even entertain that idea." She grabbed his suit coat lapels. "There's no way I'm sitting in a gas station bathroom hugging my knees and covering my head while my Evie is out there scared. She's probably crying for me."

"Look at the roads—" He waved to the street full of branches and overturned vehicles. "They're blocked here too. Only a truck or heavy-duty SUV would stand a chance of getting through."

"I'll run, walk or crawl my way there. It's not that much farther."

He bit off another curse and scrubbed his strong jaw with one hand. "Fine. If I can't convince you, then we might as well get moving. Hopefully, my truck can four-wheel it over the debris and drive that last two blocks a lot faster than you can walk. Are you okay with that?"

"Seriously? Yes. Let's go." Relief soaked into her, nearly buckling her knees.

Whit led her back to the redbrick building and into the parking garage, his muscular arm along her back helping her forge ahead. Time passed in a fugue as she focused on one thing. Seeing her daughter.

Thumbing the key remote, Whit unlocked the large blue truck just ahead of them and started the engine from outside the truck. She ran the last few steps, yanked open the passenger door and crawled inside the top-of-the-line vehicle, surprisingly clean for a guy, with no wrenches or files or gym bag on the floor. No child's Halloween costume or box of recycling like what she had in her destroyed car, and— Oh, God, her mind was on overdrive from adrenaline. The warmth of the heater blasted over her wet body. Her teeth chattered. From the cold or shock? She wasn't sure and didn't care.

She could only think of her child. "Thank you for doing this, Whit."

"We may have had our differences, but these are extraordinary circumstances." He looked at her intensely for an instant as he set his hat on the seat between them. "Your daughter will be fine. That day care building may look small but it's rock solid, completely up to code. And that's me speaking as a professional in property management."

"I understand that in my mind." Megan tapped her temple. "But in my heart?" Her hand trembled as it fluttered to her chest. "The fears and what-ifs can't be quieted."

"You're a mother. That's understandable." He shifted the truck into four-wheel drive and accelerated out of the parking lot, crunching over debris, cracked concrete and churned earth. "How did the shelter fare in the storm?"

Her gut clenched all over again as she thought of all the precious charges in her care. "I wasn't there. I'd already left to pick up Evie when the warning siren went off. The kennel supervisor is in charge and I trust him, completely, but telephone service is out."

She felt torn in two. But she had a stellar staff in place at the shelter. They were trained to respond and rescue in disaster scenarios. She'd just never expected to use that training to find her child.

Already the rain was easing, the storm passing as quickly as it had hit. Such a brief time for so much change to happen. And there could be worse waiting for her—

The worst.

Her chin trembled, tears of panic nearly choking her. "I was supposed to take the whole afternoon off to go to a movie with Evie, but we had a sick employee leave early and a mother dog in labor dumped off with us… If I had kept my promise I would have been at the afternoon matinee with Evie rather than copping out for a later show. God, she must be so terrified—" She pressed her wrist to her mouth to hold back a sob.

"You can't torture yourself with what-ifs," he said matter-of-factly. "There was no way to see this coming and no way to know where it would be safe. You were doing your job, supporting your child. Deep breaths. Be calm for your kid."

She scrubbed her wrist under her eyes. "You're right. She'll be more frightened if she sees me freaking out."

Whit turned the corner onto the street for the Little Tots Daycare. The one-story wooden cottage was still standing but had sustained significant damage.

The aluminum roof was crunched like an accordion, folded in on the wooden porch. Already other parents and a couple of volunteer emergency responders were picking through the rubble. The porch supports had fallen like broken matches, the thick wooden beams cracked and splintered so that the main entrance was completely blocked.

Megan's heart hit her shoes.

Before she could find her breath, Whit had already jogged to her side of the truck and opened the door.

"No," she choked out a whisper. She fell into his arms, her legs weak with fear, her whole body stiff from the accident. Pain shot up her wrists where, she realized, she had burns from the airbag deployment.

None of it mattered. Her eyes focused on that fallen roof. The blocked door. More acid churned in her stomach as she thought of her little girl stuck inside.

"I've got you," Whit reassured her, rain dripping from the brim of his Stetson.

"I'm okay. You can let go. I have to find my daughter."

"And I'm going to help you do that. I have construction experience and we need to be careful our help doesn't cause more damage."

No wonder the other parents weren't tearing apart the fallen debris to get inside.

"Of course, you're right." Hands quaking, she pressed a palm to her forehead. "I'm sorry. I'm not thinking clearly."

"That's understandable. We'll get to your daughter soon. You have my word."

Whit led her past the debris of the front porch, then around to the side, where the swing sets were uprooted, the jungle gym twisted into a macabre new shape. Painted Halloween pumpkins had scattered and burst. He called out to the handful of people picking at the lumber on the porch, offering advice as he continued to lead Megan around to the back of the building. The gaggle of frantic parents listened without argument, desperate.

She couldn't imagine a world without her daughter.

In her first trimester, she'd planned to give her baby up for adoption. She'd gotten the paperwork from a local adoption agency. Then she'd felt the flutter of life inside her and she'd torn up the paperwork. From that point on, she'd opted for taking life one day at a time. The moment when she'd seen her daughter's newborn face with bright eyes staring trustingly up at her, she'd lost her heart totally.

Evie was four years old now, those first sprigs of red hair having grown into precious corkscrew curls. And Megan had a rewarding job that also paid the bills and supported her daughter. It hadn't been easy by any stretch, but she'd managed. Until today.

Whit guided her to the back of the building, which was blessedly undamaged. The back door was intact. Secure. Safe. She'd been right to come with him. She would have dived straight into the porch rubble rather than thinking to check....

Megan yanked out of Whit's grip and pounded on the door. Through the pane she could see the kids lined up on the floor with their teachers. No one seemed in a panic.

The day care supervisor pulled the door open.

"Sue Ellen," Megan clasped her hand, looking around her to catch sight of her daughter. "Where's Evie?"

"She's okay." The silver-haired supervisor wearing a smock covered in finger paints and dust patted Megan's hand. The older woman seemed calm, in control, when she must be shaking in her sensible white sneakers. "She's with a teacher's assistant and three other students. They were on their way to the kitchen when the tornado sirens went off. So she's at the other end of the building."

Sue Ellen paused and Megan's heart tripped over itself. "What are you not telling me?"

"There's a beam from the roof blocking her from coming out. But she's fine. The assistant is keeping the kids talking and calm."

Megan pressed a hand to her chest. "Near the porch? The collapsed roof?"

Whit gripped her shoulder. "I've got it."

Without another word, he raced down the corridor. Megan followed, dimly registering that he'd clasped her hand. And she didn't pull away from the comfort. They finally stopped short at a blocked hall, the emergency lighting illuminating the passageway beyond the crisscross of broken beams and cracked plaster. Dust made the image hazy, almost surreal. The teacher's assistant sat beside the row of students, Evie on the end, her bright red curls as unmistakable as the mismatched orange and purple outfit she'd insisted on wearing this morning because the colors reminded her Halloween was coming.

"Evie?" Megan shouted. "Evie, honey, it's Mommy."

"Mommy?" her daughter answered faintly, a warble in her voice. "I wanna go home."

Whit angled past Megan and crouched down to assess the crisscross of boards, cracked drywall and ceiling tiles. 'Stand back, kids, while I clear a path through."

The teacher's assistant guided them all a few feet away and wrapped her arms around them protectively as fresh dust showered down. With measured precision, Whit moved boards aside, his muscles bulging as he hefted aside plank after plank with an ease Megan envied until finally he'd cleared a pathway big enough for people to crawl through. Evie's freckled face peeked from the cluster of kids, her nose scrunched and sweet cherub smile beaming. She appeared unharmed.

Relief made Megan's legs weak. Whit's palm slid along her waist for a steadying second before he reached into the two-foot opening, arms outstretched. "Evie, I'm a friend of your mommy's here to help you. Can I lift you through here?"

Megan nodded, holding back the tears that were welling up fast. "Go to Mr. Whit, honey."

Evie raised her arms and Whit hauled her up and free, cradling her to his chest in broad, gentle hands. Megan took in every inch of her daughter, seeing plenty of dirt but nothing more than a little tear of one sleeve of her Disney princess shirt, revealing a tiny scrape. Somehow she'd come through the whole ordeal safely.

Once they reached the bottom of the rubble, Whit passed Evie to her mother. "Here ya go, kiddo."

Evie melted against Megan with one of those shuddering sighs of relief that relayed more than tears how frightened she had been. Evie wrapped her tiny arms around Megan's neck and held on tightly like a spider monkey, and it was Megan's turn to feel the shudder of relief so strong she nearly fell to her knees.

Thank you, thank you, thank you, God. Her baby was safe.

"You're okay, sweetie?"

"I'm fine, Mommy. The t'naydo came and I was a very brave girl. I did just what Miss Vicky told me to do. I sat under the stairs and hugged my knees tight with one arm and I held my friend Caitlyn's hand 'cause she was scared."

"You did well, Evie, I'm so proud of you." She kissed her daughter's forehead, taking in the hint of her daughter's favorite raspberry shampoo. "I love you so much."

"Love you, too, Mommy." She squeezed hard, holding on tightly as Whit helped the other students through.

Once the last child stepped free, Whit urged everyone to file away from the damaged part of the building. He led them down the hall to where Sue Ellen had gathered the children in the auditorium, playing music and passing out cookies and books to the students whose parents hadn't arrived to pick them up. The school nurse made the rounds checking each child, dispensing Band-Aids when needed.

Whit's hand went to the small of Megan's back again with an ease she didn't have the energy to wonder about right now.

"Megan, you should see the nurse about your scratches from the accident. The air bag has left some burns that could use antiseptic too—"

She shook her head. "I will later. For now she's got

her hands full with the children and they need her more."

Evie squirmed in her arms. "Can I get a cookie? I'm reallllly hungry."

"Of course, sweetie." She gave her daughter another hug, not sure when she would ever be okay with letting her out of her sight.

Evie raced across the gym floor as if the whole world hadn't just been blown upside down. Literally.

Whit laughed softly. "Resilient little scrap."

"More so than her mom, I'm afraid." Megan sagged and sat down on the metal riser.

"All Evie knows is that everyone is okay and you're here." Whit sat beside her, his leg pressing a warm reassurance against hers. "Maybe we should get you one of those cookies and a cup of that juice."

"I'm okay. Really. We should go back to clearing the debris outside." She braced her shoulders. "I'm being selfish in keeping you all to myself."

"All the children are accounted for and the teachers have them well in hand. It's getting dark. I think cleanup will be on hold until the morning."

What kind of carnage would the morning reveal? Outside, sirens had wailed for the last twenty minutes. "I should take Evie and check back in at the shelter. Local animal control will need our help with housing displaced pets."

"Civilians aren't allowed on the road just yet and you don't have a car." He nudged her with his shoulder. "Face it, Megan. You can actually afford to take a few minutes to catch your breath."

The concern in his brown eyes was genuine. The warmth she saw there washed over her like a jolt of pure java, stimulating her senses. Why hadn't she ever noticed before what incredibly intense and expressive eyes he had? Sure, she'd noticed he was sexy, but then any woman who crossed his path would appreciate Whit Daltry's charismatic good looks. And in fact, that had been a part of what turned her off for the past three years—how easily women fell into his arms. She'd let herself be conned by a man like that and it had turned her life upside down.

But the warmth in his eyes now, the caring he'd shown in helping her get to Evie today presented a new side to Whit she'd never seen before. He might not be romance material for her, but he'd been a good guy just now and that meant a lot to a woman who didn't accept help easily.

She slumped back against the riser behind her. "Thank you for what you did for me today—for me and for Evie. I know you would have done the same for anyone stranded on the road." As she said the words she realized they were true. Whit wasn't the one-dimensional bad guy she'd painted him to be the past few years. There were layers to the man. "Still, the fact is, you were there for my child and I'll never forget that."

He smiled, his brown eyes twinkling with a hint of his devilish charm. "Does that mean I'm forgiven for refusing to let the shelter build on that tract of land you wanted so much?"

Layers. Definitely. Good—and bad. "I may be grateful, but I didn't develop amnesia."

He chuckled, a low rumble that drew a laugh from her, and before she knew what she was doing, she dropped her hand to his shoulder and squeezed.

"Thank you." She leaned to kiss his cheek in a heartfelt thank-you just as he turned to answer.

Their lips brushed. Just barely skimmed, but a crackle shot through her so tangibly she could have sworn the storm had returned with a bolt of lightning.

Gasping, she angled back, her eyes wide, his inscrutable.

She inched along the riser. "I need to get Evie…and um, thank you."

She shot to her feet, racing toward her daughter, away from the temptation to test the feeling and kiss him again.

That wasn't what she'd expected. At all. But then nothing about Whit had ever been predictable, damn his sexy body, hot kiss and hero's rescue. She'd been every bit as gullible as her mother once. And while she could never regret having Evie in her life, she damn well wouldn't fall victim to trusting an unworthy man again. She owed it to Evie to set a better example, to break the cycle the women in her family seemed destined to repeat.

And if that meant giving up any chance for another toe-searing kiss from Whit Daltry, then so be it.

Two

Six Weeks Later

The wild she-cat in his arms left scratches on his shoulders.

Whit Daltry adjusted his hold on the long-haired calico, an older female kitten that had wandered—scraggly and with no collar—onto the doorstep of his Pine Valley home. Luckily, he happened to know the very attractive director of Royal's Safe Haven Animal Shelter.

He stepped out of his truck and kicked the door closed, early morning sunshine reflecting off his windshield. Not a cloud in the sky, unlike that fateful day the F4 tornado had ripped through Royal, Texas. The shelter had survived unscathed, but the leaves had been stripped from the trees, leaving branches unnaturally bare for this region of Texas, even in November. The town bore lasting scars from that day that would take a lot longer to heal than the scratches from the frantic calico.

He should have gotten one of those pet carriers or a box to transport the cat. If the beast clawed its way out of his arms, chances were the scared feline would bolt away and be tough as hell to catch again. Apparently he wasn't adept at animal rescue.

That was Megan's expertise.

The thought of seeing her again sent anticipation coursing through him as each step brought him closer to the single-story brick structure. Heaven knew he could use a distraction from life right now. For six weeks, ever since they'd shared that kiss after the tornado, he'd been looking for an excuse to see her, but the town had been in chaos clearing the debris. Some of his properties had been damaged as well. He owned multiple apartment buildings and rental homes all over town. And while he might have a lighthearted approach to his social life, he was serious when it came to business and was always damn sure going to be there for his tenants when they needed him.

He'd thrown himself into the work to distract himself from the biggest loss of all—the death of his good friend Craig Richardson in the storm. It had sent him into shock for the first couple of weeks, as he grieved for Craig and tried to find ways to help his pal's widow. God, they were all still in a tailspin and he didn't know if he would be in any better shape by the memorial service that was scheduled for after Thanksgiving.

So he focused on restoring order to the town, the only place he'd ever called home after a rootless childhood being evicted from place after place. And with each clean-up operation, he thought back to the day of the storm, to clearing aside the rubble in the day care.

To Megan's kiss afterward.

Sure the kiss had been impulsive and motivated by gratitude, and she'd meant to land it on his cheek. But he would bet good money that she'd been every bit as affected by the spontaneous kiss as he was.

Granted, he'd always been attracted to her in spite of their sparring. But he'd managed to keep a tight rein on those feelings for the three and a half years he'd known her because she'd made it clear she found him barely one step above pond scum. Now, he couldn't ignore the possibility that the chemistry was mutual. So finally, here he was. He had the perfect excuse, even if it wasn't the perfect time.

And Megan wouldn't be able to avoid him as she'd been doing since their clash over the site where she'd wanted the new shelter built. A battle he'd won. Although from the sleek look of the Safe Haven facility, she'd landed on her feet and done well for the homeless four-legged residents of Royal, Texas.

Tucking the cat into his suit coat and securing her with a firm grip, he stepped into the welcoming reception area, its tiled surfaces giving off a freshly washed bleach smell. The waiting area was spacious, but today, there were wire crates lining two walls, one with cats, the other with small dogs. They were clean and neat, but the shelter was packed to capacity. He'd heard the shelter had taken in a large number of strays displaced during the storm, but he hadn't fully grasped the implications until now.

The shelter had a reputation for its innovative billboards, slogans and holiday-themed decor, but right now, every ounce of energy here seemed to be focused on keeping the animals fed and the place sparkling clean.

He closed the door, sealing himself inside.

The cat sunk her claws in deeper. Whit hissed almost as loudly as the feline and searched the space for help. Framed posters featured everything from collages of adopters to advice on flea prevention. Painted red-and-black paw prints marked the walls with directions he already knew in theory since he'd reviewed the plans during his land dispute with Megan.

A grandmotherly woman sat behind the counter labeled "volunteer receptionist." He recognized the retired legal secretary from past business ventures. She was texting on her phone, and waved for him to wait an instant before she glanced up.

He swept his hat off and set it on the counter. "Morning, Miss Abigail—"

"Good mornin', Whit," the lady interrupted with a particularly thick Southern accent, her eyes widening with surprise. The whole town knew he and Megan avoided each other like the plague. "What a pleasant surprise you've decided to adopt from us. Our doggies are housed to your right in kennel runs. But be sure to peek at the large fenced-in area outside. Volunteers take them there to exercise in the grassy area."

She paused for air, but not long enough for him to get in a word. "Although now I see you're a cat person. Never would have guessed that." She grinned as the calico peeked out of his suit jacket, purring as if the ferocious feline hadn't drawn blood seconds earlier. "Kitties are kept in our free roam area. If you find one you would like to adopt, we have meet-and-greet rooms for your sweetheart there to meet with your new feline friend—"

"I'm actually here to make a donation." He hadn't planned on that, but given all the extra crates, he could see the shelter needed help. So much of the post-tornado assistance had been focused on helping people and cleaning up the damaged buildings. But he should have realized the repercussions of the storm would have a wider ripple effect.

"A donation?" Miss Abigail set aside her phone. "Let me call our director right away—oh, here she is now."

He pivoted to find Megan walking down the dog corridor, toward the lobby, a beagle on a loose leash at her side. He could see the instant she registered his presence. She blinked fast, nibbling her lip as she paused midstep for an instant before forging ahead, the sweet curves of her hips sending a rush of want through him.

Her bright red hair was pulled back in a low ponytail. He ached to sweep away that gold clasp and thread his fingers through the fiery strands, to find out if her hair was as silky as it looked. He wanted her, had since the first time he'd seen her when they crossed paths in the lawyer's office during the dispute over a patch of property. He'd expected to smooth things over regarding finding an alternate location for the new shelter. He usually had no trouble charming people, but she'd taken to disliking him right away. Apparently her negative impression had only increased every time she perceived one of his projects as "damaging" to nature when he purchased a piece of wetlands.

He'd given up trying to figure out why she couldn't see her way clear to making nice. Because she had a reputation for being everyone's pal, a caring and kind-hearted woman who took in strays of all kinds, ready to pitch in to help anyone. Except for him.

"Megan," the receptionist cleared her throat, "Mr. Daltry here has brought us a donation."

"Another cat. Just what we were lacking." Megan's smile went tight.

He juggled his hold on the fractious fur ball. "I do plan to write a check to cover the expense of taking in another animal, but yes, I need to drop off the stray. She's been wandering around in the woods near my house. She doesn't have a collar and clearly hasn't been eating well."

"Could have been displaced because of the storm and has been surviving on her own in the wild ever since, poor girl. Animals have a knack for ditching their collars. Did you take her to a vet to check for a microchip?"

"I figured you could help me with that. Or maybe someone has come by here looking for her."

"So you're sure it's a girl?"

"I think so."

"Let's just pray she's not in heat or about to have kittens."

Oh, crap. He hadn't thought about that.

Megan passed him the dog leash and took the squirming cat from his arms. Their wrists brushed in the smooth exchange. A hint of her cinnamon scent drifted by, teasing him with memories of that too-brief kiss a month ago.

She swallowed hard once; it was the only sign she'd registered the brief contact, aside from the fact that she kept her eyes firmly averted from his. What would he see in those emerald-green eyes? A month ago, after her impulsive kiss, he'd seen surprise—and desire.

He watched her every move, trying to get a read on her.

"Hey, beautiful," she crooned to the kitty, handling the feline with obvious skill and something more...an unmistakable gift. "Let's get a scanner and check to see if you have a chip. If we're lucky, you'll have your people back very soon."

Kneeling, she pulled a brown, boxy device from under the counter and waved the sensor along the back of the cat's neck. She frowned and swept it over the same place again. Then she broadened the search along the cat's shoulders and legs, casting a quick glance at Whit. "Sometimes the chip migrates on the body."

But after sweeping along the cat's entire back, Megan shook her head and sighed. "No luck."

"She was pretty matted when I found her yesterday." He patted the beagle's head awkwardly. He didn't have much experience with pets, his only exposure to animals coming with horseback riding. The cat and dog were a helluva lot smaller than a Palomino. "I combed her out last night and she's been pissed at me ever since."

She glanced up quickly, her eyes going wide with surprise. "You brushed the cat?"

"Yeah, so?" He shrugged. "She needed it."

Her forehead furrowed. "That was kind of you."

"Last time I checked, I'm not a monster."

She smiled with a tinge of irony. "Just a mogul land baron and destroyer of wetlands."

He raised a hand. "Guilty as charged. And I hear you have need of some of my dirty, land-baron dollars?"

He looked around, taking in a couple of harried volunteers rushing in with fresh litter boxes stacked in their arms. The dog sniffed his shoes as if checking out the quality of his next chew toy.

The stuffing went out of her fight and she sagged back against the wall. "Animal control across town is full, and we're the only other option around here. People are living in emergency housing shelters that don't allow pets. Other folks have left town altogether, just giving up on finding their animals." He could hear the tension in her voice.

"That's a damn shame, Megan. I've heard the call-outs for pet food, but I hadn't realized how heavy the extra burden is for you and the rest of your staff."

"Let's step into my office before your kitty girl makes a break for the door. Evie's in there now, but it'll only take a second to settle her elsewhere so we can talk." She rested a hand on the front desk. "Miss Abigail, do you mind if Evie sits with you for a few minutes?"

"Of course not. I love spending time with the little darlin'. You don't let me babysit near enough. Send her my way."

Megan looked at Whit, something sad flickering in her eyes. "Evie's taking the day off from school. Come this way."

He followed her, his eyes drawn to the gentle sway of her hips. Khaki had never looked so hot. "I'm sorry to add to your load here, but I meant it when I said I want to make a donation to help."

She opened a metal baby gate and ushered the beagle into the room. It was a small room with a neat book-shelf and three recycling bins stacked in a corner. Two large framed watercolors dominated the walls—one of an orange cat and the other of a spotted dog, both clearly painted by a child. The bottom corner of each was signed in crayon. *Evie.*

The little minx peeked from under the desk, a min-iature version of her mom right down to the freckles on her nose. "Hello, Mr. Whit."

She crawled out with an iPad tucked under her arm, then stood, her red pigtails lopsided. Evie's face was one hundred percent Megan, but the little girl had a quirky spirit all her own. Evie wore a knight's costume with a princess tiara even though Halloween had already passed and Thanksgiving was rapidly approaching. Her mother smoothed a hand over her head affectionately, gently tightening the left pigtail to match the one on the right. "Miss Abigail wants you to sit with her for a few minutes, okay? I'll be through soon."

Evie waved shyly, green eyes sparkling, then sprinted out to the front desk, carrying her iPad and a foam sword.

Megan gestured for him to step inside the small office, then closed the gate again. "You mentioned writing a check, and I'm not bashful about accepting on behalf of the animals. I'll get you a receipt so you can write it off on your taxes."

"Where will you put this cat if you're already full?" he asked as the beagle sniffed his shoes.

"I guess we'll learn if she gets along with dogs since she'll have to stay in my office for now." She crouched down with the cat in her arms. The pup tipped his head to the side and the cat curled closer to Megan but kept her claws sheathed. Nodding, Megan stood and settled the cat onto her office chair.

"She likes dogs better than she likes me, that's for sure." He shook his head, laughing softly.

"I guess not every female in this town likes crawling into your arms." She crinkled her freckled nose.

He would have thought she was jealous. She *had* been avoiding him since the tornado. He would have attributed it to her being busy with cleanup, but his instincts shouted it had something to do with that impulsive kiss. "I feel bad for adding to your load here. Could you use more volunteers to help with the extra load here? I'm sure some of my buddies at the Texas Cattleman's Club would be glad to step up."

"We can always use extra hands."

"I'll contact Gil Addison—the club president—and get the ball rolling. Maybe they'll adopt when they're here."

"We can only hope." Her hand fell to the cat's head and she stroked lightly. The cat arched up into the stroke, purring loudly. "I'm working on arranging a transport for some of the unclaimed pets to a rescue in Oklahoma. A group in Colorado has reached out to help as well, but we're still trying to find a way to get the animals there. And since the Colorado group is a new rescue, I need to look over their operation before entrusting our animals to their care. Except I don't know how I'll be able to take off that much time from work for the road trip, much less be away from Evie for that long. She's still unsettled from the trauma of last month's storm. But, well, you don't need to hear all about my troubles."

"My personal plane is at your disposal," he said without hesitation.

"What? I didn't realize you have a plane. I mean I know you're well off, but...."

Her shoulders braced and he could almost see another wall appearing between them. He appreciated that she wasn't impressed by his money, but also hated to see another barrier in place.

Still, the more he thought about flying the animals for her, the more the idea appealed to him. "Make the arrangements with the rescue and whatever else needs to be done as far as crating the animals. I assume you have procedures for that."

"Yes, but...." Confusion creased her forehead. "I

don't know how to say thank-you. That's going above and beyond."

"There's nothing to thank me for. This is a win-win." He got to help the animals, score points with Megan and spend more time with her to boot.

"But the cost—"

"A tax write-off, remember? Fly animals as far as you need them to go and your time away will be reduced considerably." This idea just got better and better, not only for the animals, but also by giving him an "in" to see Megan, to figure out where to take this attraction. "This isn't a one-time offer either. You're packed with critters here. If there's help out there, take it and my jet will fly them there."

"I can't turn you down. The animals need this kind of miracle if we're going to find homes for them by the holidays." She exhaled hard. "I need to get to work placing calls. There are rescues I hadn't considered before because of the distance and our limited resources. Rescue work happens fast, slots fill up at a moment's notice."

"And this little gal?" He stroked the cat's head and for once the calico didn't dig her claws in. Perched on the back of the chair, she arched up into his hand and purred like a race car.

"Are you sure you don't want to keep her?"

He pulled his hand away. "I can't. I'm at work all the time, which wouldn't be fair to her."

"Of course." Megan looked disappointed in him, even though he'd just offered her thousands of dollars' worth of flight hours.

But then, hadn't he said it? Offering his plane was easy. Taking care of another living being? Not so easy.

"I should let you get to work on lining up those rescues." He pulled a business card from his wallet and plucked a pen from the cup on the edge of her desk. He jotted a number on the back of the card. "This is my private cell number and my secretary's number. Don't hesitate to call."

When he passed her the card, their fingers brushed. He saw the flecks of awareness sparkle in her eyes again. He wasn't mistaken. The mutual draw was real, but now wasn't the time to press ahead for more.

"Thank you again." She flipped the card between her fingers, still watching him with suspicion, their old conflicts clearly making her wary. "Would you like to name your kitty cat?"

"That's not my kitten."

"Right," she answered, a smile playing with her plump lips that didn't need makeup to entice, "and she still needs a name. We've had to name so many this past month, we're out of ideas."

He thought for a second then found himself saying, "Tallulah."

"Tallulah?" Her surprise was a reward. He liked unsettling her. "Really, Whit? I didn't expect such a... girly name choice."

"That was the name of my mom's cat." She was briefly theirs, but when they'd moved, the cat ran away. Then his father had said no more pets. Period.

"It's a lovely name."

He nodded quickly then turned to leave.

"Whit," she called, stopping him short, "about what happened after you helped me get to Evie that day...."

Was she finally acknowledging the impulsive, explosive kiss? The thought of having her sooner rather than later... "Yes?"

"Thank you for helping me reach my daughter." She

looked down at her shoes for an awkward moment before meeting his eyes again. "I can never repay you for that...and now this."

"I don't expect repayment." The last thing he wanted was to have her kiss him again out of gratitude.

The next time they kissed—and there would be a next time—it would be purely based on mutual attraction.

The stroke of Whit Daltry's eyes left her skin tingling.

Standing at the shelter's glass door, Megan rubbed her arms as she watched Whit stride across the parking lot back to his truck. His long legs ate up the space one powerful step at a time. His suit coat flapped in the late afternoon breeze revealing a too-perfect, taut butt. Her head was still reeling from his surprise appearance, followed by the generous offer she couldn't turn down.

After six weeks of reliving that brief but mind-blowing kiss, she'd seen him again and would be spending an entire day with him. Somehow, because of that day they'd gone from avoiding each other to.... What? She wasn't sure exactly.

Maybe he'd gotten the wrong idea from that kiss and thought she was looking for something more. But she didn't have time in her life for more. She had a demanding job and a daughter, and both had taken a hard hit from last month's tornado.

And speaking of her child, she'd left Evie long enough. Thank goodness Miss Abigail had been so accommodating about helping with Evie. The retired legal secretary had even babysat a couple of evenings when Megan got called out to assist with an emergency rescue. Evie had been particularly clingy this past month.

And she couldn't blame her. That nightmarish day still haunted Megan as well; she often woke up from dreams of not reaching her daughter in time, of the whole roof of the preschool collapsing.

Dreams that sometimes took a different turn with Whit arriving, of the kiss going further....

Megan watched his truck drive away, a knot in her stomach.

It would be too damn easy to lean on those broad shoulders, to get used to the help, which would only make things more difficult when she was on her own again. Megan turned away from the door and temptation, returning to reality in the form of her precious daughter sitting on Abigail's lap as they played on the iPad together. Evie's knight's armor was slipping off one shoulder, her toy sword on the ground beside her tiara.

Megan held out her arms. "Come here, sweetie."

She gathered Evie into her arms and held her on her hip. Not much longer and her baby girl would be too big to carry around. This precious child, who wanted to be a "princess knight" for Halloween and cut through tornadoes with a foam sword. Megan had hoped her daughter would relax and heal as they put the storm behind them, but now Thanksgiving was approaching and Evie was still showing signs of trauma.

The holidays were tough anyway, reminding her that she was the sole relative in Evie's life. She was a thirty-year-old single mom.

And damn lucky to have landed in this small town full of warmhearted friends.

"Thank you, Abigail, for helping out even after the school finished repairs. You've been a lifesaver."

The roof of Little Tots Daycare had been reconstructed quickly, but the dust and stress had taken its toll on the kids and the workers. Some had gotten the flu.

Others, like Evie, had nightmares and begged to stay home. Her daughter conquered pretend monsters in iPad games and dress-up play.

Abigail rocked back in her chair. "My pleasure. She's a doll." She pinched Evie's cheek lightly. "We have fun readin' books on the iPad. Don't we, Evie?"

Bringing her daughter to work wasn't optimal, but Megan didn't have any choices for now. "Thanks again."

"I'm always a call away. The benefit of being re-tired. Maybe we'll see Mr. Daltry again tomorrow. Now wouldn't that be nice if he became a regular volunteer?"

As much as Megan wanted to keep her distance, she couldn't ignore all the amazing things Whit had done for her.

Evie patted her mother's cheek with a tiny palm. "Where did the nice man go?"

"He brought a kitty to stay with us here."

She stuck out her bottom lip. "We don't like people who dump their pets. Does this mean I can't like him anymore?"

"He didn't dump the kitty, sweetie. He saved her from being cold and hungry in the woods." Although she had to admit she was disappointed he hadn't offered to keep the cat. She struggled not to resent his wealthy lifestyle. Everyone knew he was a self-made man who'd worked hard to build a fortune before his thirty-fifth birthday. "Tallulah lost her family and had nowhere else to go. We're going to help her find them again."

"'Lulah?"

"Right. That's her name."

"She can come home wif us and live in our house. I'll get her a costume too."

They already had three cats and two dogs, all of which Evie had been dressing up as part of her medieval warrior team. The costumes transformed them into horses, elves, queens and even a unicorn.

Their house was full.

And Megan was at her limit with work and her daughter. "You can visit Tallulah here while she waits to find her family. We have our kitties and doggies at home to take care of and love."

Evie patted Megan's face again. "Don't worry, Mommy. I'll tell Mr. Whit to keep 'Lulah."

If only it worked that easily. "I need to work a little longer, just a few phone calls and then we can go home for supper. We'll make a pizza."

"Can Mr. Whit share our pizza?"

Abigail laughed softly from her perch behind the counter. "I think Mr. Whit wants to share a lot more than pizza."

Evie looked up, frowning. "Like what?"

Megan shot Abigail an exasperated look before kneeling to tell Evie, "Mr. Whit is sharing his airplane to help send some of the puppies and kitties to forever homes before Thanksgiving."

"He shares his plane? See. He is very nice. Can I play my games, please?" Evie squirmed down with her iPad, her foam sword tumbling from her hand. "I'm gonna play a plane game this time." Her daughter put on her tiara and fired up a game for touring the states in a puffy airplane.

Megan glanced at the receptionist. "I don't want to hear a word about Whit's visit today, Abigail. And no gossiping."

She glanced over her shoulder to see if other volunteers were listening in. Luckily, most of them were occupied with exercising animals, folding laundry and washing bowls. The only person even remotely close enough to hear was Beth Andrews, Megan's favorite volunteer.

"Gossip?" Beth chimed in. "Did I hear the word gossip? That would surely never happen in the town of Royal where everyone stays out of each other's business. Not."

Beth wasn't a known gossip, but was definitely known for helping out everywhere; she was very involved in the community. The leggy blonde owned Green Acres, a local organic farm and produce stand. Beth's business had taken a big hit from the tornado. That made her generosity and caring now all the more special, given how rough life had been for her lately. The homemade goodies she brought to the animals were always a treat. Beth had that willowy thin, effortless beauty that would have had women resenting her if it weren't for the fact she was so darn nice.

Abigail stroked her phone as if already planning a text. "It's a gift having a community that cares so much. Like how Whit Daltry just showed up to make a big donation."

Beth arched a blond eyebrow. "You two are speaking to each other?"

Megan shrugged her shoulders and examined her fingernails. "He's helping with the overflow of animals. I can work with anyone for the good of the animals."

"Everyone's had their lives turned upside down since the twister. To lose over a dozen lives in a blink…to have our friend Craig gone so young…." She paused with a heavy sigh. "No one has been exempt from the fallout of this damn storm. Even our mayor was critically injured. And that poor Skye Taylor…"

"What tragic bad luck that she came back to town after four years on such a terrible day. How is she doing?" Megan rubbed her arms again, feeling petty for stressing over her life, thinking of Skye Taylor, found seriously injured and unconscious after the storm, her baby delivered prematurely. And since Skye was still in a coma, she hadn't even met her child. Megan shivered again, even though she didn't know the woman personally. As a mother, she felt a bond. Thank God Evie was safe. That's what mattered most. She would figure out how to heal her daughter's fears.

Clearly agitated, Beth thumbed a stack of shelter flyers. "Drew checked in with the family and Skye is still in a medically induced coma and the baby girl—Grace—is in the neonatal intensive care unit."

Abigail sighed. "And the doctors still don't know who the father is?"

Did this qualify as gossip? Megan wasn't sure, but if the talk could help find the father, that would be a good thing. "I've never met her, but I heard a rumor Skye ran off with the younger Holt brother despite their parents' protests. So I assumed he was the dad."

Beth tucked a stray curl back into her loose topknot, scrunching her nose. "I recall hearing mentions of an age-old feud between the Holts and Taylors. Abigail, do you have any idea who started it?"

"I haven't a clue. Quite frankly, I'm not sure they do either, anymore."

Beth shook her head slowly. "How sad when feuds are carried on for so long." She stared pointedly at Megan. "So what's this with Whit Daltry coming to the shelter to see you? And you actually spoke to him rather than running out the back exit?"

"Running out the back? I wouldn't do that." Okay,

so maybe she had avoided him a time or two but hearing it put that way made her sound so…wimpy. And she didn't like that one damn bit. "I think we've all done some reevaluating this past month. If he wants to offer his private plane to transport homeless animals to new homes, who am I to argue?"

Beth laughed softly. "About that flight… Look how neatly he tied in a way to see you again. Coincidence? I don't think so."

Not even having a clue how to respond to that notion, Megan clasped her daughter's hand and retreated to her office. The second she closed the door, she realized she'd done it again. Run away like the coward she'd denied being.

But when it came to Whit Daltry and the way he flipped her world with one sizzling look, keeping her cool just wasn't an option.

Three

Whit parked his truck in the four-car garage of his large, custom-built home in Pine Valley. With a hard exhale, he slumped back in the seat. He'd spent the whole day at work thinking about seeing Megan at the shelter when he'd brought in the cat. Knowing he'd locked in a reason to see her again pumped him full of excitement. Life had sucked so badly the past month. Feeling alive again was good. Damn good.

He reached for the door and stepped out into the massive garage, all his.

Growing up, he'd lived in apartments half the size of this space, which also held a sports car, a speed boat and a motorcycle. He liked his toys and the security of knowing they were paid for. Since the day he'd left home, he'd never bought anything on credit. His college degree had been financed with a combination of scholarships and two jobs. Debt was a four-letter word to him.

His father had showered his family with gifts, but too often those presents were repossessed or abandoned as the Daltry family fled creditors yet again. His parents had passed away years ago, his dad of a stroke, his mom of a broken heart weakened from too many years of disappointment after disappointment.

Every time they'd moved to a new place, his mother wore that hopeful expression that this time would be different, that his father wouldn't gamble away the earnings from his new job, that they could stay and build a life. And every time she was wrong. Most times that hope would fade to resignation about a week before his dad announced the latest cut-and-run exit for the Daltry family. Whit came to appreciate the advance warning since it gave him the opportunity to tuck away some things before the inevitable pack-and-dash.

He'd built this house for himself as a tribute to leaving that life behind. But he'd waited to start construction. He'd refused to break ground until he had the money to pay for every square foot of it. People viewed him as lighthearted and easygoing—true enough, up to a point. No way in hell was he sinking himself into debt just to make a show of thumbing his nose at the past. He knew the pain of losing everything as a kid and he refused to go through that again. He'd been damned lucky his home in Pine Valley hadn't sustained any damage from the storm.

As he stepped from the garage into the wide passageway, he thought of all this empty space. He made a point of donating to charities, even throwing in elbow grease as well when called for, like pitching in with the never-ending cleanup after the tornado.

And now working with the animals? Except he

wasn't. He'd left that cat at the shelter. He'd meant everything he said about not having time for a pet, but Megan had asked about temporary fostering and he'd rejected that out of hand. He knew he'd disappointed her with his answer. Or rather confirmed her preconceived negative notions about him.

Maybe if he got a couple of cats to keep each other company. Cats were more independent, right?

As he opened the door to the kitchen, his cell phone rang. He fished it out of his pocket and the caller ID showed...Megan Maguire?

His pulse kicked up a notch at just the sight of her name. Damn, he needed to get a grip. Pursuing her was one thing. Giving her this much control over how he felt? Not okay. He needed to keep things light, flirtatious.

He answered the phone. "Hello, pretty lady. What can I do for you?"

"Seriously?" she asked dryly. "Do you always answer the phone that way?"

"Megan?" he answered with overplayed surprise. "Well, damn, I thought it was my granny calling."

She laughed, her voice relaxing into a husky, sexy melody. "You have a granny?"

"I didn't crawl out from under a rock. I have relatives." Just really distant ones who had cut ties with his branch of the family tree long ago because of his father. "Actually, my grandmother passed away ten years ago. My cheesy line was totally for your benefit, I just didn't expect it to fall so flat. So let's start over."

That might not be a bad idea: to call for a do-over in a larger way, erase the past three and a half years.

"Sure," she said. "Hello, Whit, this is Megan Maguire. I hope I didn't disturb your supper."

"Well, hey there, Megan." He opened the stainless-steel, oversized refrigerator and pulled out an imported beer. "What a surprise to hear from you. What do you need?"

He sat in a chair at the island where the cooking service he'd hired left a dinner in a warmer each night. He couldn't cook. Tried, but just didn't have the knack for more than grilling and he worked too late to grill. He twisted open the beer and waited for her to answer.

"I was just loading my dishwasher, and this weird panic set in that maybe you weren't serious earlier."

"About what?" He tipped back a swig of the imported brew.

"Did you really offer your plane to transport animals?"

"Absolutely. I don't make promises I can't keep." His father was the king of broken promises, all smiles and dreams with no substance.

"Whew," she exhaled. "Thank goodness. Because I asked a contact in Colorado to check out the rescue. I also spoke with the veterinarian the rescue uses and everything appears perfect. So I called them and they can still take a dozen of our cats, a huge help to us and to local animal control. Am I being pushy in asking how soon we can transport them because I would really like to see them settled before Thanksgiving?"

"Not pushy at all." This was Thursday, with turkey day only a week away. He had a meeting he couldn't miss on Friday, but the notion of spending the weekend with her was enticing as hell. He'd hoped this would work out. He just hadn't realized how quickly the plan would come together. "Glad they have space to accommodate. I could see you're stuffed to the gills."

"Feeding and caring for so many animals is depleting our budget in a hurry." Her voice was weary, tempting him to race over to her house with his pre-cooked dinner. "We try our best to plan for disasters, but having just built the new shelter, we're stretched to the max."

He couldn't feed her tonight, but he could lighten some of her load. "I also meant it when I said I'll talk to the Cattleman's Club about rolling up their sleeves and opening their wallets. We can help. We're about more than the Stetson hats and partying."

"I honestly don't know what to say to all of this generosity. You've really come through for us with so much, especially offering your plane. Thank you."

"Glad to help. Can you have the animals ready to fly day after tomorrow? I'm free to fly them to Colorado on Saturday."

She gasped. "*You* are flying the plane? I thought you would have a pilot…."

Had he failed to mention that part of his offer? Would she go running in the opposite direction? Not with the cats' well-being at stake. But might she try to send someone else from the shelter in her place? Had he just roped himself into a weekend with her kennel supervisor?

That didn't change his promise. He didn't break his word.

But he would definitely be disappointed to miss out on the chance to get closer to Megan.

He clicked speakerphone and placed his cell phone on the slate island. "I do have a pilot who flies me around if I need to have a meeting or entertain en-route. But I'm a licensed pilot too, quite proficient, if I do say so myself. What do you say? Let's make a week-end out of it."

"A weekend away together in Colorado?" The shock in her voice vibrated through the phone line. "Are you trying to buy your way into my life?"

"Now that stings." And oddly enough, it really did. He wanted her to think well of him. "I will concede that I'm trying to get your attention, and bringing the cat today offered an excuse to see you again, but it's not like I concocted a fake stray to meet you. Flying the other cats to Colorado is the right thing to do for the shelter and for our community. Even a hard-ass like me can see that. If you doubt my motives, bring your daughter along. She's a great kid."

The silence stretched and he checked the menu card with his meal—balsamic skirt steak with corn po-lenta—while he waited. Her answer was suddenly a lot more important than it should have been. But he wanted more time with her. Hell, he flat-out wanted her. He had since the first time he'd seen her. The tor-nado had just made him reevaluate. Life was too short and too easily lost to put off pursuing goals.

And right now, his goal was to discover if the chem-istry between him and Megan was as explosive as that one kiss led him to believe.

"So, Megan? About Saturday?" He rolled the beer bottle between both palms, anticipation firing in his gut.

"Without question, Evie would love the adventure. I'm not able to offer her much in the way of vacation or special trips. She's also been hesitant to stay at the sitter's...." Megan drew in a shaky breath. "Saturday it is then."

A thrill of victory surged through him, stronger than any he'd experienced in a damn long time.

"Excellent. And hey, feel free to make more calls and line up a place for the extra dogs and we can make it a weekly outing. Wait—before you accuse me of using the animals to get to you, the offer still stands if you want to send one of your staff in your place."

She laughed dryly. "Let's take it one week at a time."

But he knew she wouldn't be able to turn down the offer. He'd found the perfect in with her. "And by the way, a trip that long won't all fit into one day. Be sure to pack an overnight bag."

Megan held a clipboard and cross-referenced the information on the printout with the card attached to each cat carrier lined up inside Whit's aircraft. The plane could easily hold a dozen or more people, but those sofas and lounge chairs were empty. The kitty cargo had been creatively stashed beneath seats and strapped under the food station bar.

Most of the felines were already curled up and snoozing from the sedative she'd administered prior to crating them. Three of the cats, though, were staring back at her with wide, drugged eyes and the occasional hiss, hanging on to consciousness and looking at her suspiciously. Sheba, an all-black fluff ball, had come from a home where she was an only pet and queen of her domain, but after her owner passed away, the extended family had dumped their mother's beloved pet at the shelter. Sheba had been freaked out and terrified ever since. She needed a home environment, even a foster setting, until an adopter could be found. Skittles, an orange tabby stray, had been found at the shopping mall with no name tag, no microchip and no one to claim her. If she went much longer without a home setting, Megan feared Skittles would turn feral. And the third of the cranky passengers, Sebastian, was a gorgeous, very huge Maine Coon cat that desperately needed more space to move around than the shelter could offer.

Provided the Colorado group was as wonderful in person as her contact and the vet indicated, by evening the twelve cats would be with a rescue that only operated with foster homes until adoptive homes were found. No more shelter life for them.

She rested a hand on top of a crate, exhaustion from the past month seeping through her. Maybe now that she had some help in sight, her body was finally relaxing enough to let all those extra hours catch up with her. She still could hardly believe this was happening— and thanks to Whit Daltry, of all people. The last man she would have expected to go the extra mile for her.

But the very man who'd done more than that for her when he'd helped her reach Evie after the tornado.

Megan stole a quick glance to check on her daughter, currently sprawled out asleep on one of the leather sofas. They'd had to get up early to ready the cats at the shelter. Evie had insisted on wearing a cowgirl outfit today—with the ever present tiara, of course.

Footsteps sounded outside on the metal stairs, and a second later Whit filled the hatch. He looked Texas-awesome, with broad shoulders—as if Texas ever did anything half way. He wore a chambray button-down with the sleeves rolled up. And his jeans—Lord help her. The well-washed denim fit him just right. Her mouth watered. He ducked and pulled off his hat to clear the hatch on his way inside.

"Everything's a go outside whenever you and Evie are ready to buckle in." His boots thudded against the carpeted floor as he walked to Megan and rested a hand on her shoulder.

Static sparked through her so tangibly she could almost believe crackles filled and lit the air. Whit's clean soap scent brought to mind the image of a shared morning shower, a notion far too intimate to entertain, especially when they had to spend the next two days in close confines. She eased away from him under the guise of flipping the page on her clipboard. Except it was already the last page so she looked too obvious.

Quickly, she flipped all the papers back into place.

Whit stuffed his hands in his jean pockets. "We might as well talk about it."

"Talk about what?" How she couldn't peel her eyes off his strong jaw? Could barely suppress the urge to step closer and brush her cheek along the fresh-shaven texture of his face? She was having a hard time remembering why she had to stay away from this man.

"When you kissed me."

"Shhhh!" she whispered urgently. "Do you want someone—Evie—to hear?" Her daughter was a great big reason she needed to tread warily with any man she let into their lives.

He stepped closer. "Okay, how's this?"

His voice rumbled over her like the vibration of quiet thunder in a summer rain. Desire pooled low in her belly, her breasts tingling and tightening as if the first drops of that summer storm were caressing her bare skin.

Damn. She was in deep trouble here.

She clutched the clipboard to her chest. "I didn't kiss you that day. Not exactly."

"I remember the day well. Your lips on mine. That's a kiss," he bantered with a devilish glint in his eyes.

"But just so that we're clear, none of this trip today is contingent on there being another kiss."

"I meant to kiss your cheek as…a thanks." A mind-melting, toe-curling thanks. "You're the one who turned your face and made it into something more."

He dipped his head and spoke softly, his breath warm against her ear. "And you're the one who smells like cinnamon and has this sexy kitten moan. I dream of hearing it again."

She fought back the urge to moan at just the sound of his voice and the memories his words evoked. "I thought you were taking the animals on this flight as a totally philanthropic act."

"I am."

She tipped her chin and stood her ground. "Then what's this flirting about?"

"I'm a multitasker." He knocked on the clipboard still clasped against her breasts. "Let's get strapped in and ready to roll."

An hour later, Megan rested her arm along the sofa back and watched the puffy white clouds filling the sky. The plane cruised as smoothly as if they were cushioned by those pillowy clouds, not a bump yet to disconcert her.

Shortly after takeoff, Evie had asked to join Whit. Megan had started to say no, but apparently he'd heard and waved her daughter up front to the empty co-pilot's seat. As a single parent, Megan was so used to being the sole caregiver and primary form of entertainment for her daughter—especially since the tornado. This moment to relax with her thoughts was a welcome reprieve.

Hell, to relax at all seemed like a gift.

The cats were all happily snoozing now in their tranquilized haze. No more evil eye from the three stubborn ones that had stayed awake the longest.

Her gaze shifted back to her daughter up front. Evie, rejuvenated from her nap, was now chattering to Whit. He sat at the helm, piloting them through the skies with obvious ease and skill. His hands and feet moved in perfect synch, his eyes scanning the control as he seamlessly carried on a convoluted conversation with her four-year-old daughter.

"Mr. Whit, I'm a cowgirl," Evie declared proudly.

"I see that," he answered patiently as if she hadn't already been peppering his ear with accounts of every detail of her life from her best friends at school—Caitlyn and Bobby—to what she ate for breakfast this morning—a granola bar and chocolate milk in the car on the way to the shelter. "Last week, you were a knight with a sword."

"A princess knight," she said as if he was too slow to have noticed the difference.

Megan suppressed a smile.

"Right," Whit answered. "You always wear that pretty tiara."

"This week, I'm keeping the monsters away with my rope." She patted her hip where the miniature lasso was hooked to her belt loop. "It's a lassie."

"Lassie? Oh, lasso. I see," he said solemnly. "You're going to rope the monsters?"

Megan swallowed down a lump of emotion at how easily he saw through to her daughter's fears.

"Yep, sir, that's right," Evie answered with a nod that threatened to dislodge her tiara. "Rope 'em up and throw 'em in the trash."

He stayed silent for a heart-stopping second before he

answered with a measured calm, "You're a very brave little girl."

Evie shrugged. "Somebody's gotta do it."

Megan choked back a bittersweet laugh as her daughter parroted one of her mommy's favorite phrases.

Whit glanced at Evie. "Your mommy takes very good care of you. You're safe now, kiddo."

"But nobody takes care of Mommy. That's not fair."

Megan blinked back tears at the weight her little girl was carrying around inside. He didn't seem to have a ready answer to that one. Neither did Megan.

Evie hitched up her feet to sit cross-legged, picking at the Velcro of her new tennis shoes. They hadn't been able to afford cowgirl boots, not with new shoes to buy. "I'm not sure what I'll be next. Gotta look through my costume box and see what'll scare the monsters."

"Where are these monsters?"

"They come out of the sky with the wind." Evie pointed ahead at the windscreen and made swirly gestures with her spindly, little-girl arms. "So I'm riding wif you in the plane. I'll get 'em before they scare other kids."

Megan tipped her head back to hold in the tears. She had seen this flight as a welcome distraction for her child. She hadn't considered Evie might be afraid, and certainly not for this particular reason. But it made perfect sense, and somehow Whit had gotten more information on the fears in one simple conversation than Megan had been able to pry out of her strong-willed child in the past month.

Evie wiggled her feet. "I got new shoes. They light up when I walk."

"Very nice."

"My princess sneakers got messed up in the tora-na-do." She pronounced the word much better these days than a month ago.

They'd all had lots of practice with the word.

Whit glanced at Evie for an instant, his brown eyes serious and compassionate. "I'm so sorry to hear that."

"They were my favorites. But we couldn't find ones just like 'em. I think these lights are a good idea. I coulda used the lights the day the tora-na-do made the school all dark."

Megan's stomach plummeted as surely as if the plane had lost serious altitude. Was every choice her child made tied into that day now? Megan had thought the shoe-shopping trip had been a fun day for Evie, and yet the whole time her daughter had assessed every choice using survivalist criteria. Megan blinked back tears and focused on listening to Evie.

"Mommy says lots of little girls lost their shoes too and we need to be glad we gots shoes."

"Your mother is a smart lady."

Was it her imagination or had he just glanced back at her out of the corner of his eye? A shiver of awareness tingled up her spine.

"I know, and I wanna be good like Mommy so Santa will come visit my house."

His head tipped to the side inquisitively. "Santa will see what a very good girl you've been today. I suspect you're always a good girl."

"Not as good as Mommy."

Megan frowned in surprise, her heart aching all over again for what her daughter had been through and how little Evie had shared about that. Until now. Somehow Whit had a way of reaching her that no one else had. Megan was grateful, and nervous to think of him gaining more importance in her life.

Whit waited a moment before answering, "Why do you think that about yourself, kiddo?"

Evie just shook her head, pigtails swishing and tiara landing in her lap. "Let's talk about something else. Caitlyn and Bobby are my bestest friends. Are you Mommy's new bestest friend?"

Four

As the sun set at the end of a chilly day, Whit cranked the heat inside the rental car, an SUV that had been perfect for transporting the twelve cats to their new foster families with the Colorado rescue group. They'd just finished their last drop-off. Mission complete.

Megan had insisted on inspecting every home in spite of the long day and the Colorado cold. But in the end, she was satisfied she'd found a great new rescue to network with in the future.

Glancing at the rearview mirror, Whit watched Megan strapped her daughter into the car seat, a task he'd learned she never allowed anyone else to take over no matter how many stops they made. Evie had been patient, excited even, over seeing her mom in action. And the couple of times the kid had gotten bored, she'd been easily distracted by the snow flurries—which had necessitated a side trip to pick up a warmer snow suit and snow boots.

Evie had been hesitant about covering her costume and her trepidation stabbed Whit clean through with sympathy for the little tyke. Finally, he'd been able to persuade her even cowgirls needed cold weather gear more appropriate for Colorado—which was a helluva lot colder than Texas.

Megan tucked into the passenger side as they idled outside a two-story farmhouse belonging to an older widower inside who'd made a fuss over his feline visitor. She rubbed her gloved hands together in front of the heat vent and then swiped the snowflakes off her head.

"I miss Texas," she said between her chattering teeth. "If you ever hear me complain during the winter, just remind me of this day."

That implied they would keep in contact after this weekend. He was making progress in comparison to their previous standoff. Did this mean she'd forgiven him for claiming the land she'd wanted for the shelter? He wasn't going to push his luck by asking. He intended to ride the wave of her good mood today and build some more positive memories.

Megan deserved to have some fun and recreation.

He'd seen firsthand how she carried a ton of worries around for one person, between taking care of her daughter alone and spreading her generous heart even thinner for these homeless animals. Who looked after Megan? Who gave her a break from life's burdens?

He turned his heater vents in her direction as well. "You accomplished a lot in one day."

"It's a relief to have them settled, and so quickly." She reached back to Evie and squeezed her daughter's hand. "Did you have fun?"

"I like the plane and the snow." She kicked her feet. "And my new boots that Mr. Whit bought me."

"Good, I'm glad, sweetie. We'll get a Happy Meal before going back to the…hotel." She swallowed, her eyes darting nervously to Whit. "Thank you again for arranging everything."

He put the SUV into drive and pulled out onto the tree-lined suburban road, leaving the last foster home behind. "What about other rescues? Did you find more places that can help out with some of the animals back home?"

Her green eyes lit with excitement. "I have a line on a couple of breed-specific rescues that might be able to take a few of our beagles and our German Shepherd." She touched his arm lightly; it was the first physical contact she'd initiated since that kiss. "But I can't keep asking you to take off work to fly around the country."

"I have a private pilot and I'm guessing if you already know the reputation of the rescue, then the animals can fly alone with him." While the obvious answer would be to lock in their weekends with more of these flights together, he also knew a more subtle approach would win Megan over. Just as he'd told Evie, her mama was smart and Whit was drawn to that part of Megan as well. So he opted for a smoother approach. "This doesn't always have to be about us spending time together. Not that I'm complaining. What? You look surprised."

He bit back a self-satisfied smile and steered out onto the rural mountain road into a smattering of five o'clock traffic.

She tipped her head to the side, the setting sun casting a warm glow over her face. "You would pay your pilot to fly just one or two dogs at a time?"

"Sure, although I've also got an idea for recruiting some of my friends to help out." He accelerated past a slow-moving vehicle backing up traffic. "A number of them own planes, short range, long range, and we all like to pitch in and help. Sometimes we just need pointing in the right direction."

"Even if you don't get to see me and make moves to follow up on…." She glanced up at the rearview mirror and watched Evie playing with her iPad. "Even if you know there won't be a replay of what happened a month ago."

"I can separate work and personal, just as I can separate personal and philanthropic. And," he ducked his head closer to hers, "I can also blend them when the situation presents itself. Like today."

Evie kicked the back of her mother's seat. "Can I have my Happy Meal, please? 'Cause if I have to wait much longer, I'm gonna starve and then it would be a Sad Meal."

Whit choked on a laugh. God, this kid was a cute little imp. "Absolutely, kiddo, we can get supper for you. And then after supper, I have plans."

Megan sat up straighter. "Plans?"

Damn straight. He had an agenda full of fun for a woman who didn't get much in the way of recreation. "Unless you have an objection, we'll have dinner and ice skating before we turn in for the night."

Ice skating.

Megan never would have guessed the mega-wealthy, smooth operator Whit Daltry would plan a night of ice skating and burgers. Granted, they were the best burgers she'd ever eaten. But still, the laid-back quality of fun appealed to her.

He'd also taken Evie into account, something else that set him apart from other men who'd asked her out for a date—except wait, this wasn't a date. She didn't have time for dating.

Right?

She sat on a bench by the outdoor skating rink, eating the last of her sweet potato fries and watching Whit lead her daughter carefully as she found her balance on the children's skates. Moonbeams and halogen lights created the effect of a hazy dome over the crowded ice, which was full of people getting into the Christmas spirit early. His patience was commendable. A person couldn't fake that. He genuinely had a knack with kids.

Megan could see her daughter's mouth moving nonstop as she chattered away, her breath puffing clouds in tiny bursts. Whit nodded periodically. Other skaters whipped past, but he kept up the slow, steady pace with Evie, making sure to keep her safe.

She stopped and tugged his hand, so cute in her puffy pink snowsuit next to Whit, who towered over her in his blue parka. He knelt, listening intently. Then he stood, scooping her up and skating faster, faster, faster still. Evie's squeals of delight carried on the wind, mixing with music piping through the outdoor sound system. Megan's heart softened, a dangerous emotion because this could be so easy to get used to, to depend on. To crave.

Him.

She exhaled a very long stream of white vapor. She needed to steel herself and tread warily. She ate three sweet potato fries. Fast. Feeding her stomach because she couldn't address the deeper hunger.

Whit and her daughter circled the rink twice before he skidded to a stop in front of Megan's bench. He held Evie confidently. Her cheeks were pink from the cold, her little girl's smile wide and genuine for the first time since the twister tore apart their lives.

Megan scooted over on the bench to make room for them to join her. She patted the chilly metal with her gloved hand. "You're very good at ice skating for a Texan."

Whit lowered Evie to sit between them. "My parents moved around a lot when I was growing up, all over the U.S., actually. I spent some time ice skating on ponds because we couldn't afford the admission to a rink."

That explained why his accent wasn't as strong as others who lived in Royal. But she'd assumed he still came from a privileged background because he fit so seamlessly into the elite Texas world typified by the TCC members. She tried to picture him as a kid fitting in at all those new places. He'd earned all that confidence the hard way. She understood that road well.

"What other skills did you pick up over the years?" Megan passed her daughter the box of fries.

"You'll have to wait to find out." He stretched his arm along the back of the bench and tugged a curly lock of her hair.

"A man of mystery." Had she actually leaned into his touch? The warmth of his arm seared her through her coat and sweater and the temptation to stay right here burned strong.

"Just trying to keep you around."

Evie dropped her fry and looked up with worried green eyes. "Where's Mommy going?"

"Nowhere, sweetie." She gathered her child close to her side, love and the deep importance of her role as Evie's mom twining inside her. "I'm staying with you."

Her daughter continued to stare up at her. "Are you sure?"

"Absolutely."

Evie looked down at her ice skates, chewing her lip before turning to Whit. "You said I could pick somethin' from the gift shop."

Megan gasped, ducking her head to meet her daughter's eyes. "Evie! You shouldn't ask Mr. Daltry to buy you things. He's already been very generous with this trip for the kitties and then entertaining us with ice skating."

He squeezed Megan's shoulder. "It's okay. Evie's right. I offered, downright promised. And a person should always do their best to keep their promises."

Megan raised her gloved hands in surrender. "Sounds like I'm outvoted."

"Yay!" Evie giggled.

Whit hefted her up, keeping his balance on the ice skates. "Did you have something already picked out, kiddo?"

She bobbed her head, pigtails swinging around her earmuffs—which she had instead of a hat so she could still wear her tiara. "I wanna get the snow princess costume so I can freeze the monsters."

Megan's stomach plummeted. This night may have felt like a magical escape from real life. But she couldn't afford to forget for a second that her everyday reality and responsibilities were still waiting for her once this fantasy weekend was over.

This night was all she could have with Whit.

The more time he spent with Megan on this trip, the more Whit was certain he should take his time with her, get to know her. Win her over gradually once they got home.

For now, here in their cozy ski chalet, he needed to

keep his distance. He needed to bide his time. Rushing her tonight could well cost him all the progress he'd made. Megan wasn't the type to be interested in a one-night stand, and quite frankly, he couldn't imagine that once with her would be enough.

The chalet was a three-bedroom in Vail, with a full sitting room and kitchen that overlooked a lake. He'd originally gotten three bedrooms to assure Megan that he respected her privacy, while still leaving their options open. But that timetable had changed.

He'd just finished building a fire in the old-fashioned fireplace when Evie's bedroom door opened and Megan stepped out. Her hair was loose and curlier than normal around her face after their evening at the windy ice rink. She still wore her jeans and green fuzzy sweater, no shoes though, just thick socks. Her toes wiggled into the carpet as if she was anchoring herself in the room. Finally, he had her alone and today of all days he'd resolved to bide his time.

It would take all his restraint to keep himself in check.

Tucking aside some extra logs to keep the fire burning for a few more hours, he stepped behind the wet bar and pulled out a bottle of sparkling water. "Would you like something to drink? The bar is stocked. There's juice and some herbal tea…"

"Any wine? Preferably red." She slid a band off her wrist and tugged her hair back to gather it into a low ponytail. "One glass won't incapacitate me."

"Oh, sure," he said, surprised. He scanned the selection and found a good bottle from a reputable California vineyard. He poured a glass for her, water for himself. He passed her the crystal glass.

She savored a sip and smiled, sinking down in the

middle of a pile of throw pillows on the sofa. She could have chosen the chair, but she'd left room for him to sit, even sweeping aside one of the pillows to clear a space. Intentional or not? He kept his silence and waited while she gazed into the fire for a long moment.

"Thank you for everything, Whit. For bringing us here, for going to so much trouble to arrange such a special evening for Evie too." Megan tucked her legs to the side, the flames from the fire casting a warm glow on her skin. "It was an incredible way to end an already wonderful day."

As she shifted, her socks scrunched down to her ankles, revealing a tiny paw print tattoo. How had he never noticed that before? Did she have others hidden elsewhere on her body? His gaze fixed on that mark for an instant before he took his tumbler and sat in the leather chair beside her.

Was that a flicker of disappointment in her eyes?

"No trouble at all," he said. "This has been a nice change of pace from eating alone or playing darts at the club."

"You aren't fooling me for a second." Her green eyes twinkled with mischief. "Your life is much more fast-paced than that."

"If you're asking if I'm seeing anyone, the answer is no." Although the fact that she would ask gave him hope he was on the right track playing this cool, taking his time. "You have my complete and undivided attention."

Her eyes went wide and she chewed her bottom lip. "Really?"

He angled back, hitching a booted foot on his knee. "That was impressive seeing you in action today. You were amazing interviewing the foster families and sifting through all that paperwork. I had no idea how much detail went into ensuring the animals are safe and well cared for."

"I'm just doing my job, a job I'm very happy to have. I get to do the work I love in an environment that is flexible about letting my daughter join me. It's the best of both worlds and I intend to be worthy of keeping the position."

"Well, I don't know a lot about the animal rescue world, but from what I can tell, whatever they're paying you can't be nearly enough for how much heart you pour into saving each one of those cats and dogs."

"We're all called to make a difference in the world. This is my way," she said simply and sipped her wine, her eyes tracking him with a hint of confusion.

Keep on course.

And he found himself actually wanting to get to know her better. Staying in the chair and finding out more about Megan wasn't such a hardship. "What made you choose this line of work?"

"I've always loved animals."

"But it must be more than that."

She eyed him over the rim of her glass. "Most people accept the simple answer."

"I'm not most people."

He stared back, waiting even though he wanted to close the space between them and lay her down along that sofa. He burned to cover her, kiss her. Take her.

"Well, while other girls were reading *Little House on the Prairie* or Nancy Drew novels, I devoured everything I could find on animals, their history, how to care for them, how to train them." The more she spoke, the more she relaxed on the throw pillows piled on the corner of the sofa. "I had these dreams of going to the big dog shows with my pup Snickers. I watched the shows over and over again so I could train him to do all the moves."

She was so buttoned up and proper, all about the rules, he hadn't expected such a quirky story from her. He wanted to know more. "What happened?"

Megan rolled her eyes and lifted her glass in toast. "Somehow I missed the memo that the dog show was just for purebreds."

"What kind of dog did you have?"

"A Jack Russell-Shih Tzu mix. Absolutely adorable and somehow unacceptable." She shook her head. "Wrong."

"I'm sorry you didn't get to have your big show with that pup."

Her gaze narrowed to a steely determination he'd seen before, except he'd been the cause of her ire then.

"Oh, I made sure Snickers still had his moment in the sun. I trained him to ride a skateboard, made a video and sent it into the *Late Night* show. Imagine my mom's surprise when they contacted us. I went on the show. And my dog was famous for a week."

He leaned back with a chuckle of admiration. "If you did that today, you'd get a reality show."

"You could be right."

"You were famous for more than a week. I remember that story now...."

"I ran the talk show circuit until my fifteen minutes of fame was up."

He blinked in surprise. "Somehow I didn't guess you were a limelight seeker. I envisioned you more as the studious type, the crusader in a more conventional way. Now I see where Evie gets her showmanship."

She laughed. "We've never really spent enough time with each other to form opinions."

"You must have been fearless." His mind filled with images of her as a child, as quirky and incredible as little Evie. "Most kids would be scared to put themselves in front of the camera that would broadcast them to the whole world."

"I was hoping my father would see me." She sipped her wine and stared into the flames crackling in the fireplace.

"Your dad?" he prompted.

"My biological father wasn't in my life. He made child support payments and sent a birthday card with a check each year, which puts him one step ahead of Evie's dad, who hasn't so much as bought her a pair of shoes." She cleared her throat. "But back to my father. I know he saw the show because he mentioned it in my next birthday card. He'd noticed, but it didn't change a thing." She shrugged. "I found out later he was married. I worry about Evie, since her father's chosen not to be a part of her life."

"I imagine it doesn't help to hear that missing even a minute with Evie is his loss."

She held up a hand. "Stop, I don't want sympathy. I love my daughter and I've worked hard to build this life. I just want her to have an easier path, to find a man who will value what a gift she is."

"That makes sense."

She leaned forward, elbows on the arm rest. "I'm not sure you're hearing me though. I can't afford to make another mistake in a relationship. I have to be a good example as her mother, as a woman."

Was she tossing him on his ass before they even got started? He angled forward, and suddenly the space between them wasn't so great after all. "That doesn't mean you can't have a social life."

"I need to be careful for my daughter." She nibbled on her bottom lip. "So things like dating, especially now, need to be on hold."

She half rose from the sofa and her mouth was a mere inch away from his as he sat in the leather chair beside her. Her pupils widened with unmistakable arousal. But she'd just said she wasn't interested in dating. He had to be misreading her...unless...she wanted a one-night stand, which was ironic as hell since she was the first woman he'd had serious thoughts about dating in a very long time. Before he could wrap his brain around that thought—

She kissed him.

Five

Shimmers of desire tingled through her.

Megan settled her mouth against his. It was no impulsive "thank you" this time. She'd thought it out, planning to make the most of this evening with Whit. She could indulge in this much before returning to everyday life and responsibilities.

She'd spent so much of the past three and a half years annoyed at Whit, resisting the attraction. Until now. She'd been tempted, seeing the altruistic side of him that she'd heard about but he'd done his best to keep hidden from her. Then watching him with her daughter totally slayed her.

Just one night. That's all she could have. And she intended to make the most of it.

Her lips parted against his, encouraging… *Yes.* His tongue traced along her mouth, sweeping inside to meet hers. Kissing. She'd longed for a man's kiss, the bold give and take, the hard planes of a masculine body.

Of his body.

Whit.

She'd been attracted to him from the start, and resented those feelings since they'd been at odds over the property dispute. Not to mention he wasn't particularly known for being environmental friendly. She'd given him an earful once over his purchase of a piece of wetlands.

However, even if they hadn't been adversaries, she'd been wary of dating because of her little girl, who was less than a year old then. The memory of Evie's father's betrayal had still been so fresh. She'd been struggling to put her life together and Whit had threatened to rock that. She'd been tempted though, then deeply disappointed when he quickly squelched those fantasies by being a ruthless land baron, causing her constant headaches.

The ache was lower now, pooling between her legs. She thrust her fingers into his hair, and something seemed to snap inside of him. His muscular arms wrapped around her, hauling her closer until her chest pressed to his and she sat on his lap. She wriggled against him and straddled his legs, kneeling on the leather chair. His low growl of approval rumbled against her, flaming the heat inside her higher, hotter.

His hands slid down her back in a steady caress to cup her hips. The steady press of his fingers carefully sinking into her flesh had her writhing closer. It had been so long since she'd languished in these sensations of total, lush arousal. Maybe she was feeling emotional in the wake of the storm's destruction, leading her to want something more.

And judging from his response, he felt the same. She'd known he was attracted to her too. She couldn't miss that in his eyes. But feeling the thick length of his arousal against her stomach sent her senses reeling.

His mouth moved along her jaw, then down her neck, his breath caressing along her overheated skin. Her head fell back to give him better access and with each breath she drew in the scent of his aftershave mixed with the sweet smell of fragrant smoke wafting up from the fireplace.

He stroked her arms, then ran his hands up over her shoulders to cup her face. The snag of his callused fingertips sent a thrill through her. He was a man of infinite finesse and raspy masculinity all at once. Would they go to her bedroom or his? She had condoms in her purse. Always. She loved her daughter but she wouldn't risk an unplanned pregnancy.

The thought threatened to chill her and she sealed her mouth to Whit's again, her fingers crawling under his sweater to explore the solid wall of his chest. His touch trailed back down her arms in a delicious sweep until he clasped her wrists.

And pulled her hands away from him.

She blinked in confusion. "Whit?"

He angled back, his brown eyes almost black with emotion. "You're beautiful. I've fantasized about what your hair feels like so many times."

Then he cradled her hips in his palms again and shifted her off his lap and onto the sofa. Were they going to take things further out here? She opened her mouth to suggest they go to her room when she realized he wasn't sitting down again.

She reached up for him, ready to follow him wherever. He took her hand and pressed a kiss to her palm.

His eyes held hers. "Thanks for an amazing day. I look forward to tomorrow." He squeezed her hand once before letting go. "Goodnight, Megan. See you in the morning."

Cool air chilled over her flaming face. The first time she'd kissed him she could write off as an accident and save her pride. But not now. And he'd clearly been turned on and into the moment. So why the rejection?

Damn it all, she didn't have time in her life for games. Anger took root inside her, fueled by frustrated desire. As far as she was concerned, he could take his mixed signals and stuff them.

She would communicate with him on a professional level for the animals. But beyond that, she was done throwing herself at Whit Daltry.

As Whit landed his plane on the runway back in Royal, he couldn't help but compare this journey home to their flight out to Colorado. Yesterday's trip had been full of chatter and fun. The whole day had been one of the best he could remember. And he wanted more of them—with Megan and with Evie. Which meant he had to stay the course. As much as he'd wanted to follow through on Megan's invitation last night, he sensed she wasn't as ready as her kiss indicated.

So today, he sat up front alone at the plane's helm, while Evie stayed in the back napping beside her mom. The craft glided along the runway, slowing, slowing, slowing. He taxied up to the small airport that serviced their little town, the only place that had ever felt like home.

Megan had stayed quiet all day for the most part, giving only one or two answers to his questions about her work. Had he offended her last night? He'd only intended to ramp her interest, to take his time rather than rush her and risk her bolting. And now she'd bolted anyway after one of the most explosive kisses of his life. Only a kiss, damn it.

A cinnamon-scented moment.

The memory of that instant with her had him hard and wanting her now. But from the steely set of her jaw and straight spine, another kiss wasn't welcome. He had some serious backpedaling to do.

He steered the plane into the appointed parking spot. His employees converged outside to service the plane, unload the luggage and all the empty animal crates. He opened the hatch and lowered the steps while Megan unbuckled her napping daughter. Megan hefted Evie up into her arms and paused by Whit, her eyes scrubbed free of any emotion.

"Thank you for everything," she said with a careful smile.

He touched her elbow. "It was a good weekend."

"I should get home to relieve the pet sitter. Evie and I need to tackle washing before Monday hits." She nibbled her bottom lip, anger flickering in her eyes.

Well, hell. That cleared up any questions. He didn't have to wonder if he'd upset her by giving her time and space. And in the process, he'd denied them both an incredible night together for no reason at all. He needed to let her know he wasn't rejecting her, just…giving her time to adjust to the change in their relationship. "Do you need help with anything? I'll have the crates delivered back to the shelter."

"Thank you," she said tightly, then looked away for a second, adjusting her hold on her daughter before meeting his gaze head-on again. "Listen, about last night when I kissed you—"

He tapped her lips. "Would you like to spend Thanksgiving together?"

Her eyes went wide with shock. "What?"

"Let's spend Thanksgiving together." He hadn't planned on that particular offer, per se, but it made perfect sense now as a way to show her he was serious. "Last night wasn't a game to me. Your place or mine, whichever you want. I don't expect you to cook for me."

"What is going on with you? You're giving me whip- lash." She cupped Evie's head. "You plan to make the meal?" She laughed skeptically.

"If you don't mind ptomaine poisoning." He scratched the back of his neck. "Actually, I have a cook- ing service and they'll cater Thanksgiving. Unless I got a better offer from you and Evie."

"No." She shook her head without hesitation. "I'm sorry. But no. Spending the holiday together would give Evie the false expectations about the two of us."

She was turning him down?

Okay, now he was truly confused. "We just spent the weekend together. How is an afternoon of turkey a problem?"

"You didn't hear me. It's Thanksgiving. A holiday. That's for families." Her throat bobbed with a quick swallow. "Last night, I, uh, I didn't mean to give you the wrong impression with that kiss."

"What impression was I supposed to get?" He braced a hand on the open doorway, trying to get a read on her. She'd kissed him, made it clear she was ready for sex but didn't want anything—close. Damn. She'd wanted a quickie with him and nothing more.

Now he was mad.

"Whit, you don't have to worry about me throwing myself at you anymore."

"Seriously?" he said, unable to believe he'd so misread this woman. "You expect us to go back to avoiding each other after the weekend we just spent together?"

"Not at all. I can behave maturely as I trust you can too. We both have to live in this town." Without another word, she descended the stairs and stepped out into the sunshine. The rays streamed over her hair, turning it into a beacon, and he couldn't peel his eyes away.

Damn, she was hot when she was all fired up. Of course she was hot any time. And while he'd misjudged her intent with the kiss Saturday, he hadn't misread her interest. For some reason she thought a one-night stand would suffice, but she was wrong.

He would give her some space for now. Holidays were tough. He got that. But after Thanksgiving?

They would not be ignoring each other.

Monday morning, Megan carried her sleepy daughter with her into work. The familiar chorus of barking dogs greeted her, reminding her of her responsibilities here, to all of the animals still in need of homes. Saturday's placement of twelve cats had been an amazing coup for such a small shelter. She couldn't afford to turn down Whit's generous offer of his plane, but she also couldn't put her heart at risk again.

The weekend with Whit had been better than she could have dreamed. He'd been charming, helpful, generous. He'd been amazing with her daughter.

And he'd been a perfect gentleman.

She was the one who'd gone off the rails and kissed him. She'd literally thrown herself at him. Again. Sure, he'd responded, but then he'd pulled away. She was starting to feel silly.

Except she knew she hadn't misread the signs. He wanted her too. So why did he keep pulling away? She'd all but promised him a night of no-strings sex and he'd still walked.

Usually guys bailed out because she had a kid. Those guys were easy to spot. They were awkward with Evie. But Whit wasn't that way.

Had he freaked out that there was a child in the picture at the last minute anyway? She didn't think so. His eyes had still smoked over her at every turn Sunday. But she hadn't felt up to the embarrassment of doing a postmortem on how he'd walked away from taking that kiss to its natural conclusion.

Damn it, she didn't have time for these kinds of games in her life. Which was the very reason she'd wanted one night, just one night with him.

She nodded to Beth at the front desk and walked past to settle Evie in her office on the small sofa. Evie had chosen a doctor's costume today, to cure all the people and animals hurt in the tornado. The post-Halloween sales had filled Evie's costume box to overflowing. Every time Megan or one of her friends offered to buy her a toy, Evie shook her head and picked another outfit. Megan had thought about counseling, even discussed it with the preschool director. Sue Ellen had pointed her in the direction of some videos the other children in the preschool had watched together, but so far those hadn't effected any changes in Evie.

Megan sagged against the open door frame.t

Beth waved from the desk. "Good morning. How was your weekend?"

She dodged the question that she didn't even really know how to answer. "You're here early."

Beth cradled a mug of herbal tea, the scent of oranges and spices drifting across the room. "The kennel supervisor let me in. I wanted to see your face when you came to the shelter today."

Alarms sounded in Megan's mind. "Is something wrong?"

"Things are very right." Beth set aside her mug. "A dozen guys—and women—from the Cattleman's Club spent the weekend volunteering."

Another reason to be grateful to a man she'd spent the past three and half years resenting. "Whit said he intended to ask them to help out...."

And she was grateful. She'd assumed a couple of them would come by to play with the dogs.

"Well, they did more than help out. In addition to doing the regular cleaning and exercising the dogs, they fixed the broken kennel run and cleared an area behind the play yard that's been full of debris. They said they'll be back after Thanksgiving weekend to build an agility course for the dogs and add a climbing tree for the cat house." Beth winked, her eyes twinkling with mischief. "You must have really impressed him."

Megan's knees felt wobbly. He'd coordinated all that effort this weekend while she'd been thinking about a quick fling? She'd had Whit Daltry all wrong. All. Wrong.

"Whit mentioned putting in a call, but I had no idea how much they would do. Especially when everyone is still dealing with the upheaval in their own lives."

"They care about each other and our community. They just needed pointing in this direction to help. It's okay to ask for help every now and again, Megan. You don't have to be a superwoman."

She nodded tightly. "For the animals, absolutely."

"For yourself."

Megan stayed silent, uncomfortable with the direction of the conversation. She was happy with her life, damn it. She was looking forward to spending Thanksgiving with her daughter, eating turkey nuggets and sweet potato fries.

Memories of Evie's laughter at the ice skating rink taunted her with all she might be missing.

"So?" Beth tipped back the office chair and sipped her tea. "How did things go with you and Whit on the great kitty transport?"

"Fantastic. The rescue is all foster-home-based, so every cat is now placed with a family until an adopter is found." Megan opted for impersonal facts. She walked to the shelves by a small table and straightened adoption applications and promotional flyers. After Thanksgiving, she would need to put up a small Santa Paws tree for donations. So much to do. She didn't have time for anything else. "I even made some notes for our shelter on how they handle their foster system."

"Sounds like Whit is really bending over backwards to mend fences with you."

Megan crossed her arms over her chest that still yearned for the press of Whit's body against hers. "As you said, we all need to do what's best for the community right now."

"Sure, and sometimes it's personal." Standing, Beth said, gently, "Like now."

"I never even implied—"

"You don't have to. You're blushing!" Beth pointed, her nails short and neat. She stepped closer and whispered, "What happened while you were in Colorado? Come on. I tell you everything. Spill!"

"There's nothing to tell." Sadly. Megan had wanted more and still didn't know why he'd pulled away. "My daughter was with me. How about we discuss your love life? Yours definitely has more traction than mine. How are things with you and Drew Farrell? Have you set a date?"

"Weeellll, a Valentine's wedding would be nice, but we'll see." She set aside her mug with a contented sigh. "For now, we're enjoying being together and in love. Repairs are still going on at my house. Once they're done, we'll decide if I'm going to sell or stay at Drew's."

"How's Stormy?"

Beth had adopted a cocker spaniel mix from the shelter, similar to her dog Gus that had died. Stormy had stolen Beth's heart when she'd volunteered after the tornado. "Full of mischief and a total delight."

"And the cats?" She stalled for time.

When Drew first dropped Beth off at the shelter after the storm to help Megan with cleanup, Megan encouraged Drew to take a couple of cats home with him. He'd insisted he was allergic to cats, but Megan could tell he and Beth were both enchanted. Since the kittens had come from a feral litter, placing them would have proved difficult at a time when they were already packed. Megan had mentioned the possibility of him needing barn cats—and it was a match made in heaven.

"They spend more time indoors than in the barn. Drew pops a couple of antihistamines and watches ball games with them in his lap." Home-and-hearth bliss radiated from her smile. "It's adorable."

Megan didn't begrudge Beth that joy, but God, it stung today of all days. "I'm happy for you both. For Stormy and the cats too. Thank you for taking them."

"Our pleasure."

Hearing how easily Beth said "our," Megan couldn't help but ask, "You and Drew were enemies for so long. How did you overcome that negative history so easily?"

"Who said it was easy?"

"Oh, but—"

Beth rested a hand on hers. "It's worth the effort." She sat back with a sigh. "I'm still in the 'pinch me' stage with this relationship. It's everything I didn't dare to dream of growing up."

Beth was a jeans-and-cotton-shirts kind of girl, with a causal elegance she didn't seem to realize she had. If anything, she was a little insecure in spite of all her success, sensitive about her past and the whole notion of having grown up on the wrong side of the tracks.

Megan gave Beth an impulsive hug. "It's real." She leaned back with a smile. "I've seen the way he looks at you and I'm so happy for you, my friend."

"Thank you." Beth hugged Megan back. "By the way, I noticed you dodged answering my question about Whit. I only ask because I care. I want you to be happy. You deserve to have more in your life than work."

"I have my daughter." Megan sat at the table set up for people to fill out adoption applications, the Thanksgiving holiday suddenly looming large and lonely ahead of her.

Beth walked to the table and sat in the chair across from her. "And when Evie grows up?"

"Then you and I can have this talk again." She fidgeted with a pen, spinning it in a pinwheel on the table.

Beth's eyes turned sad. "I'll respect your need for privacy." Standing again, she started to return to the front desk, then looked back over her shoulder. "Oh, in case you wanted to tell the Cattleman's Club thank-you in person, this weekend they're having a big cleanup in preparation for Christmas decorating."

Whit couldn't remember having a crummier Thanksgiving. Thank God it was finally over and he could spend the weekend helping out at the club with cleanup and decorating.

His invitation to spend Thanksgiving with Megan and her daughter had been impulsive—he'd originally just planned to send some flowers as part of his gradual pursuit. So he'd been surprised at the level of disappointment when she'd turned him down for dinner. That frustration had gathered steam with each day he waited and she didn't return his calls.

His catered turkey meal had tasted like cardboard. He'd ended up donating the lot to a homeless shelter. There had been invitations from his buddies in the Cattleman's Club to join them and their families for the holiday, but he hadn't felt up to pretending. No doubt part of his bad mood could be chalked up to the memorial service planned for Craig next week.

He just wasn't up to being everyone's pal today, either, but he'd promised to help and so many of them had chipped in to volunteer at the shelter. This club was the closest thing to family he had.

Launched by some of the most powerful men in town, the Texas Cattleman's Club had stood proud in Royal, Texas for more than a century. The TCC worked hard to help out in the community while also being a great place for members to get away from it all and to make contacts.

To be invited into the TCC was a privilege and a life-long commitment. And for a man who'd grown up as rootless as he had, that word—commitment—was something he didn't take lightly.

He climbed a ladder to hook lights along a towering tree outside the main building, an old-world men's club built around 1910. The tree was taller than the rambling single-story building constructed of dark stone and wood with a tall slate roof. Part of that roof had been damaged by the tornado, as were some of the out-buildings.

Looking in through the wide windows, he could see other club members and their families decorating the main area, which had dark wood floors, big, leather-up-holstered furniture and super-high ceilings. TCC president Gil Addison was leading a contingent carrying in the massive live tree to be used inside.

What would Megan think of all the hunting trophies on the wall? He'd never thought to consider her feeling on that subject given her work in animal rescue. But he sure as hell hoped it wasn't a deal breaker.

He hooked his elbow on the top of the ladder, look-ing out over the stable, pool, tennis courts and a re-cently added playground. Evie would love this place. He could almost envision her in her tiara, fitting right in with the rest of the kids. Except a person had to be a member to have full use of the facilities.

How had he gotten to the point in his mind where he was envisioning Evie and Megan here?

"Whit?"

A voice from below tugged his attention back to the present.

He looked down to find one of his pals from the Dal-las branch of the TCC, Aaron Nichols, partner in R&N Builders. Aaron had been overseeing the repairs to the club, but didn't appear to be in any more of a merry-making mood than Whit was. But then given the fact Aaron had lost both his wife and his kid in a car ac-cident several years ago, Whit could see how holidays must be particularly tough.

Which made him a first-class ass for feeling sorry for himself over being alone for Thanksgiving.

Whit hooked the lights along the top of the tree, wrapping and draping. "Hey, buddy, what can I do for you?"

Aaron handed up more lights, controlling the strand as it unrolled. "Just here to help. Shoot the breeze. Everyone's asking about you inside."

"Yeah, well, somebody's gotta take care of the tree out here." That had always been Craig Richardson's job.

Aaron nodded with an understanding that didn't have to be voiced. "Have fun on your big rescue mission?"

As if Whit hadn't been asked that question a million times already. Folks had expected him to bring Megan today. He'd entertained that notion himself while in Colorado, but she'd shut him down.

"We helped place a lot of cats, eased the burden on the shelter. It was a good day." He kept the answer brief and changed the subject. "Thanks for the cleanup at the shelter last weekend." Whit hooked the light over a branch. "I appreciate so many of you pitching in."

"We help our own," Aaron said with a military crispness he hadn't lost in spite of getting out of the service. "We would have gone sooner if we'd realized how tough things were at the shelter."

And Megan wasn't one to ask for help easily. He admired her independent spirit, her grit, the way she fought for her daughter and the animals. He just hadn't realized how much he would flat-out enjoy being with her too.

He hauled his attention back to the present rather than daydreaming like a lovesick teenager. "Everyone's been up to their necks in repairs. Sometimes it's difficult to tell where to start."

As he reached for Aaron to feed him more lights,

Whit caught a glimpse of a car approaching with a woman at the wheel.

There was a time when women weren't allowed at the club unless they were accompanied by a male member. But a few years ago the TCC had started allowing women to join, a huge bone of contention that caused great friction in the organization.

Now, however, almost ten percent of its members were females. Two years ago they'd added an on-site day-care center, which had created even greater discord. But this year, things had finally begun to settle down and feel normal for the TCC members. Watching everyone pull together today, Whit could see there was a real sense of camaraderie the club hadn't experienced in a long time.

So a woman coming to the club on her own wasn't a surprise or big deal. Except this woman had unmistakably red hair. Whit knew her from gut instinct alone, if not sight. His pulse sped up and he decided that this time, he wouldn't just bide his time. He'd known and wanted her for years. Aaron Nichols's presence had served to remind him how fast second chances could be taken away.

Whit tossed aside the strand of lights, leaving them tangled in the tree branches for now, and climbed down the ladder. Because he'd found the perfect distraction to lift his holiday mood and make him feel less like Scrooge.

Megan Maguire had come to the Texas Cattleman's Club.

Six

Megan told herself she was not coming to the Cattleman's Club to see Whit. Absolutely *not*.

Holding a Tupperware container full of homemade brownies, she exited her new-used compact purchased after the tornado took out her other car and hip-bumped the door closed.

Evie had wanted to bake on Thanksgiving so they would be like a real family. Real? The comment had sent Megan into a frenetic Betty Crocker tailspin that produced dozens of brownies.

She was proud of the life she'd built, damn it. She was an independent woman with a satisfying career and a great kid.

This morning hadn't been very easy though. Evie had thrown a screaming fit over the thought of wearing regular clothes to a playdate with Miss Abigail's great nieces. The counseling videos and books recommended by the preschool director just weren't working with

Evie. Finally, Megan had surrendered to the request for a homemade costume made out of cut up sheets. In the big-picture view of things, it was most important that Evie wanted to play with other kids again without her mom present. But Megan had had to draw the line somewhere. When Evie had wanted to be a zombie, Megan suggested she be a mummy instead. Somehow a mummy princess seemed more benign than a zombie princess. What four-year-old knew about zombies?

Megan adjusted her hold on the container of brownies and picked her way around the big trucks and SUVs in the parking lot. Halfway to the looming lodge, as she was passing a golf cart loaded down with fresh evergreen boughs and spools of red ribbon, she felt as if she was being watched. She tracked the sensation to a towering pine tree with a ladder beside it. Whit stood at the base, his boot on the bottom rung, Stetson tipped back on his head.

Of course she'd known he would be here today.

But she didn't know what she would say to him. At all. She'd been off-kilter this week, questioning herself. She'd spent all of Thanksgiving imagining what it would have been like to share the day with him. Had he been alone on the holiday because of her decision?

His offer to spend the day together had intrigued her the more she thought about it. But it also had her reliving their kiss in Colorado. Had she really thought she could just sleep with him for one night and then walk away? This was a small town. They would run into each other.

Often.

That was good motivation to tread warily, because if things exploded between them, there could be lasting fallout. Not just the upheaval it would cause for

Evie to lose a male figure in her life, but Megan also had to think of her job and how a big blow-up between her and Whit could make living in this town together awkward. She had to put Evie first and her daughter was happy here.

"Hey, hello, Megan," a female voice called out from a row of cars over.

Megan turned to see Stella Daniels waving as she got in her sedan to leave. The administrative assistant from the mayor's office had become an unexpected hero after town hall had taken a direct hit in the tornado. With Mayor Richard Vance still in the hospital, Stella was serving as the unofficial leader of Royal, giving interviews to the major networks and making heartfelt pleas for federal aid. Her quiet calm was just what the town needed in a crisis.

Megan could use some of that calm for herself.

Waving back, she smiled, then grappled to keep the plastic container from tumbling out of her arms. Stella ducked into her car; the organized woman was likely headed back to the office or off to inspect more cleanup efforts, even on the weekend.

Megan balanced the brownies again, turning back to the ladder only to find Whit gone. But it wasn't more than a second before Whit's broad hands came into view, sliding underneath the container.

"Can I help you with that?" he asked, his broad flannel-clad shoulders angling beside hers, their elbows bumping lightly as he shifted to help.

"Thank you. I brought these to thank the club for all their hard work at the shelter." She handed the three dozen turtle brownies to Whit.

"That's what we do." He glanced back over his shoulder. "Right, Aaron?"

Startled, she looked past Whit, surprised she hadn't even noticed Aaron Nichols was there as well. Just as she hadn't noticed Stella until the woman had called out. Megan had been one hundred percent focused on speaking to Whit. She'd seen that easy smile too many times in her dreams. Remembered the feel of his touch on her waist. Her hips...

Aaron clapped a hand on Whit's shoulder. "We can finish up later." He tipped his head to Megan. "Good to see you, Megan. Be sure this bozo doesn't keep all the brownies for himself. See you inside." He pivoted away and went into the lodge.

And then Megan was alone with Whit for the first time since before Thanksgiving. She searched for something to say to fill the awkward silence, finally asking, "What was Stella Daniels doing here?"

She tried not to let her gaze roam all over Whit. No easy task, that.

"She came to ask for help out at town hall. They're still plowing through debris and there's concern about lost files."

"If anyone can restore order in the chaos, Stella can." The town was lucky to have someone so competent leading recovery efforts during such a tumultuous time. "She's done some great work in organizing reconstruction during the mayor's recovery."

Mayor Vance had suffered massive injuries while working out of the town hall when the tornado hit. Stella seemed unsure of herself at times, but she was proactive in rounding up help where it was needed. And the Cattleman's Club was definitely the place to check, full of powerful movers and shakers in the community.

"The club is all in to do what we can." Whit's molten brown eyes held her for another long instant, making her skin tingle. "How was your Thanksgiving?"

She swallowed hard, thinking about how she'd been too much of a coward to return his calls. "Evie and I had a feast of chicken nuggets and sweet potato fries, then made turkey paintings using our handprints. The front of my refrigerator is full of artwork." She paused for an instant before asking, "How was your Thanksgiving?"

"Lonely," he said simply, without even a hint of self-pity, more like a statement of fact.

Surprise kicked through her, quickly followed by guilt that he'd spent the day alone after reaching out to her. "You didn't spend the day with friends?"

"They have families, like you do." He shrugged his broad shoulders. "But hey, it wasn't a total wash. I watched ball games and ate a catered meal."

The Whit she'd spent time with recently, the Whit who was standing here with her now, didn't fit the image of the man she'd known for over three years. She wasn't sure what to make of him now. She'd been so sure he was a wealthy, ruthless charmer.

Maybe he really was just a nice guy who wanted to be with her. What the hell was wrong with her that she'd been upset because the man had acted like a gentleman and didn't jump all over her during their trip? "I'm sorry you spent the day alone. After all you did for the shelter it was small of me not to include you in my Thanksgiving."

"I didn't want you to include me in your holiday out of gratitude." He looked past her, trees rustling overhead. "Where's Evie today?"

"Playing with Miss Abigail's great nieces." She took the brownies back from him under the guise of securing the lid but really to occupy her jittery hands. It had been Evie's idea to give the extra brownies to Whit, but Megan had been wary of showing up on his doorstep. Bringing baked goods to the whole Club offered her a face-saving option.

A smile played with his mouth, a sexy mouth that kissed like sin. "What's our princess dressed as today?"

Our? Had he noticed the slip of the tongue?

"She wanted to be a zombie, but I thought that was a little dark for a kid that young. We opted for a mummy, like 'Monster Mash.'"

"Good call." He frowned, his hand tucking under the brim of his Stetson to scratch his head before he settled the hat back into place. "She's still having a tough time?"

"I've talked to the day-care director about it. Sue Ellen suggested some videos and books with tips on how to promote discussion with a child after a traumatic experience. I have the name of a counselor too." She swallowed hard. "I hope we won't need to use it. I figured I would give her another week to ease back into a routine. Hopefully she'll get excited about Christmas celebrations at school."

"Hopefully," he echoed.

She should go. She reached and opened the container, releasing the intoxicating scent of chocolate. "Would you like an advance sampling of the brownies as an olive branch? Well, a chocolate kind of olive branch?"

She took one out to offer it.

He leaned in to bite off a corner of the brownie while she still held it. "Hmmm…" He hummed his appreciation as he chewed. "Damn, these are good."

His praise warmed her on a chilly day. "I'll take that as a compliment, coming from a man who can afford to eat at the best of the best restaurants."

"The cooking service I use has never brought anything as good as this." He popped the rest of the brownie in his mouth and reached for another.

"Over-the-top flattery." She scrunched her nose and set the container aside on the golf cart. "That can't be true."

"Sure it is." His smile was as bright as the dappled sunlight in the tree branches. "A cooking service is a luxury, but it's a necessity for me unless I want to eat at a restaurant every night, which I do not. I get to kick back in front of my television at night like a normal guy."

"A normal guy with a cooking service." She toyed with a strand of lights dangling off the cart.

"A cooking service I may have to fire since apparently they have been feeding me substandard brownies."

Damn it. How could she not like a guy who said things like that? She couldn't hide a smile.

"Evie and I will make some more just for you to thank you for the flight." The offer fell from her mouth before she could overthink it.

"I should say no, given how busy you are. But I'm going to be utterly selfish and accept." He finished off the second brownie.

"It's the least I can do after all your help. And you were so patient with Evie last weekend."

"That's a good thing. So why are you frowning?"

And there was the crux of things, her real reason for coming here with the brownies when she knew she would run into Whit. "My daughter is hungry for a father figure in her life. I just don't want her to build false hopes based on some nice gestures from you."

"Is that why you turned down my request to spend Thanksgiving together?" He raised an eyebrow.

"Yes, in part," she said carefully.

"You gotta know I think she's a great kid and I enjoy her company as well."

Yet another reason to like Whit. His affection for Evie was genuine.

Megan sagged back against a fat oak tree, bark rough even through her thick sweater and jeans. "She's a kid in a fragile state of mind. I'm not...comfortable risking anything upsetting her."

"Okay, okay...." Exhaling hard, he pressed a hand to the tree trunk, just above her head. "I can see where you're coming from on that, given the tiara and tornado-butt-kicking costumes."

"I'm glad you understand my predicament. I'm her mother. I have to put her needs first."

"You're a great mom too, from everything I've seen." His head angled closer. "I have to wonder though. Why did you kiss me in the hotel? Call me arrogant, but I wasn't mistaken in thinking you're interested...." He stroked her loose hair back over her shoulder. "Unless you were using me as a one-night stand. In which case you should be upfront about that. I'm not passing judgment. Just asking for honesty."

His touch sent a shiver down her spine. "Point taken."

"Exactly." His hand glided down to her shoulder blade, his fingers tangled in her hair.

Thank heaven everyone was inside, though the possibility that someone could catch sight of them through a window helped keep her in check. And heaven knew she needed all the help she could get to restrain her from throwing herself at him again. Her daughter's well-being had to be first and foremost in her mind.

"Whit, I'm just asking you not to use her to get to me.

She's a little kid who still believes in fairy tales where princesses can always win in the end."

"What about her mom?" He cupped the back of her neck, massaging lightly. "What does *she* believe in?"

His question stunned her silent for three heartbeats. "What does that matter?"

"Because, honest to God, I want to get to know you better."

His words filled the space between them with so much hope and possibility, she was scared as hell to step out on that ledge and risk a big fall.

So she settled for sarcasm. "You want to sleep with me."

"True enough." He eased his hand around to palm her cheek, caressing with his thumb. "Can you deny you're attracted to me?"

"Your ego is not your most attractive quality."

He chuckled softly. "What is, then?"

"Searching for compliments?" She tipped her chin. "I wouldn't have expected that from you."

He ducked his head. "Megan, I'm searching for a way to get through to you, because make no mistake, I want to spend more time with you. A lot more. I always have." His words and eyes were filled with sincerity. "I was able to keep my distance when I thought the feeling wasn't mutual. But now that I know you're attracted to me too? I'm all in."

Her breath hitched in her chest. "What does that mean?" Nerves made her edgy.

"A regular date, dinner with me."

Dinner scared her a lot more than the notion of no-strings sex. "I can't leave Evie alone and she can't stay out that late."

"What time does she go to sleep?"

She chewed her bottom lip, already seeing where he was going with this. "At eight."

"Then how about getting a sitter and we go out after she falls asleep."

"And this gossipy small town we live in?"

"There are plenty of places other than Royal to find dinner. We can get to know each other better talking during the drive."

She hesitated, wanting to agree but unable to push the words past her lips.

A smile stretched across his handsome face, giving him a movie-poster twinkle in his eyes. "I'll take that as a yes. See you tomorrow at eight-fifteen." Stepping back, he picked up the brownies again. "Let's take these inside so we can get started making plans for the evening."

The next day, after finishing up at the Cattleman's Club, Whit rushed home to shower and make plans for his evening with Megan. God, he needed her and not just for the distraction of forgetting about Craig's upcoming memorial service. But for the chance to be with her, talk to her, find out why she had this tenacious hold over his thoughts.

She'd clearly had reservations, but she'd still agreed. She'd been emphatic though that he couldn't arrive until after eight once she had Evie in bed.

As if he didn't understand how important it was to be careful of the little girl's feelings.

But one victory at a time.

He finished his shower and pulled out a suit, more ramped for this date than he could remember being... ever.

An hour later, he shifted his sports car into park

outside Megan's cute three-bedroom bungalow south of downtown. He'd left the truck at home tonight and opted for his silver Porsche. He wanted to make the evening special for her. He had things back on track to win Megan over. Tonight was a big step in the right direction.

He'd considered bringing her flowers, but didn't want to be obvious. So he'd opted to buy her a catnip plant. He'd actually bought two, one for her and one for his greenhouse even though he didn't have a cat. He'd also picked up a citronella plant that repelled mosquitoes to give him an excuse to stop by the shelter.

Walking up the flagstone path, he took in the multi-colored lights on the bushes and a little wooden sign that read *Santa, please stop here.* He climbed the steps and knocked twice just under the holly wreath on the door.

Dogs barked inside and he could hear Megan shushing them just before she opened the door. The sight of her damn near took his breath away. She wore a Christmas-red dress, the wraparound kind with a tie resting on her hip. Those strings made his fingers itch to untie the bow, to sweep aside the silky fabric and reveal the hot curves underneath. His gaze raked down her body, all the way to her bare feet, that tiny paw tattoo on her ankle tempting him all the more.

And he would have told her just how incredible she looked with her hair flowing loose to her shoulders except two dogs ran circles around his legs. He planted one hand on the door frame and gripped the terra-cotta pot with the catnip plant in the other. Some kind of Scottie mix in an elf sweater yapped at him while a border collie bolted out around the porch, then back inside.

"Sorry for the mayhem." Megan rolled her eyes.

"Piper and Cosmo just need a good run in the back yard before I go."

"No problem." He passed her the plant. "Catnip."

"Thank you, how thoughtful. Truffles, Pixie and Scooter will have a blast with it." Her smile was wide and genuine, her lips slicked with gloss. "Come on inside. Evie is asleep and Abigail should be here soon to watch her. Beth helps out, but since she's with your friend Drew…I just want to keep any talk to a minimum."

He swept off his Stetson as she stepped aside to let him in. He focused on learning more about her from her house to distract himself from the obvious urge to keep staring at her.

Her home was exactly how he would have imagined: warm and full of colors. A bright red sectional sofa held scattered throw pillows and three cats. Her end tables were actually wood-encased dog crates. A toy box overflowed in a corner.

And there were photos everywhere. Of her with Evie. Of them with the dogs. The cats too. Years of her life not just on the mantel but also in collages on the walls.

She held up the sprig of catnip. "I'm just going to water this."

He followed her into the kitchen and sure enough, the refrigerator front was decorated in finger-painted turkeys and a cotton ball snowman. He noticed her recycling station tucked just inside the laundry room, with its neat stacks of bundled newspapers and rinsed milk jugs in labeled bins. "I should take lessons from you on recycling."

"You should," she said pertly.

Chuckling softly, he looked past all those precise

labels, and saw a large crate with a familiar calico cat inside.

"Is that the same cat I brought to the shelter?" He pointed. "Tallulah? I thought she was staying in your office."

"Tallulah came down with an upper respiratory infection, so I brought her home to keep a closer watch over her." She turned off the water and set the plant on the counter. "I've been crating her to keep her separate from the other animals."

He knelt beside the extra-large enclosure, wriggling his fingers through the wire. The kitty woke, arching her back into a long stretch. She was a damn cute little scrap. "Is she going to make it?"

"She's doing much better now." Megan leaned a hip against the doorframe, crossing her arms over her chest as she watched him with curious eyes. "She's on medication. I've been keeping her at home with me at night to make sure she's eating and hydrated."

As if on cue, Tallulah went to the double bowl and lapped up water.

Whit stood again, inhaling Megan's cinnamon scent. "Do you often take animals home from work?"

"We all do. There are never enough foster homes, especially right now."

"And I added to that burden by bringing in Tallulah. I'm sorry about that."

"You're a confusing man, Whit Daltry." She studied him intently.

"If it makes you feel better, I'm not even close to understanding you yet either. But everything I've seen so far, I like." Unable to resist for another second, he tipped his head and brushed his mouth against hers.

The soft give of her lips and that sweet moan of hers

had him reaching for her. She didn't lean in, but she wasn't pulling away either. So he moved slowly, carefully. And savored the feel of her.

He slid his hands behind her, along her waist, the silkiness of her dress teasing his hand with thoughts of how silky her bare skin felt. He tasted her, drawing her closer and just enjoying the moment. Things couldn't go any further, not with the babysitter due to knock on the door at any second.

So he enjoyed just kissing Megan, learning more about the way the two of them fit together. Her arms slid around his neck and she pressed those sweet curves against him as her fingers toyed with his hairline. Such a small gesture, but each brush of her fingertips sent his pulse throbbing harder through his veins.

He backed her against the door and she stroked her foot up the back of his calf. A growl rumbled in the back of his throat, echoing the roar in his body to have this woman, to take her even though his every instinct shouted he would lose her if he moved too fast.

The doorbell rang, jarring him back to his senses.

For now.

A date.

She was on a no-kidding, grown-up date.

Megan couldn't even bring herself to feel guilty. Her child was asleep and well cared for and she was enjoying an adult evening out with a sexy, fascinating man.

The valet drove away to park the Porsche as she and Whit climbed the steps of the restored mansion-turned-restaurant. She had heard about the French cuisine at Pierre's, but never had the spare cash or free time to try it for herself. Her heels clicked on her way up the stairs and she couldn't miss the way Whit's eyes lingered on her legs.

A rush of pleasure tingled through her.

Sure, she loved being a mom and enjoyed her job, but it was nice to slip into a dress that wasn't covered with ketchup or cat hair. She tucked her hand into the crook of Whit's arm as they stepped over the threshold into the warm, candlelit restaurant. Her fingers moved against the fine weave of his suit jacket.

A string quartet played classical carols in the foyer, elegant strains swelling up into the cathedral ceiling. She was so preoccupied with taking it all in she almost ran smack dab into an older couple. She started to apologize, then realized—damn it—they weren't the only Royal residents who'd ventured outside the city limits.

She forced herself to relax and smile at Tyrone and Vera Taylor. "Good evening. Imagine running into you two here."

She'd hoped to keep her relationship with Whit out of the public eye a while longer, but she should have known that would be next to impossible, in most any local restaurant given their wide circle of friends.

"Whit?" Tyrone said. "What are you—? Oh, well, hello, Ms. Maguire."

"Good evening, sir," Whit answered the silver-haired man. Tyrone had a reputation for riding roughshod over people, but Whit met him face on without a wince.

Megan considered asking them about their newborn grandbaby in the NICU, about their daughter Skye still in a coma, but rumor had it Vera wasn't enthused about being a grandmother. The possibility of that poor little baby being unwanted hurt Megan's already vulnerable heart. So she simply said, "You and your family are in my thoughts."

"Thank you," Vera answered tightly before turning to her husband. "Tyrone?"

The blustery man clapped Whit on the shoulder. "We'll let you get to your meal. I'll see you at the town hall cleanup…and of course at Craig Richardson's memorial service."

"Yes, sir." Whit nodded curtly.

Megan wondered if the others noticed the tension in Whit's shoulders at the mention of his dead friend. She tucked her hand into the crook of his arm again and squeezed a light reassurance.

The maître d' arrived and saved them from further awkward conversation by leading the Taylors to their table while the hostess guided Whit and Megan to theirs—thankfully on the other side of the room.

Megan settled into her seat, the silver, crystal and candlelight a long way from chicken nuggets and fast food on the run. Music from the quartet filled the silence between them until their waiter took their order. They both settled on the special: rack of lamb, white grits and Texas kale.

As she stabbed at her salad, she realized just how quiet Whit had gone and knew with certainty that the mention of his friend Craig had hit him hard.

"Are you okay?" She rested a hand over Whit's. "We don't have to do this tonight."

"I want to be here with you." He flipped his hand over to squeeze hers. "I'm good."

"You don't have to be Mr. Charming all the time." In fact, she sometimes wanted a sign to know what was real about him, what she could trust, because lately he seemed too good to be true. "We can call it a night and reschedule."

His thumb caressed along the sensitive inside of her

wrist. "No. I need a distraction and you're a damn fine one."

"Thank you, I think." She tipped her head to the side. "I'm just so sorry for your loss."

"Me too. It was just so…." The tendons in his neck stood out, and even in the dim candlelight, she could see his pulse throbbing along his temple. "Losing him in that tornado was just so unexpected."

She agreed on many levels. The whole town of Royal, Texas, had been tipped upside down by that storm. "Do you think we're both just reacting to all that life-and-death adrenaline?"

His gaze snapped up to meet hers. "What I feel for you has nothing to do with a natural disaster."

"But I kissed you that day and that changed things between us."

"Lady," a smile finally tugged at his handsome face, "I was attracted to you long before that kiss."

She'd suspected, but hearing that gave her a rush far headier than it should have. "I thought I was just a great big pain in the butt since I moved to town."

He glanced down again. "Craig used to tell me I should just sweep you off your feet."

"You told him how you felt?"

Whit shook his head. "I didn't have to. Craig guessed. He said it was obvious every time I looked at you." And his eyes held hers again now, full of heat and intensity. "But you shut me down cold right from the start. And I can't blame you. We had our disagreements. I thwarted your business plans. And you were quite vocal in your disapproval of my company buying wetlands. I thought I was saving us both a lot of grief by steering clear. Then you kissed me, and all bets were off. I would have acted sooner but when we got the news about Craig…."

The confirmation that he'd been wanting a relationship with her for so long rattled her more than a little. "You've been grieving."

"I have…still am." He glanced down for a couple of heartbeats before swallowing hard and looking back up at her. "But that doesn't stop life from happening. And it doesn't stop me from thinking about what happened between us that day. We can't ignore it."

Her face flamed. "I'm embarrassed that I kissed you."

"But you liked it." He leaned back in his chair, watching her over the candlelight. "So did I."

She couldn't deny it to him or to herself any longer. She wanted Whit, and she wanted him for more than just one night. "Obviously I liked it."

He leaned closer, took her hand across the table, the heat in his eyes smokier than the candle between them. "Then let's do it again."

Seven

After Whit's suggestive comment, dinner had passed in a blur of anticipation as she waited for this moment. To be in Whit's sports car heading to his house. To be alone. Together.

A part of her knew she'd done a grave disservice to the fine cuisine, but she could only think of the promise in Whit's eyes. Now they were finally at his house for after-dinner drinks and whatever else came next.

The garage door slid closed behind them, sealing them inside one of the four bays, where they were surrounded by other signs of his luxurious lifestyle. She'd seen the truck, but there was also a boat. A motorcycle. She gulped back a nervous shiver and concentrated on the man in the seat next to her instead. He was about more than expensive toys and an extravagant lifestyle. Whit was real. This was real. She was going to act on her feelings for this man. The attraction that had been simmering between them for days—weeks, years— would finally be fulfilled. She'd ached for him, dreamed of him.

Shifting in her seat, she smoothed her fingers over the red silk hem where it had ridden up one knee just a little. She'd dressed with care, wanting to be noticed. Yet the silk fabric had teased her too, clinging and skimming along her skin every time she moved.

Whit turned to her, the leather seat creaking. Her temperature spiked and heart pounded. She met his gaze and knew what was coming. She'd been waiting all evening....

He sketched his mouth over hers lightly. Once. Twice. Nipping her bottom lip and launching a fresh shower of sparks through her veins.

Then he eased back and looked into her eyes. "Going inside doesn't commit to anything more than you want."

She angled her head to the side and lifted an eyebrow. "Really? Are you going to kiss and bolt again?"

"Not a chance." He tucked his hand behind her head, his fingers massaging a sensual promise into her scalp. "I just want you to know I care about you."

The simple words were filled with layers of meaning she wasn't ready to delve into just now. Still, she held them close, savoring the heady warmth of being cared about by this handsome, magnetic man.

"I want to see the inside of your house." She stroked his face with one hand and reached for her door handle with the other. "So let's go."

"Yes, ma'am." He scooped up his Stetson. "I'm happy to oblige."

As she stepped out of the low-slung sports car, Whit was already holding the door open for her like the perfect gentleman he'd been all evening. His palm low on her back, he guided her past his Porsche and truck toward the door. The warmth of his hand seared through her silky dress. The silence wrapped around her as they climbed the three stairs into his house.

And holy cow, what a house.

Mansion would be a more appropriate word. She slipped off her heels and padded barefoot down the corridor leading to the main foyer. She wriggled her toes against cool marble, then into the plush give of a Persian rug. She tipped her head back to stare up the length of the stairway, up to the cathedral ceiling with a crystal chandelier. The scent of lemony furniture polish and fine leather teased her nose. Whit stood silently at her side.

God, the place was quiet compared to the constant mayhem of her home, with Evie's laughter, dogs barking, and kids' television shows playing. Curious to learn more about this man full of contradictions, Megan glanced at the dining room to her left, with its heavy mahogany table set, then turned to the living room on her right. She stepped through the archway, taking in the tan leather sofas and wingbacks, tasteful while still being oversized for a man. She trailed her fingers along the carved mantel above the fireplace.

"What do you think?" he asked from behind her, his footsteps thudding on the hardwood floor.

"It's…" She searched for a word to describe the surroundings that had clearly been professionally decorated, just as his meals were professionally prepared. The place was pristine. High-end gorgeous. Yet missing all the touches that made a place a home. There was no clutter, no scars on the furniture from the wear and tear of making memories.

And there were no pictures, just knickknacks on

the shelves and gallery artwork on the walls. But no photos. That tugged at her heart as sad, so very sad. "You have a lovely home."

His hands fell to rest on her shoulders, his chin against her hair. "It's a damn study in beige and I never realized that until I compared it to your place tonight. Kinda like how your brownies taste better than anything the best catering service could offer."

With every word, he made her heart ache more for him. She turned in his embrace and slid her arms around his neck. She saw so much in his eyes. So much caring and even a hope for things she wasn't sure she could give him.

But she couldn't think about that now. She refused to ruin this night by borrowing trouble from what might come. For now, she just wanted to enjoy this new connection and all the heady promise of his touch.

She stroked the back of his neck along his close-cropped hairline. "Do you really want to talk about paint swatches and recipes? Because I have something a lot more interesting in mind." She gripped his shoulders, her fingers flexing against hard male muscle. "The only question in my mind is, do you prefer the leather sofa or your bedroom?"

Megan's proposition fueled Whit's already smoldering need for her. Dinner had been a delicious torture as he waited to get her in his home, in his bed.

Although right now, the sofa sounded fine to him.

He skimmed the back of his fingers along her face. "You're sure this is what you want?"

"Are you kidding?" She tugged his hair lightly. "I thought I'd made my wishes abundantly obvious."

"I just want you to be clear." He cupped her face,

resting his forehead on hers. "This won't be a one-night thing."

She hesitated, but only for an instant before whispering, "I hear you."

"And you agree." He needed to hear her say it. He'd waited too long to have this woman in his arms to wreck it all now.

"How about this." She angled closer into his embrace, her cinnamon scent filling his every breath. "It isn't a one-night stand, but we're still going to take it one night at a time."

He'd wanted more, but she hadn't said no outright. He was a smart man. He'd made progress, and he wasn't going to wreck his chance with this amazing woman.

He wrapped his arms around her and pressed her soft body to his. "I can live with that for now."

"Good, very good." She swept her hands into his suit coat and shrugged his shoulders until the jacket fell to the floor. "Because you've been filling my dreams for a very long time."

"I would bet not as long as you've been in mine."

"Really?" Her green eyes went wide, her voice breathy. "Tell me more."

"Yes, ma'am. I'd heard about the hot new director at the shelter, then I saw you and you were—are—so much more than hot." He took a step toward the wide leather sofa, then another step. "But you shut me down cold because of the property dispute."

"I noticed you all right." She tugged at his tie, loosening it and pulling it free from his collar. "But yes, you made my life more than a little difficult by putting up roadblocks for the original shelter plans. And you're right that I don't approve of your company's history of buying up wetlands. But, to be honest, there's more. I was still wrapped up in getting my feet on the ground with Evie and being a mom."

"It didn't have to do with trusting men because of Evie's father?" he couldn't resist asking.

"This conversation is getting too serious." She backed toward the sofa, their feet synching up with each step. "Can we return to the part where you tell me I'm beautiful and I tell you I admire your abs?"

"You like my abs, do you?"

Her fingers stroked down again until she cupped his butt. "I like a lot about you, Whit Daltry."

"Nice to know." He leaned down to kiss her just as she arched up to meet him.

The taste of their after-dinner coffee mingled with the flavor of pure Megan. A taste he was coming to know well and crave more with each sampling.

Every time he held her, it was only more intense. He leaned forward at the same time she fell back. They landed on the leather sofa in a tangle of arms and legs and need. The sweet give of her curves under him sent desire throbbing through him, making him ache to be inside her. The silk of her dress as she writhed against him only tormented him with the notion of how much better her skin would feel. He wanted her now on the sofa and again upstairs. But he also wanted to make this moment perfect for her. No rushing.

Although that was getting tougher to manage with her tugging his shirt from his pants and working his belt buckle open. He toyed with the hem of her dress, his knuckles brushing the inside of her knee and drawing a husky moan from her lips.

He'd been fantasizing all evening long about untying her wraparound dress, and he intended to fulfill that fantasy. Soon. For now, he lost himself in the pleasure of kissing her, stroking along her creamy thigh. Taking his time. Taking them both higher and higher still until the need was a painful razor's edge.

Drawing in a ragged breath to bolster himself, he lifted off her. The image of her kissed plump lips, her flame-red hair splayed across the buff-colored sofa, was pinup magnificence.

She looked up at him with a question in her sparkling green eyes. She extended a hand. "Whit? Where are you going?"

"To carry you to my bedroom." He scooped her into his arms and against his chest.

Her gasp of surprise made him smile.

She got past her surprise quickly, though, and toyed with the top button of his shirt. "Luckily for both of us, that's exactly where I want to be."

He headed back into the foyer and past the stairs with long-legged strides that couldn't eat up the distance to the master suite fast enough.

Finally, finally, he crossed the threshold into his room. He'd never thought of it as more than a place to sleep. Houses—homes—weren't things to get attached to.

Just short of the four-poster bed, he set her on her feet. As she slid down his body, she thumbed free two more buttons on his starched cotton shirt.

She angled back as if to sit on the edge of the bed and he stopped her with a hand to the waist.

"Wait," he said, "we'll get there soon enough."

He dropped to his knees, his hands grazing over her breasts on his way to hug her hips. Her husky sigh urged him on as he eyed the tie of her dress, the loops right there for the taking, releasing. He took one end of the sash between his teeth. He looked up at her, holding her gaze with his. Her hands fell to his shoulders, but not to push him away. In fact, she swayed a bit, her fingers digging into his back, as if she was bracing herself to keep her balance. She dampened her lips with her tongue.

He tugged, slowly, imprinting the moment on his mind. Her dress parted and with a shrug of her shoulders she sent it slithering off into a pool at her feet. His breath lodged in his chest, then he exhaled in a long, slow sigh of appreciation.

The sweet swell of her breasts in red lace, the curve of her hips in crimson satin panties had him throbbing harder with the urge to be inside her. Now. And thanks to her bikini undies, he found the answer to his question about whether she was hiding more tattooed paw prints. She had a tiny trail along her hip bone. He took the edge of her panties in his teeth and let it lightly snap back into place.

"Megan, you are…beautiful beyond words. More than I even imagined, and what I imagined was already mighty damn awesome." His hands trembled as he reached to stroke her arms. Sure, he'd touched before but the feel of naked flesh was so much more intimate now that her curves were bared.

A flush swept over her lightly freckled skin. "And you, Whit, are seriously overdressed for the occasion."

She tugged him back up to stand again and unbuttoned his shirt the rest of the way, one deliberate move at a time, kissing each inch of exposed skin. Her licks and nibbles had him bracing a hand against one of the bed posts to keep from stumbling to his knees again. He kicked off his shoes while she made fast work of unzipping his pants and shoving them down and off. Her eyes widened with appreciation and she stroked the length of him. He gave up and let gravity take them both onto the mattress.

Whit laid her back on the bed, his bed. In his room. His house. Finally, he had her here after three and a half long years.

He stretched out on top her, hot flesh meeting flesh. Her curves melded to him, enticed him, made him ache all the more to be inside her.

The thick comforter gave underneath them. He stroked up the creamy satin of her skin, cupping her lace-clad breasts. Her nipples tightened against his palms. A low growl rumbled in his chest and he took one of those hard pebbles in his mouth, teasing and circling with his tongue through the fabric.

He reached a hand behind her and unhooked her bra. Then, yes, he took her in his mouth again, bare flesh this time, and she tightened with pleasure at the stroke of his tongue. Her fingers dug deeper into his shoulders, cutting tiny half moons in his skin.

The moment was so damn surreal. He'd been hoping for this chance to be with Megan since the day he'd met her. He'd held himself in check because she'd shut him down cold for so long.

She wasn't cold now. Not even close.

Megan matched him stroke for stroke, taste for taste, exploring him as he learned the landscape of her naked body. Each panting breath came faster and faster, hers and his, and he knew restraint was slipping away. He angled off her to reach into the bedside drawer and pull out a condom.

She smiled a thanks before plucking the packet from him. She tore the wrapper open, her eyes intent but her hands trembling. He understood the feeling well. She pressed a hand to his shoulder and nudged him onto his back.

With a smooth sweep of her leg, she straddled his legs. Her fiery red hair tumbled over her shoulder in a gorgeous tangled mess of curls. He reached to cradle her breasts in his palms, his thumbs circling. Her eyes fluttered closed for a second before she looked at him again and rolled the condom over him, one deliberate inch at a time, never taking her eyes off him.

He cupped her hips and drew her closer until his erection pressed against her damp cleft. She rocked against him and his fingers dug deeper into her flesh. Much more and this would be finishing too soon.

He lifted her from him and lowered her back to the bed, sliding on top of her again. She hitched a leg around his, gliding her foot along his calf and opening for him. He nudged against the warm, moist core of her, pressing and easing inside with a growl echoed by her sigh. He thrust deeper as she arched up with a with gasping "yesss."

Her hips writhed against his, her arms looped around his shoulders and holding him close. She gasped and whispered in his ear, nonsensical words that somehow he understood. He moved inside her, the velvety clamp of her body around him so damn perfect. Like her.

The need to pleasure her, to keep her, pulsed through him along with each ragged breath. He linked fingers with her, their clasped hands pressing into the comforter as they worked together for release. Damn straight he'd been right to wait for her, because being with Megan was more than special. This woman had him tied in knots from wanting her.

And even as he chased the completion they both craved, he was already planning the next time with her, and the next. But first, he had to be sure she felt every bit as rocked by the moment as he did. Whatever it took. He pulled a hand free and hitched her leg higher around him, kissing and stroking as he filled her.

Her head dug back into the pillow, thrashing, her gasps coming faster and faster, the flush on her chest broadcasting how close she was to…flying apart in his arms.

She arched against him, her arms flinging up to lock tighter, draw him closer and deeper as she dug her heels in and rode through each shivering echo of her orgasm.

The bliss on her face sent him over the edge with her.

He growled as his release shuddered through him again and again, each ripple of pleasure reminding him how much and how long he'd wanted this woman.

And how damn important it was to keep her.

Good sex mellowed a person.

But great, incredible, unsurpassable sex?

That made Megan nervous. She'd been looking for a brief, no-strings affair. What she and Whit had just shared made an already complicated relationship even more tangled.

Megan sat on a barstool at Whit's kitchen island, wearing his white linen shirt, while the man himself foraged in the refrigerator. He'd tugged on a pair of jeans and nothing more and heaven help her, he offered up an enticing view. His perfect butt in denim…his broad, bare shoulders… She swallowed hard and looked away.

She'd just had the best sex of her life. She should be rejoicing. Instead, she kept thinking about all the ways this could go so horribly wrong. And if it did, that failure would be in her face every single day because living in such a small town made it all but impossible to ignore each other.

Regardless of her intention to keep things light, tonight was a game changer. She knew that. To protect herself and her daughter, Megan would have to tread warily. Easy enough to do since her feelings for him made her jittery.

For now? Her best move would be to get to know as much about him as possible and figure out quickly whether or not to run.

Whit grabbed two bottled waters and closed the refrigerator. He opened a cabinet and pulled out two cut crystal goblets. He poured them each a glass and set them on the island just as the microwave dinged. He'd warmed their crème brulee dessert they'd brought home rather than waiting any longer at the restaurant.

He snatched up a potholder, pulled out the warm pudding and placed it on the island. The image of him all domestic and sexy had her mouth watering.

She eyed the empty bottles and walked to the counter, letting her hip graze his as she passed. "I'll just toss these for you. Where's the recycling?"

"Thanks. Check the door beside the pantry."

She tugged open the door to reveal a line of high-end built-ins, labeled with brass plates. "Be still my heart. This is amazing."

She smiled over her shoulder at him, then opened the bin marked *glass*. She found it empty and pristine, clearly never used. She tamped down disappointment and tossed the two bottles inside. She turned back to find him standing right behind her with a sheepish grin on his face.

Whit slanted his mouth over hers. "Forgive me?" He kissed her again, then teased her bottom lip lightly between his teeth. "I promise to try to be more earth-friendly in the future. Scout's honor."

"I wish you would do it because it's a good thing to do and not just to impress me." She enjoyed the bristle of his five o'clock shadow, savoring the masculine feel of him. "But I'll take the win for our planet however I can get it."

He chuckled softly against her mouth. "I appreciate your willingness to overlook my shortcomings."

His hands tucked under the hem of the shirt, cupping her hips in warm, callused hands. Goosebumps of awareness rose on her skin and she stepped closer, her feet between his as she flattened her palms to his bare chest. His heartbeat thudded beneath her touch, getting faster the longer the kiss drew out.

In a smooth move, he lifted her and set her on the island, his fingers stroking along her legs as he stepped back. "Food first. Then maybe we could share a shower—in the interest of conserving water, of course."

His promise of more hung in the air between them. He opened the silverware drawer and passed her a spoon.

Megan tapped the caramel crackle on top of the crème brulee, Whit's shirt cuffs flopping loosely around her wrists. "So I told you why I went into animal rescue. What made you decide to go into property development?"

He raised an eyebrow, his spoon pausing halfway to his mouth. "You say that like it's a something awful."

"I'm sorry. I didn't mean to sound…judgmental." She winced as she set her spoon down and folded back the shirt cuffs. "But I guess I wasn't successful in holding back."

"Well, I do have three and half years' worth of cold shoulders from you to go on."

"Help me to understand your side." She spooned up a bite and her taste buds sang at the creamy flavor. Of course, her senses were already alive and hyper-aware after both of the spine-tingling orgasms Whit had given her.

"I like building things. I like helping businesses and people put down roots." He stood at the bar beside her, so close he pressed against her thigh.

"You can build things anywhere. Why destroy wetlands with high-rise office buildings?" Damn it. There came her judgmental tone again. But she had values. She couldn't hide what she believed in just because it might stir old controversies.

"I'm not destroying the wetlands around here." He said with an over-careful patience. "I'm relocating them, responsibly and legally. Tell me how that's a problem."

At least he was asking. He'd never opened the door to discussion before, just shut her down.

But then hadn't she done the same?

Now was her chance. "By relocating you're creating a manmade, imitation version of something that already exists in nature. Why not leave nature alone?"

He scooped up a spoonful of the crème brulee. "I guess we'll have to agree to disagree on the word imitation."

"You say you care about the animals and environment by relocating the wetlands." Frustration elbowed its way into her good mood. She set her spoon down and tried another approach to help him see her side of things. "In order to save animals, I needed the best facility and location possible, which you blocked. Legal and ethical aren't always the same."

He quirked an eyebrow. "You landed on your feet. The animals are cared for. I made sure of that."

"What?"

"I made sure the piece of land you ultimately built on was affordable."

She wasn't quite sure what to do with that piece of information. She rubbed a finger along the rim of her crystal goblet. "Are you saying you offered up a diversion so I would back away from the property you wanted?"

"Do we have to rehash this now?" He tempted her with another spoonful of his caramel custard dessert.

"I think we do." She took the spoon from him, licked it clean and set it down. "I would have been closer to Evie the day of the tornado if the shelter had been built where the original plan called for."

"Fine." He leaned back and crossed his arms over his chest. "I can't make business decisions based on personal convenience and be successful."

"I understand that. Obviously." She searched his eyes for a sign of easing, but his expression was inscrutable. "But you also shouldn't pull your heart and humanity out of your job."

His eyes narrowed and chin tipped up as he reached to skim her hair over her shoulder, his hand lingering to stroke the sensitive spot behind her ear. "How can I make you get over that grudge?"

"I'm not sure. Show me you've changed...." She struggled to think, tough as hell to do with his touch enticing her to just sink into his arms again. "Or convince me you didn't do anything wrong."

"Megan," he said, exasperation dripping from that one word. Then he kissed her in an obvious attempt to distract her. "You're trying to pick a fight with me so I won't get closer. Am I wrong?"

His breath was warm along her face.

She whispered, "You're not wrong."

He nodded, then pulled back, his hand trailing along her arm. "Tell me how teaching your dog to ride a skateboard led you to become a shelter director rather than, say, a lion tamer?"

She grasped the safe topic with both hands, grateful for the reprieve. "I was always the little girl bringing home stray kittens and lost dogs. My mother was terrified I would get bitten or scratched, and looking back I can totally see her point." She shrugged. "But nothing she said stopped me—you may have noticed, but I'm very stubborn. So my mom signed me up for this thing called 'Critter Camp' at our local Humane Society. It was a summer camp for kids. We learned about animal care, animal rights, responsible ownership and yes, animal rescue."

"Sounds like a great program."

"My mom had to work overtime to pay for it." The memory pulled her under, back to those days of her mother scrimping to support her child. Megan understood the fear and weight of that responsibility well. "I didn't realize that until I was older, begging to go to the camp for the fifth year in a row. But I was hooked. I looked into the animals' eyes and they needed me. But they also saw how much I needed them. People don't always realize that they save us just as much as we save them."

"Why haven't you started a critter camp here? I'm certain it would be a huge success."

A dark smile tugged at her mouth and she dropped

a hand to his knee, squeezing. "Are you sure you want the answer to that?"

"I wouldn't have asked unless I wanted to know." His hand fell to her leg, his calluses rasping along her sensitive inner thigh.

She swallowed hard and tried to think past the delicious sensation. "Lack of space because of the plot of land we had to take as the consolation prize when you blocked the purchase of our original choice."

"You said you were content with the second location." Concern creased his forehead, but his hand inched higher.

She clamped his wrist. "It's farther from the schools, which makes logistics tougher for after-school programs. There are a host of other reasons—"

"Such as?"

"We need space to enlarge the dog park, and then there's the budget." She moved his hand back to the counter. "But if you start writing checks to the shelter and offering flights for animals, while generous, that does not buy you time with me. If you want to make a donation, I'll gratefully accept as the director. But we have to keep that separate from me—Megan, the woman."

He clasped her hand and brought it to his mouth, kissing her knuckles. "That said, will Megan, the *sexy* woman, have dinner with me again?"

Another brush of his mouth along the inside of her palm made it tough for her to think, but then that was a problem even when they weren't touching. She needed time to get her head together. She needed to figure out if it was even possible to let this play out regardless of the consequences.

That wasn't something she could figure out now.

"I'm helping with the town hall cleanup tomorrow afternoon while Evie naps. We can talk about it then." She slid off the barstool. "I should get dressed and go home. I have to think about all that's happened between us."

He held on to her hand. "Remember what I said about one-night stands. I don't do them."

Could she trust in those words when neither of them knew what the future held? She searched his eyes and saw he believed what he said. For now.

Somehow that only made matters more complicated. "I remember." She let go. "I'll see you tomorrow—at town hall."

Eight

The next day, Whit spent hours sifting through the rubble inside a town hall office, his buddy Aaron helping, but there was still no sign of Megan. This whole place was a lot like the mess of his life. His evening with Megan had been right on track. He'd been so certain they were making progress.

Then somehow things had derailed near the end for reasons that went a helluva lot deeper than his unused recycling bins. He still wasn't sure how they'd steered off course. It was as if they'd both self-destructed by discussing things guaranteed to drive a wedge between them.

And she still hadn't shown up for the town hall cleanup effort as they'd planned.

After their argument last night, they'd both thrown on their clothes and he'd driven her home, silence weighing between them in the dark evening streets. It was around one o'clock when they arrived, and he'd insisted on walking her to her door, where he gave her one more searing kiss. But she'd drawn the line there. She didn't want him to come inside where Abigail waited, babysitting Evie.

Work boots scuffling through dusty and crumbled brick, he took another garbage bag from Aaron. The job was too mindless to take his thoughts off Megan and what had happened last night. He trusted Abigail to keep her word to stay silent about their date until they—until Megan—was comfortable revealing the news to the town. But this had gone beyond Abigail. Given that they'd run into the Taylors at the restaurant last night, the whole town would know soon enough anyway.

As if there wasn't enough to keep everyone occupied. Like rebuilding the town.

The perimeter of town hall had been secured but there was no quick fix to all the destruction, especially inside in the few areas of the building still standing. Town hall had been almost totally destroyed. Only the clock tower had survived unscathed, but since the tornado, the time had been perpetually stopped at 4:14. The planning committee had decided to rebuild on the same location, but the cleanup effort would take time. They had to be careful sorting through the mess. Even in the digital age, there was so much damn paperwork.

Outside, Tyrone Taylor was barking orders to people as if it was his place to take charge. The guy seemed to think he ran the town. Luckily for them, Stella Daniels was there, and she had a quieter approach. A far more effective one at that. She let Tyrone bluster away and quietly followed up behind him giving direction and thanks.

Whit scanned the crowd outside the cracked window, over the parking lot, looking for Megan but she still hadn't shown. He hadn't heard from her since he'd driven her home. He'd called in the morning to offer her a ride over, but she hadn't answered. Was this a replay of the day the tornado hit when she'd shut him out after the kiss?

Being with Megan had been even more incredible than he'd expected. And his expectations had been mighty damn high.

He ground his teeth and focused on what he could fix. "Hey, Aaron, wanna help me lift this bookshelf and put it back against the wall?"

"Sure thing." Aaron squatted and braced both hands under one side of the walnut shelf. "Okay, Whit, on three, we lift. One. Two. Three."

Whit braced his feet, hefting and pushing alongside his friend until the bookcase was standing upright again. Files and thick hardbacks littered the floor where it had fallen. They were dry, but some had been soaked in the past, their pages curled and dirty brown. "We can put the undamaged items on the shelf again and stack the ruined stuff on the desk. The staff can decide what's crucial to keep."

"Sounds like a plan to me." Aaron scooped up two large volumes and paused, half standing, then pointed to the window. "Check out who just arrived—your shelter director lady friend."

Whit pivoted fast, then realized he'd given himself away with how damn eager he was just to see her. But he kept looking as she picked her way around a trash dumpster and a pile of broken boards. The sun streamed down on her fiery red hair, which was held back in a loose ponytail. Her jeans and shelter sweatshirt might as well have been lingerie now that he knew what was underneath. She could have been wearing a burlap sack and he would still want her.

Aaron stepped up beside him at the window. "So you and Megan Maguire have made peace with each other."

"We weren't at war." His denial came more out of habit than anything else; he was still focused on Megan, who was now talking to Lark Taylor, a local nurse passing out surgical masks for people to wear in the dusty cleanup.

"Like hell you two weren't constantly at odds," Aaron said. "You can't rewrite history, my friend. We all know how contentious things got over that land dispute when she wanted that site for the shelter. What I can't understand is how you got her to overlook how you buy up wetlands to build. She went ballistic last time it was mentioned."

As if Megan could hear their conversation—or feel the weight of Whit's stare—she turned, her eyes meeting his through the window with a snap of awareness as tangible as a crackle of static. He waved in acknowledgment, then turned back to cleanup detail. "We stay away from controversial topics these days."

Aaron didn't let him off the hook so easily. "Ah, you are seeing her. I always thought you had a thing for her under all that bickering."

Whit didn't like being transparent but he couldn't outright deny the obvious. "Why are you so all fired up to know about my personal life?"

"Oh, I get it. Who's trying to keep it quiet?" His friend elbowed his ribs like they were in freakin' high school. "You or her?"

Whit leveled a stare at his pal, who was grinning unrepentantly. "Do you want my help with this mess or not?"

"Somebody's touchy."

Touchy? That was one way to put it.

He was frustrated as hell that Megan appeared to have returned to their old ways of avoiding each other. Damn it, last night had been a game changer.

Ignoring each other simply was *not* an option anymore.

Megan said bye to Lark and went in search of Beth. She wasn't sure if she wanted advice or a buffer, but she just wasn't ready to face Whit yet, and she couldn't stand out here shuffling her feet indefinitely.

A voice whispered in the back of her mind, asking her why she'd bothered to come here if she really wanted to avoid him.

Truth be told, Megan wanted to rush into town hall and find Whit, to touch him or even just look at him. And the strength of that desire was the very reason she had to stay away until she found her footing again. No man should have the power to rock her with just a simple glance through a window.

She needed to get her head on straight fast because given the way people kept looking at her and whispering to each other, she suspected that Vera Taylor hadn't wasted any time in spreading the word about seeing her with Whit at the restaurant last night. Vera liked to pretend she was the expert on couples and marriage and everything else, but the senior Taylors were poster children for all the reasons marriage made people miserable.

But then on counterpoint, she saw the Holt family patriarch and matriarch bringing refreshments to the volunteers. Watching David and Gloria Holt lodged an ache in Megan's chest. Seeing them resurrected dreams she'd buried five years ago when Evie's father had walked out, leaving Megan pregnant and alone. The Holts were such a team, married for decades and still so deeply in love. Word around town was that David still brought his wife flowers every week. And Megan was glad Gloria had delivered her baked goods to boost the TCC's spirits after Megan's brownies. It was no contest: Gloria was renowned for her blue ribbon fruit pies.

Finally, she spotted Beth's blond head. Just last week, she and her friend had decided to create compost heaps for rubbish wherever possible. It wouldn't take care of all the recyclable debris, but it would help.

"Sorry I'm late," Megan said, kneeling beside a box of moldy computer paper that had been soaked by rain.

Beth swiped a wrist over her forehead, brushing back her hair. "The Holts are adorable, aren't they? Real soul mates."

"If you believe in that kind of thing, I guess." She tugged on the facemask Lark had given her and passed another to Beth.

Her friend pulled the elastic bands around her ears. "You don't believe in soul mates?"

"Years ago I did. I imagined finding him, getting married and starting a family." She looked up and shrugged, tossing a moldy ream of paper into the pile. "It's obvious things didn't work out that way. But I have my daughter. I love her and I don't regret having her for even a second."

But she couldn't deny life was tougher. Choices were more difficult.

"You don't mention Evie's father often. I've never wanted to pry, but it's tough not to feel judgmental of the guy when you're working so hard to do everything on your own."

"Thank God I found out what a selfish jackass he is before I married him." Still, the fallout for her daughter wasn't so clear-cut. "My only regret is the pain Evie will feel when she realizes he abandoned her. She doesn't ask about him now, but someday, she's going to want answers. Telling her he lives very far away won't be enough."

"There must have been some positives that drew you to him in the first place."

The oak tree branches rustled in the afternoon breeze as Megan tugged on work gloves. "I was blinded by his charm." She dug deeper into the rubble to move past bad thoughts. "He went out of his way to romance me with dinners and trips, gifts that seemed thoughtful as well as extravagant. It was like a Cinderella fantasy after the way I grew up."

"You're a big-hearted person who sees the best in people." Beth reached to give her arm a quick squeeze. "The only person I've ever heard you criticize is Whit."

"And people who abandon their animals." She scrunched her nose under the mask.

"Surely he ranks a level above them."

"Of course he does." Megan kicked through layers of dirt until she found more paper goods for the compost heap and some limp file folders that could go to the recycling pile. "I just don't want to repeat the past. I let myself believe in love at first sight. I was wrong. It takes time to get to know a person, to trust them."

"You've known Whit a long time." Beth loaded branches into a wheelbarrow for a bonfire later. "There's no issue with love at first sight here."

"I didn't say I love Whit Daltry." The L word. Her chest went tight. She tore off the mask to breathe deeper.

"I never said you did. You're the one who got defensive." Beth pulled off her surgical mask and guided Megan toward a park bench. "Where there's smoke, there's fire. And I'm seeing lots of smoke steaming off the two of you."

Megan sat down beside her friend, toying with the mask and snapping the elastic ear bands. "I've learned the hard way that attraction isn't enough. And I have Evie to consider now."

"You're not the only single mom to have been in this situation before, you know." Beth squeezed Megan's wrist. "There's happiness out there for you."

She looked out over the volunteers who'd turned up in droves, a town full of people who'd welcomed her into their fold. "I am happy with the life I've built."

"Fair enough. Still, there can be love and a partner for you. There can be a man who wants to be a father to that amazing daughter of yours. But you'll never know if you don't try."

Megan heard the logic in Beth's words, but accepting what she was saying was easier said than done. "I think we're all just feeling our mortality because of Craig and the others who died. We're all reacting out of grief and adrenaline, a need to affirm life."

"Or the tornado could have torn away your defenses and is making you face what you've been feeling all along."

"Okay, Dr. Freud." Megan bumped shoulders with her friend. "Do you think we can back off analyzing for a while?"

The crunch of footsteps on downed branches gave her only a second's warning. She looked over her shoulder and found Whit approaching. Denim and flannel never looked so good. She smoothed back the wisps of loose hair into her ponytail before she could stop herself.

Beth stood abruptly as Whit leaned against the bench. "I think I'm going to head inside and see if Drew needs help. Good to see you, Whit." She scooped up her mask and jogged toward the clock tower.

The sounds of traffic being routed around town hall mixed with birds chirping. The world was almost normal again.

Almost.

Whit gestured to the scarred bench. "Mind if I sit?"

"Of course I don't mind." That would be silly, and she didn't even one hundred percent understand the turmoil inside her.

"I noticed that your car's blocked in so I'm offering you a ride if it's not clear when you're ready to leave." His hard thigh pressed against hers. He pointed to where utility vehicles had recently arrived and boxed in her compact.

She eyed him suspiciously. "Did you have something to do with my car getting blocked in?"

"Why would I do that?" He palmed his chest in over-played innocence.

"You're funny." And she was being prickly for no reason. She rested her hand on his knee.

He covered her gloved hand with his. "Just trying to keep you happy. When are we going to make it official and tell folks we're seeing each other? They all know anyway."

Panic made it tough to breathe even without the surgical mask. "I need time to figure out what to tell Evie."

"Well, people are already talking so you should figure that out soon before someone says something in front of her."

"I know, I know." She sagged back on the bench, accepting she'd reached a crossroad with Whit. Beth's words knocked around in her mind. Had Megan just been hiding from her feelings for Whit all along? She tugged off her work gloves. "We just need to be careful with Evie. She's fragile right now."

His thumb stroked the inside of her wrist. "Do you think she's going to be jealous of the time we spend together?"

"Just the opposite. She likes you." And that had a whole different set of potential landmines. "You're really good with her and that's scary too. Her heart's going to be broken when we—"

Irritation flickered through his dark brown eyes. "You're dooming this before we're even off the ground yet."

Was she? She reminded herself of the conversation with Beth. "I want to try. I just need time. Okay? Let's finish helping out and then you can drive me home if I'm still blocked in."

"Evie will be there. What will you tell her?"

She chose her words carefully. This was such a damn big step for her. She hoped he understood just how much. "That you're Mommy's very good friend." She tugged another surgical mask from her pocket and passed it to him. "Let's get back to work."

Whit hadn't had a role in blocking Megan's car but he was more than happy to ride the good luck that fate had dealt him. Now he had time alone with her to figure out why she was so spooked.

Not spooked enough to avoid him altogether though, because she could have asked Beth to bring her home. But she hadn't. Instead, Megan had worked beside him tirelessly at town hall, as if she didn't already carry a full load at the shelter, and agreed to a lift in his truck when they were done.

Sun dipping into the horizon, he pulled up and parked outside her cottage. "You fit right in here. You'd think you've lived here all your life."

"It's a welcoming town." She dusted off the knees of her jeans. She'd really dug in to help at town hall today.

She worked hard all the time and he couldn't help but want to make things easier for her.

Whit angled toward her, enjoying the way the setting sun brought out highlights in her hair. "Are you planning to stay in Royal?"

She blinked in surprise. "I don't have any plans to leave."

"That's not the same as planning to stay." He stroked a loose strand behind her ear.

"What about you?" she countered. "What if your business expands and there's a great opportunity to take things global or something?"

"No matter how large my company grows, Royal will always be where I've planted my roots," he said without hesitation. "This is the only place I've ever been able to call home. That's not something I'm willing to throw away."

She shook her head slowly. "Home is family, not a place. If I got an offer from another shelter for a significant pay raise, I would have to consider it, for Evie's future." She cupped his face. "Why are we discussing this now? It's a what-if that may not ever happen. Let's focus on this moment."

"Right, of course." His hand slid behind her head and he guided her to him and kissed her. It was just one of those simple kinds of kisses. But he was finding there were so many ways to savor this woman and they'd barely even begun.

She eased back and smiled. "I need to let Miss Abigail go. Do you want to come inside and have supper with Evie and me? It's nothing fancy. Just hot dogs, macaroni and cheese, maybe apple slices with peanut butter."

"Peanut butter?" He kissed her nose. "Now that's an offer I can't turn down." He stepped out of the truck.

She was trying, and that was more important than he wanted to admit to himself right now. He needed to keep his focus on the moment.

He followed Megan into her house, the warm space full of color and clutter reminding him again how his place didn't come close to feeling like a home. Tails wagging, Piper the Scottie and Cosmo the Border Collie raced across the room to sniff his shoes. The cats Truffles, Pixie and Scooter lounged on the back of the red sectional sofa in the same spots he'd seen them last time, as if they hadn't moved.

Evie jumped up from her Barbie house, wearing an angel costume with a halo and tiara, the two headpieces jumbled on top of each other. She ran to her mother and flung her spindly arms around Megan's waist. "Mommy, I missed you." She peeked up, a little bit of gold garland from the halo dropping over one eye. "Hello, Mr. Whit."

Miss Abigail scooped up her purse and sweater from the sofa beside one of the snoozing cats. "Well, hello, Whit. This is a surprise."

Megan kept her arms around her daughter. "My car was blocked in. Whit offered to bring me home."

"Right." Abigail winked. "Have fun, sweetie, and

call if you need me to babysit. Anytime." She patted Whit on the cheek. "Treat her well."

The door closed behind the retired legal secretary. He took heart in the fact that Megan hadn't even bothered denying Abigail's assumptions.

Megan eyed him nervously, then blurted, "Would you mind keeping an eye on Evie while I change and cook supper?"

He could tell what that cost her. "Thanks, of course I can." He looked over at Evie's toys. "We'll play—"

"Tea party," the little girl squealed, and ran to the coffee table.

Megan's laugh tickled his ears as she left the room.

Whit sat on the sofa. "How's Tallulah?"

Evie arranged a tiny pink plate in front of him and one on her side, then placed two more on the table and whistled for Piper and Cosmo, both of whom were apparently familiar with the game and sat beside her. "My mommy's taking very good care of your kitty cat."

He didn't bother mentioning it wasn't his cat. From the mischievous glint in Evie's eyes, he suspected she was exerting some subtle pressure of her own. "Your mother is a very good person."

The little girl nodded her head and placed a plastic slice of cake on each plate. "My mom helps doggies and kitties."

"That's her job as a grown-up."

"I wanna job." She placed a saucer under each teacup then poured from the toy pitcher that made a *glub, glub, glub* sound.

"Your job is to learn your letters, to eat your vegetables and play."

"We are playing. Is the tea good?"

"Oh …." He pretended to sip from the cup that was smaller than a shot glass. "Very good."

She fished around in her pocket and pulled out two dollar bills and a quarter. "Mommy gave me this to buy treats when I go back to school. But I'm buying shoes for the kids that lost their shoes in the tora-na-do."

Whit set the tiny cup down carefully, his heart squeezing inside his chest at the weight this little girl was carrying on those small shoulders. Megan's words about having to be cautious for her daughter's sake rumbled around inside him.

"Kiddo, I think that's a very good idea."

She hung her head and poured more pretend refills. He couldn't stop thinking about that tiara and those costumes she always wore. He felt so damn helpless.

He'd been doing some nosing around on the internet about kids and trauma and had stumbled on an article about therapy dogs being used at schools. He wondered if he should run that idea by Megan now rather than later. Or would she think he was intruding?

As he looked into Evie's green eyes that carried far too many burdens and fears for one so young, he could understand Megan's need to protect her daughter.

Evie's nose scrunched, making her look so much like a mini-Megan. "I can't drive. And if I tell my mommy what I wanna do it will ruin the surprise."

"Are you asking for my help to surprise your mother?"

"Would you?" Her eyes went wide and hopeful. "Please?"

"Can do. In fact, I have an idea." He held out his hand. "If you pass me your iPad we can order shoes online now. Together we can buy lots of shoes."

"You're gonna buy some too? I like that." She sprinted to the sofa and jumped up beside him.

Was she going to hug him? He braced himself.

She rocked back on her heels, her forehead furrowed and worried. "I had two more coins but I bought a sucker. My mommy wouldn't have bought herself a sucker. I should have gotten somethin' for her instead."

He tugged one of her crooked pigtails. "Maybe we could get something for your mommy while we buy those shoes."

"Like flowers or candy. Mommy likes chocolate—and recycling." She grabbed her iPad off the end table.

He reached for the tablet. "Chocolate and a new recycling bin for your mom."

"Yay!" She wrapped her arms around his neck and squeezed tight. "You're a good boy, Mr. Whit."

God, the little minx was well on her way to wrapping him around her little finger.

On her way?

Too late.

The sense of being watched drew his gaze across the room. Megan stood in the archway between the living room and dining area, holding Tallulah in her arms. Her green eyes glinted with tears. She'd told him she was wary and she had every reason to be given her past. He needed to prove to her he could change, that he was a man worthy of a chance. He didn't know where they were going yet, but he damn well knew he couldn't walk away without digging deeper. Trying harder.

He patted Evie's back and looked at her mom. "Megan, I have an important question to ask."

She blinked in surprise while Evie spun around in her angel dress, humming a tune from the show that had just been on TV.

Megan sniffed and nodded. "Okay. What is it?"

"Can I take my cat home today or do I need to fill out an adoption application at the shelter when you open on Monday?"

Nine

Megan was so stunned by Whit's request to adopt Tallulah, she almost dropped the cat. She adjusted her hold on the calico and stepped closer to the man who continued to turn her world upside down. "Excuse me? You want to do what?"

"You said Tallulah's better now." He stepped closer to stroke the cat, his knuckles grazing Megan's breasts. "So I thought I could take her home, like you asked me."

She eyed him suspiciously. "Are you doing this just to impress me? Because if so, that's the wrong reason to adopt an animal. A pet is a lifelong commitment. If we…break up," the words lodged in her throat for an instant, "you still need to be committed to keeping and loving Tallulah."

He nodded solemnly. "I understand that. We may disagree on a lot of things, but I would never walk out on a commitment. That's why I didn't keep her the first day. I wasn't sure I could care for her the way she deserves. I'm certain now that I can."

Was he talking in some kind of code? Adding layers to his words? Talk of the future made her jittery when she was barely hanging on in the present. "Okay then. When would you like to take Tallulah?"

"I'll need to get supplies for her." He scratched his head. "I'll stop by the pet store on my way home. They'll let me bring her inside, right? I know I'm not supposed to leave an animal in the car."

She stifled a smile. He really was trying. "How about this, Whit? Let me gather some supplies to get you through the night and then you can shop at your leisure tomorrow for the things she'll need. I've got a flyer on file I can email you. We give it to all adopters."

"Thanks. I appreciate that." He leaned in and whispered in her ear, the warm rumble of his voice so close that it incited a nice kind of shiver. "Will Evie be upset to see Tallulah go?"

Megan rested a hand on her daughter's hair, no easy feat as she maneuvered around the halo and tiara. "She understands Tallulah isn't ours. Don't you, sweetie?"

Evie nodded. "Me and Mommy are rescuers. We find good homes for kitties and puppies. Tallulah is Mr. Whit's cat. I'll go get her bed and stuff." She looked up at Whit. "You won't forget about the shoes?"

He knelt down to look Evie in the eyes. "I won't forget. I promise." He tugged a pigtail. "And I always keep my promises."

"Good deal. Thanks." Evie kissed him on the cheek then sprinted to the laundry room where the kitty supplies were kept.

Megan drew in a shaky breath. Seeing flashes of

how good life could be with Whit around was tougher than she thought.

He looked at the tiny pink cup in his hand and shrugged sheepishly before setting it down on the coffee table. "About Tallulah—you're not going to call me out on all the BS reasons I gave you about why I couldn't keep a cat in the first place?"

She had questions, but not so much about the cat and certainly not right now with Evie a room away. "I don't believe in saying 'I told you so.'"

"Good to know. I hope there's a lot of information on that list. I've never taken care of an animal on my own before." His eyebrows pinched together and he stuffed his hands in his pockets as if having second thoughts. "I wouldn't want to screw this up."

"I'll be happy to give you our adoption briefing." She held back a smile since she didn't want to hurt his feelings. She truly was touched by his concern. If only more people were this careful. "The most important thing for her now is to get lots of TLC while she bonds with you. So, are you cool with letting her sleep in your lap while you watch ball games?"

"I think I can handle that." He rocked back on his boot heels.

"Sounds good." She rubbed her cheek against Tallulah's dark furry head before passing over the cat. "Let me go dig up an extra scratching post for her to use at your house."

"Would you like to come to dinner at my house tomorrow night?" Whit secured the cat in one arm so he could scratch her under the neck with his other hand. "You can give me that briefing and check on Tallulah."

He was asking her to take a big step. Another meal together. Spending time in his home and in his life. But no matter how nervous those ideas made her—and they still did—she couldn't deny the warm hopefulness that sparked to life insider her either.

Despite the risk, she wanted to try.

The next evening, Whit stepped into his house with Megan and it felt so damn right to have her here it shook the ground under him. She was becoming more and more a part of his life with each day that passed.

Last night's hot dogs with mac and cheese had tasted a helluva lot better than any of his catered dinners. But then he knew that was due to the people at the table with him. Then he'd taken his cat home. And holy hell, it still surprised him that he'd decided to get a pet. Except it felt right. Still did. His house didn't feel so damn empty with the cat checking out his furniture and deciding which places were worthy of her. Tallulah had sniffed out every corner and seemed to approve of his leather ottoman in the living room. His bed had gotten cat props too; Tallulah had curled up on the pillow next to his head as if she'd been sleeping at his place every night.

He'd actually had a good time using his lunch break to pick up cat gear and drop it off at his house. The calico had leaped off the ottoman in full attack mode when he tossed her a feather squeak toy and before he knew it, he'd spent an extra twenty minutes watching her chase a catnip ball and wrestle a fur mouse.

But by the time dinner rolled around he'd been damn near starving. He and Megan had decided to have supper at her house again, then her neighbor would watch Evie after the child went to sleep.

He'd asked Megan to come to his house for dessert.

He hadn't wanted to leave his cat alone any longer. Megan's smile told him he'd said the right thing.

She kicked off her shoes and lined them up by the door. "I can't believe you really ordered all those shoes with Evie."

"She's got her mother's entrepreneurial spirit. You've done a good job with her." He slipped an arm around her waist.

"Motherhood is the most important job I've ever had."

"Your commitment shows." His parents had vowed they loved him but they hadn't been big on teaching moral responsibility.

"How's Tallulah?"

"Come say hello to her and see for yourself." He guided her to his study where he'd closed Tallulah in for the evening. The space had a sunroom too, where he'd set up her litter box and food. "I put her in here for the day while she gets acclimated. I thought she would enjoy the sunshine through all the windows. I did some reading on the internet last night on cat care."

He pushed open the double mahogany doors and Megan gasped. She pointed at the six-foot scratching post he'd bought, complete with different levels and cubbies for climbing and snoozing.

"Oh, my God, Whit." She walked to the carpeted and tiered post he'd parked between two leather wingback chairs and reached into a cubby to pet Tallulah. "You obviously went shopping too."

He hefted his cat out and leaned back on the dark wood desk, scratching Tallulah's ears the way she liked. "I just stopped by the pet store on my lunch break and picked up a few essentials."

"A scratching post the size of an oak tree is an essential?"

"It looked cool? What can I say?" He was planning to talk to his contractor buddy Aaron about ordering mini solarium windows for Tallulah to hang out in.

"I wish all our animals could land this well." She dusted cat hair off his suit jacket.

"She needs something to keep her occupied while I'm at work." Tallulah purred like a freight train in his ear. "And I read online that if I want to save my furniture from her claws, she has to have an appropriate outlet for scratching at home."

Megan had perched on the arm of a wingback. The warmth in her eyes told him he was saying all the right things.

"I also read—" He stopped when the realization hit him. "You already know all of this."

"But it's nice hearing you're excited about having her. Not just in your house but in your life."

And he had to admit, it surprised him too. "I always thought I would be a dog person."

"It doesn't make you any less macho."

"Thanks. I'm not concerned with proving my masculinity."

"Hmm, I have to admit, your confidence about being tender with the cat is very appealing." She trailed a lone finger down his arm in a touch as enticing as any full-on stroke. "If you want a dog though, I'm more than happy to help you find the perfect one for your lifestyle."

One step at a time. "Tallulah needs time to adjust to her new home first."

"Spoken like a natural pet owner. That's really nice to hear." She flicked a cat toy dangling from one of the levels of the scratching post. "Although if you bought Tallulah this, I wonder what you would buy for a dog."

His mind churned with possibilities, like one of those agility courses the Cattleman's Club was working on for the shelter. "I bought one of those climbing trees for Safe Haven too."

"Truly?" she squealed, giving him an enthusiastic kiss with the cat squirming between them. "You do know me better than I gave you credit for."

He tucked Tallulah back into one of the cubbies attached to the climbing post. "You'll even find bottles and paper in the recycling. Will that get me another kiss?"

She laughed and looped her arms around his neck, kissing him again, nothing standing between them now but too many clothes. Her mouth on his felt familiar and new all at once. He knew so much about her, yet there was still so much more of her to explore. And he had a plan in mind for the next few hours to discover more about what pleased her.

Ending the kiss, he angled away while unfastening the clasp holding back her hair. "I'm learning fast that the way to your heart is less traditional than a bouquet of flowers."

She shook her hair free in a silky, wavy cloud around her shoulders and his hands. "Oh, I should share some of the catnip you gave me with Tallulah."

"I have some of my own." He slid an arm around her waist. All day, he'd been fantasizing about showing her his favorite part of the house. "Come with me. There's a part of my home you haven't seen yet."

She eyed him curiously. "I'm intrigued. Lead on."

He steered her into the hall again, toward the back of the house. "This way."

She tucked herself against his side. "Thank you again for helping Evie with the shoe donation drive."

"We shopped for some new video games too."

She stiffened and her footsteps slowed. "I have to approve all of her new games."

"Uh, sure," he said, wishing he'd thought of that himself. But he didn't have nieces or nephews. "Kids are new territory to me too, like the pets. Except I can't exactly shut a kid in a room with a climbing tree and a bowl of food."

"Not unless you want to end up in jail," she said with a laugh in her voice that let him know she wasn't angry with him. "I know you meant well. I just need for you to consult me on anything having to do with Evie."

"Sure, of course." He pushed open the back door into his landscaped yard. "For what it's worth, they were all labeled for her age group and I know the video game developer."

Walking beside him along the flagstone path, she glanced up at him, a hint of frustration in her eyes. "Not all video games are educational."

"You're right, and I do hear you." He guided her toward the left, under an ivy-covered arch. That led to a cluster of trees in the very back of his property. "I'll be more careful about consulting you when it comes to anything with Evie."

"I'm sorry for being prickly." She slid her arm under his suit coat and around his waist. "This is new territory for me too."

"You haven't dated anyone since you had Evie?" Where the hell had that question come from and why was her answer so important?

"In case you haven't noticed, there isn't much spare time in my life between my job and my daughter."

"No one at all?" He stopped at the concrete steps leading into his greenhouse, tucked away in the privacy of a circle of trees.

She took his lapels in her hands. "You're my first venture back into dating since Evie was born."

"I don't want to be your rebound guy." And he meant that. He'd already accepted that he wanted more than a short-term affair with her.

"It's been nearly five years since Evie's biological father walked out of our lives. I'm far past the rebound zone, don't you think?"

Five years? The bastard had walked out before Evie was even born? Whit had heard the jerk wasn't a part of Megan's life, but this was even worse than he'd thought. He let that information roll over him again now that he had a better feel for how much commitment and effort it took to raise a child. He knew logically, of course. But his admiration for how hard Megan had worked grew even more. For that matter, he understood a little better just how tough it must have been for her to let go of that control.

She smoothed his lapels back in place and turned to the greenhouse. "What do we have here?"

He thought about pushing the discussion further, then reconsidered. Better to take his time so he didn't spook her. And luckily for both of them, taking their time had deliciously sensual implications tonight. "Through this door, we have our dessert."

More than a little intrigued, Megan opened the greenhouse door and peered inside the dimly lit building. Warmth and humidity wafted out, carrying a verdant scent of lush life. She stepped inside, expecting some fancy garden typical of the rich and famous. But instead, she found a more practical space, filled with tomato plants and tiered racks of marked herbs, potted trees lining the center of the aisle to give room for their branches to spread. Curiosity drew her in deeper and deeper.

She reached up to tap lemons, limes and even an orange. "This is incredible."

"Glad you like it. The catnip is a recent addition, over that way." He pointed toward the back right corner.

She came around a tree and found a two-seat wrought-iron table set up with plates, water glasses and in the center…a fondue pot? Whit reached past her to turn up the flame.

"Chocolate sauce?" she asked.

"There's a pear tree that's producing, thanks to the climate control in here. When Evie told me you like chocolate, it all came together." He plucked a pear from a branch. "Why the suspicious look?"

"I'm trying to figure out why you're going to so much trouble to win me over?"

"You're worth it." He set the pear on a stone pottery plate and sliced through it with a paring knife.

"I'm appreciative, but why me when you could expend far less effort for any number of women around here?"

"I don't want them." He swirled the piece of fruit through the chocolate. "Just you." He offered her the dripping slice.

She bit into the end, the sweet fresh pear and gooey chocolate sending her taste buds into a flavor orgasm. She sank into the chair. "Okay, totally amazing," she said, reaching for another slice. "And I'm totally surprised."

"How so?" he sat across from her, their knees bumping under the small table.

"Well," she said, swirling the slice in the chocolate and stroking her toes along his ankle. "I wouldn't have expected you to be so…thrifty."

"I think I was just insulted."

"You're wealthy. Filthy-rich wealthy."

He resisted the impulse to get defensive and forced himself to answer logically. "That doesn't mean I'm wasteful. I've worked damn hard to get to where I am, but there are plenty of people who work just as hard for a lot less, like my mom did. I recognize that there was luck that partnered up with my work ethic."

"Well, your gardener has really outdone himself here." She picked up one of the heavy silver spoons laid out in the fondue display and swirled it through the sauce.

"The hits just keep coming." He laughed. "I don't have a gardener." He popped a slice of fruit in his mouth.

She dropped the spoon in surprise. "You tend all of this yourself?"

Her gaze roamed the neat rows of tomato plants again. The bins of gardening tools and the bags full of potting soil tucked under the plant shelves affirmed that all this work had been done right here. He hadn't just grabbed a bunch of plants from a nursery to decorate his greenhouse. What a lot of work. And patience. She remembered all the times she'd mentally accused him of not caring about the environment and felt a pang of guilt.

"Having money doesn't mean I should stop taking care of things myself." He held up a hand. "The catering service is a survival thing. I may have a green thumb, but my skills in the kitchen suck. It was less expensive to hire out than to continue throwing away food. Makes economic sense."

"But you don't have to pinch pennies." So much about this man was different than what she'd assumed for the past three years. She hadn't expected him to be so generous and thoughtful, and now to find this "green" side to him? Her head was reeling.

"I grew up in a feast-or-famine kind of childhood. When my dad had a job, we lived well, really well." He tugged an orange from a low-hanging branch and began peeling the ripe fruit. "And then he inevitably got fired and we skipped town, chasing a fresh start. At one point we lived in an RV for about eight months. Even at ten years old, I knew if we'd lived more frugally at the place prior, we would have had enough to carry us through the lean times."

Her heart ached for that little boy with so much upheaval in his life. "How is it that's never shown up in your official bio—or at least the grapevine gossip?"

"My life story is no one's business," he said with the brash confidence she'd seen so often in the past.

Now she saw that confidence with new eyes, saw the man who'd taken adversity and let it drive him to success. She couldn't help but respect that.

She scooped the peels into her hand. "A thrifty woman like myself would recycle this into potpourri."

"Hmm, I'm beginning to see merits in your recycling drive." He brought an orange slice to her mouth.

She held it in her teeth, tugging his tie until he leaned across the table to share the bite with her. The fruit burst in her mouth just as their lips met. His eyes held hers as they both ate and watched each other. He kissed a dribble of juice off her chin.

She loosened his tie. "You're a naughty man."

"Lady, I haven't even gotten started yet." He sank back in his seat again, yanking his tie the rest of the way off.

The night outside and the steamed windows inside provided more than enough privacy. It also helped that the greenhouse was tucked away in a cluster of pine trees. They were alone. Truly alone.

Megan's body came alive with anticipation and possibility.

This humid greenhouse was like a tropical retreat in the middle of their everyday small town. What a gift to have such a lush hideaway from the world nestled right here in Whit's backyard.

Standing, he draped his tie over a branch and shrugged out of his coat. She couldn't look away, wondering how far he would go. He flung his coat over the back of his chair and the swoosh of it landing snapped something inside her.

Without taking her eyes off him, she tugged her polo shirt from work over her head. His eyes widened in appreciation and then she lost track of who got undressed faster. She just knew somehow her bra had landed alongside his tie on the orange tree.

She would never again be able to eat an orange without tingling all over.

Whit reached behind a stack of bags full of soil and pulled out a quilt. He'd clearly thought this through and prepared. He shook it on the ground beside the table and took her hand in his. She stepped into his arms and savored the feel of masculine skin against her bare flesh. The rasp of bristle and muscle. A hum of pleasure buzzed through her, melting her as he lowered her onto the blanket.

She trailed her fingers along his shoulders. "This is the most perfect night. You're an ingenious man."

"You inspire me." He pulled an orange slice from the table and held the piece of fruit over her stomach with slow deliberation.

Delicious anticipation shivered through her a second before he squeezed the juice onto her one sweetly torturous drip a time.

"Whit," she gasped just as he dipped his head to sip away each drop.

He glanced up the length of her. "Should I stop?" he asked, kissing his way upward.

Her elbows gave way and she sank back. He snagged the rest of the orange from the iron table and drizzled more juice along one breast, his mouth soon following. She arched up into his caress and gave her hands free rein to enjoy this intriguing, sexy man who'd found his way into her life.

She let herself be swept away in sensations and desire. He was an intuitive lover, lingering when she sighed, in tune to the cues of her least sound or movement. His mouth skimmed lower and lower still until her knees parted and…yes…he sipped and licked, nuzzling at the bundle of nerves drawing tighter. He coaxed her pleasure closer and closer to the edge of completion.

For so long she'd been alone, and while she'd told herself she didn't need more in her life, right now she knew that was a lie. She needed this. This man.

The thought sent a bolt of ecstasy through her. Her fingers gripped his shoulders and dug in to let him know just how much she needed him to stay with her for every wave of pleasure. And he did, as each wave rippled through her.

Her arms fell to her sides as she breathed in ragged

gasps, her mind still in a fog. But even in her afterglow haze, need already built inside her again.

Soon, the goal of having Whit reach those heights with her had her reaching for another orange.

Ten

Tucking Megan to his side, Whit trailed his fingers up and down her arm, making the most of their last minutes together tonight. He understood she had to be home soon to relieve the sitter, but he wanted more time with Megan. He'd never dated a single mother before.

More importantly, he'd never been with anyone who captivated him the way she did, dressed or undressed. Although right now he was enjoying the hell out of the undressed Megan. Her silky hair teased along his arm in a fan of red. He'd explored every inch of her soft, pale skin.

He kissed a smudge of chocolate off her nose. Chocolate and oranges would long be his favorite flavors. He'd discovered a lot about her this evening, and intended to make the most of the time they had left before she sent the sitter home at midnight. "Penny for your thoughts."

Megan rubbed her foot along his calf. "Why do you

have a greenhouse full of fruits and vegetables if you order your food catered?"

He propped up on one elbow and gestured at the plants on either side. "There's a theme here, if you look closer," he said, surprised at her question but glad to have a chance to extend the evening. "Fresh fruits and vegetables for a salad or salsa. I may not be able to cook, but I can chop. Plus, free tomatoes are a great way to make friends with your neighbors."

"Just being neighborly?" she pressed. "I think there's more to your answer than that."

"Believe it or not, I like roots." If he wanted more from her, he would need to give more of himself. "I moved around so much as a kid, this place reminds me I'm here to stay."

One of those happy-sad smiles played on her lips, which were still plump from kissing. "You break my heart sometimes."

"How so?" He tensed. He didn't want her pity. Part of him wanted to pull back, but that would mean letting her go. And with her hands sketching lazy circles all over him, staying put seemed a better option.

"With those images of you as a kid longing for a home." One of her hands slid up to cradle his face.

"You're a nurturer." He kissed her palm.

"You're a builder and tender too, you know." She gestured to the greenhouse. "You just have to learn to see that in yourself."

Okay, enough of this kind of talk. It was one thing to share parts of their past. It was another altogether to submit to a cranial root canal. "This conversation is getting entirely too serious."

"Then why did you bring me out here and show me this part of your life?"

Why had he? Every time he got close to that answer, he mentally flinched away as if he were getting too close to a flame. He settled on the easy answer. "Because I had been fantasizing about making love to you out here, about tasting the fruit on your skin."

She paused and he could see in her eyes she wasn't buying into his dismissal of her assessment. Then she nodded as if conceding to give him space on the issue and arched up to nibble his bottom lip. "You taste mighty delicious yourself."

"I've developed a new appreciation for fondue."

She flicked her tongue along his chin before pressing her mouth to his collar bone, then settling back into his arms. "I appreciate the dessert and the thought that went into arranging such an amazing evening, and all you've done for Evie and for the shelter as well."

"I would like to pamper you every day if you would let me." He massaged along one of her narrow shoulders, then down her back, skimming along her curves and around her hip where he knew her tattoo trailed across her skin. He could get so used to this. "The way I see it, you don't get much time to relax between work and being a mom."

"I love my daughter and my job. That's always been enough." Yet as she said that, her eyes fluttered closed and she melted against him.

"That doesn't mean you can't have recreation."

"Is that what you are?" She tipped her face to look at him. "My recreation?"

"I'm just trying to be a help. We all need a break every now and again, right?" He couldn't hold back the burning question any longer. "Where does Evie's father live?"

Her body went rigid under his touch and she rolled

away, sitting up and gathering her clothes. "Not here. He's not a part of her life and chances are he never will be."

"But he knows about her."

"Of course," she answered indignantly, tugging on her panties, then her bra. "I would never keep that a secret. The minute he found out, he cut ties and ran."

The bastard. Whit wanted to find the guy and pummel him for the pain he'd caused Megan and her amazing daughter.

"He doesn't pay child support, does he?" Whit tugged on his suit pants.

She shrugged and pulled on her shirt. "He snowed me. Completely. Last I heard he was in the Keys heading for the Bahamas."

"Hey." Whit cradled her face in his hands. "It's not your fault he's a loser. He missed out on an amazing family." Whit's own father may not have been much of a provider but at least he'd been there.

"My fault or not," she gripped his wrists and stared straight into his eyes, "Evie will grow up knowing her father didn't want her and there's nothing I can do to change that."

She pulled away to slip on her khakis, her rigid back telling him she was holding on by a thread while rebuilding defenses he'd apparently blasted with one simple question.

Whit could see he didn't just need to be careful for Evie's sake. Megan was every bit as wounded by the past as her daughter. She just didn't wear the costumes.

And now he prayed like hell his idea to help with Evie wouldn't backfire.

"What's the matter with you?"

Beth's question cut through Megan's fog as she

picked at her lunch salad the next day. Evie had taken her lunch box and joined Miss Abigail at the front desk.

Megan sagged back in her office chair, the squeak in the old seat mixing with the muffled sound of a couple of dogs in the play yard. The kennel runs were quieter today than usual thanks to some new calming CDs brought in by one of the volunteers. If only that music could help calm her spinning thoughts.

Even the salad reminded her of Whit's greenhouse and how hard he was trying on her behalf. Yet she couldn't shake the jittery feeling that things would fall apart, and the closer she let herself get to him, the worse the breakup would hurt.

Tossing aside her fork, Megan reached for her water instead, staring at the photo on her desk of beach day in Galveston when Evie was two. She'd scrimped and saved for that trip, convinced she needed to start making special memories with her toddler. "I'm just preoccupied."

"Because of Whit?" Beth unpacked her navy blue lunch sack that could have passed for a purse. "How did it go last night?"

"Did you know he has this massive greenhouse where he grows fresh fruits and veggies?"

Beth's eyebrows shot up. "No, I didn't know. And you think he would have told me since I have an organic farm. We could have shared clippings—" She stopped. "Wait. This is about you."

Megan tapped the catnip plant. "He brought this for the kitties. And he's rolling out all the stops romancing me and I have to admit, he seems so sincere."

"Seems?" Beth absently thumbed her engagement ring, spinning it around on her finger.

Admitting her insecurities, even to her close friend,

was tough for Megan. But God, if she didn't work through this and she blew it with Whit without even trying… "I don't trust my instincts when it comes to men. And he's known for being ruthless."

"In the work world," Beth pointed out. "That's different."

"Is it?"

"He adores Evie. He's not faking that. Evie would sense that a mile off." The natural blonde beauty smiled. "Remember that banker guy who pretended to be in the market for a dog so he could hit on you about six months ago? Evie made a point of getting peanut butter and jelly on his ties so you would see him freak out over kid germs."

Megan laughed at the memory. "She's a great little bodyguard." But even that thought was sobering in light of her daughter's fears since the storm. "Can I afford to let Evie grow any more attached to Whit when I'm not sure where the relationship is headed?"

"Unless you intend to spend your life alone, at some point you have to trust again," Beth said with undeniable reason.

"I could wait until Evie's eighteen." Except after last night's sex, fourteen years felt like an eternity.

Her friend stayed diplomatically silent and bit into an apple.

The noise level in the lobby grew. New voices and a squeal from Evie drew Megan's attention away from her pity party, thank heaven, because talking was just making her feel worse today.

She rolled back her chair and stood. "Beth, I should see what's going on out there."

She stepped into the lobby, her eyes drawn immediately to Whit. What was he doing here in the middle of the workday? Then she noticed Evie petting a golden retriever. Megan's instincts went on alert at the thought of her daughter petting a possible stray with an unknown vaccination history. Except then she saw the dog was wearing a "service dog" vest. What did all of this have to do with Whit's arrival?

He turned to face her—and he wasn't alone. A sleekly pretty woman with dark hair stood at his side. Jealousy nipped. Hard.

Megan smiled tightly and knelt beside her daughter. "Sweetie, that vest means this is a working dog. We don't touch dogs with this special vest."

Her daughter—dressed as a Ninja Turtle today—grinned. "I asked. She said it was okay and Mr. Whit said it was okay. He brought the dog for my preschool class."

Megan glanced up at him, confused. "What's going on?"

Whit set his Stetson on the receptionist's desk. "I talked to the day-care director about bringing in a therapy dog for the kids given all they went through with the tornado. The local school psychologist recommended this group in Dallas and contacted the other parents to clear it. I said I would check with you to save her a call, and well, here we are. The dog handler said she's even interested in evaluating the dogs here for training."

Introductions were made in a blur and the next thing she knew her wonderfully intuitive friend Beth was offering to walk the dog handler—Zoe Baker—back to the play yard.

Megan's head was spinning in surprise. Of course it was a great idea, but having someone take over decisions for her daughter so totally felt…alien. But there wasn't much she could say since he'd gone straight to the school and she didn't want to cause a scene that would upset Evie.

Still, she ducked her head and said, "Could we talk for a minute. Alone."

Miss Abigail knelt beside Evie. "Would you like to come with me to play with the cats? Your mom told me a new litter of kittens was just brought in."

Evie skipped alongside Abigail with a new spring in her step Megan hadn't seen in a month.

Whit swept his hat off the desk and followed Megan to her office. "I meant this to be a surprise, to show you I care about you and Evie, that I respect your work with animals."

"Okay," she said cautiously, "but why not consult me? This is my child. And animals are my area of expertise."

He scratched his head, wincing. "You're right. I should have. I was thinking about Evie's fear of going back to school and then I saw this article about the group in Dallas and I got caught up in the moment wanting to surprise you. Like with the catnip."

"This is a much bigger deal than catnip."

She couldn't help but feel defensive. "I don't want to push her before she's ready."

"Hey," he took her shoulders in his hands, "I'm not questioning your parenting. Thinking of her made me wonder about the other kids. So I spoke with some of the dads at the Cattleman's Club and asked if their kids were having trouble this past month. This is for all of them. Not just Evie."

"You talked to the other parents…about their children?" Her lips went tight, anger nipping all over again.

But she couldn't help but remember how carefully he'd studied the instructions for taking care of Tallulah. Thinking about that kind of thoughtfulness applied to her daughter touched her. "Which other children?"

"Sheriff Battle said every time his son hears a train he thinks the tornado's coming back." He turned his hat around and around in his hands. "When I saw that article about therapy dogs going into nursing homes and schools, it got me thinking. Ms. Baker uses shelter dogs, which I knew would be appealing to you. I even learned there's a difference between service dogs, therapy dogs and emotional support dogs. Anyhow, what do you think? Aside from the fact I've been pushy, when I should have consulted you."

"I actually think that's a great idea. I'm kicking myself for not thinking of it." She sagged back against the edge of her desk. "You sure acted on this quickly."

"You've had your hands full. And I figured why wait. The day-care staff is expecting us this afternoon. I'm hoping Evie will be excited to take the dog to show off to her friends."

"I still wish you'd consulted me. We talked about this yesterday."

He flinched. "Guilty as charged and I truly am sorry. It seemed like a good surprise in my head. Would you have said no if I told you?"

Sighing, she conceded, "Of course not."

But that wasn't the point.

He scratched the back of his neck. "My buddies thought it was funny as hell that I was asking about kid stuff so word got around fast. The press is involved now too, planning to cover it. I figured it would be a good chance to talk about shelter dogs and how full your rescue is."

And he'd done all this for her when she'd given so little of herself in return. She'd just held back and questioned and worried. "You're really going all out to win me over."

"Busted." He slid his arms around her waist. "I want to be with you."

She toyed with his tie and knew he wouldn't give a damn if Evie painted it with jelly. "I'm still the same pain-in-the-butt person who's fighting with you over what parts of Royal you choose to develop."

"And I'm still the same guy who's going to argue there's a way around things."

"We're going to argue," she said with certainty.

"At least you'll be talking to me rather than ignoring me."

"Hey," she tugged his tie, "you ignored me too."

He tugged her loose ponytail in return. "I gave you space when it looked like you were going to cause a scene."

Before she could launch a retort, he kissed her silent, and this man knew how to kiss. Her arms slid around his neck and she knew without question he was a good man who would try like hell for her.

Which was going to make this hurt so much worse if it didn't work out.

Whit was mighty damn pleased with how the therapy dog issue had shaken down.

He stood in the back of the Little Tots Daycare classroom with Megan while all the kids sat in a circle on a rug. The town had done an amazing job at getting the facility functional quickly so the children could get back into a regular routine, the kind of reassurance they needed after such a frightening event.

Their teacher was reading them a book about tornadoes. The golden retriever was calm, but alert, carefully moving from child to child as if knowing which one was most in need of comfort, whether with a simple touch of his paw or resting his head on a knee, or just letting a dozen little hands burrow in his fur.

As the teacher closed the book, she looked up at her students. "What do you think about the story we just read?"

Beside Evie, a little girl with glasses admitted, "I was scared."

"Not me," said the boy in tiny cowboy boots sitting on the other side of Evie.

"Yes, you were," the girl with glasses retorted. "You were crying. I saw you wipe boogers on your sleeve."

Evie raised her hand until the teacher called on her. "I was scared," Evie said. "I told my mom I held Caitlyn's hand 'cause she was scared. But it was really me. I was the fraidy cat."

The retriever belly crawled over to Evie and rested his head on her leg. Evie rubbed the dog's ears, her eyes wide and watery.

The teacher leaned forward in her rocking chair. "We were all afraid that day. That's why we have the drills. So we know what to do in an emergency."

Evie kept stroking the dog and talking. "What if another tora-na-do comes to our school? What if it hurts Mommy's car again, 'cept it gets Mommy too?"

Megan started to move forward, but Whit rested a hand on her arm. It was hard as hell for him to hear the little imp's fears too, but she was talking. Thank God, she was talking. Megan's hand slid into his and held on.

The teacher angled forward, giving all the right grown-up answers that Evie took in with wide eyes, both her hands buried in the dog's fur.

Evie kept talking, but she smiled periodically. Something that didn't happen often.

Megan's chin trembled. "This is so incredible to watch," she whispered.

"I wouldn't have even thought twice about the article if not for you." He ducked his head to keep their voices low so as not to disturb the class. "You do a good job educating about your work at the shelter."

"Thank you." Her cheeks flushed a pretty pink.

"I knew about service dogs for the disabled and I'd heard there were studies showing that owning a pet lowers blood pressure." He scanned the group of little ones up front with the dog. "But this is a whole new world." In more ways than one.

"I think of it all as the balance of nature."

"That makes sense."

"Taking care of our resources." She looked up at him pointedly.

"Hey, I've started recycling water bottles and cans because of you."

She clapped a hand to her chest. "Be still my heart."

"Are you making fun of me?" He raised an eyebrow. "I happen to think that was a very romantic gesture on my part."

"It is sweet. But you would be wise to remember, sometimes I don't have much of a sense of humor when it comes to things like this. You just caught me on a good day."

"Fair enough." He had a feeling there was a lot more to learn about Megan before he could banish the wary look that still lurked in her green eyes. "I will keep that in mind."

He glanced at his watch, and damn, he was running late. When he woke up this morning, he hadn't thought there was a chance in hell he could get through the day of Craig's memorial service without a bottle by his side. But Megan and Evie had given him a welcome distraction. They were good for him.

"Do you have a meeting?" she asked.

"I need to go home to change and get some things together for Craig's memorial service."

She pressed a trembling hand to her mouth. "Oh God, Whit, I'm so sorry. How selfish of me not to think about how difficult today is for you." She touched his shoulder lightly. "What can I do?"

"This helped keep my mind off things."

"I'll meet you at the church."

"You don't have to—"

"I want to be there for you."

He brushed his hand along her back, which was as much contact as would be appropriate here in a classroom full of kids. But he knew how tough it was for Megan to spend time away from her daughter and appreciated her being there for him. "I'll see you tonight."

This wasn't a day when he could feel joyful by any means, but suddenly the weight didn't seem as heavy.

Since her parents' death, Megan had avoided funerals and memorial services, but she'd wanted to be here for Whit. As she stood in the church vestibule with Whit after the service, she was relieved it was over, and certain that attending had been absolutely the right decision.

It had been emotional experience for everyone. Not just mourning their friend, but also remembering that fateful day all their lives had been forever changed so quickly. Paige Richardson's husband was taken from her in an instant.... A thought that had Megan reaching for Whit's hand.

Whit's words about his friend had brought tears to her eyes, reaffirming how important it was to be here for him. He was trying so hard and there was danger in a relationship that was too one-sided. It wasn't fair to him.

At least the service had been in the evening so she wouldn't be spending as much time away from Evie. Her daughter had been excited talking about going to preschool tomorrow. She'd chattered about her friends and all the fun activities coming up for December.

Megan stood silently at Whit's side while he gave his condolences to Craig Richardson's widow Paige and his twin brother Colby, who'd returned to town from his home in Dallas.

Everyone was making small talk, doing their best to hold it together. Then Whit took her elbow and guided her outside, shouldering through the crowd and into the chilly night full of stars. In the dark, the scars from the storm didn't show. It was almost if it never happened. Except tonight reminded her too well it had.

She tucked her arm in his. "Are you okay?"

"Hanging in there. It's hard to believe he's been gone for over a month." Whit sighed, cricking his neck to the side as they walked to his truck.

"Did I hear right that R&N Builders is helping out with the reconstruction?" Colby Richardson and Whit's friend Aaron Nichols were partners in the business.

"You did. Colby has offered all the services of his very successful company to help," Whit confirmed, although his forehead was still furrowed over what should have been a good piece of news.

"I'm sure you'll be glad to have more time with your friends, especially now."

"Hmm."

She squeezed his arm as they walked. "Something's bothering you?"

"The whole evening is just surreal. Especially seeing Colby with Paige."

"Because Colby is Craig's twin?"

He shook his head. "Because Colby and Craig each went out with Paige in high school. There is still a lot of tension between Colby and Paige."

"It must be difficult for her to have him around reminding her of her dead husband."

"Maybe so." He nodded, stopping beside his truck and opening the door for her. "Tonight sure makes a person think hard about what's important."

"That's an understatement." She climbed inside, thinking back to the first time she'd sat inside this vehicle, terrified for her daughter.

He settled behind the wheel without starting the truck. "It meant a lot to me to have you here."

"Of course I was here for you."

He stretched his arm along the seat, his fingers toying with her hair. "I think we both know what we have going is about more than sex."

His words stirred up a flurry of nerves in her belly. "Are you saying you're thinking about happily ever after and white picket fences?"

"I'm saying you mean something to me." He angled toward her, his eyes intense in the darkness. "And yeah, that scares the hell out of me, but this isn't casual. Not for me."

"Well, it scares the hell out of me to think about letting a man in my life again." As terrified as she was to say the words out loud, tonight had reminded her there were no guarantees in life. She linked her fingers with his. "But it scares me more to think about not trying at all."

Eleven

Whit couldn't remember being this nervous—and genuinely pumped up—about a Friday night date.

But then he'd never proposed to a woman before.

The diamond solitaire damn near burning a hole in his suit coat pocket, he shifted gears on his Porsche as he drove through Royal with Megan at his side. They weren't hiding out in some tucked away place. He'd chosen a restaurant near his Pine Valley home, where the odds of running into friends were high. Megan had agreed. The whole town knew they were dating. Evie had accepted him into their routine this past week.

And soon, everyone would see the ring on her finger.

Things were moving fast, sure, but during the week since Craig's memorial service, Whit had felt as if he and Megan had lived two lifetimes together. Their lives fit together. More than fit. They were good together and he didn't want to lose that. He'd been searching his whole life for a steady home life to build a family. Megan was the perfect woman for him.

Steering through the night streets, he noted the Christmas lights just beginning to crop up in windows and could see the efforts to rebuild the town starting to bear fruit. There was still a lot of work to be done, but then couldn't that be said about life overall? Everything was a work in progress. And he looked forward to meeting the challenge with Megan at his side.

God, she was gorgeous in a green lace dress, her thick hair swept up into one of those loose kinds of topknots that somehow stayed in place but begged his fingers to set free. She was such an intriguing mix of contrasts. On the one hand, a no-nonsense kind of woman not afraid to get her hands dirty whether she was working with animals or building a compost heap. On the other hand, an elegant woman as comfortable curled up reading her daughter a book as she was dressing up for a five-star evening out. Megan's confidence didn't come from a sense of entitlement or wealth. It came from within. From having tackled life head on and made her way in the world.

He respected that.

Megan trailed her fingers along the window as they drove past the Royal Diner, still closed due to damages from the storm. "Evie and I used to have supper there on days I would work late."

"Amanda will reopen," he said. "It's just going to take a while. I hear she and Nathan took out good insurance on the place. With luck the diner will be even better than ever."

"Like the hospital?" She smoothed a hand over her green lace dress. "I almost feel guilty getting all dressed up to have fun when there are still people dealing with the chaos of the aftermath."

"There's nothing wrong with enjoying yourself. You work hard and deserve a break. I think even the people who are struggling take comfort from seeing life returning to normal around them. It's good to do regular things. Support local businesses." He rested his hand on top of the steering wheel. "I know a perfect diner Evie will love when you two move in with me—I guess I should say, 'What if you and Megan moved in with me?'"

Wait, that wasn't what he'd meant to say. He was going to propose, then ask her to move in while they were engaged. But damn it, the words were already out there, so he held his peace as he stopped at a red light and waited for her response.

"What did you say?" she asked carefully.

"I have plenty of space." The light changed and he accelerated, weighing his words. "It's a gated community, so you two would have more security. And Evie would enjoy the Pine Valley community stables and pool. I'm thinking she could use some jodhpurs. Maybe for Christmas?"

"Maybe," Megan said noncommittally. To the riding clothes or moving in?

He needed to shift into damage control ASAP.

"Is that a no to moving in?" If so, that didn't bode well for his plans to propose.

"You've sprung this on me rather quickly. Can we talk more about it, please?" Her fingers clenched and tangled together in her lap. "I have a lot to consider with Evie. She's only just stopped wearing costumes—thank you again for bringing the therapy dog to her school. You were right about that."

Did that mean she trusted him more? "I did it for all the kids. And for the animals too. I'm glad Ms. Baker was able to take two off your hands."

"You and me both." She twisted in the seat toward him. "I didn't mean to be short about moving in together. You just caught me unaware."

He glanced at her beautiful face, full of worry. "It's okay. Like you said, we can talk more later. We have time."

They had time and he had plans. He knew the right opportunity would present itself for the proposal. And he'd even chosen a gift for her he thought would let her know just how much he cared about her as a person and accepted their differences.

She smiled, and it damn near took his breath away. "Taking our time. I like the sound of that."

Megan had barely tasted a bite of the appetizer, soup, salad or main course. Her mind was still on Whit's surprise suggestion that they live together. Things were moving so fast, she felt as if she was still stuck in the tornado sometimes.

But with each minute that passed, she found herself considering the possibility more seriously.

They were all but spending every waking hour outside of work together. Evie didn't even question his presence. If anything, her daughter questioned when he would arrive. She'd even asked if he could pick her up from day care. He was everything Megan could have hoped for in a man, on so many levels. So much so, it scared her sometimes how well things were going. Maybe that's why she was nervous about moving in together. It was like tempting fate.

The waiter cleared away their dinner plates and brought dessert. "Mr. Daltry," the waiter said, "just as you ordered, our chef made this especially for your celebration. A dark chocolate and orange tart with toasted almonds. I hope it is to your satisfaction."

Orange and chocolate? Surely not a coincidence?

The twinkle in Whit's eyes confirmed he'd intended the treat as a reminder of their time together in the greenhouse.

"I'm sure it will be perfect," Whit answered smoothly. "Please pass along my thanks."

Megan pressed a hand to her mouth to stop a laugh as the waiter left them alone again. "You're wicked."

"Just reminding you of all the wonderful times we can have together in the future." His hand gravitated to his suit coat, smoothing his lapel as he'd done a number of times throughout the dinner.

Was he as nervous as she over this? In a strange way she found it comforting, more of a sign he took this big step seriously.

"About what you said in the car regarding moving in together, I'm still not ready to say yes outright, but I want to think about it. And for me that's huge."

His hand fell away from his jacket and she linked fingers with him.

"Whit, we have something wonderful started. Let's not rush."

"Sure, of course," he agreed, but the tight lines of his mouth indicated that she'd let him down.

Couldn't he see how hard she was trying by letting herself be swept into his world so fast? She thought they'd really made progress. And it wasn't as if she just had herself to consider. A move would be a lot of upheaval for Evie at a time when she was just settling back into school and enjoying herself.

Megan tried to think of a better way to help Whit understand—to ease that tense expression on his face—when a cleared throat from behind him drew her attention upward.

Colby Richardson stood there with his hands shoved in his pockets. His resemblance to his late brother Craig was shocking. The man had a closed-off air emotionally, but that was understandable given what he must be going through. "Sorry to interrupt your dinner, but I wanted to congratulate you."

Megan looked up in confusion. Whit couldn't have already told people of his plans to move in together, could he? Whit stood, as if to quiet the man, which only fueled her concerns—and confusion.

"Thanks, Colby. I appreciate that. Could I treat your table to another round of drinks?" Whit asked, clearly trying to divert him.

"Of course. I see you have a bottle of champagne on its way over. I should leave you both to celebrate your big purchase."

Megan frowned. "Big purchase?"

"Yes," Colby said. "Whit managed quite a coup this week in scooping up the stretch of wetlands on the edge of town."

Her insides chilled faster than that bottle of bubbly in the ice bucket. "You bought up the wetlands?"

"Yes," Whit shuffled his feet, "but it's not exactly what you're thinking."

Colby backed away. "Sorry to have spilled the beans prematurely. I'll just leave the two of you to talk. Good evening."

The clean-cut real estate mogul turned and made a beeline to his table, leaving Megan alone with Whit again.

She restrained the urge to snap at Whit. He was a businessman, first and foremost. She knew that. She shouldn't be surprised that he'd proceeded as planned. He'd never misled her about who he was.

Still, she couldn't stem the deep well of disappointment pooling in her stomach.

"Megan? Do you want to hear what I have to say?"

She shook her head. "It doesn't matter." She folded her napkin in her lap, wishing she could sweep this disagreement away along with the breadcrumbs. "I understand we're different people. I'm not angry."

It cost her, but she would make peace. Try harder. Damn it, she was trying harder.

"But you're upset with me." Tension threaded through his shoulders, his jaw flexing.

She met his eyes and answered honestly. "Disappointed."

"Megan, our careers are separate. I respect your professionalism and I expect you to respect mine."

"Okay," she answered carefully, "but that doesn't mean I'm going to compromise my principles."

"You're calling me unprincipled?"

She struggled for a way to wind back out of this discussion that was playing out like too many confrontations they'd had over the years. Had the past couple of weeks just been a fluke, with reality now intruding once again? "We've had this disagreement for years. Did you think I was magically going to change because we…"

She couldn't even push the last words free without her voice cracking. She snatched up her water glass, her hand trembling with emotion.

He held her eyes without speaking for what felt like an eternity. Dishes and silverware clanked. The candles flickered between them, the dim chandelier above casting more shadows than light.

Finally, he shook his head. "You've already made up your mind about me. It's clear we have nothing left to say to each other."

How dare he act disillusioned with her? In the span of a couple of weeks, she'd done an about-face on so many of her stances to be with him. She was even willing to overlook this land purchase, as much as it galled her, and accept that they were different.

But now she suspected in spite of all his words to the contrary, he didn't want to be with her after all. Because it wasn't good enough for him that she would compromise on this issue. He needed her to be on his side. Think like him. Cheer on his plan to destroy wetlands she felt passionately about.

Why couldn't they just leave it be? Like so many men she'd seen in the past, he was okay to let their relationship self-destruct. He'd found an out and taken it. The knowledge burned all the way down her throat. She shot up from her chair before she did something humiliating like burst into tears.

Or worse yet, accept anything he said as truth just to stay with him.

Anger and frustration making his blood boil, Whit strode through the restaurant after Megan. He angled past the Richardson family at one table, the sheriff and his wife at another, and barely registered that they spoke to him because his focus was fully on Megan.

He charged past a Christmas tree covered in golden lone stars and white twinkling lights. Whit pushed through the door and stopped beside Megan, who was standing under the restaurant awning. "Megan—"

"The doorman is calling a cab for me." Her arms were crossed tight over her chest as her teeth chattered, her face every bit as chilly as her body language.

He held up a hand to stop the doorman from hailing

a taxi. "Damn it, that's not necessary. I brought you here. I'll drive you home."

"That would be awkward." She squeezed her eyes closed and then nodded to the doorman, silently signaling him to flag down a ride. "Please, just let me go. You already made it clear we have nothing left to say to one another."

Her struggle to hold back tears tugged at him. Damn it all, the last thing he wanted was to hurt her. But pride held him back from telling her the truth about that land. He needed her to believe in him. "You're upset. I get that." He took her arm and gently guided her away from the restaurant's main entrance. "But this isn't the place."

She let him steer her a few steps to the side. "The facts won't change if we're in your car."

"The facts?" He bit back a weary sigh. "You don't understand—"

"How about this for facts?" Her arms slid to her side, her hands clenched in tight fists. "You've been buying up land since the tornado. Taking advantage of people's pain. So fine. Tell me how I'm wrong," she finished defiantly.

"Taking advantage?" He searched for the words to make her understand, for the words to keep her in his life. "I've been buying property from people who needed to cut their losses. If I wasn't there to buy from them, they would lose everything rather than walking away with the money to start over. We've discussed this before."

He'd spent his childhood seeing his family's life repossessed. He wasn't lying when he told her he tried to help people in his town as best he could. He swallowed back the past and focused on the present, on Megan.

She shook her head. "And destroying the wetlands?

How is that 'helping' people? Sounds like you're making excuses. You can justify it however you want, but I don't see it the same way."

The sound system hummed with a symphonic version of "Have Yourself a Merry Little Christmas," as if mocking him with memories of a holiday spent in a homeless shelter until his dad landed on his feet again. Granted, they had all gotten gifts that year, courtesy of a local church group.

Even if he told her his real reason for buying the wetlands, that wouldn't change who he was. "You're employed by a non-profit organization and get paid a salary. I own a business where people only get paid if I make a profit. That's how life works."

She held up a finger, her hand shaking with restrained emotion. "Don't speak to me like I'm a child. There are plenty of people who make a profit without compromising their values."

"I follow the letter of the law in my business practices." He wasn't like his father, damn it.

"Just because something is legal doesn't mean it's morally right."

Okay, now she was stepping over the line.

"And what makes you the authority on right and wrong? There can be a middle ground if you'll stop being judgmental and—"

Gasping, she backed up a step. "Is that what you think of me? That I'm uptight and judgmental just because I live my life by a moral code that isn't identical to yours?"

He looked into her eyes and didn't see any room for changing her mind. She'd dug in her heels deeply. He recognized the look from the three years he'd known her. These past few weeks had been an anomaly. She wasn't interested in a real relationship with him.

"I think you're just looking for a reason to break it off with me. I think you're so locked onto the past that you're convinced every man is like your dad or Evie's dad. So much so, that you never really gave me a chance. Not three and a half years ago and not now."

"That's not fair," she whispered.

"None of this is." His hand gravitated to the ring box in his pocket again by habit, but he left it inside. He met her gaze and willed her to see the love in his eyes, to understand how he felt. To trust him.

To trust *in* him.

For an instant, he could have sworn he saw her stance softening and he reached to caress her arm.

The taxi rolled to a stop at the front entrance.

She pulled her hands in tight again, closing herself off from him, from what they could have had together. "Goodnight, Whit. I just…I can't do this."

Looking so damn beautiful that she took his breath away and broke his heart, Megan rushed past him and slid into the cab.

The taxi's taillights disappeared into the night like fading Christmas lights. His big night with Megan was over and he'd botched it from the start. He'd been so busy making plans for them, looking for angles to persuade her and win her over. All the while missing the most important thing of all.

This wasn't about winning a deal like some business merger. This was about having Megan in his life forever. This was about being in love with her. Somehow, he'd never once used that all-important word and because of that, he'd lost her.

Twelve

After a sleepless night, Megan took out her frustration by trying to restore order to some part of her world. She grabbed the bottle of disinfectant and moved on to spritz the next cat kennel. Her gloved hands scrubbed with a vengeance.

She'd spent most of the night crying and second-guessing herself. Today was supposed to be a day off. She should have been spending it with Whit. Evie had even asked to go to a friend's house to play, her costumes and fears fading. Which left Megan alone in her too quiet house. So she'd come to the shelter to get her mind off things, but it wasn't working.

Somehow she and Whit had shifted from considering moving in together to broken up in the span of one dinner, and all because of a land purchase.

A land purchase they had been at odds over for months. She should have seen the signs, but she'd been so blinded by how much she enjoyed being with him. Her eyes watered again. She sniffled and rubbed her wrist under her nose.

Footsteps echoed in the corridor and she blinked faster to clear her eyes—as if that would make any difference given how puffy they were. God, she hoped whoever it was wouldn't stop and talk. She just wanted to clean and clean until she dropped into an exhausted sleep and didn't have to think.

The footsteps stopped right outside the doorway.

"Soooo?" Beth's voice called. "How did your big date with Whit go last night?"

Megan could have diverted an employee or regular volunteer. But there would be no escaping Beth.

Eyes stinging from the sharp scent of bleach, she spoke over her shoulder, keeping her face averted. "The meal was five-star quality."

"Everyone knows the place is great." Beth pulled up alongside her. "It's one of those restaurants where guys take women to propose. Megan? Sweetie? Are you okay?" Beth dipped her head to make eye contact.

Megan flinched and scrubbed harder. "Would you like to help me here? I'm expecting a call from a grant writer any minute." Her words tumbled over each other as she sought to distract. "The guy's going to donate his services to help us put in a proposal to help fund a voucher spay/neuter program."

Beth grabbed a second bottle of antiseptic spray and tore off some paper towels. "Abigail and I can finish up here. On one condition."

She tucked her head into the steel kennel. "What's that?"

Her friend rested a hand on her shoulder. "Can you take off the glove so I can see the ring?"

Is that what her friend thought? This day just got worse.

Megan knew the moment had come. She couldn't hide anymore. "There's no ring."

She couldn't even begin to think about all that didn't happen between them last night. All her hopes…up in flames.

"Oh. Really? I could have sworn that he planned to…" Genuine confusion was stamped on Beth's face. "I mean…"

Seeing her friend's certainty was bittersweet. "Just because he takes me out to eat doesn't mean he planned to propose."

Beth took Megan by the shoulders gently and turned her. "Those are dark circles under your puffy eyes. Were you crying? Honey, what's wrong?"

Megan sagged back against the empty kennels they used for new cats to get acclimated before going into the free roaming facility. "We had a…really bad argument, and, well, it's over between us."

"No," Beth whispered, "that's not possible."

But it was. She knew that all too well. "I heard about his land grab…the wetlands."

Beth's eyes narrowed. "Who told you that?"

"Colby Richardson. We crossed paths at the restaurant last night."

"What did Whit say when you asked him for his side of things?"

"I said I…I mean, we talked about it." She chewed her bottom lip, thinking back over their argument and trying to remember when things really went off the rails. "He didn't deny it."

Beth nodded, but stayed silent.

Alarms jangled in Megan's mind. "You're trying to say there was a good reason for what he did?"

She thought back over the evening. It had been the perfect setup for a proposal. He'd even asked her to move in on the drive over. He was clearly serious.

Reflecting on how quickly things had spiraled out of control, she started to question why she hadn't asked rather than just assume. At the time it had seemed as if asking would have given him a chance to lie. But now she wondered if she had subliminally sabotaged the evening because deep down, she was afraid to trust any man again. Just as Whit had accused her of doing.

She looked at Beth, guilt stinging over the way she'd jumped to conclusions when Whit had done nothing but try to see and meet her needs. Her eyes watered again and she didn't bother hiding the emotion from her friend. "I should have asked him about the land purchases."

Beth hugged her close. "Sweetie, it's hard to push aside a lifetime of insecurities. I understand that well." She angled back and smiled. "But the risk is so very much worth it."

Megan eyed her friend suspiciously. "You wouldn't happen to know why he bought the wetlands?"

Beth shrugged. "You should be asking him."

"I'm asking you, because I think you know the answer."

"And if I did?" Beth replied enigmatically, "I think it would be wrong for me to tell you. A relationship needs to be built on trust and if I give you the easy answer, then you will have missed an amazing chance to make things right between you."

Beth's words sunk in. Deep. As Megan looked back

over her time with Whit, once she'd gotten to know him, he'd been honest, thoughtful, generous. Loving.

The way she'd assumed the worst and walked away had to have hurt him. He had plenty of friends, but no family that had ever come through for him. His father had let him down time and time again.

Even skipping out on bills.

And God, she'd accused Whit of being dishonest. She squeezed her eyes shut and rested her head against the cool steel kennel. At every turn since the tornado, she'd seen his quietly philanthropic spirit. He wasn't the type to shout his good deeds from the rooftops. He didn't seek thanks or accolades.

He was a good man.

And she'd messed up, big-time.

She'd been so afraid of getting hurt, she'd turned her back on the love of a lifetime. As she peeled off her gloves, she made up her mind—she owed Whit an apology. She was done being scared.

In his greenhouse, Whit dug his hands into the dirt and pulled the catnip from its original pot. The plant had taken off, outgrowing the small container. He'd come out here today to get his thoughts together. About half-way through the night he'd gotten past his pride. Sure, he'd hoped for more trust from Megan. But he'd pushed too much too fast. He needed to back up and regroup.

He wasn't a quitter. He'd worked to build a better life for himself and now he realized how narrow his view of success had been. It wasn't about the house. It was about the people. He just had to figure out the right way to win her back.

He dropped the catnip into a larger container and scooped more potting soil around the exposed roots.

He'd made a lot more headway with Megan when he'd given her simpler gifts. But damn it, he'd thought buying the wetlands for her and leaving them untouched was the right decision.

Damn it, he still did. He just needed to find the right time to try again.

The greenhouse door opened and he called out for the deliveryman, "You can leave the crate of plants by the door."

"I don't have any plants to offer." Megan's voice carried down the long walkway. "Can I stay anyway?"

The sound of her, here, where they'd shared such an amazing night, was like water poured on parched soil. Incredible relief. Hope for new life. But he needed to tread carefully rather than steamrolling her as he'd done too often in the past.

Whit pulled his hands out of the dirt and grabbed a rag. "Did you leave something here last week?"

She walked toward him, every bit as gorgeous in jeans and a T-shirt as she'd been in her lace gown last night. "I did, actually."

Damn, disappointment kicked through him. "What did you leave? I'll keep an eye out for it."

"You already have it in your hands, Whit." She stopped in front of him and pressed her palms to his chest. "I left my heart here with you."

Had he heard her right? "Megan, about last night and the wetlands—"

"Wait." She tapped his lips. "Let me finish. It's important. I brought something for you, but I need to say some things first. I want you to know that I trust you. I know you have an answer and a reason for whatever you've done. We may not agree, but I do respect your right to do as you see fit. We are different, you and I. And that's a good thing too."

"You really mean that."

He was stunned to *his* roots that she gave him her trust so fully. He'd been so used to working like hell for everything in his life. He'd never expected something so perfect, so incredible to land so smoothly in his arms.

"Absolutely." She sounded so sure of herself. Of him. The constant worry in her green eyes was nowhere in sight.

"God, Megan, I l—"

She tapped his mouth again. "I'm still not finished. I need for you to listen. I know I said some unforgivable things last night and I'm sorry. I should have asked for your side of the story rather than assuming."

He held her with his eyes. "I haven't given you a lot of time to trust me. I realize trust has to be earned."

"And you've done that. More times than most people in this town know and probably far more than I've realized." She stroked his face. "I looked back and realized that you use your money and influence to help so many people without ever taking credit."

He shrugged off those words. "It's easy for me to help. Doesn't put a dent in my bank balance. That's not a sacrifice."

She shook her head. "I think for a kid who was homeless a few times, it probably is a lot tougher to let go of the security of extra money in the bank than you let on."

God, she humbled him and amazed him and made him fall in love with her all over again. "You see me through far nicer eyes than I deserve."

"And you see yourself through a much harsher lens than you should."

Relief shuddered through him as he began to accept

that she'd given him a second chance. He wrapped his arms around her waist, hauled her to his chest and just held her, a simple pleasure he would never take for granted again.

He nuzzled her hair, her cinnamon scent tempting his nose and giving him ideas for something new to add to his garden. "What made you change your mind? Who told you about my plans for the wetlands?"

"No one told me about your plans." She angled back to look at him. "I meant it when I said I'm here because I trust you."

"Megan," he said hoarsely. "I bought the tract of land to give to you. It will stay just as it is as a tribute to how damn lucky I am to have you in my life."

Her eyes went misty and then bright with tears. "Are you kidding? Oh my God, Whit." She hugged his neck, kissed him, hugged him again, then dabbed her eyes. "I'm so sorry for doubting you. Can you forgive me?"

"There's nothing to forgive. You're here." He stroked along her back, loving the way she felt in his arms. Loving her, period. "You said you'd brought something for me. What is it?"

"Oh, right." Her tears vanished and she smiled mysteriously. "A couple of things actually for your—our?—house." She reached into her purse and passed him two silver picture frames. The first had a photo taken at the ice rink in Colorado of him with Megan and Evie. The second picture was of Evie on the sofa holding Tallulah, with Truffles, Pixie and Scooter sleeping along the back, while Piper and Cosmo stood by the coffee table set for a tea party.

A lump rose in his throat.

He hauled her close with a ragged sigh. "God,

Megan, I love you so damn much. The thought of spending another night wondering if I'd lost you forever…"

"You'll never have to wonder again." She arched up on her toes and brought her lips close to his. "I love you, too, Whit Daltry. Today, tomorrow and forever. Me, you, Evie and our menagerie of animals—we're a family."

"I like the sound of that." A lot. Deciding to leave his heart very much in *her* hands, he knelt on one knee in front of her. "Megan Maguire, will you do me the honor of being my wife, my lover, my love for the rest of our lives? Will you allow me the honor of being a father to Evie and any brothers or sisters we might give her in the years to come? Because there is nothing more that I want than to build a life with you by my side. I love you, Megan. I have a ring too, inside—"

"Yes, yes, with or without a ring, yes." She sank to her knees and took his hands in hers. "Of course, I'll marry you, live with you, love you, for the rest of our lives."

He reached for that quilt he'd never gotten around to putting away and snapped it out onto the floor, then remembered what a mess he was. "We should shower. Together. In the interest of conserving water, you know."

She whispered against his lips. "Oh, we will. But first I have some plans for you and those oranges."

He had some plans for her too. And a lifetime to fulfill them right here in Royal, Texas, where finally he'd put down real roots, thanks to Megan's love.

* * * * *

He took her into the ballroom so they'd conclude this business with her boss, and he could have her all to himself again.

Eliana spooled away from him, flashing him an exquisite smile. "I'll go finish my own mission."

Before he could stop her, an erratic movement caught his eye.

Ferreira.

Rafael's enemy was on a collision course with them.

Before any of them could move, Ferreira was pulling Eliana into his arms.

Aggression erupted, almost bursting Rafael's head. *He* was her boss? And he was on hugging terms with her?

Then the words Ferreira kept saying as he clutched Eliana sank into Rafael's mind.

Ellie, my baby girl, you're okay.

Rafael stared at the woman he'd lost his mind over, in the arms of the man he was here to destroy.

And everything crashed into place.

* * *

From Enemy's Daughter to Expectant Bride
is part of The Billionaires of Black Castle series:
Only their dark pasts could lead these men
to the light of true love.

FROM ENEMY'S DAUGHTER TO EXPECTANT BRIDE

BY
OLIVIA GATES

Published in Great Britain 2014
by Mills & Boon, an imprint of Harlequin (UK) Limited,
Eton House, 18-24 Paradise Road, Richmond, Surrey, TW9 1SR

© 2014 Olivia Gates

ISBN: 978-0-263-91483-2

51-1114

Harlequin (UK) Limited's policy is to use papers that are natural, renewable and recyclable products and made from wood grown in sustainable forests. The logging and manufacturing processes conform to the legal environmental regulations of the country of origin.

Printed and bound in Spain
by CPI, Barcelona

Olivia Gates has always pursued creative passions such as singing and handicrafts. She still does, but only one of her passions grew gratifying enough, consuming enough, to become an ongoing career—writing.

She is most fulfilled when she is creating worlds and conflicts for her characters, then exploring and untangling them bit by bit, sharing her protagonists' every heart-wrenching heartache and hope, their every heart-pounding doubt and trial, until she leads them to an indisputably earned and gloriously satisfying happy ending.

When she's not writing, she is a doctor, a wife to her own alpha male and a mother to one brilliant girl and one demanding Angora cat. Visit Olivia at www.oliviagates.com.

To Pat Cooper.
I'm so honored and grateful my writing
has struck such a chord within you.
Your reviews have literally changed my life.

<u>Prologue</u>

He woke up in darkness again.

His cheeks were wet, his heart battering his chest, and his screams for his mother and father still shredding his throat.

"Get up, Numbers."

The vicious voice had terror expanding in his chest. The first time he'd heard it, he'd been terrified, thinking it was a stranger in his bedroom. But he'd soon realized it had been even worse. He'd no longer been at home, but somewhere narrow and long with no windows and no furniture. He'd been on the freezing ground, hands tied behind his back. That voice speaking heavily accented English, the language he knew so well, had said the same thing then.

And that had been how this nightmare had started.

"Seems Numbers wants another beating."

That was the other man. He believed he'd never see anyone but these scary men ever again. And they called him Numbers. It was why they'd taken him. Because he was good with numbers.

He'd been offended when they'd first said that about him. He wasn't "good with numbers." He was a mathematical prodigy. That was what his parents and teachers and all the experts who'd sought him had said he was.

He'd corrected them, and he'd gotten his first ever slap for it. It had almost snapped his neck, sending him crashing into the wall. As the shock and pain had registered, he'd realized that this was real. He was no longer safe and protected. Anything could and would be done to him.

At first, that had made him angry. He'd said if they returned him to his parents, he wouldn't tell them they'd dared lay a hand on him. The two men had laughed, just like he'd always imagined devils would. One had told the other that this Numbers kid might take longer to break than they'd thought.

He'd still insisted his name wasn't Numbers, and the other man had backhanded him on his other cheek, even more viciously.

As he'd lain on the ground, shaking with fear and helplessness, the men had told him what to expect from now on.

"You'll never see your parents or leave this place again. You now belong to us. If you do everything we tell you, the moment we tell you, then you won't be punished. Not too bad."

But he'd disobeyed their every order ever since, no matter how severely they'd punished him for it. He'd hoped they'd give up on him and send him home. But they'd only grown more brutal, seemed to be enjoying hurting and humiliating him more, and the hope that this nightmare might end had kept dwindling.

"Shall we give Numbers a choice of punishments today?"

He heard his tormentors snickering, could barely see their silhouettes towering over him out of the eye that wasn't swollen shut. And in that moment, he gave up.

It finally sank in that what he'd endured their abuse so long for would never happen.

This nightmare would never end.

His captors would never stop their cruelty, his parents would never rescue him and no one else would ever help him. It would never stop getting worse.

And if this was what his life would be like from now on, he no longer wanted to live.

But he couldn't even kill himself. All he had in his cell were metal bowls for dirty water and slimy gunk and the bucket he used for a toilet. There was no way to escape them even through death. Except maybe…

The idea took hold in a second. He'd tried everything except playing along. Maybe if he did, they'd think they'd broken him, and let him out of his cell. He could escape then.

Or die trying.

One of the giants kicked him in the ribs. "Up, Numbers."

Gritting his teeth against the shriek of pain, he rose.

A terrible laugh. "Numbers finally obeys."

"Let's see if he really does." The other monster shoved his foul-breathed face in his. "What's your name, boy?"

The burning liquid in his shriveled stomach rose to his mouth. He swallowed it with the last thought of resistance. "Numbers."

A slap stung across his sore cheek, if not as hard as usual. They'd punish him anyway, just not as badly when he obeyed. "And why are you here?"

"Because I'm good with numbers."

"And what will you do?"

"Everything you say." Another slap left his ears ringing, his head spinning, yet he continued, "The moment you say it."

In the faint light coming from outside, he saw them exchange smiles of malicious satisfaction. They believed they'd succeeded in breaking him. And they had. But he didn't intend to live long enough for them to enjoy their victory.

And they did as he'd thought they would—they dragged him out of his cell. Too weak to walk, he hung between them, his bare feet and the knees exposed through his tattered pants scraping on the cold, cobbled ground.

Barely able to raise his head to look where they were taking him, he got glimpses of soaring, blackened columns and arches, with a roiling gray sky between them. The whole place looked like a medieval fortress from one of the video games his father had gotten him. The one thing he noticed or cared about now was that the walls between the columns were low enough to jump over. To escape…or fall to his death.

Then one of the monsters said, "If you get near the walls, you'll get caught, beaten then thrown back in your cell for twice as long as it took to break you the first time."

So even *that* plan was impossible. But he couldn't go on like this anymore. He couldn't take it.

Before he begged them to just kill him and be done with it, they pulled open two towering wooden doors, dragged him across the threshold and hurled him to the rough ground.

When he finally managed to raise his head, he saw that they were in a huge hall with rows of tables filled with silent boys who'd all turned at their entrance.

"This worm is your newest addition. If you see him doing anything you're not allowed, report him. You'll have a bonus."

With that, his two jailers turned and left him on his knees facing the boys. His pride surged back under their scrutiny, had him staggering to his feet, the initial hope he'd felt when he'd realized he wasn't alone here draining away. He knew boys could be cruel to those smaller and weaker.

And from a first sweep around the room, he was probably the youngest around.

He stood, trying not to hug his aching side, not to show weakness, and almost sagged back to his knees in relief as they turned back to their food and whispered conversations.

So they were all afraid to even raise their voices as the boys in his old school had, who'd been free to laugh and joke. These boys were prisoners like him. They'd been broken before him.

Painfully good smells of hot food hit him, making him dizzier with hunger. Trying to appear steady, he headed toward the source of the aromas.

He was struggling to reach the lid of one of the massive containers when a hand raised it. He hadn't felt its owner's approach.

It was an older boy with a shaved head and piercing black eyes who was already as tall as his own father. But instead of being intimidated by the boy's size and fierce looks, he felt…reassured by his presence.

"My name is Phantom. What's yours?"

His real name rose to his tongue before he swallowed it. This boy might be waiting for him to do something "they weren't allowed to," like tell his real name, so he could report him and get a bonus.

To be on the safe side, he only said, "Numbers."

The boy's winged black eyebrows rose. "That's your specialty? But you can't be older than seven."

"I'm eight."

At his indignation, the boy's gaze gentled. "The first month—or three in your case—of starvation made us all look smaller. You must now eat well, so you can grow as big and strong as possible."

"Like you?"

Phantom's lips twitched. "I'm not done growing. But I'm working on it."

The older boy filled a bowl of steaming stew that smelled mouthwatering compared to the rotting messes he'd been unable to force down for what he'd just now realized had been the past three months. He'd had no way of knowing how long it had been until Phantom had told him.

After handing it over, Phantom filled himself a bowl, then beckoned for him to follow. "If you warranted a name according to your skill that young, you must be a prodigy."

It pleased him intensely that this huge boy with the soundless steps and penetrating eyes could see him for what he was. Even after his jailers had stripped him of everything that made him himself.

Encouraged, he asked, "How old are you?"

"Fifteen. I've been here since I was four."

The boy had answered his next question before he'd asked it, telling him that what his jailers had said was true.

He'd never leave here.

They reached one of the tables and Phantom gestured for him to sit down. There were five other boys, each looking as different as could be from the other, all older than him, but none as old as Phantom.

Two boys scooted along the bench to make space for him as Phantom introduced him to them, his lips somehow not moving, so it would appear to the guards who flanked the hall that he wasn't talking at all. Each of the boys introduced himself. Lightning, Bones, Cypher, Brainiac and Wildcard.

As they continued to eat, each of them asked him something, about his past life. He emulated the boys in stealth, telling them truths without revealing facts. Then they started giving him equations, which he solved with perfect accuracy no matter how convoluted they made them.

By the time they finished eating, he felt he'd known these boys for a long time. But the guards were announcing the end of the meal, and all the boys stood up to leave the hall.

Unable to control his anxiety, he clung to Phantom's arm. "Will I see you again?"

Phantom gave him a stern look, making him remove his hand before the guards noticed. But his voice was gentle when he said, "I'll see that you're brought to our ward."

"You can do that?"

"There's a lot you can do around here, if you know how."

"Will you teach me?"

Phantom raised his eyes to the other boys. And it was then he realized they weren't just fellow prisoners who sat together for meals or shared the same ward. These boys were a team. And Phantom was asking their approval before he let him join them.

Suddenly, this was all he wanted in life. To be part of their team. His old life was gone. And he just knew he wouldn't have a new one without these boys.

He watched each boy give Phantom a slight nod, each filling him with hope he'd thought forever dead.

Before Phantom started walking away, leaving him behind, he said, "Welcome to our brotherhood, Numbers. And to Black Castle."

One

Twenty-four years later

Rafael Moreno Salazar stood in the shadows, looking down from the mezzanine of his newly acquired mansion in Rio de Janeiro.

The grand ball was in full swing. All the major names in the marketing world were enjoying his exclusive hors d'oeuvres and free-flowing Moët et Chandon and waltzing to the elegant music of his live orchestra. And he hadn't yet made an appearance.

He was leaving his guests to…stew, letting their curiosity about him and his intentions reach a fever pitch.

He'd been doing that since his announcement. That Rafael Salazar—the enigma who'd revolutionized financial technologies—was shopping for a marketing partner in the Western hemisphere. Although the announcement's impact was already huge, he'd kept stoking interest by deepening his mystery. Then he'd added a pinch of spice. A handful of dirt, really.

As he always did with potential clients and associates, he'd let info leak that his background was in organized crime. As it was. Just not in the way people imagined. He and his brothers had had their own shadow operation in their beginnings.

Heads of state had been fascinated by his avant-garde methods from the start, but they hadn't courted him aggressively except when they'd found out those methods had been forged in the crucible of crime and tested through the ingeniousness of corruption.

But he hadn't been sure the marketing tycoons he was baiting would be as open to dealing with someone who dabbled in the world's grayest zones and was one of those zones' most ambiguous figures.

But instead of being repelled, it seemed everyone thought any illegal skills and liaisons he commanded would make him an even more lucrative partner. And if he was as formidable as it was rumored, he'd also be invulnerable. They could all do with a partner bullets bounced off.

And there they were, the hopeful candidates, pretending to be enjoying his lavish party and trying to be gracious to one another. But he could feel them seething with frustration, wondering whom he'd favor if and when he finally deigned to grace his own ball.

"Will you finally make an appearance tonight, Numbers?"

He slanted a calm glance at the man who'd appeared silently at his side. "I just might this time, Cobra."

The Englishman he'd called Cobra for the past twenty years curled a ruthless lip as he examined the scene. Rafael had told him the same thing on three previous occasions.

To the world, he was Richard Graves—the name he'd picked when they'd manufactured their new identities. At forty-two, Richard looked like a Hollywood movie star, and at first glance, he could pass for Rafael's older brother. They had almost the same build and coloring, only Richard's jet-black hair was threaded with discreet silver. On closer inspection, however, their bone structure revealed their different ethnicities, with Rafael being of Portuguese Brazilian stock.

But there was one other major difference between them, and it wasn't on the surface. It was in their specialties.

Though Rafael had been trained to be deadly, his main power lay in his mind. He'd rarely relied on his prowess in violence but was the go-to guy to liquidate targets financially. Richard was code-named Cobra for the best reasons. He was the total package of lethality. His liquidations had always been the literal kind. He now hid the deadliness that made him the ultimate assassin behind a facade of refinement. Until you examined him. Or he examined you. Rafael didn't know any mere mortals who could withstand his scrutiny.

But Richard's days of eradicating scum were behind him. Or so he said. But whether this was true or not, he now eliminated threats in the worlds of business and politics with an equally ruthless precision. With Richard as his partner and protector, Rafael felt confident that the past would never catch up with him…and that the future could hold no worries.

Richard pulled back, leveled probing eyes on him. "Aren't you playing this with too much deliberation? You waited years to concoct this plan—I thought you'd be a bit more eager to finally put it into action."

Rafael jerked one shoulder. "I'm in no hurry."

"Really? Could have fooled me." Richard huffed. "Seriously, all you've done for two months is set up such events, then stand in the wings watching. Don't you think you've done enough reconnaissance?"

"After twenty-four years, you think two months is too long for me to savor the anticipation of my revenge?"

"Put that way, no." Richard made a sound of self-deprecation. "Seems I'm the one who can't contain my impatience. You've always been the most methodical, *patient* person I know. That is, along with your dear, relentless Phantom. But you still have one up on him. On anyone. You see the intricacies of probability as simple equations when they're a maze to the rest of us."

Rafael didn't contradict him. He'd long known that the fluke of his mathematical ability did make him see the world in a different way.

But no matter what he'd just claimed, Richard was as clear-sighted as he was in his own way when it came to his concerns. However, when it came to Rafael's, Richard had zero tolerance. He'd killed for him, would no doubt do so again if need be. He'd die for him. The feeling was absolutely mutual.

It never stopped amazing him that he'd not only been blessed with such a "brother" but with seven. Even though they were down to six these days.

Shaking away the disturbing memory of how they'd lost Cypher, seemingly forever, he sighed. "Maybe I'm discovering revenge is a dish best served cold."

At Richard's unconvinced grunt, Rafael chuckled, then sipped his champagne, swirling the sweet taste of vicious expectation.

His revenge *would* be cold. As bitterly cold as the prison he'd grown up in. As agonizingly slow as time had sheared past there. As grimly inexorable as the hatred he'd nursed all those years for those who'd had a hand in his enslavement.

Twelve interminable years of enduring his enslavers' dehumanizing as they'd molded him into the mercenary the Organization would later lease to the highest bidders. Their patrons ranged from top names in politics and commerce to those in organized crime, espionage and war mongering.

He'd been one of a few hundred boys, picked from all over the world. Some kidnapped from their families, others bought or bartered, many more plucked from orphanages, the streets or chaos-torn zones. They'd all been way above average, physically and mentally. Some were gifted. Like him and his brothers.

The Organization's "recruiters" chose their potential operatives using unerring criteria, and they went to great lengths to "acquire" them. They delivered them to that prison in the depths of the Balkans, where they were kept segregated from the world in that sinister fortress his brothers had named Black Castle.

The Organization acquired children as young as possible, the easier to shape them. The ones they acquired a bit older, like him, or younger but strong enough to resist, like his brothers, they broke first, before they put them in training.

Training was a euphemism for the hell, both physical and psychological, that they put them through to forge them into lethal weapons. Once they graduated to fieldwork, they were sent out in teams according to the skill set each mission required. They performed under the airtight surveillance of their "handlers." Death rewarded any attempt to escape.

Yet he'd survived escaping and, before that, the years of oppression and abuse. Not that it had been because of his own strength. He'd had none left after that first period of isolation and torture. If he hadn't met his brothers, he wouldn't have lasted much longer. Then, four years later, Richard had taken him under his wing, too. Richard and his brothers had saved his sanity, and his life.

Phantom, now Numair Al Aswad, had fulfilled the promise he'd made that day in the dining hall when he and the boys had recognized him as a kindred spirit. From that point on, they'd made life worth living, their brotherhood replacing the family he'd lost. After proving himself worthy of their total trust, they'd included him in the blood pact they'd sworn. That they'd one day escape and become powerful enough to bring the entire Organization down.

To that end, Phantom had maneuvered the Organization into constantly teaming them up together until they became their prized strike force. This inseparable unit had been vital to their very long-term plans.

Phantom had also made them believe they'd eradicated their individuality, had turned them into inhuman weapons to be pointed wherever they pleased.

Once they'd become trusted and depended on, they'd been granted more autonomy, until that laxness had allowed them to execute their escape.

When they'd finally broken out, they'd gone deep underground, using their combined covert expertise to forge new identities....

"Reminiscing?"

Richard, his onetime handler, always read him with uncanny accuracy. It was how he'd found Rafael and the others after they'd escaped—by tracing him.

His brothers' handlers had thankfully had no insight into their true nature. But since Richard had been assigned to him when he'd been twelve, an unbreakable bond had developed between them. Richard, ice-cold and implicitly trusted by the Organization, had hidden it perfectly. But there'd been no hiding anything from his brothers. Especially from Phantom and Cypher. Those two saw *everything*. And seeing his growing rapport with Richard had made them more apprehensive by the day. Their trepidation had proved wellfounded when Richard had found them.

They'd distrusted Richard as totally as Rafael trusted him, considered him one of their enslavers. Their decision had been unanimous. Richard had to die.

Rafael hadn't known whom to fear for more. Richard was

the most lethal operative the Organization had ever had and certainly capable of wiping them all out. There'd been only one way he could avert that catastrophic situation.

He'd declared he'd stake his life on both sides, so if there was any killing, they had to kill him, too. Thankfully, they'd trusted him and his judgment implicitly, and it had been enough to make them all back down.

Yet even after he'd proved their escape plans wouldn't have worked without Richard's covert help, they'd still suspected Richard's motives. It had taken proof that Richard had been a hostage of the Organization himself for them to believe that he wanted to bring them down, too.

It had still taken his brothers ages to warm up to Richard. Never in Numair's case. Rafael remained the link between them, since he didn't relish tearing Richard and Numair's fangs out of each other's flesh.

Those two had never had a truce, not even while they'd collated their unique skills to guide their brotherhood into building their joint enterprise. The one thing they'd ever agreed on was the name of their business—the name they'd given their prison, where they and their brotherhood had been forged. And so Black Castle Enterprises had been born.

Their business now spanned the world, with each becoming a billionaire in his own right. Each was also on a personal quest. Some searching for the family they'd been taken from, others for the heritage they'd been stripped of, some for a new purpose in life. But beyond planning the Organization's downfall to save other children from their same fate, they had one more quest in common. Investigating how they'd ended up in the hands of the Organization.

Rafael had recently found out exactly how.

"Ferreira is down there?"

Richard's question brought him out of his musings. "Of course."

"So when will you put the man out of his misery?"

Rafael glanced fondly at his friend. "I wouldn't put it past you to mean that literally."

Richard gave him his patented predatory smile. "Oh, no. I think your plan is a much worse fate. I couldn't have thought of a more diabolical one."

"High praise from the man who puts 007 to shame."

Not one for false modesty, Richard only said, "You know I'm a fan of subtle and protracted torture."

Indeed. And his impending torment of Ferreira would have an abundance of both elements. Disgracing him and oh-so-gradually stripping him of his wealth would only be the beginning.

"Your plot is far more effective than putting a bullet in his brain. I just wish you'd get on with it."

"So you no longer disapprove of my direct approach?"

Richard shrugged. "A remote one remains better. It would be the perfect setup if he didn't realize where the blows were coming from. But that's logic talking. And there's more than logic involved here. You need the satisfaction of looking that git in the eyes as you stick the knife in and turn it."

Richard had originally advised against getting close to Ferreira, with the inherent drawbacks and dangers that entailed. It now warmed Rafael that his friend not only understood his need, he empathized. He wanted this for him. This gratification. This closure.

And he would come close. He'd make Ferreira taste everything he'd ever hungered for…before snatching it away. Rafael would have a front-row seat to his betrayal and desperation.

Putting his glass down, he sighed. "But you're right. It's time I got that satisfaction. I won't single Ferreira out tonight, though. I'll dangle myself, pretend to take pitches, let the mystery around me build a bit more, before…"

Something sizzled at the back of his neck. As if a soft hand stroked him there, or a hot breath blew over his skin.

Frowning, he turned to investigate the source of the disturbance. It couldn't be someone's gaze. He wasn't in anyone's line of sight.

As expected, no one was looking his way. But those sensations only increased, enveloped his body and…

Everything seemed to fade as his senses converged on the beacon of disruption. A woman.

Framed in the ballroom's doorway, she stood as if at a loss for what to do. She was swathed in an ethereal off-the-shoulder cream evening gown, gleaming hair swept away from a face that seemed almost unreal before cascading to a tiny waist that…

"Before what?"

He blinked Richard's question away, resuming his focus on her. Though he'd never suffered anything like this before, he knew what it was. A bolt of attraction. More than that. Recognition…of the woman who translated his every fantasy into glorious reality.

He had to be imagining this. But all his senses told him he wasn't. This felt real.

One way to find out. Get closer.…

"What are you staring at, Numbers?"

This time Richard's intrusion annoyed him. He realized his reaction was exaggerated, but he didn't want to talk, couldn't risk shattering this moment.

As if afraid he'd startle her out of her indecision, which afforded him the leisure to examine her, he whispered, "Her."

Richard stepped forward. "Who? That woman at the door?"

Surprised, he turned to him. "You see her?"

Richard scowled. "You asleep on your feet again?"

He hadn't slept in over twenty-four hours, but that had nothing to do with his reaction to her. "I'm wide-awake.

Though she does belong in a dream. She looks like she's just stepped out of a fairy tale."

Richard's incredulity surpassed his. "You're serious?"

"I am. I…"

His thoughts stalled. She'd started walking into the ballroom, but her uncertain steps, her darting eyes and the way she fiddled with the long chain of her purse revealed her discomfort. Everything about her unconscious grace and reluctant demeanor made something rev behind his sternum. It intensified with her every step until he had to rub the heel of his hand against it.

"How could this be real?"

"It isn't."

Richard's response startled him. He hadn't realized he'd spoken out loud. "How can you say that?"

"I can because she's just another pretty blonde."

He looked at his friend as if he'd grown a third eye. "She's *not* blonde. Are you even talking about the same woman?"

Richard seemed about to argue, then changed his mind. "Whatever. Just go initiate your incursion."

"It won't be an incursion. I will approach her with utmost finesse."

Richard frowned. "I'm talking about Ferreira."

"Forget Ferreira. I'll…"

Rafael stopped as he realized something. He *couldn't* approach her. He'd been scrupulous about keeping any photos of himself out of the media. But if anyone knew what he looked like, they were down there at the ball. He didn't want to risk anyone recognizing him, not now that he'd decided against making an appearance. This evening had suddenly become all about establishing contact with this magical being.

He turned to Richard. "Cobra, bring her to me."

His former handler blinked. "What's wrong with you,

Numbers? You've never reacted to a woman like this before."

"She's not just 'a woman.'"

Richard snorted. "Oh, yes, that's right. She just slithered out of a fairy tale."

Rafael gritted his teeth, impatience shooting through him. "Just go down and get her up here."

"You want me—the man famed for putting people at *such* ease—to approach a woman I don't know and command her to come with me…to meet another man she doesn't know? A man who currently looks deranged? You expect this fairy being to be a total moron, too?"

Richard's derision tripped some still functioning logic circuits. That scenario did seem implausible.

But he *had* to get that woman alone.

Suddenly, another idea came to him. "I'll go down with you and stand outside the ballroom. You just get her to me. I'll take it from there."

"I'm your protector, not your pimp, Numbers."

"Oh, shut up. And move it."

With one last glance as if to a madman, Richard turned and headed downstairs. Rafael dogged his steps, scenarios crowding in his overheated imagination.

What if this excitement fizzled out once he saw her up close? Worse, what if it didn't…but she didn't reciprocate it? Or what if she *was* interested, but like all other women, her attraction was based purely on his looks, wealth and power? Worst of all, what if she was already taken?

No. This last possibility he categorically rejected.

She wasn't taken. He just knew it.

At the edge of the ballroom, Richard looked back as if hoping he'd come to his senses. Rafael only shoved him forward.

Grunting a curse, Richard walked away, cutting through

the crowd. At six foot six, he towered a head above everyone, making it easy for Rafael to monitor his progress.

Then he saw her. Pressing to the periphery, as if taking refuge from the crowd, wishing she were anywhere but there.

Everything inside him tightened, anticipating the moment Richard pointed her in his direction. Or something. He had no idea what his friend would do or say to get her to cross the ballroom to meet him.

Richard was feet away from her when she suddenly turned her elegant head. And looked straight into *his* eyes.

A bolt hit him through the heart. A growl escaped his lips as the current forked within him. Then again as her eyes widened and her tense features went slack.

He wasn't imagining this. She'd felt his focus, and it had made her home in on him, even across the distance and with him in shadows. He'd had the same effect on her.

And without volition, holding her mesmerized gaze, he raised his hand and…beckoned.

Her stare faltered, her throat worked. Peach stained her chiseled cheekbones and her gaze darted around, as if unable to believe she was his target.

Look back. Look back at me.

As if against her will, her eyes dragged back to his.

Satisfaction surged through him. She'd felt his need and had been unable to resist it. Testing his theory, he beckoned again, taking a step backward deeper into the shadows.

She stepped forward, looking surprised, as if she hadn't intended to move. He took another step back. She once again moved in his direction, the confusion on her exquisite face deepening. This live wire of attraction that had sprung to life between them *was* reeling her in to him. He hadn't needed Richard's help after all.

The steely Englishman glared down at her as she bypassed him in a daze. Realizing his mediation was no longer needed, he shook his head in exasperation and strode away. Richard fell off Rafael's radar as he focused on the vision he held in thrall, just as she held him. He continued to recede and beckon, drawing her toward him.

It took forever for her to weave through the throngs of people who turned to stare at her trancelike advance. Then at last, *at last,* she entered the deserted corridor. He took her deeper into his home where no one would come. She kept advancing after he stopped. Lips parted, eyes wide, face tilted up, she finally halted within arm's reach. The sconces illuminated her face and figure in golden radiance and soft shadow.

She was more than he'd thought from afar, her impact on him fiercer up close.

And she most definitely wasn't blond. Such a mundane word didn't describe her cascade of spun silk with its thousand shades. Each strand had the tones of Rio's beaches, its Sugarloaf Mountain and its sunrays at every time of day.

In contrast, her skin, from forehead to fingertips, was flawless cream. As for her body, it was *the* body sculpted to his every requirement, to accommodate his every desire and demand. At once willowy and womanly, unconscious femininity screamed in its every line and swell and curve.

Richard had been wrong about something else, too. She wasn't pretty. Or beautiful. She transcended such descriptions. From the intelligent forehead to the elegant nose to the lush lips, her face was a tapestry of perfections, embodying his every taste and fantasy. But it was her eyes, where her essence resided, that snared him. Wide, heavily fringed, a magnificent shape and slant, he'd thought he'd imagined their color as she'd approached. He hadn't. They were an intense, luminous tawny. The hue of fire. And just as dangerous.

But *her* effect wasn't about her physical attributes. Something about her just made him want to…devour her. He'd never been so ferociously attracted, or aroused. It was incomprehensible, but all he wanted was to unwrap her then bury himself inside her.

Even in his state, he realized that course of action wasn't advisable. Even if she was willing. Which, from her glazed stare and agitated breathing, she probably was.

"Obrigado, minha beleza."

He heard his hungry rasp, thanking her, calling her *his beauty* in his mother tongue. Though most of tonight's guests weren't Brazilian, he had a feeling she'd understand. And though he only thought in Portuguese and hadn't spoken it since he'd been abducted, it felt the only language personal enough, intimate enough, to do this moment justice.

"Wh-what for?"

His breath caught. She *had* understood, yet answered in English. Cultured, American English. And she sounded as shaken as she looked. Her voice was a soft, sultry caress, made to moan enchantments in his ear, against his flesh, in long, pleasure-drenched nights.

"For coming when I summoned you."

She blinked, as if emerging from a trance. "Summoned me?"

She obviously took exception to his choice of words. He wanted to tease her, say that she *had* obeyed his summons. But he couldn't talk—he needed to make that first contact. Holding her gaze, he reached out and cupped her cheek.

His breath hissed out as her flesh filled his palm, as he absorbed its texture and heat. She trembled in his grasp, pouring molten steel into his erection. Then her eyes darkened into burning coals and singed away his control.

Two urgent, stumbling steps had her back to the wall, plastering her between its unyielding barrier and his. Hot resilience cushioned his aching hardness and ripped a rumble from his gut. Her echoing gasp filled his lungs with her scent. A hint of jasmine, a mist of pheromones, a gust of compulsion. Hunger writhed inside him until he could no longer bear not tasting her.

Holding her stunned eyes with his, he hovered over her trembling lips for one last anticipation-laced moment. Then he obliterated the distance between them.

A spark arced between their lips, making him jerk up. Her eyes displayed shock, too; her lips trembled with it. But the rise and fall of her breasts was that of excitement, not distress. Then arousal seeped into her eyes, weighing down her lids, and made her lips swell, as if he'd already ravished them.

She wanted this. Wanted him. Like he wanted her.

And he didn't want just a kiss anymore. He wanted everything.

They'd exchanged two sentences—phrases—and he knew nothing about her. But this would follow no rules. The passion that had exploded into existence between them obliterated any.

He would take her first. As she wanted him to. Everything else would come later. Satisfying this overpowering hunger was the most important thing now. The only thing that mattered.

He bent, swept her up in his arms. She only gasped and went limp against him, her eyes enormous orbs of surrender.

Triumph and elation fueled his strides to his study. Kicking the door shut, he put her back on her feet and pressed her against it. Her feverish eyes assured him this was exactly what she wanted. Everything with him. Now.

"*Sim, beleza, sim...tudo comigo...agora.*"

And he crashed his lips on hers.

Two

Ellie was drowning. In pleasure. The pleasure of this man's kisses. The man she'd met only minutes before.

But it was okay to drown. Since this had to be a dream.

In the waking world, it was unthinkable for her to lose her head at the sight of a man, let alone her sense of self at his touch. Perfect pleasure like this couldn't possibly exist. Not for her. She was the last woman on earth to get zapped by attraction at a literal hundred paces. And then came this man. *He* was what proved this must be a dream. He *couldn't* be real.

No real man could have compelled her like this. Even the way he'd materialized out of the darkness had been unreal.

One thing explained all this. She must be dozing off in her car, lost in the most outrageously erotic dream ever.

Which figured. After two days of continuous work, exhaustion had been another reason she'd hated having to go to that ball. She'd been asleep on her feet by the time she'd dragged herself home at three to throw on "something appropriate," then driven to that mansion in Armação dos Búzios, the "Hamptons of Brazil." The damn place was over two hours away. And she'd been lost an extra half hour before finding it.

After she finally did at six o'clock, she had memories of valet parking and walking through the ingeniously landscaped, multilevel gardens into the splendid, four-level edifice sprawling over what she thought was no less than ten thousand square feet. Outside, each spray of indirect illumination enhanced every white-painted arch, column and molding in its neo-Renaissance architecture, giving it the grandeur of a temple or cathedral. Inside, the pervasive, festive lighting came from an abundance of all-crystal chandeliers and antique brass *lampadaires,* giving the Portuguese-French–style gilded interior the feel of a fairy tale. Then she'd reached the ballroom, which was right out of one.

She remembered pausing at the threshold, wrestling with her dislike for crowds, then finally walking in since braving it was preferable to being subjected to more pleading.

Then as she'd kept to the periphery, avoiding the forced gaiety, she'd felt as if she was hit by lightning. Her eyes had jerked to the bolt's origin. And she'd met his gaze.

As her heart had stumbled like a horse on ice, he'd raised a hand made of elegance and power, and beckoned.

Breath hitching, she'd looked around to see who he was beckoning to. Once sure he was actually motioning to her, she'd had no thought of resisting. He'd kept receding, and she'd kept moving toward him, no volition involved. Then she had been within touching distance, and nothing had remained in her stalled mind but…wow. *Wow.*

Even at five-foot-ten with four-inch heels, she was dwarfed by him. Besides his towering height, his shoulders, torso and arms were daunting, his waist and hips narrow, his thighs formidable. And his legs went on forever.

And that was what she could see through his slate-gray suit. She couldn't even imagine what his body would look like out of it.

But one thing she saw clearly. His face.

Ruthless planes and stark angles composed his forehead, nose and jaw. His cheekbones slashed so sharply against his polished teak skin, she felt she could cut herself on them. His lips were sculpted from decadent sensuality. Put together, his features were a standard of male beauty no one would ever come close to measuring up to. Not in her eyes.

But what captivated her went beyond his physical endowments and sexual magnetism. It wasn't even those stormy eyes, surrounded by lashes as raven-black as the layers of his vital hair, and slanted to the same mysterious angle as his dense eyebrows. It was the entity that looked back at her through them.

Then he'd thanked her, for coming when he'd *summoned* her.

The dark spell of his voice hadn't stopped annoyance from registering at his arrogance. Even when nothing else could describe the way she'd walked to him as if in thrall. Then he'd cupped her cheek and the world disappeared.

Nothing was left but his touch, and the building urge for something…more. And he gave her more. Like a hungry panther, he backed her against the wall only to hover over her lips, tantalizing her with the dizzying scent of his maleness and desire.

She started trembling, fearing her heart would stop if he didn't kiss her. Then he did. And that intensity between them manifested into a literal spark, zapping what remained of her coherence. She looked up into his eyes when he jerked away, confessing her helplessness. And a change came over him.

As overriding as his approach had been up till that point, there'd been restraint in it. But now his eyes explicitly said there'd be none from this point forward. He wouldn't stop at a kiss. He wanted more. Everything. Then he told her just that.

Yes, my beauty, yes. Everything with me. Now.

On some level, she realized this was insane. But when he swept her up into his arms, she melted in his hold, let him take her wherever he would.

Then he crossed into a semidark room, an opulent study. He set her back on her feet only to press her against the door. Before she could draw another breath, he thrust his tongue deeper in her mouth as he undid her hair clip. Her hair swished down over his hand, and he combed his fingers through it, sending pleasure cascading to every root. Then his other hand found her zipper and slid it down.

She moaned a sound she'd never before produced—the sound of relief-laced shock—as her bodice released her breasts with a rustling sigh. His lips swallowed her moans, drugging her with delight. One thing kept repeating in her brain.

She'd wake up any moment now.

But she didn't wake up. And now she knew she wouldn't.

This was just too overwhelming to be a dream.

This was real.

Another shock zigzagged through her as his fingers splayed against her back, and her flesh almost burst into flame. She jerked away from the burning, then pressed back for more. And he took his onslaught to the next level.

He yanked up her skirt, cupped her buttocks beneath her panties and hauled her up against him. She gasped at his grip over her intimate flesh, at his effortless power. Gasps became moans as he ground the steel of his erection against her core, flooding it with another rush of liquid heat.

Something scalding rumbled from him as he tugged one thigh, splaying her around his hips. Then he thrust against her to the same rhythm his tongue plunged inside her mouth.

His powerful chest rubbed against her breasts, the friction of their remaining clothes pricking her nipples into pinpoints of agony.

She trembled in his hold as his lips burned a trail from her lips down to her neck, settling there to ravage her with tugging kisses that sent pleasure hurtling through her blood with each savage pull.

It felt as if all existence converged on him, became him, his body and breath, his hands and mouth. She was no longer herself, but a mass of needs wrapped around him, open to him. The flowing throb between her legs escalated to a pounding that needed *something* to assuage it. When it tipped into sheer discomfort, she cried out.

He shuddered against her, as if her cry electrified him, then he snapped his head up and crashed his lips on her wide-open mouth, thrusting deeply.

She plunged into his taste again as his tongue dueled with hers, as his lips and teeth mastered her. This was nothing like the slow seduction she'd imagined her first intimate encounter would be. This was an invasion, a ravaging. And she wanted it that way.

In unison with her feverish need, he snatched her off her feet again, crossed the room. Lowering her on a massive couch that would accommodate his full length, he straightened and looked down at her. In the dim light coming from somewhere in the spacious room, his gaze reflected the illumination, sparkled silver, devouring her. Hers druggedly luxuriated in gliding over his awe-striking figure.

Then he finally came down over her, his powerful limbs a prison of muscle and maleness.

"Estou louco de desejo por você, minha beleza única."
I'm mad with wanting you, my unique beauty.

She would have said the same to him, if she could. But all she could do was silently arch up to help him when his hands dipped beneath her to undo her bra. He peeled it off and spilled her swollen breasts into his palms. She lurched as he growled his appreciation, pressing them together, mitigating their ache, heightening her fever. Then he bent and showed her there was more exquisite agony, grazing one nipple then the other with his teeth, swirling them with his hot tongue. By the time he suckled them, she was writhing beneath him as he built to long, hard pulls.

Then he blew his scorching confessions on them. "You made me lose my mind with a look. Then I touched you, tasted you, felt you like this, beneath me, open for me, needing me."

She could only nod jerkily, her teeth starting to clatter as his hands squeezed her buttocks, then slid her soaked panties off her quivering legs. He then discarded his jacket, undid his shirt and flung it open before pressing back over her. His silky hair-roughened flesh rubbed her into a frenzy, then suddenly…he stilled.

Disentangling their bodies, he rose on extended arms and loomed above her. "You're trembling all over. Are you afraid?"

Surprise made words catch in her swollen throat. "O-only that my heart might stop…or I might faint."

Something more dangerous than anything he'd exposed her to spread on his face. A smile. Predatory, starved, unbearably arousing. "I feel the same. Minus the fainting. My heart might stop if I don't have you naked beneath me." But instead of extracting her from her undone dress, he bunched it at her midriff. "Next time, I'll worship you from your lashes to your toenails. But now I need to be inside you. Say you need me, too. Say you can't wait. Say it."

There was no voice left in her. She was coming apart, the pounding in her core rising to a frantic hammering. Her head jerked on a nod, a tear slipping from her left eye.

He swooped down, closed his lips over her earlobe, catching the moisture. With his first nip, she arched up into his arousal with a cry, her legs falling open, giving him license to take, to possess.

His breathing as harsh as hers, he rose to his knees, and in barely suppressed urgency, released himself. Her heart rammed her ribs. With intimidation at the size of him.

Then he took his erection in his hand, and she could only lie there, waiting for him to do whatever it took to satisfy this gnawing hunger. Her heart thundered, expecting him to drive into her, filling that maddening emptiness he'd created inside her, bracing for the pain. But he didn't, only squeezed his eyes shut on what sounded like a vicious curse. When he opened them, they almost vaporized her. Then pushing her thighs wider apart, his hand slid beneath her, tilting her hips. His gaze swept downward, dragging hers with it. With a stuttering heart, she watched him open the engorged lips of her sex, then, making no attempt to penetrate her, he rubbed the scorching length of his manhood between them.

The pleasure was so acute she bowed up on a shrill cry.

His other hand clenched her buttocks, he bent and clamped her lips in a fierce kiss.

"Do you feel how wet and hot and ready for me you are?"

He glided up, nudging her most sensitive knot of flesh. She shrieked in his mouth, ecstasy almost too sharp to bear. He circled her swollen knot with his crown until everything in the world focused on the point where his flesh tormented hers.

"Please, please…"

She pleaded with him even when she didn't know if she could accommodate him. But this…this was what she'd been waiting for all her life. This was why she'd never been tempted to share her body with a man. Because she'd never experienced anything like this mind-searing, caution-annihilating lust.

His lips possessed hers again, swallowing her pleas as he thrust against her, prodding her nub over and over.

The pleasure became an unbearable pressure that clamored to unfurl. When she felt she could stand it no more, he quickened his tempo and snapped the tension inside her.

He pinned her beneath him as she bucked and shrieked, release tearing through her. Continuing to pump his hardness against her quivering flesh, he drained her of the last spasm of pleasure her body needed to discharge.

She slumped beneath him, depleted, sated, her intoxicated gaze fixed on him as he rose to his knees between her splayed legs. Pumping his erection, groans gusted from his depths as he climaxed, his blazing eyes never leaving hers.

She'd never known anything as incredible as the sight and sound of him in the grip of orgasm, nor felt anything as fulfilling as knowing she'd given him as much pleasure as he'd given her. Breathing slowing down, she spiraled into a chasm of satisfaction and melted deeper into the plushness beneath her....

Awareness flooded back into her as she felt him gently wiping her belly before he came down over her, claiming her lips in luxurious kisses. It was as if after devouring her, he was now sipping her, savoring her. Each clinging kiss solidified the intimacy they'd shared, and told her the explosive episode had been a prelude to a deeper passion.

When he finally raised his head it was to reach above her. A light burst on. Even though it was soft and soothing, her eyes squeezed shut. When she opened them again, she found him looking down at her indulgently.

"What—what just happened?"

She hadn't intended to speak. Certainly not to say something that moronic. But she had, her voice deep, husky and nothing like she'd ever heard it.

Expecting ridicule to enter his gaze, his hypnotic eyes only turned serious. "No idea. Nothing like this has ever happened to me before. But if I have to guess, I'd say... magic."

Relief swamped her. He didn't consider her bewilderment an act, or stupid. And he felt the same way.

She exhaled in relief. "In the absence of any other explanation, I'd have to agree."

Yet now with the madness-inducing arousal sated, embarrassment started to submerge her.

What had she done?

She sank deeper into what she now saw was an oversize, dark green and gold silk brocade couch, acutely conscious of their state of undress, of every inch of his flesh that was still pressed into her most intimate parts.

As if attuned to her needs, as he'd seemed to be from the start, he rose off her, slid to the ground and kneeled beside her. After forcing his unabated erection into his pants, he retrieved her panties. Navigating the high-heeled shoes he'd left on her, he slid the panties over her shaking legs, caressing and kissing his way from her foot up. Her senses had ignited all over again as he fitted the damp garment back on her hips. And that was before he pressed a hot kiss on her core through the fabric, and almost blew out any fuse left intact in her brain.

As she struggled to deal with the new blow, he rearranged her skirt over her legs, then eased her up to a sitting position. He was so tall he was on her same level even on his knees. Before he pulled her bodice up, he cupped her heavy breasts in his large palms and saluted each gloriously sore nipple with a soft kiss. Every string holding her up gave. She slumped forward against his endless chest.

He received her weight with a shuddering groan. Then after a final kneading caress, he scooped her breasts back in her bra, rearranged the bodice over them, reached behind her and pulled her zipper up.

Brushing her hair back, he cupped her jaw and claimed her parted lips. He drew back, pausing for a moment before he came back over her, plundering her lips and body.

Deepening their kiss, he rose and pushed her back against the couch. When he finally tore his lips away, her head was swimming and her body had ignited all over again.

"It's actually physically painful to stop ravishing you." His teeth gritted. "I thought taking the edge off would cool us down long enough for us to get introduced. Seems I was wrong."

"Ellie." Her name left her in a rush as he moved to gather her to him again. Her heart would burst if he resumed kissing her. "My name is Ellie."

"Ellie." He frowned as he sat back, repeated the name as if tasting it. Then he shook his head. "It doesn't suit you."

"Why, thanks!"

His lips pursed at her sarcasm, an imperious eyebrow raised in disapproval. "How could your parents see the glorious baby you must have been and give you such a nondescript name? Ellie? What's that supposed to mean?"

"My parents actually gave me a pretty lofty name. I extracted a nickname from it as everyone thinks it makes me sound like a character from a medieval play."

"I take back my condemnation of your parents if they gave you a distinguished name. What is it?"

"Eliana."

His eyes suddenly grew soft. "Eliana. God has answered."

He understood the meaning of her name. He was the first one to ever do so.

He took her hand, pressed his lips in her palm. "Now, *that* is you. You must have been their every prayer answered. As you are the answer to my every fantasy."

Her blood blazed as it rushed to her cheeks. "You're poetic, too? Isn't it enough you're…all that?" She made an encompassing gesture, then rushed to splay a hand over his chest as he surged toward her. "We aren't anywhere near introduced yet, and if you touch and kiss me again I—I…"

"You'll catch fire again."

She turned her head against the couch. "I can't deal with the way I did the first time, so give me a chance to…"

A gentle finger on her chin brought her eyes back to his. "I thought I was imagining it before, but you *are* shy."

"Pretty laughable, I know, after…after…"

"You went up in flames in my arms?" he completed for her again. "I find your shyness no such thing. But I felt it even through your mind-blowing response." She hid her face in his chest, felt his chuckle rev below her cheek. "Don't be even shier now. You affected me the same way, minus the shyness part. *Meu Deus*…the way you surrendered to me, as if you couldn't help yourself, as if I'd overwhelmed you."

"No 'as if' about it. You more than overwhelmed me." She burrowed deeper into him, arousal mingling with relief as he crushed her harder in his embrace.

So this was what desire was all about. This was what had been missing all her life. Him. She must have felt him out there, have instinctively known that accepting anything less, with anyone else, would be shortchanging herself.

Out loud, she whispered, "So this is the kind of crazy attraction that drives people to commit insanities, huh?"

His beautiful lips curved. "Delightful insanities."

She couldn't have put it better. "Yes."

"But even in my insanity, some fail-safe mechanism kicked in and pulled me back from possessing you without protection."

She gaped at him. That hadn't even crossed her mind!

Then the enormity of the whole situation hit her. Hard.

He smoothed a hand over her flaming cheek. "I only did so for you. Another unprecedented thing for me."

"You mean you usually don't consider your…partner?" she croaked, reeling with belated shock at her own folly.

"I usually consider my partner *and* myself. This time I only considered you. This was so out of the blue, progressed with such blinding speed…at the last moment I thought you might not even realize what you were risking. So even though it was beyond me to stop pleasuring you, I had to protect you."

"Oh…" She found no words to express what she was feeling. This was…huge. He could have just taken his pleasure, but he hadn't. He'd put her safety before his own carnal needs. Her hands squeezed his arm in gratitude, loving the sheer power her fingers felt beneath them. "Thank you."

He gathered her tighter to him and planted a kiss on her forehead. "Anything for you, *minha beleza,* anything at all." He drew away to look down at her. "But now that I'm not about to have a heart attack with arousal, I will procure all precautions, and props."

Props? The word ricocheted in her imagination as he leveled the full force of his gaze on her.

"Give me your promise."

"Wh-what promise?"

"That you'll spend the night in my arms."

"Oh…"

She *really* had to stop saying that!

"Then after this night, the next night. And the next."

Throat closing at his intensity, she murmured, "Wouldn't you want to see how one night goes before committing to more?"

"I know how this night will go. I will pleasure you to within an inch of your life, make it impossible for you not to crave more." At her head shake his eyebrow rose again, what she felt certain sent powerful men cowering. "How can you think this won't happen?"

"Because I have no idea if *I* can make it impossible for *you* not to crave more nights."

"Have I blown a fuse in there with too much pleasure already?" One finger gently tapped her temple, his smile lazy assurance itself. "It's the only explanation as to why you'd even consider something so ludicrous."

"If you say so," she mumbled.

"I do. Now give me your promise." At her hesitation, he frowned. "Are you worried I might turn out to be a nutcase?"

She coughed. "That is one thing that didn't even cross my mind."

"So you're saying you trust me?" He dragged his teeth along her neck like a vampire searching for the sweetest spot for a bite. Her head fell back, giving him the exposure he needed to find the best one.

A shudder of acute pleasure shook her whole frame as he took that nip. "I'm saying I couldn't even think about anything beyond what you made me feel. If you didn't notice, I haven't exactly been functioning on any logical level since you…'summoned me.'"

He raised his head, pure male satisfaction gleaming in his eyes. "No, you haven't. But neither have I."

It was so gratifying that he confessed her equal effect on him so openly. "I was and still am operating purely on instinct."

"And your instincts are telling you to trust me?"

"I can't explain it—" she dived into him again, nodding against his hot-velvet flesh "—but they do." She looked up, whispering what felt like a pledge. "I do trust you."

His eyes blazed in response. "Implicitly?"

She nodded again.

"You won't freak out when I make unusual demands in bed?"

Her eyes grew wider as his filled with that predator's gleam that made her pulse race in anticipation.

Still, she had to ask. "Define unusual."

"Unusual in quantity…not quality." Before she could tell him that wasn't much better, he added, "At least, not too unusual in quality."

"There you go again with unrealistic expectations."

His lips twisted. "You think I'm false advertising?"

"It's me who has performance...or rather conformance anxiety. I don't think I can meet your demands in quantity. It's out of the question I could in quality."

"Just leave everything to me. As you've done so far." He took her on his lap, caressing her all over. "Any complaints?"

"Only one." She fidgeted over the massive hardness beneath her, the simmering inside her flaring up again. "That you seem to have created a monster."

Those perfect teeth flashed as he pressed her against his arousal. "You want more."

"I want *you*," she moaned.

"Not as much as I want you. Ah-ah-ah..." He placed a silencing finger on her lips when she started to protest. "You just have to trust me again on this. Now...your promise."

She pushed out of his arms, trying to scramble off his lap. "I can't. My brain feels like I was in a collision and I..."

He let her separate them, his face suddenly chiseled from granite. "Are you regretting it?"

"God, *no*. It was...beyond magical. But...but..."

"It's too much, too fast."

She nodded, anxiously probing his reaction. And it felt as if a cool balm had spread over her burning flesh. There was only self-deprecation on his lips, empathy in his eyes.

After the way she'd surrendered to him, another man would have accused her of leading him on, then playing hard to get. A few men had even called her a tease.

But he wasn't like those men. He was like no other.

She wanted to kiss him for being so wonderful. But a kiss might destroy his control, the only thing that stopped *her* from getting in over her head. More than she already had, that was.

"It isn't too much or too fast, not for me," he said, his voice a dark caress. "Every second with you is how I'll define perfection from now on. But I will slow down—for you." He swept her into his arms again and she succumbed on a ragged sigh, sank back into the luxury of his embrace. "But there are so many more intimacies I need to share with you, many untold pleasures. I need to keep kissing and touching and talking to you. So when everyone goes away, you'll stay."

"Yes." Then she frowned. "But what do you mean *stay?*"

"The night. In my bed. In my arms."

"I got that. But stay where?"

"Stay here, of course."

"*You're* staying here?"

"I should think so. I own the place."

And suddenly, all the details she'd missed—in him, in what he'd said, which should have made sense before now but hadn't—coalesced. Into one big wrecking ball.

It swung into her so hard, it knocked her out of his arms again. "You're…*him?*"

Three

Ellie gaped at the man who'd given her her life's most intense experience. He was...he was...

"I've been referred to in some extremely unflattering ways before," he drawled. "'Him' wasn't among them."

"I mean *you're*...that man?"

"'That man' is also not what I want to hear on your lips."

"God...it's just... Okay, stop! Let me breathe." Shaking her head, she splayed her hand on his chest as if to ward him off, but really to steady herself. "You're...Moreno Salazar?"

He took her fluttering hand to his lips. "To you...I am only Rafael." He punctuated his words by suckling each finger. "You will moan my name into my lips...scream it against my flesh...all through the night."

She was a molten mass by the time he pulled her other hand, wound her arms around his neck. But she still had to say...something. Anything.

"But you said you won't make love to me."

That wasn't the issue here. Or what she'd meant to say.

He kissed the arms hanging limply around his neck. "I think I proved there are other ways of pleasuring you."

"But I thought you understood, agreed that I need to—to…"

"Regroup? Yes, I know. And I won't do anything to cross your comfort zone anymore."

This man seemed to be reading her hectic mind, defusing her agitation, saying just the right thing.

But… "That's still not it."

"Then what is it?"

"You even have to ask? It's who you are. It changes everything."

His lips stilled on the sensitive flesh of her inner arm, then he raised his head, a spectacular frown descending over his leonine brow. "It changes nothing. I'm still the man you lost your mind over, the man you wanted with every fiber of your being. And that's the man I'll remain to you."

"Yes, but you're also Rafael Moreno Salazar, and I'm here attending your ball because my…boss is here to court your favor. And this complicates everything."

"This complicates nothing, I tell you."

"Oh, but it does. It tangles business with pleasure in a way I couldn't have expected in my wildest dreams. Now I can't spend the night with you. I don't even know how everything will be affected by what we've already shared."

Ellie's arms slid off his shoulders and she slumped back. She felt as if he'd hurtled out of her reach when just minutes ago she'd felt he was closer to her than anyone had ever been.

She pitched forward, dropped her head in trembling hands. "Oh, God, why couldn't you have just turned out to be just another guest here, just a regular man?"

"Well, I'm not." He pulled her back into the cradle of his arm. "Which is why I can have you. A regular man wouldn't dream of coming near you." Before she could scoff at the exaggeration he'd said with such conviction, he went on just as seriously, "But I don't care that business interests are involved. I'm even thankful they are, since they brought you here. I'm in your boss's eternal debt for being the reason I met you. So if he is any good, I'll do business with him. And that will have nothing to do with us."

She squirmed to put some distance between them. "How can you say that in the same breath you say you'd do business with my boss for me?"

"I did stipulate he be at least 'any good' at what he does. I won't prove my interest in you by gambling on a losing proposition. I'm into winning and would go to any constructive lengths to win you."

"Constructive lengths." A giggle escaped her. "Now, that's an innovative way of putting it. Though you didn't have to go to any lengths, constructive or otherwise. You stood there and cast your spell, and I ran and flung myself into your arms."

"You neither ran nor flung yourself. But you will."

She sighed, acknowledging his confidence. "So will you always be the magnet, with me the helpless iron filings, or is there hope of you doing some running yourself?"

"Command me, and I'll run as long and as hard as you wish." His fervor felt so real. But why not, when she felt the same? "I *would* have run to you this time, too, but I had to draw you away from the crowd."

Something slotted in her mind with a thud. "You didn't intend to make an appearance tonight, did you?"

His shrug was dismissive. "Whatever my intentions, I saw you…and nothing else mattered after that."

"Same here. But you were going to pull another no-show tonight, right? Do you keep gathering people so you can watch them when they think you're not around? Is this your method of vetting prospective partners?"

"It's currently a partner. In the singular."

"Oh. I didn't realize you're looking for only one."

"I am." The flare in his eyes said he was no longer talking about a *business* partner.

A thrill darted through her, and she sighed as he gathered her closer, soaking up his warmth and desire. "You do know the moment you touch me you nullify my thought processes, don't you?"

"Not touching you is like holding my breath. I can only do it for so many minutes at a time. So will you stop pulling away? We can discuss whatever you like, for as long as you like, just with you in my arms."

Sighing again, she relaxed in his hold, resigned to the fact that she wasn't strong enough to resist both her need and his.

His lips curved. "So you think I'd judge those I'm considering for such a vital partnership by spying on them in a party? Would I disqualify them for stepping on their partner's feet or talking with their mouth full?"

"I bet you'd see everything you need to make an accurate judgment in observations like those. Just like you always do."

His eyebrows rose. "How do you know what I always do?"

"Are you kidding? The past couple of hours are worth a year of intensive…exposure. And I'm connecting what I've just learned about you with what I've long known of you."

"And what, pray tell, do you think you know about me?"

"Well, as a virtuoso in your field, you have such non-linear, multidimensional analytic powers, you have the world begging for your Midas touch. You got where you are by judging every situation and person you've dealt with throughout your career perfectly. As perfectly as you judged me from a literal hundred paces."

He wove his fingers into her hair, wrapped a handful around his wrist and inhaled it. "Get yourself out of any comparison. Nothing with you had anything to do with anything I've ever experienced before. There was no judgment involved on my part, not when you zapped me from a literal hundred paces, too. And you did that to me when I had my back to you."

She blinked. "Really?"

"Really. I was at the mezzanine when your aura lashed me with a thousand volts of delight." He bent and kissed the tops of her breasts that bulged above the now too-tight bodice. "We've already agreed there was magic at work."

"Yes." There was no contradicting him on that point. "So you're not orchestrating events only to watch the attendees, at least to weed out those who prove to be blatantly unsuitable?"

"Don't you think someone as exceptional as you advertise me to be would let résumés choose for me?"

Suddenly she realized what was going on. They'd moved from blinding passion, bypassing any expected awkwardness in the wake of its temporary sating, and plunged right into delightful banter. The seamlessness of it all had her heart soaring.

She cupped his jaw, luxuriating in the ruggedness that filled her palm. "I would have thought so, if you haven't just promised to give my boss preferential treatment if he passes the lamentable level of 'any good.' Or maybe I just mess with your thought processes, too."

Blistering intensity suddenly filled his eyes, making her heart falter. Then he covered her hand with his. "Do you realize this is the first time you've touched me?"

Her mouth dropped open. "I've been touching you non-stop since about a minute and a half after setting eyes on you."

"No. You didn't touch me once. You let me touch you. This is your first voluntary touch."

She gaped at him, everything rewinding and replaying. And he was right. She hadn't touched him once!

She'd just stood or lain there and let him do whatever he wanted, inciting him only by total surrender.

"I was too overwhelmed to do anything but let you possess me. But let me compensate both of us."

Her other hand reached for his face, gliding up his cheek, moaning at the wonder of his feel, before doing what she'd been aching to do. She slipped her fingers into the hair at his nape, and the thick mass slid like living silk between them, urging her to take more. His breath caught as she bunched a handful of his locks, then tugged.

Next second she was flat on her back, with him on top of her, hips driving between her spread thighs, his febrile, wrenching kisses no longer resembling his previous ones.

Her reaction was an even fuller submission. And a deeper madness. Now that she was aware of the risks, she wanted to release him from his promise, tell him to just take her now, come what may.

But to her dismay, Rafael only tore his lips from hers. Flinging himself off her, he sat up and pitched forward, both forearms resting on his knees, hair raining over his forehead to hide his eyes as he struggled to regulate his harsh breathing.

"I thought touching you was mind-altering…but you touching me is insanity inducing." He slanted her a voracious glance as he took her hands and pulled her up. "Leave the touching to me tonight. Until I train myself to withstand your touch without pouncing on you and ravishing you."

Trembling all over, she sat up, every cell in her body rioting against his decree. She now wanted nothing but to touch him, craved nothing but his ravishing. Even thinking of the consequences wasn't deterring her. Which did prove that exposure to him *was* insanity inducing.

But it meant so much, that he'd applied brakes—for her—against the demands of his very…obvious desires. It meant even more that he confessed to a weakness. Something Rafael Moreno Salazar had never exhibited in the eight years of his meteoric rise to the top of a field he'd singlehandedly revolutionized.

The fact that *that* man and *her* man were one and the same was still too much to get her head around. She hadn't even started to scratch the surface of the implications. No matter what he said, she knew being who he was *would* cause problems.

But for now she had him, in those moments of perfection when she was the world to him. As he was to her. And really, what was the point of looking ahead? She had no illusions there would be a continuation once they exited this magical interlude.

But they were still there now.

Feeling she'd be poking a dragon, yet unable to stop, she slid her hand across his shoulders, caressing her way down his back to his waist, delving beneath his open shirt and repeating the journey up, then down, then lower still. The exquisite pleasure of having this freedom, this privilege, was intoxicating.

He caught her against him, crushing her in his arms, his face set in stark lines of savage hunger. And she did another first. She brought his lips down to hers.

Initiating this kiss made it so different, enabling her to set its taste and temperature, sweet and scalding at once. He let her savor him—for about thirty seconds. Then he pushed out of her arms, exploded to his feet.

He scowled down at her. "If you don't want to be on your back, naked and with me buried all the way inside you, you better not touch or kiss me again."

She rubbed the heel of her hand against the itch behind her breastbone. "And you better find a shortcut in your training because now that I've touched and kissed you, I don't want to do anything else."

"You better stop saying things like that, too. They have the same effect on me."

Her lids grew heavier as she slumped under the weight of craving. "Whatever you say."

He took an explosive step toward her, before stopping, vibrating with control. Then he gritted, "Enchantress."

She sighed, rubbing the itch harder. "Sorcerer."

Suddenly his lips spread into a wide smile as he sat down, keeping a two-inch no-touching zone between them.

"I'm keeping score of your transgressions, and I'll get satisfaction for each and every one. But first, I need the subject of business closed permanently." Seriousness suddenly replaced his intimate teasing. "It won't be preferential when I give your boss precedence over equally qualified candidates. Personal preference *is* an acceptable decisive factor when all things are equal. He might not land *the* partnership, but for you, I'll give him something he's worthy of. I bet he's way above 'any good.' You wouldn't work for someone inept."

Giving in to wild impulse, she combed the raven satin away from his forehead, her breath catching as his eyes flared and his whole body tensed. "On what do you base such belief?" Suddenly a suspicion hit her. "You don't think I rely on something other than my professional skills, do you?"

The darkening of pained arousal in his eyes abruptly became affront. "What? *No.* That's something I'd feel at a *thousand* paces." He took her by the shoulders, his face set in adamant lines. "A major part of the judgment you so laud is instinct, and that told me everything I need to know about you. And then, your effect on me transcends my judgment, not nullifies it. Now that I choose to employ it, I can see you're acutely intelligent but burdened with unwavering integrity. You'd only rely on your personal merits no matter how many more lucrative paths were at your disposal."

Her eyes glazed over his lips. Everything he said was so lyrical, it kept deepening his spell. And beyond that, and his hypnotic voice, there was that accent she couldn't pinpoint. And it was the sexiest thing she'd ever heard.

And if that wasn't enough, and he'd ignite her while reciting the ingredients of a salad dressing bottle, he'd gone and said all those incredible things about her. No one had ever held her in such high regard before. And for it to come from Rafael Moreno Salazar—a man whose analyses governments and giant multinational corporations paid millions for—that was beyond enormous.

She surged, clung to his lips in a kiss of gratitude.

By the time she swooned away and lay back, transported by his taste and testimony, he was growling like a starving lion.

"You're treading nonexistent ice, Eliana."

Hearing the name she'd never liked on *his* lips, enunciated with such elegance and command, she suddenly loved it. In fact, she couldn't imagine him calling her anything else.

She sat up, pressed another kiss to his jaw. "You can't say things like that and expect me not to pounce on you."

Unlocking his gritted teeth, he shot her a warning glance. "I'd stake my history as an unerring analyst on every word's accuracy. And if your agency warranted an invite…" He raised an eyebrow. "I assume your boss *is* invited?"

She giggled. "I assure you he's not gate-crashing."

"Then this validates my theory that he is way above the 'any good' level. And if he invited you, then you have a prominent position within his agency. And to have that so young, you must be superlative in your specialty."

"I'm not *that* young."

"I know you're over eighteen. If not by much. I'm almost having dirty old man pangs here."

"You're only thirty-two!"

His lips twisted at her exclamation. "You've researched

me well. But that still makes me ten or more years older than you are. You can't be more than twenty-one."

"I'll be twenty-four in three months."

His eyebrows rose, but he only said, "That's less than three years older than my estimate."

"Three years make a huge difference. Especially to me. I graduated high school two years early, earned my undergraduate degree almost four years ago and I'm on my second masters degree now. And because of my home environment, I've had hands-on experience in my current job since I was twelve."

"See? My analysis was accurate. You follow no rules, and your prowess has nothing to do with your age." He tugged her flush against him, spoke against her lips, singeing her with his breath and words. "And I've changed my mind. Forget your boss. I'll steal you away from him. Name your terms. Whatever they are, I'll meet them."

That made her push him away. "Stop right there. For God's sake, you don't even know what my specialty is!"

His shrug was self-assurance incarnate as he stretched her back on the couch and came down full-length beside her. "Whatever it is, I always need unique minds and exceptional talents on my team. It's how my conglomerate got so big so fast, by offering candidates everything they'd never get anywhere else in terms of freedom, resources and remuneration."

She did know that. But never in a million years had she imagined she'd be headhunted by him under any circumstances. And for him to do that while they lay entwined like this…

She feebly pushed at him as he bent to nuzzle her neck. "I do know your methods, but…no, okay? This wouldn't only complicate matters…it would mess them up beyond repair. People still think I got my current position because of nepotism. With you, they'd think I got it because…"

"Because you send me out of my mind with desire and it's literally painful to keep my hands off you?" He gathered her tighter against him. "I can't describe how profoundly indifferent I am to what people think. You're exactly the kind of rare talent I aggressively pursue."

"*Rare...?* Come on!"

"You said I got where I am by reading people perfectly. I read you better than I've ever read anyone. So you either don't know how rare you are or are too modest or too held back by other's opinions. I'm the one to free you from all that, the one to give you everything you need to fulfill your potential. You are exactly what I need. On all fronts."

She stared into his eyes, head spinning. He had no reason to sweet-talk her. She'd already promised him the night. And as many nights as he'd want her. He meant all that.

A smile broke his intensity. "But as I'll take it slow in courting you in pleasure, I will do the same as I court you in business."

"Don't. Please, Rafael…"

He shuddered against her, his fingers digging into her buttocks, grinding her into his hardness. "Yes, say my name. Say it, *minha beleza*."

"*Rafael.*" That came out a long moan of protest. "Please… stop talking about business in any form. I want to keep things purely like this—between us, man to woman. This is all that matters to me."

He eased his hold on her, rose on his elbow, brooding down at her. Then he exhaled. "As you wish. For now."

Then in one impossible move, he was on his feet with her swept up in his powerful embrace. She wrapped her arms around his neck, not to secure herself or to help him, but because she loved it.

He smiled down at her. "You must be starving. Let's dine while we wait the ball out, and then…"

She jackknifed, making him spill her to her feet.

"I have to get back to the ball!"

He detained her as she whirled away. "You certainly do not. You didn't want to be there in the first place."

As her gaze darted around, searching for her purse, his words sank in. "How do you know I didn't want to come?"

His smile was all knowing, as she was really beginning to think he was. "I told you I can read you."

Something hot and sweet expanded inside her. He did interpret her so accurately it was scary. Wonderfully so.

She caressed his hard cheek and he caught her hand, buried his lips in her palm. "I'll never stop being thankful that I dragged myself here. But I do have to go find my...boss. He must think I've driven off a cliff by now."

After a moment's contemplation, he let go of her hand and walked away. He located the purse that had fallen from her what felt like days ago by the door.

He brought it back to her. "Call your boss. Give him some excuse for not attending the ball."

Ellie blinked up at him. "Now that you mention calling, I can't imagine how he hasn't called me a million times." She pounced on her purse...and groaned when she didn't find her phone. "I must have left my phone in the car, or even back in the apartment. I was half-asleep at the time. Oh, God, he must be going out of his mind thinking something happened to me."

Rafael frowned, but silently bent to reach for his jacket. Producing his phone, he handed it to her.

She shook her head. "I'd have to explain why I'm calling from someone else's phone, whose it is—and I assume you don't want me to tell him it's yours?"

"I don't mind."

She rolled her eyes. "I do. You have no idea the interrogation your name would instigate. And I don't want to invent a story. I'll just go reassure him in person."

She turned away and he buttoned up his shirt, tucked it

in, shrugged on his jacket and fell in step with her, taking her around the waist. "I'm not letting you out of my sight."

She kissed his chest. "I'll only be ten minutes."

"Not one minute. Not without me."

She leaned her head against his shoulder, loving his unyielding…everything. There was no point in arguing. This man got what he wanted. Period. And she was what he wanted now. Who was she to stand in the way of his desires?

Sighing her pleasure, she still had to point out the obvious. "Though I never found photos of you, I can't say I looked very hard. What if someone out there did and recognizes you? Your plan to keep stirring the marketing scene into butter with your elusiveness will come to an abrupt end."

"I'll be worth not letting you out of my sight."

Delight heightening, she teased, "But if people recognize you, you'll be swamped. This might postpone our…plans."

"If I suspect it will, I'll go on a rampage and chase everybody out." He pressed an openmouthed kiss on her lips. "Now quit stalling."

Laughing, tucked into his side, she walked out of the study where her life had changed forever, feeling she was stepping out into a new universe filled with endless possibility. A universe with him at its center.

For however long she had with him.

Walking back to the ballroom with Eliana, Rafael realized how far away his study was. When he'd been carrying her there, it had only felt ten paces away.

"This place is amazing."

He looked down at the magnificent human flower nestled into his side. He felt as if her flesh was an extension of his, her smile and voice and eyes the fuel of his heartbeats. The past hours had been the most incredible, ecstatic stretch of life he'd ever had.

She was looking around as she strode by his side, as if it was the first time she'd seen the place. It was. She'd had eyes only for him on her first passage through it.

He nuzzled her cheek, truly unable to stop touching her. "It was a mansion that was converted into a boutique hotel. I was driving down the coast when I saw it and decided to spend the night. The next day, I bought it. I refurbished it but preserved most of what I liked about it in the first place."

Her eyes poured that all-out appreciation over him, not attempting to temper it or to hide how much she loved being with him. "It must have tremendous tourist appeal, especially in its current lavish condition."

"I didn't buy it for commercial purposes."

Her eyes widened. "You plan to live here?"

In the space of a heartbeat, he saw a whole lifetime in which he did—with her. But something stopped him from sharing the vision when so far he'd been telling her everything as it occurred to him. Probably out of fear he'd alarm her, as he had when he'd made those business offers. It had been only then that she'd resisted him. He wouldn't risk another premature move.

"I haven't thought about it." He'd only had revenge on his mind since he'd come to Brazil. Until he'd seen her. Now anything but her felt inconsequential. "I always acquire whatever my gut tells me to, then decide what to do with my acquisitions later. This place presented the best setting for this ball. But though I'm used to living in spacious, isolated places, this mansion might be too much for only me."

"You have no one to share the place with…?" She stopped, mortification suddenly flooding her gaze, stiffening her body. "It didn't even occur to me to ask if you have a—a family."

Thanks to Ferreira, he no longer did.

But that wasn't the family she was asking about. She

was belatedly horrified at almost sleeping with a man who might turn out to be married.

Before entering the ballroom, he took her by the shoulders. "Do I transmit sleazy cheater vibes to you?"

That delightful flush flamed across her cheekbones as her eyes escaped his rebuking ones. "You know what vibes you transmit to me. The kind that short-circuit my mind."

He raised her face to his, felt a pang at the uncertain vulnerability in her eyes. Hugging her fiercely, he knew he'd do anything to never see that look in her eyes again.

"Even short-circuiting, you pegged me right in every way. I have no one, *minha beleza*. I'm totally free to worship you. As I will. From now on."

Her eyes cleared at once. And she didn't question his "from now on" statement the way she had when he'd proposed nightly meetings before. He was grateful because he no longer considered those enough. He now realized what it meant to want someone constantly in his life. It was how he wanted her.

He realized something else: What he saw in those enchanting eyes shouldn't be there, according to logic and the too-limited time they'd had together. But it had been there from the start, was now a blaze that fired his blood, eradicated the cold in the recesses of his heart. Trust. Not limited to her belief in her safety with him, and not the kind he'd seen in his brothers' eyes. This was unique. All hers. And all-out. In him.

Unable to wait to tell her how proud he felt to have it, he took her into the ballroom so they'd conclude this business with her boss and he could have her all to himself again.

A few feet in, it was as if he'd hit a force field head on. And…of course…what but that living storm he had for a partner would cause such a disruption?

Richard was striding toward them. He couldn't wait to brag how right he'd been about Eliana. Not that he expected anything but castigation and scorn. With his brothers seemingly heartless, just like he'd thought he was before finding Eliana, Richard was the one who was truly merciless. As his friend zoomed closer, Rafael saw he wasn't attempting to hide the demon believed to share his body. Not wanting Eliana to see him the first time with it manifested, he shot Richard a warning glance before turning to Eliana with a smile.

"Eliana, please meet my partner, Richard Graves."

Temporarily distracted from searching for her boss, she graciously extended her hand toward Richard. "Pleased to meet you, Mr. Graves."

Richard didn't take her hand, didn't even look at her as he stepped toward Rafael and hissed, "I need a word—*now.*"

"Oh, please, go." Eliana spooled away from him, flashing him an exquisite smile even when it was clear Richard's incivility had rattled her. "I'll go finish my own mission."

Before he could stop her or tell Richard what he could do with his word, an erratic movement caught his eye. Ferreira. He was on a collision course with them.

Before any of them could move, Ferreira was pulling Eliana into his arms.

Aggression erupted, almost burst Rafael's head.

He was her boss. And he was on hugging terms with her?

Then the words Ferreira kept saying as he clutched Eliana sank into his mind. Then exploded like depth charges.

"Ellie, a minha menina, você está bem."

Ellie, my baby girl, you're okay.

Rafael stared at the woman he'd lost his mind over, in the arms of the man he was here to destroy.

And everything crashed in place.

Eliana was Ferreira's daughter.

Four

Ellie wished it were true the ground split and swallowed people up. She could have used a vanishing act right now.

First, Rafael's partner ignored her—after a split-second glance that had made her feel that if he ever got her alone, no one would ever find her again.

Then, just as she was trying to pretend to Rafael that his partner's barely leashed aggression hadn't knocked the breath out of her, her father pounced on her out of nowhere.

He was now squeezing her breath out. And swamping her in "baby girls," something they'd agreed he'd never call her in public.

She'd taken the job with his agency over other positions only when he'd promised he'd never give her preferential treatment. But lately she'd been feeling she'd soon be forced to leave, even if she loved her job and was perfect for it. The moment they discovered her boss was her father, no one took her seriously. It was why she hadn't told Rafael. She'd feared he'd reach the same conclusion everyone invariably did. She'd thought this particular bit of info could wait until he got to know her better.

Too late now. She'd been outed in the most embarrassing way. That taught her to get major stuff out of the way first. Not that she considered *that* major. Nothing about her was. It was Rafael who had the market cornered on humongous stuff.

Needing to see his reaction, she struggled to turn her head, but she was inescapably mashed into her father's shoulder. All she could see in her compromised position was Richard Graves. He was striding out of the ballroom, without having that "word" he'd almost dragged Rafael away to have.

At least that reduced the awkwardness. He was one scary dude. She wouldn't wish to meet him in a dark alley, with fewer than the three hundred people around. And Rafael at her side.

Then another thought hit her, pushing her dismay to the maximum.

What could Rafael possibly be thinking about what was happening right now?

"Daddy, oxygen alert."

Her father lurched away at her choking protest, still holding her by the shoulders, his feverish eyes roving over her.

"Where have you been? I drove back to your apartment when I kept getting your voice mail, hoping you'd just fallen asleep. I went out of my mind with worry, banging on the door, knowing how lightly you sleep, thinking you'd fallen and injured yourself...until I remembered you gave me a key. I rushed in to find the place empty and your phone dead and hurried back here hoping you arrived but..."

"I'm *so* sorry you got so worried." She raised her voice over the cacophony of the ball and his frantic reproach, feeling terrible. He'd done over four hours worth of driving. The whole time she'd been with Rafael. "I just got...uh...lost..."

Which was sort of true. She had for a while on the way, initially. Then she had, totally, in Rafael's arms.

Before her father launched into another tirade, she turned him toward Rafael, who was looking at him as if he was some revolting life-form. Probably because he didn't realize who he was. Or found his over-the-top agitation off-putting. Or both.

Wincing at the whole mess, she touched Rafael's arm, feeling a pang at how absolutely vital he'd become to her, how even this simple touch, in this situation, sent her heart scattering its beats at his feet.

"Rafael, this is my father, Teobaldo Ferreira."

Rafael's gaze panned to her and her heart clapped so hard her breath snagged in her throat. There was something in his eyes, something…weird. As if he'd forgotten who she was. Which she had to be imagining. This must be how he looked as his formidable mind processed new situations and variables.

Seeming to gather his wits at last, and even clearly unsure who Rafael was, or unable to believe he was the same man he was desperate to do business with, her father extended his hand to him.

Rafael stared down at her father's hand.

She winced. She knew he hadn't wanted to make any contact with his candidates tonight, and her father *was* one. But right now, this wasn't about business, but about a simple salute between her overprotective father, and Rafael—the man who'd just demolished the foundations of her existence.

She rose on tiptoe so her words were for his ears only. "Just say hi and leave. I'll catch up with you."

She tried to capture his gaze, to exchange the delight of anticipation of the night to come. Her heart fluttered at the heavy-lidded look in his eyes then stumbled in confusion, as without a word or another look, ignoring her father's hand as his partner had ignored hers, he turned and walked away.

"What was this all about? Who's that man?"

Tearing her stunned gaze away from Rafael's receding back, she looked dazedly at her father, her mind racing.

She didn't want to validate his suspicion about Rafael's identity. If her father realized she was suddenly on such personal terms with the man whose favor he was so fervently hoping to court, he'd subject her to endless interrogation, or ask to be introduced properly—or both. This didn't only mean lost time, but more important a premature crop of those complications she'd predicted. And she didn't want the real world to intervene now, didn't want them to stop being the man and woman who'd found this pure passion for each other, and become the tycoon and the daughter of a hopeful business partner.

But…how could Rafael just leave like that? If he chose not to shake her father's hand because he didn't want any contact with business people tonight, she could understand. It was a bit excessive, stung a little, but she would never bring any issues with her father between them. But the way he'd looked at her, then walked away, even after she'd explained her father's identity…

Stop. Her mind must be playing tricks on her after all the upheavals of the past hours. She must be beyond exhausted now, operating on pure adrenaline…and other hormones. And those weren't conducive to rational observations.

Someone must have caught his eye, someone important he couldn't postpone greeting. Then he'd be back.

"What's going on with you tonight? Talk to me, *querida.*"

Blinking, she realized she'd been staring at her father vacantly as her mind churned.

Forcing herself out of her fugue, she gave him a hug, his beloved presence grounding her as it always did. "I'm really so sorry I caused you such worry." Heat rushed to her face with memories of why she had. "I came as soon as I could to reassure you I'm fine. But I have to go now."

"You called that man Rafael. Is he who I think he is?"

Her hungry gaze sought out Rafael, found him standing at the entrance of the ballroom. So he wasn't coming back. He was waiting for her to join him. To begin their first night together.

She turned to her father, urgency coursing in her blood. "Please, Daddy—don't ask me anything now, okay?" She kissed his lean cheek. "I'll tell you everything later."

Looking almost pained with curiosity and anxiety, he stared down at her. "As long as you *are* fine?"

At his worried question, she nodded as her gaze dragged back to Rafael—and her breath caught.

A woman was approaching Rafael—statuesque, flaming red tresses cascading down to her buttocks, dangerous curves in a strapless black dress. She looked as if she was in a trance. Ellie knew that *she* must have looked exactly the same as she'd gravitated toward him hours earlier.

Making a conscious effort to breathe again, Ellie absently answered her father's further demands for assurance, no longer anxious to leave him. She'd better stay put until Rafael sent his admirer on her way.

The woman reached him. Rafael brooded down at her as she talked then he raised his eyes and looked straight at *her*.

After her heart zoomed at the touch of his gaze, it slowed down to a wary rhythm at the emptiness she saw there. Hoping to reestablish the connection meeting his partner and her father had interrupted, she forced a smile only he would understand on her lips.

It faltered when he continued to cast that blank gaze at her. It froze along with her blood as the beautiful redhead put her arm around him and they turned and walked out of the ballroom.

Tremors invading her every muscle, her mind tripped over rationalizations. He must be trying to get rid of that woman without making a scene. When he did, he'd come back. Or not. He expected she'd follow him out. That must have been what he'd been telling her with that vacant stare.

She turned to her father. "See you tomorrow, okay?"

Before he could say anything, she rushed away.

Once outside the ballroom, she felt as if a thundercloud had descended. Then she saw the source of the darkness.

Richard Graves was leaning a formidable shoulder against the gold-paneled wall, watching people like a bored predator deciding which one he'd pick off first, nursing what looked like a straight whiskey. At the sight of her, he lazily unfolded to his full height, making her feel as if the world had shrunk.

Collecting herself, she nodded. "Mr. Graves."

"Looking for Rafael?"

Acutely uncomfortable under his laser gaze, but feeling trapped since she didn't know where to look, she said, "I'll wait until he comes back."

"You'll wait till morning, then. That's the soonest I see him being done with that redheaded ballistic missile."

Her heart boomed painfully. It wasn't *what* he'd said, she told herself. It was Graves himself. She didn't get intimidated easily, but this man—she bet he scared monsters. And for some reason, he'd decided he didn't think much of her.

Not that she cared. She only cared about Rafael's opinion.

"You're mistaken, Mr. Graves. Rafael is…" She couldn't go on. Her throat closed under his pitiless stare and the growing uncertainty and confusion. What *was* Rafael doing?

"Rafael is with—or rather *in*—that redhead now." He had the look of someone taking intense pleasure from pouring acid in an infected wound. "Seems he promised *you* an intensive exercise in his bed, but had a change of plans. Not to mention a huge upgrade in exercise-mat quality. Me, alas, I don't have anything better to do for the night. I might be persuaded to accommodate you in his stead."

She bit her lip to stop it from trembling at his barrage. "Why are you being so...vicious?"

He shrugged. "I'm actually being kind. I'm saving you further embarrassment—if you feel such a thing—and am offering you an alternative, so your night's...efforts aren't a total waste."

Dazed, unable to believe someone would talk to her so offensively, she choked, "I don't know why you disliked me on sight..."

"Instant judgments. And executions. Just two of my many shining qualities."

Corrosive heat surged behind her eyes as she searched his caustic stare. "Are you telling me the truth?"

"That Rafael took that redhead to his quarters and is probably having sex with her as we speak? Yes."

She tore her gaze away, heart flailing as for one last time she silently begged Rafael to come back, prove this cruel man wrong.

But Rafael wouldn't come back.

And every idealistic rationalization was knocked down, replaced with the sordid truth.

Rafael had probably come out to the ball with her because he wanted to see if there was someone who'd appeal to him more before he wasted the night on her. And he *had* found a more beautiful woman, no doubt one who wouldn't dream of asking him to defer his pleasure. And he'd just forgotten about her. He hadn't even deemed her worth another word or glance, as if those hours of magic hadn't happened.

But it hadn't been magic. Not between them. The magic had been all his. A sorcerer casting his dark spells on a willing victim, entertaining himself while he pulled the strings of hundreds of others by remote control.

Graves knocked back the rest of his whiskey before leveling harsh eyes on her. "You're better off. Rafael is way out of your league."

She stared at this man of granite who hacked at her with such pitilessness. But what hurt most was that he was right. About everything.

He rolled his shoulders back, seeming to grow even more menacing as he tossed her a suggestive glance. "I'm even more out of your league, but if you're interested…"

"Enough…*please*."

And she ran away, out of this mansion she'd entered what felt like a lifetime ago, undamaged and oblivious. She now left it with a chasm in her heart, one torn open by the wanton cruelty of the only man she'd ever let her guard down with, the first tears of a deluge scouring down her cheeks.

Ferreira's daughter.

The two words revolved in Rafael's head until he felt it would burst.

He'd lost all sense of time, all sense period, since he'd realized who Eliana was. He'd had to get away before he did something catastrophic. But shock and rage only got more out of control the more they sank their talons in his flesh.

Eliana, the woman he wanted with every fiber of his being, who'd stormed his barriers and brought down his defenses, was the daughter of his slave broker.

Rafael, this is my father, Teobaldo Ferreira.

And he'd once been Rafael's father's best friend and partner.

He remembered all too clearly when Ferreira had been a constant presence in his family's life. Her father hadn't changed much in the twenty-four years since he'd last seen him. As a matter of fact, at sixty-four, he'd aged *very* well. Contrary to Rafael's own father, who'd aged beyond his years. Thanks to Ferreira's heinous crime against him, the man he used to love and trust.

He remembered how *he'd* loved and trusted him. Tio Teo,

he'd called him. His frequent visits had been one of the most anticipated pleasures of the child he'd been.

Then, during his investigations into his abduction, he'd found that just prior to it, his father had dissolved his partnership with Ferreira. Once he'd dug into the events, he'd found conclusive evidence that there had been only one person who could have orchestrated his abduction. Ferreira.

But remembering the man he'd run to greet whenever he'd come visiting, who'd shown him such affection and attention, he'd rejected the evidence, reinvestigated from scratch. He hadn't wanted it to be him. He'd wanted it to be anyone *but* him. But every inquiry had led to the same results. And Ferreira's motivations had been ironclad, too.

Arranging for his abduction would have hit two birds with one stone. Taking revenge on his father, the man he'd publicly accused of destroying him, and accruing enough money to make up for the major losses Ferreira thought he'd caused him. The Organization paid *very* well for their select subjects. He and his brothers had been the most select and costly of their acquisitions. Whoever had sold them had known their worth, had demanded top dollar…and gotten it. In his case, Ferreira.

After he'd gotten conclusive proof, Rafael had concocted the perfect revenge for him. He intended to initiate a real collaboration with him, giving him a taste of the profits and the boost in status, letting his ambitions and greed soar, before he smashed him down from an incredible height. Then he planned to send Ferreira to prison, as he'd sent him. He didn't intend for him to ever get out. Not in this lifetime.

Yet he still hadn't rushed to exact his revenge. The truth was he still struggled with superimposing the image of the monster who'd sold him into slavery onto that of the indulgent uncle he'd loved. He still hadn't relished a face-to-face meeting.

Then he'd seen Eliana and everything but her had ceased

to matter. It was literally the last thing he could have anticipated, for Ferreira to be her father.

A roar tore from his depths.

Something detonated against the wall.

Then the door burst back on its hinges and Richard exploded in, gun drawn and ready to blow any intruder away.

His partner's all-seeing eyes summed up the scene, before tucking his firearm back into the holster at his side. "Redecorating already?"

Rafael turned to where Richard had pointed, staring at the extensive damage to the exquisite plaster wall and the smashed remains of his executive desk and everything that had been on it. He hadn't even thought he could lift it, let alone toss it into the wall. He hadn't gone berserk like that in…ever.

Richard closed the door then approached to circle him. "I thought that redhead would defuse you better than that."

"What redhead?"

"Forgotten her already? You're in worse condition than I thought."

Rafael shook his head, struggling with the adrenaline crashing in his system. He had to get himself under control. Before he had a heart attack.

"How did you find out?" The word Richard had wanted to have with him must have been about Eliana's true identity. Once Ferreira had descended on them, it had become redundant, and he'd left, letting him deal with it on his own.

"About your fantasy girl being Ferreira's daughter? How didn't *you*? Didn't you investigate the man to death? The first thing you must have known about him was his family history."

"I already knew his three sons from his first marriage. The youngest was my age. They were my best friends when we were in and out of each other's homes, even after he divorced their mother two years before my abduction. I found out he remarried right after it and had a daughter with his second wife, who died three years later. So yes, I know everything about him, but I considered the details of his personal life irrelevant to my plans."

"That's the one flaw I see in your plan—that you don't intend to incorporate damages to his personal life."

"His children have nothing to do with his crimes."

"Are you certain about that?"

"I'm certain they had nothing to do with my abduction."

"Becoming tycoons themselves at such a young age suggests they might have shared their father's villainy before each laundered his image and history."

"Like us, you mean?"

"Exactly. Just without our reasons."

Rafael shrugged. "Regardless of any other transgressions they may or may not have committed, I'm only acting as judge, jury and executioner in the crime pertaining to me."

Richard gave a conceding head tilt. "Your prerogative. But you're the man who never misses or forgets a thing, and Eliana isn't a name you hear every day. Didn't it ring a bell?"

A million bells could have rung and he wouldn't have heard them. He'd been that far gone under her spell.

"The only way it didn't is if she gave you a nickname."

"She did, but told me her real name almost at once."

"Did she tell you those as soon as you met?"

"There was no chance for that until much later."

Richard made a satisfied gesture. "There you go."

He frowned. "There I go what? What difference does it make if she told me her name at first or later?"

"Timing is the difference. Later you were submerged under her spell and no longer able to add one and one."

Just what he'd been thinking, even if his view of her spell's nature and Richard's were worlds apart.

"How could you possibly assign devious intent to her actions when this whole thing has been a total coincidence?"

Richard looked at him as if his IQ had dropped a hundred points. "I can because she's Ferreira's daughter, the woman who works with him, and whom he brought here instead of his senior partners to use as bait for you. And it would have worked spectacularly, if not for the tiny detail they're oblivious of—who you really are, and that you're the one reeling him in."

He waved Richard's incriminating theories away. "That's preposterous. You *know* I'm the one who sought her out and that she didn't even know who I was."

Richard's lip curled. "She knew enough about you to cast a spell in your general direction and wait for you to reveal yourself by going after her."

He gaped at him. "You actually believe such nonsense?"

Richard shrugged. "The world, especially this part of it, is full of inexplicable things. Just like this compulsion that came over you when she walked in."

"That's called attraction. That's supposed to be an inexplicable magic, at first at least. Then I touched her, talked to her, and all was explained. To me, she's…perfect."

It was Richard's turn to gape at him. "See that? That's not you talking. I'm starting to think a curse breaker is in order."

"We've progressed from spell to curse? What we shared…"

Richard gave a harsh snort. "Dear Lord—shared? You've had what with that woman? Three, four hours?"

"Time is irrelevant when something is that powerful."

Richard shook his head, regarding him with a mixture of dismay and disparagement. "Seems I'll have to dig deep to find someone who specializes in such potent curses. And there I'd hoped hers was broken when you took off with that redhead. What did you do with her anyway?"

"*What* redhead?"

Richard stared at him. "You really don't remember her?"

Suddenly, he vaguely recalled something. A woman talking while he'd heard nothing but the cacophony of his own thoughts, saw nothing but Eliana across the ballroom. Then the woman was clinging to him and dragging him out of the ballroom. Once outside, he'd shaken her off without a word and stormed to his study from another path that didn't traverse the ballroom.

"No wonder you don't remember that temptress who was wrapped around you. You were still wrapped around Ferreira's daughter's pinkie even as you walked away from her."

It had been the hardest thing he'd ever done. He'd felt as if his heart was being dragged out of his body with every step he took away from her. Then he'd reached the ballroom's threshold and had been unable to go farther. Every cell in his body screamed to get away, but screamed louder to stay close, to not lose sight of her. Everything inside him still rioted, demanding that he return and spirit her away to their promised night....

"Lower the volume, mate." At his start, Richard smirked. "I can hear you thinking of going back for her. But before you go any further down that road, let me underscore that she's the daughter Ferreira lavished his love on while he deprived you of your family and them of you. He sent you to hell where you could have been killed after untold abuse. You can't let that daughter interfere with your revenge on him."

He knew that, but it was all too much to take in....

Richard snapped his fingers. "Snap out of it, mate."

"Get your hand out of my face, *mate*." Suddenly, his fury was back at maximum. "And you actually thought I'd walk away from Eliana and take that woman to bed? Just like that?"

"I would have. But then you're not me. You're no longer you, for that matter." Ice-cold deliberation entered Richard's eyes. "But this Ferreira's-daughter thing *can* work in your favor."

"What the hell do you mean?"

"Think about it. What have you learned about her?"

Rafael glowered at him. If he thought he was going to share anything that had happened between them…

Then he realized. Richard was asking about *Ferreira's* Eliana, not his.

He exhaled heavily, recalling the details he'd archived in his mind as extraneous about Ferreira's then-unknown only daughter. "She was born in the States, and her mother, an Anita Larsen, was an American born to Scandinavian parents." He now understood it was that amalgam of ethnicities that had produced her unique beauty. "Her parents named her Eliana, believing that God had answered their prayers when she was born, after her mother had two early miscarriages…."

He'd said almost the same thing when he'd commented on her name, but hadn't made the connection then when he should have.

Yet, if he had, would it have made a difference? Would he have aborted their intimacies? Could he have? Or had it already been too late from the moment he'd laid eyes on her?

At Richard's go-on gesture, he exhaled again. "She attended university in San Francisco, double majored in business management and child psychology, already has an MBA in the first and is earning another in the second." Which was exactly what she'd told him minus her exact specialties. And he hadn't had a inkling of realization. "But why are you asking? You must have found all this out yourself."

"I did. But you're not mentioning the relevant part. That Ferreira's wife died, leaving him their three-year-old daughter as all that remained of her. That's what makes this such a golden opportunity. Using his daughter against him would make your revenge a hundred times more potent."

Instant abhorrence of the very notion made bile rise to his throat. "If I wanted to involve his family in my revenge,

I would have used his sons. They're the ones who don't see eye to eye with him."

Richard again looked at him as if he feared he had permanent brain damage. "You got that in reverse. Those sons are from a loveless marriage of convenience that imploded after years of cold war. They'd long drifted into their own lives and would make very dull blades. But the daughter he had with the only woman he ever loved—his most beloved person in the world—now, that's a lethal weapon."

"No."

At his adamant rejection, Richard shrugged. "I guess it's just as well you're vetoing the idea. You probably wouldn't be able to use her now, not after you took another woman to bed."

"I did no such thing!"

"Not according to what she now believes."

Rafael gaped at him for long, mute moments. Then he exploded. "*You* made her believe that."

Richard met his apoplectic anger with calm disregard. "When you walked away, I thought your episode of insanity was over and you'd take that woman to bed to cleanse your palate. So when Ferreira's daughter ran out after you, I took it upon myself to make sure she didn't try to insinuate herself under your skin again."

She'd run after him. Even after he'd left her without a word. And Richard had...

"For full disclosure's sake," Richard added, "I also offered to have sex with her in your stead."

The next second, Richard was flat on his back, and Rafael's hand felt broken.

Coming to stand over Richard, who'd pulled himself to his elbows, he growled with rage and pain, "Stay down."

Richard struck out one leg, swiping both of Rafael's from under him. He twisted in midfall, coming down in position to launch into a fight.

Richard did that elastic rebound move that no one his size should be able to do, landing in a crouching stance. The right side of his jaw was already swelling.

"I don't feel like sending you to intensive care, Numbers, but touch me again and I will."

"You can try, bastard."

Richard unfolded to his full height just as Rafael did, his gaze exasperated. "You got it that bad, huh?"

"If you touched her, Cobra, I swear…"

"Please. I just wanted to see how she'd react. She fled from the monster sobbing, predictably." Richard suddenly took him by the shoulders. "You can't let her derail you. Forget her."

"I *can't*. I have to have her. Whatever the cost."

"Even if it is letting her father go unpunished?" Richard asked.

"That's the one thing I won't do for her."

"There's that at least. But you won't even consider that she might have come here with an ulterior motive?"

"No. Besides all evidence to the contrary, I can fathom people."

"Really? Did you fathom her father?"

"I was a child."

"I meant tonight."

Rafael gritted his teeth. He hadn't. Beyond being shocked, beyond knowing Ferreira was a monster, he still hadn't *felt* it.

Richard read his answer in his silence. "You seem to have a serious glitch in your judgment where this family is concerned." A beat. "Did you know that, besides being groomed to be her father's right hand, she does a lot of charity work and volunteering? And that her main focus is orphanages?"

Rafael's heart stopped. Then it boomed out of control.

Unable to bear Richard's presence anymore, he hissed, "Leave."

Richard gave a shrug that said his work here was done then walked away.

At the door he turned, flexing his jaw. "See to that hand. I hope it's broken. It should be a reminder of what this woman has cost you—and will continue to cost you if you don't stay away from her."

Staring after Richard, the pain in his hand throbbed as he stood over the wreckage he'd caused, in the room where he'd found perfection with Eliana. A metaphor for how everything was in ruins at his feet.

Orphanages and helpless children…this was where he couldn't afford rationalizations. That could be too much of a coincidence. And the implications could be…gruesome.

Orphanages were a perfect recruiting ground for the Organization, full of children no one would defend or miss. So had Ferreira found his sale too lucrative? Was he still supplying children? Was she working with him, getting to know those children, to pick the best specimens…?

Deus. He couldn't even contemplate that his Eliana…

But his Eliana might not be real. The only Eliana might be Ferreira's.

If that were true, if everything he'd felt from her was a perfect facade, if she was her father's accomplice, he'd crush both of them to dust beneath his feet.

Five

Ellie felt as if something had been crushed inside her.

She kept pressing her hand to her chest, as if to hold the damaged part back together until it mended. But its sharp edges kept poking into her vitals.

It had been twenty hours since she'd run out of Rafael's mansion at midnight...and yes, the irony wasn't lost on her.

But she was no Cinderella and her prince had turned out to be a predator. As she should have expected, from all the improbabilities.

Ever since she'd fled the scene, she'd been counting the hours. The minutes. Waiting for the misery to subside, for the memory of everything she'd had with him to fade. But time only magnified everything and smashed the broken shards to smaller pieces.

Which was absolutely stupid...and that was precisely what *she* was. Anyone would consider her the dumbest woman on earth if they knew the speed with which and extent to which she'd been bowled over by Rafael. And that she'd gone further, done something she'd never done before. She'd *trusted* him. With her safety, with her heart, with…everything. She'd opened herself so totally, had been so completely unguarded, his unprovoked blow had caused that much damage.

It was pathetic to feel that way when she'd known him only hours. But she'd been so under his spell she'd felt she'd known him forever. Now she knew the truth. What she'd thought a perfect coming together had just been a cheap interlude between a naive moth and a bored flame.

But even knowing that, she hadn't been able to stop crying. When she *never* cried. Tears flowed again every time a memory replayed with such acuteness and clarity. Each look, each touch, each word from him. The man she'd felt so attuned to, so connected to. Who'd turned out to be just another player, only one on a level she hadn't known existed.

Not that that was an excuse. Everything inside her fluctuated from regret for all the beauty that had turned out to be a crude illusion to anger at him for being such a perfect fiend to humiliation that she'd been such an eager mark.

She'd had to run to the bathroom three times while playing with the kids so they wouldn't see her tears. Not that she'd been able to hide her condition from their anxious eyes. But their frantic questions and hugs had made her feel worse, and angry enough at herself to rein in her rampant emotions.

For these orphaned or abandoned children to feel worried and sorry for her when it was they who depended on the goodwill and intermittent care of people like her was a slap that had roused her from wallowing in self-pity.

It also made her knock herself over the head for thinking of canceling her Friday-night entertainment. She wasn't letting a hoarse voice, a puffy face and a broken heart stop her from giving the kids the weekly bedtime performance they'd come to crave over the past month.

She now announced that their entertainment was about to begin, and all the kids ran to their beds excitedly.

They were thirty-six in this ward, from seven to ten years old. She loved all one hundred and twenty kids in Casa do Sol Orphanage, but this ward was extra special and her most enthusiastic audience. And one boy really stood out. She'd clicked with him on so many levels from the first moment, too. But, unlike Rafael, she was sure Diego was who he seemed to be.

The eight-year-old now helped her make a final rundown of her props, put her phone in the portable dock and sound system, then raced back to his bed with a huge smile of anticipation on his face.

Once everyone was in bed, she started performing, complete with dramatic music and on-the-fly costume changes. She always gave them her version of fairy tales, and in this one, Snow White was a Robin Hood–like character with the Seven Dwarves as her swashbuckling sidekicks, and she saved Prince Charming from being turned into a heartless monster by the Evil Queen, who wanted him to be her consort.

Once deep into the story, she forgot everything as she jumped on beds, whirled and swooped and changed voices, wigs and clothes and had the kids kicking in bed with laughter.

"And they lived interestingly ever after."

She took an exaggeratedly deep bow at the kids' fervent applause as the music ended with a flourish.

After stowing all the props in her rolling suitcase, she went from bed to bed kissing and tucking the children in. As usual, she left Diego for last. This time she slipped him the eReader she'd promised him so he could read under the covers. He was The Book Gobbler, one of the things they had in common.

As Diego clung around her neck, he whispered in her

ear, "Will you ask your friend to come a little earlier next time so he can visit us?"

She withdrew to look down at the dark-haired, brown-eyed boy, thinking he'd assigned her an imaginary friend like the one he'd invented for himself. Smiling, she kissed his smooth, olive-skinned cheek. "So what does my friend look like?"

"He looks like a superhero."

"Does he wear a costume and cape?"

"No, he was wearing light blue jeans and a black jacket with a black T-shirt. And his left hand is in a dark blue splint."

Okay. That was pretty detailed. She didn't know Diego had such a knack for dressing his characters.

"That's regular clothes. And the splint is proof he's not invulnerable. So why do you say he looks like a superhero?"

"Because he must be seven feet tall and looks like Batman in his secret identity. He entered in the middle of your story and no one else noticed him. He put a finger on his lips, so I wouldn't interrupt you. Is he your friend or your husband?"

"No one else noticed him, huh…?" The rest caught in her throat, all hairs standing on end. With the relative silence and stillness in the ward, she suddenly felt it. That aura.

She swung her head to the door in time to see a huge shadow separating from the darkness of the entrance vestibule.

Rafael.

Heaving up to her feet, blood didn't follow to her head. She struggled to remain upright as he approached. And he was clapping…albeit with one of his hands in a splint, just as Diego had said.

"That was the best version of *Snow White* I've ever heard. And the most dynamic, entertaining performance I've ever seen. You missed your calling. You should be on stage."

He was dressed as Diego had described. So casually chic and disarmingly handsome it was painful to behold his beauty. And he clearly hadn't shaved since she'd seen him. His beard had turned him from a soul-stealing seducer to a heart-snatching pirate.

"What are you doing here?" she hissed.

Ignoring her anger, he gently swept a finger around one puffy eye and rasped, "I made you cry."

Suppressing a shudder, she stepped away. "I made me cry. But I'm done crying. Answer my question."

Instead of answering, his probing gaze left her to settle on Diego. "Thank you for not drawing attention to my entry and giving me the chance to watch Eliana's performance. Is she always that fantastic?"

Diego nodded enthusiastically. "Always. She's the only one who makes us laugh. And she's the only one who makes me think."

Something scalding came into Rafael's wolf's eyes as they swept to hers. "She's the only one who makes me… do so many things, too." He turned to Diego, extended his hand. "Rafael."

The boy put his small hand in Rafael's with all the decorum of a young prince meeting a vital new ally. "Diego."

A painful tightness gripped her throat as Rafael shook the boy's hand with utmost earnestness. It felt as if she was seeing two versions of Rafael, separated by the chasm of time and circumstance, past and present selves meeting. The way they regarded each other, the awareness in their eyes, as if each recognized something fundamentally the same about the other.

She blinked away the moisture. Where was this coming from? Rafael, the all-powerful tycoon, couldn't have anything in common with an abandoned boy like Diego. Though she knew nothing about Rafael's past, she couldn't imagine he'd ever been as disadvantaged as Diego.

But…what had his childhood been like? How had he become this complex, irresistible force of nature…?

No. Not irresistible. Not to her, not anymore. And she didn't care about his past or present. She didn't want to know anything about him, or have anything to do with him.

"I asked Ellie if she could ask you to come again, just earlier so you could visit us for a while before bedtime."

"It would be a pleasure and an honor, Diego." He slanted her a glance. "*If* Eliana approves."

Ellie tried not to gape at Rafael. It stunned her to see him treat Diego with such respect and regard. Especially after he'd snubbed her father so viciously last night. Before doing the same to her.

"Why do you call her Eliana?" Diego asked. "We all call her Ellie."

"She is Eliana to me. Do you know what that name means?"

Diego shook his head vigorously.

"It means God has answered."

"Answered what?"

"Prayers. So Eliana is God's answer to prayers."

Completely engrossed, Diego probed, "Whose prayers?"

"Her parents. Mine. And I have a feeling yours, too."

Rafael's eyes moved back to her, and the look in them, the way he'd said *mine,* made her forget how last night had ended in humiliation. But that only lasted for moments before she was back to wanting to rant that she never wanted to see him again.

But Diego clung around her neck with even more fervency than usual. "Please, let him come again."

Her fury at Rafael intensified. But she couldn't blast him in front of the starstruck boy, yet she couldn't raise expectations she'd have to disappoint, either.

"We'll see, sweetie. Go to sleep now. Or not."

Forcing a conspiratorial wink, she hugged him one last time and got up before he argued.

Walking away, she struggled not to run out of the ward. It was even worse than she'd thought. All the kids were sitting up in bed, watching Rafael with utmost fascination. They'd never seen anyone like him in their lives. Their interest and eagerness made her curse Rafael even more. Then he made it worse, smiling and waving as he bid them good-night. They all chanted a delighted response.

The moment she closed the door behind them, she turned on him. "What kind of sick game do think you're playing?"

"I never play any kind of game. I'm here to take you with me. I have a promise of untold pleasure to fulfill. And so do you."

"Are you for real? No…don't answer that. Just…"

"Senhor Moreno Salazar!"

She swung around at the excited call and found the nuns who ran the orphanage rushing closer, eyes fixed on Rafael, smiles so large they could have engulfed him whole.

Sister Cecelia, the one who'd called out, started speaking before they reached them. "Now that you've seen Ellie, if you're amenable, we'd love to give you a tour of our orphanage. I know you didn't have a chance to really see the children today, so you won't get an accurate idea of the activities and facilities we have for them, but…"

Rafael waved away her anxious explanations. "I've seen enough. And I already know you're the best since Eliana supports your establishment." He produced a checkbook and pen, scribbled for moments before cutting out a check and handing it to Sister Cecelia. "This is only until you can give me a more comprehensive list of your needs and plans."

The woman took the check dazedly, looking down at it with the other two nuns squeezing closer to get a look, too.

Their collective gasps told Ellie it was an obscene

amount. At least, to mere mortals. To him, a man who juggled billions, everything was pocket change.

"But…Senhor Moreno Salazar…this is…is…"

"Just something to get you started on those projects you told me you've been forced to put off for lack of funding." He handed her a business card. "These are my personal numbers. Call me when you're ready to discuss your projects in detail. And please, feel free to contact me *anytime* with any problems concerning the children. If you don't have project managers, accountants and attorneys you trust, or if you can't afford any, mine are at your disposal."

The sisters fell over themselves thanking Rafael for his incredible generosity. He waved away their thanks and shook their hands, assuring them he'd make more visits. Then he turned to Ellie, gesturing for her to precede him out of the building.

Feeling as if she'd fallen into another dimension, she walked ahead. Sister Cecelia fell in step beside her. Rafael followed with the other two flanking him.

"Where did you find this angel, Ellie?" Sister Cecelia all but swooned as she kept snatching glances at said angel.

So not even nuns were immune to Rafael's charms. She'd bet nothing that breathed would be.

Biting her tongue so she wouldn't put *fallen* before *angel,* she smiled vaguely, diverting the conversation to weekend plans as they made their way out of the orphanage.

The sisters stood at the door waving and sighing until she and Rafael turned the corner. Once they did, she lengthened her steps, wanting nothing but to escape him.

Without even trying, his longer strides kept him by her side, his imposing figure parting the pedestrians around them on the sidewalk like Moses parted the Red Sea.

Finally, out of breath, she ground to a halt and turned on him. *"What?"*

In answer, he just swept her up in his arms and kissed her.

Just like his first kiss, there were no preliminaries. Just off the deep end into devouring passion. And like they had in that isolated corridor, her senses sang at his feel and taste. The abrasion of his bristling beard and splinted hand stoked the fire that not even his mistreatment had doused, clamoring downtown Rio disappearing around her.

Then the images lodged into her brain. Of him looking at her as if he didn't know her, walking away without a word then disappearing with that woman…

She tore her lips away, struggling until she made him put her back on her feet. But he wouldn't let her escape the cage of his embrace.

She glared up at him. "What was *all* that about? Is making huge, empty promises to vulnerable people the way you get your kicks?"

"I never make empty promises."

"Sure, because you intend to come back to visit an orphaned boy. Because you intend to place all your resources at the disposal of destitute nuns in a backstreet orphanage."

"That's exactly what I will do."

The imperious conviction with which he said that! Last night, she would have believed him without reservations. She would have had as many stars in her eyes as the kids and nuns had when they looked at him. She would have believed him to be the superhero or the angel they believed he was. He'd been even more to her. The sum total of her fantasies. Then he'd walked away and slapped her with the truth. *His* truth.

The horrible part was that even knowing it, she couldn't *feel* it. Let alone see it. He felt and looked sincere and forthright. Not to mention even more gorgeous. The harsh shadows of the beard and what looked like haggardness made him devastating. Even the casual clothes that were nothing like his impeccable attire last night made him more ruggedly sexual. She felt downright dowdy in comparison.

His left arm holding her, the splint digging deliciously into her lower back, he gently swept her bangs away from her eyes. "You were breathtaking in that evening gown. But in this sweater and jeans, with your face scrubbed clean and your hair swinging behind you like a spirited mare's tail, you look even more…edible. And I'm starving for you."

She pushed against him harder, making him release her this time. "How do you do this trick? When you appear to read my mind? It must be your handiest one in getting stupid chicks like me to fall in your arms."

His lips thinned disapprovingly. "First, you're the very opposite of stupid. Second, I'm not interested in 'chicks.' I want only you to fall in my arms. Third, it's not a trick. We are on the same wavelength."

"Yeah, sure. How nice. Well, I can't say it was nice seeing you again. I would have rather broken a toe."

Knowing she sounded childish, she flounced away. He fell into step with her at once.

"Come with me. We need to talk." She turned to blast him and he added, "And to have each other."

His words, his tone painted such erotic images—Ellie winced with longing.

But she needed to settle one thing. "Listen—about that. Thank you for what you did last night. Or what you *didn't* do. Whatever the reason you did pull back, I'm grateful."

He brooded down at her. "I told you why I pulled back."

"Yeah, for me…and all that. I said I don't care why you did it, but I'm thankful anyway. It would have been a far worse mess if you hadn't. But you can drop the act now."

"This is no act."

She exhaled in exasperation. "I don't blame you for walking away, okay? It's what every man should do when he realizes he's dealing with a naive fool who'll be more trouble than she's worth. It's only natural you'd go for the more beautiful, sophisticated woman who actually looks like she's out of her teens, who doesn't say, 'Oops, I didn't meant to go that far that fast,' then ask you to postpone taking your pleasure until she's ready. But what I don't understand is why you're back. If the redhead you spent the night with didn't satisfy you, and you're wishing you'd stuck with your first, if inferior, choice, I'm sorry. My temporary insanity has already lifted."

"I spent the night alone, suffering the most agonizing sustained arousal I've ever experienced. And you were and will remain my only choice. After all, I choose only the absolute best."

God, how did he do this? How did he sound so…convincing?

Wanting to smack herself for wanting to believe him still, she smirked. "A likely story. But whatever the real one is, just leave me alone. As you partner so unkindly pointed out, I'm not in your league."

"Eliana…"

"Taxi!"

She streaked away from his side as the cab she'd yelled for skidded to a halt, as usual barely missing her. Cabdrivers in Brazil had perfected the art of almost hitting their passengers while stopping to pick them up.

Before Rafael could detain her, she'd jumped into the cab, counting on the driver to make it impossible for him to catch up. The driver didn't disappoint her. Even before she told him her address, he screeched away as if to continue a rally race.

She snatched a look backward as they shot through the mayhem that was Rio's evening traffic and saw Rafael standing like a monolith, feet planted apart, hands fisted at his sides, looking the image of volcanic frustration.

Biting down on the urge to yell for the driver to take her back to him, she slumped in her seat. Buckling her seat belt, she tried to let being knocked about by the nerve-racking driving and the subsequent cacophony of horns and road rage distract her.

But his face was all she saw; his taste remained on her tongue, his breath still flaying her cheeks, his hands and hardness imprinted on every inch of her flesh.

She groaned with the severity of the phantom sensations, with craving the real thing. But she'd put an end to any possibility of that. He must have expected she'd fall into his arms again, and now that she hadn't, he'd walk away. For good this time. Which was what she hoped...because any more exposure would compound the damage, scar her permanently.

She suddenly hurtled forward before being brutally yanked back by her seat belt. It took her petrified moments to realize the accident she'd been anticipating hadn't finally happened. It was only the taxi coming to a violent stop in front of her apartment building in Ipanema.

After paying the driver, and thanking him for scaring her enough to take her mind off Rafael, she left the taxi on jellified legs. They hadn't solidified much by the time she entered her one-bedroom apartment on the twenty-sixth floor.

She'd fallen in love with this place the moment she'd seen it. A beachfront unit with wonderful northern exposure, the apartment was high enough to afford her magnificent views of Lagoa Rodrigo de Freitas in daylight, and of the glittering Rio skyline at night.

Finding this place had mitigated her reluctance to be in Brazil. She hadn't wanted to move here, but two months ago, her father had begged her to join him while he pursued the partnership with Rafael. She'd agreed on the condition that she wouldn't stay with him in his villa in Copacabana. He'd been crestfallen, since he'd thought this would be a chance to have her back in his nest after she'd moved out of his Marin County home over a year ago.

Knowing how much he missed being a father hen to her,

she'd almost weakened on the living arrangements. But as long as he had her at home, he was content. She didn't want him content. She wanted him lonely, so he'd do something about the gem he had right under his nose, the gorgeous fifty-two-year-old Isabella Da Costa, who'd been his loyal PA for the past four years.

Whenever she encouraged him, her father reiterated that he was a one-woman man, and he'd lost that woman. And every time she pointed out that twenty years was too long to be alone, he insisted he wasn't alone. He had her. So she made sure he didn't, at least half of the time. Knowing how dependent he was on her for companionship, she hoped it would force him to look for it elsewhere.

But even though she'd been making headway, almost getting him to admit his attraction to Isabella, he kept insisting it wouldn't be fair to a woman to give her less than the whole heart he'd given her mother. But she knew Isabella would settle for *any* corner of his heart, and she was certain that once he left the door to his heart ajar, his smitten PA would take it over completely. He was the most loving man on earth and in time he'd give his all to the woman who loved him.

So here she was, staying out of his way, hoping he'd get it on with Isabella. She wasn't giving up hope. And neither was Isabella.

But up until last night, she'd always felt she was the older one, dealing with an emotionally ambivalent youngster. Being untouched by passion until then had made her coolly cerebral as she sat in judgment, giving sage advice.

Then Rafael had happened.

Now everything she knew about herself and the world had been rewritten, giving her true empathy for her father's turmoil. If only she hadn't had to gain that insight at such a steep price.

Leaning on the door after she closed it, she looked around

the foyer. She'd miss this place. But she'd leave right away. Without telling her father. Once back in San Francisco, she'd explain everything, and that there was no point in him staying in Brazil any longer. Rafael wouldn't give him even the minor business he'd promised her when he'd been having fun at her expense. She'd known mixing sex and business would end badly. She just hadn't thought it would go that bad, that soon.

Exhaling dejectedly, she took off her belt purse as she entered the living room…and almost keeled over in shock.

Rafael was sitting in the middle of the floral couch, his jacket discarded, his T-shirt stretched tautly over his massive chest. From the way his muscled arms were spread over the back of the couch, and those long, powerful legs were stretched out on the coffee table, he looked as if he'd been there for hours.

"How…?"

That was all she could say before she slumped against the wall, not knowing how she remained standing.

He answered her aborted question. "I ran. I took shortcuts that ensured I'd arrive long before your taxi."

"You *ran?*" she choked. "You're not even out of breath."

"I'm in very, very good shape."

He could say this again. Her gaze slid hungrily over his body before it faltered, stopped then slammed up back to his as she burst out, "How did you enter my apartment?"

"My background in crime is very, very handy."

So that had been true. He'd once been a gang member… or worse. Which did explain that lethal edge to him. She wondered how deadly he had been. Or still was. She also wondered why she wasn't in the least afraid of him. His presence here didn't frighten or even alarm her. It just annoyed her. And if she was totally truthful…thrilled her.

But then he just had to exist to do that. Even now…

Exasperated with herself more than him, she harrumphed. "That's all you have to say? You used your criminal creds to con your way past the concierge, then to pick my locks?"

He inclined his head in utmost tranquility. "Yes."

"Well, marathon man, you can run out the same way you ran in. I have nothing more to say to you."

He spread himself out even more comfortably. "But I have something to say to you. I realized I missed telling you the one relevant thing—why I walked away."

She teetered away from the wall's support but found her legs were still rubbery. "You found a woman that appealed to you more."

"As I said before, no woman has or will ever appeal to me more than you...."

"Oh, *please*."

He heaved up from his deceptively relaxed pose and in three endless strides was, like last night, plastering her against the wall. "That's all I aim to do—all I will do—please you. And pleasure you and cater to your every need."

"Rafael..."

He clamped his mouth over hers, swallowed her gasp and plunged deep. Delight went off like fireworks through every nerve ending as his hard length impacted her, as his tongue thrust into her recesses, all mental faculties shutting down.

It was he who finally raised his head, cradling hers in the crook of his arm, his eyes endless silvered twilights.

Then he took her hand, lying limply over his chest, and guided it down. Her gaze followed, her whole body lurching as he placed it over the huge hardness tenting his pants.

"You feel this? See it? That was how obviously turned on I was as I took you into the ballroom last night."

She hadn't noticed, because she'd been too busy looking for her father. But she did remember how his arousal had remained blatantly apparent through the more relaxed suit pants all the time in his study.

"I didn't care who saw it. But not even finding myself faced with your father…deflated me. I didn't want to get introduced to a man I'll work with in that state—especially when said man happens to be your father. I didn't know how to handle it so I walked away. It was immature and tactless, but once it was done, I didn't know how to undo it." His lips hovered over hers and his breath singed her face. "I waited for you to come to me, so you'd advise me how to fix my faux pas. But you didn't."

"So you left with another woman." She moaned as he bent his knees to thrust against the junction of her thighs.

"I didn't. When she steered me outside I just kept going until I went back to our place. I thought you'd rejoin me. When you didn't, I thought you'd gotten angry and left and thought it was just as well. If you'd come back, I would have taken you right there and then. Ever since, I've been investigating you."

She finally ducked out of the prison of his seduction. "I thought my details didn't matter."

"They didn't, until I had to find you. But I learned so much more about you being in your home."

Embarrassment suddenly struck her at having this immaculate entity in her messy abode. "It's a rental. But it sure must be a novelty for you, being in a packrat's place."

His lips crooked in a smile of such indulgence. "You are a collector, aren't you? But since this isn't one of your permanent homes, it means you travel with your mementos."

"Yeah, I unpack them first thing and have them covering every available surface and hanging on every wall as soon as I get anywhere I intend to stay longer than a month. And tidy is something no one could accuse me of being…."

He covered the distance she'd put between them, pulling her back into his arms. "I love your mess. I've had painstaking order my whole life. Anywhere I lived was minimalist. I do everything according to sparse equations. Then I entered your home and it was as if a warm breeze swept over me, dispelling the cold I carry within me. Everything here tells a meticulously detailed story of who you are, who you love, what matters to you. And it's just exquisite. Like you."

The barrage of beauty spilling from him had her dissolving in his arms. "God, where did you learn to...*talk* that way?"

"I never did. It just comes out of me when I'm with you. And I need you to be as spontaneous with me. I can't bear the walls you've erected between us. I need your passion-hued eyes to melt me with your all-out appreciation again."

"Passion-hued..." she repeated on a sigh.

He *was* too much. And she wanted him too fiercely.

She sighed again. "Okay. Let's do it."

Confusion crept into his eyes. "Do what?"

"Have sex."

Six

"I assume you have protection this time?"

Rafael disengaged from Eliana with the same caution he would distance himself from a bomb.

Just as guardedly, he said, "I don't."

"There's a pharmacy nearby that delivers merchandise," she murmured.

He shook his head, as if it would change what he was hearing. "What's come over you?"

She raised one eyebrow challengingly. "That's why you're here, right? The untold pleasure thing you said we promised each other? So let's cut the chase."

"You mean cut to the chase."

"No, I mean what I said. You seem to want me the more I resist, so I'm ending the chase. Let's do it."

"Stop saying *it*."

"What do you want me to call sex?"

"Don't say that, either. When I take you it won't be 'sex.'"

"You like to refer to it as 'making love'?"

"I never 'refer to it' as anything."

"You just do it, huh? Fine by me."

"I said stop it, Eliana." He scowled at her, but those eyes of hers were unrepentant. And they inflamed him even more for it. His lips twitched. "But if I must give what we'll share a name, it would be something like…plunging in passion."

The twist of her lips told him what she thought of his flowery descriptions. He couldn't fault her ridicule. He was stunned at what kept spilling from his lips himself.

He exhaled forcibly when she kept looking stubbornly at him. "Why the sudden change of mind?"

She shrugged. "I doubt I'll ever want a man like I want you, and you want to have sex—oh, sorry—to *plunge in passion* with me. Probably to uphold your record of never having a woman say no to you. But I no longer care about your motive. I just want to find out what the fuss is all about. Once you're appeased, you'll walk away again and that will be that."

"First, I don't have a record. Second, I didn't walk away in the first place."

"So you say."

"So you didn't believe my explanations?"

"They're no longer relevant. So if you want to take me to bed, I want that, too. But let's be clear about what it will be—a one-night stand or at most a very brief liaison."

His insides tightened. This was spiraling out of control, going where he never expected. "Is this what you want?"

Another shrug. "This is what will happen."

"Is this about my wealth and power again?"

"It's about everything that you are. I always held my own with anyone, but I can't with you. You are *way* out of my league."

"Stop saying that, too," he growled, exasperation soaring.

"It's the truth, as your horror of a friend said."

"Seems he has more than I thought to answer for."

"He just pointed out what I was trying not to see so I can have some time with you. But I need balance in any relationship, no matter how fleeting, and the gross imbalance of power between us is something I can't deal with."

He reached for her hands carefully, as if afraid she'd bolt away and never let him near again. "Those tiny hands turn me to mush. I am powerless where you're concerned. And since you're the one who has the will to resist me, that makes you the one with the power in this relationship."

She snatched her hands away, hugging herself in a defensive gesture. "We don't have a 'relationship.' And if you haven't noticed, that will to resist you lasted about an hour. So here I am…offering myself like I did last night. But this time I know what to expect. So take me or leave me. Your choice."

Frustration boiled over at her finality, which he knew in his bones was no act. "You believed me last night without reservations. Why do you doubt everything I say now?"

Her shoulders jerked on what felt like dejection. Then she kicked off her sneakers and sat down on the armchair by the couch, curling her legs beneath her.

She looked so small and vulnerable, nothing like the entity who'd sizzled with energy and enchantment as she'd entertained the children. Yet she was the most formidable force he'd ever encountered. Her hold on him was growing by the second. He suspected it might already be unbreakable.

She sighed. "Something changed when you walked away. And I guess I…woke up. I did try to cling to the fantasy, but you and your partner thankfully made it impossible. So though your explanation is so lame it should be true, since you could have come up with something better if you were lying, it doesn't revive the trust I felt in you. You're no longer the man I trusted implicitly, just another person I have to take my usual precautions with. That's why I need the upfront terms to guarantee I won't end up feeling like I did last night."

And *that* was where he'd miscalculated. He'd come here counting on that trust to make his justifications readily acceptable to her but hadn't realized he'd already pulverized it. And that her being so in tune with him would actually backfire. She now saw through the fakeness of his explanations, just as she had sensed the truth of his every word and emotion last night.

So he didn't deserve her trust, not where her father was concerned, but he'd meant every word he'd said to her—and about her. And now that he'd made sure her orphanage work was all benevolence, he was free to surrender to what he felt for her.

How this would work in tandem with his revenge on Ferreira, he had no idea. And for now, he didn't care. He just needed her trust and spontaneity back.

And he would do *anything* to have all of her again.

He crouched down beside her armchair, struggling not to haul her out of it and crush her in his arms. "Then give me a chance to take you back to the fantasy and I will make it a reality. I will erase the change that happened inside you."

She curled tighter, like a cat shying away from petting. "The change I felt happened inside *you*. I can't explain it, but it…hurt."

Had she felt his hatred and aggression when he'd seen her father, and it had pained her that much? She was *that* supremely sensitive to everything he felt?

"I know I didn't know you long enough to have the right to feel or say any of that…"

He took the hands twisting on her lap to his aching lips. "You have every right to feel and say anything. We already agreed what we share transcends time."

"I agreed to that when I was still under your spell."

"Then let me cast another one."

She wrenched her hands out of his. "No thanks. Sex is all I want from you now, all I have to offer. If you want to play more games, I'm no longer available for those."

"No games, Eliana. Never any games. This is deadly serious to me." He succumbed to the need to wrap his arms around her, laid his head on her breasts, listening to the music of her heartbeats. "I spent the night in a fever, my mind flooding with images and sensations. Of silk sheets drenched in your sweat, of your hot velvet limbs around me, of your cries rising in the dark."

The heart beneath his ear raced, with his every word, but when she talked her voice was as stiff as her body. "No need to fantasize anymore. Take me and be done with it."

He withdrew instead. This wasn't how he wanted her. And then there was something else.

"You said something earlier…about finding out what the fuss is all about. Did you mean me or sex in general?"

"I meant sex with you. After all the buildup, I'm warning you I have ginormous expectations."

"I will provide you with satisfaction of massive proportions." He took her hands in his good one. "But there's one thing I need to know. Are you a virgin?"

"Are you going to have sex with me now?"

He growled at the word *sex*. "No."

"Well, when you decide to make good on your promises, I'll let you know. Until then, that's privileged info." Her fiery eyes crackled with ire. "What's it to you anyway?"

"Just finding out my variables. If you're a virgin, I'll live with it. If you're not…I'll also live with it."

"Both variables sound equally unwelcome to you. Which is hard luck for you, since these are the only two available."

He stroked a finger down her hot cheek, loving the way it trembled at his touch. "I actually welcome either. I would just appreciate a heads-up as to which is the truth, as it would dictate my…approach."

Scoffing and choking on mortification at once, her eyes and lips became petulant. "Then why won't you take me to bed now and end the suspense once and for all?"

"Because I made a promise to you that I would take it slow."

"But I'm telling you I no longer want slow."

"Only because you want to punish me."

This time her scoff was pure derision. "Gee, I didn't realize taking me to bed would be such a hardship."

"You can't forgive me, so you want to have me so you can get me out of your system and get rid of me. Just wanting this is as harsh a punishment as you can deal me." Releasing her tresses from the elastic band, his groan echoed her moan as he massaged her scalp, sealed her lips with his and poured his pledge into her. "But I'm in your system to stay, *minha* Eliana."

The way she melted into his kiss—like all the parts of him he hadn't known had been missing fitting back into his being—made his head spin with hunger.

Before he forgot all the big talk about not taking her now, he released her.

She gasped, "I—I do forgive you."

His heart thundered. "You do?"

"For last night. But I can't forgive you for today."

"You mean showing up uninvited at the orphanage? Attending your performance without your consent?"

She pushed at him, furious tears surging in her eyes. "How about dangling yourself in front of those deprived kids, especially a boy like Diego? He is *starved* for an adult male presence in his life. Then you appear like a genie that could grant him his every wish, treating him as if he mattered to you and making idle promises. Didn't you think you'd be adding another letdown to a lifetime defined by abandonment?"

The lash of her disapproval felt like salt in every open wound. "I meant every promise I made to him."

She jumped to her feet, glared down at him. "That you'd visit him? Once? More? Then what? Don't you realize the hopes he could be pinning on you? And that he's already hero-worshipping you?"

He rose to his feet, met her glare with his. "Are you telling me not to see him again?"

"I'm telling you it's dangerous, it's thoughtless and it could end up damaging him. I saw his expectations soar just realizing you exist, and when you showed him interest and regard, it developed into a tangled mess right before my eyes. A fall from such heights back to the bleakness of his reality would be devastating."

She had a point. No matter that this boy so reminded him of himself at the age when he'd also found himself without a family, he had to tread carefully. He'd felt an incredible connection with Diego on sight, almost as strong as the one he'd felt with her. And although he *did* have intentions he would see through, he didn't have a clear-cut plan in place yet. So for now, he just sighed, nodded in concession.

Taking this to mean he wouldn't pursue the matter further, she exhaled. "About the check you cut to the orphanage—care to give me a number? Just so I know how bad the heart attack you gave the sisters was?"

"A million dollars." At her gasp, he elaborated, "I estimated it's what they need for immediate needs, and for rebuilding the parts of their convent and the orphanage that got damaged in the last tropical storm. But once they give me a comprehensive list of what they need for the children I'll provide them with open funding."

She gaped at him. Then she swallowed. "Thank you."

He bent and caught the convulsive movement in her throat in an openmouthed kiss. He really couldn't keep his hands and lips off her for longer than a few minutes. "Thank *you*."

Throwing her head back, giving him license to worship her, she moaned, "Thank me for what?"

He raised his head. "For guiding me to Casa do Sol. My aid work is focused on organizations for children, but so many are inferior hellholes while others use children to bait donations that end up lining the pockets of the managers. I always have to deal with inefficiency or crush corruption before I can benefit the children. When I found you've been mostly working with Casa do Sol since you came to Rio, I investigated and found out that it's the one orphanage that's above all suspicion, as well as the one offering their children the best quality of life. That's why I wrote them a check on the spot."

That appreciation he was already addicted to was back in her eyes. Now it mixed with bashfulness. "That was very... thorough of you. Not to mention very thoughtful."

"It's just a start. If you have any ideas for improving the orphanage, or specific wishes for the children, make me a list. I will make them all a reality."

"Thank you, I will." She suddenly hid her face in his chest, peach staining her cheeks. "I didn't know you had such an ongoing involvement in helping children. I'm sorry I accused you of being oblivious to their needs."

A finger below her chin raised her eyes to his. "You were looking out for the children's best interests."

"I shouldn't have interpreted your actions in the worst way just because I was angry with you. I'm really sorry."

The whole world darkened as her eyes filled. She was that upset she'd misjudged him.

He hugged her fiercely, needing to absorb her dismay. "I *am* too powerful, and your worry that I might thoughtlessly step over the vulnerable without noticing was well founded. You couldn't know what I do as I keep those activities a secret."

She buried her face in him again, shaking her head. "I still shouldn't have jumped to conclusions."

He tilted her chin up again. "You're painfully fair. I love this about you, as long as the pain you inflict in your fairness isn't on yourself."

"You don't mind if I inflict it on you?"

"I welcome anything you inflict on me. I invite it." A deep drugging kiss. "I beg for it."

After he let go of her lips, she let out a crystalline laugh. "Diego read you right on the spot, too. He said you looked like Batman in his secret identity. That guy is also a billionaire philanthropist."

"With the difference that Bruce Wayne advertises his philanthropy. I can't even bear the word."

Her eyes grew thoughtful, the warmth he'd been sorely missing flooding back in them. "So you don't like considering what you do philanthropy?"

"I just have the means to achieve things. So I do."

"And you hide your altruism while you leak info about a criminal past and affiliations. You want the world to learn about your lethal edge but not your gooey center, huh?"

He swung her around to her squealing delight, grinned down widely at her. "See? You read me like no one ever has." Putting her back on her feet, he probed, "But how did *you* know about Casa do Sol? Did you investigate them, too?"

"No. I just made visits everywhere, and they were the only ones I felt...good about."

"So again your instincts proved infallible. You read everyone, not just me. It's *your* superpower."

"It never felt like a good thing. It leaves me with precious few people in my life."

"You only need a few who *are* precious." He squeezed her tighter. "Though I'd rather you only need me."

The flush that flooded her face was adorable. Before he commented on her paradoxical shyness—given that she hadn't batted an eye while asking him to have sex—he realized his hand was hurting like hell. He'd been using it as if nothing was wrong with it.

He raised it up. "Aren't you going to ask about my hand?"

A stubborn look came into her eyes. "No."

"You don't care that I broke it?"

"Are you going to take me now?"

"No."

"Then I don't care."

He guffawed as she stuck her nose up at him. He'd never laughed that way, so elated and unfettered.

Still laughing, he swept her up, and his heart boomed at the way she clung to him, fitting into his every emptiness. The memory of her earlier rejection jolted through him, making him gather her tighter. He was never letting her recede from him again.

In her bedroom, another place full of her mementos, he laid her down on the burgundy comforter and came down half over her. She wriggled beneath him until she'd brought him fully over her, pulling him into an all-body hug.

He rose on one arm, the pain in his loins becoming agony. "You'll blow all my fuses."

She arched up into him. "Serves you right."

"It wouldn't serve *you* right."

She giggled, clung harder and brought him down between her thighs.

He groaned. "I was right. You are an enchantress."

"I was wrong. You're not a sorcerer. That sort of implies a level of benevolence. You're pure evil."

At once laughing at her pout and grunting in pain, he rolled off her. It was unheard of for him to defer having anything he wanted. But doing so with her was the most pleasurable thing he'd ever experienced.

If anyone had told him last night he'd be lying side by side with her in her bed, just to hold her and talk, when he'd never hungered for anything as much as he hungered for her, he would have thought them insane. But now, he couldn't imagine anything better as she slipped her limbs into the exact places where he needed them, holding on with the exact intensity he craved.

Sighing after she'd settled into him as if she'd been doing so all their lives, he reached over her and picked a frame off her crowded bedside table.

The photo was of a woman and a little girl, both grinning unreservedly at the photographer, throwing their arms wide as if to embrace him and the life they loved with him. The object of their all-out affection was obviously her father.

A pang twisted in his gut at yet another proof of the depth of emotions she had for that man.

Banishing Ferreira from his thoughts, he focused on this piece of her past, another detail bringing him closer to her.

"You got a lot from her."

She nodded, threading her fingers through his hair. "I also got a lot from my father."

After seeing them together, he hated to admit that was true. But then, on the outside, the man was a perfect specimen. Rafael was certain that on the inside Eliana hadn't been tainted by any trace of his weaknesses and evils.

"Whatever you got, wherever you got it, you became this one-of-a-kind amalgam."

She gave an adorable little snort. "Did you go to the University of Extravagant Descriptions? Then got a PhD in hyperbolic metaphors?"

"Hush. I have all that vocabulary that I never found use for. You're getting the benefit of it all."

"Whether I like it or not, huh?"

He tugged a thick tress. "Oh, you like it."

A sigh clasped her even closer against him. "Yes."

He kissed her forehead. "Do you remember her?"

Her eyes became suddenly turbid. "Everyone thinks that I couldn't possibly remember all that I do about her, since I was just three when she died, and that what I think are my memories are just from what Daddy kept telling me about her as I grew up. But I do remember her. Very well. Too well sometimes."

He feathered kisses all over her face, needing to take away the raw edge of memories. "Is this why you give so much of your life to orphans?" Almost every weekend, and after work almost every day. "Because you feel like one, and you feel her loss so keenly?"

"If I feel that way when I have the best father in the world, I can't imagine how those who've lost both parents, or never had anyone feel."

The best father in the world. The man who'd sent him to hell. But she had nothing to do with his crimes. And he'd keep her away from their fallout, whatever it took.

He forced down the bile that rose to his mouth. "Next time I see Sister Cecelia I'll correct her. *You're* the angel."

Her eyes widened. "You heard her?"

"I have very, very good hearing."

Her eyes grew heavy as they traveled down his body. "Everything about you is very, *very good*."

He caught her tongue in a gentle bite, sucked it inside his mouth. "I'm agonizingly thrilled you approve...as you can feel."

He ground his hardness against her and she mewled, became even more pliant against him. His head almost burst with the urge to forget his promise and just take her as she'd asked. But he had to wait. Had to deepen her involvement until she was as dependent on him as he was on her.

Insinuating a leg between his, she pressed her knee into his erection, wringing a growling thrust from him.

She chuckled, eyes telling him she considered them equal now. "But Sister Cecelia got it right, even if at the time I wanted to tell her that fallen angel would describe you better."

"It would. I've done very, very bad things in my time. I still do, when the need arises."

Her eyes grew serious. "But not to innocents."

It was a statement, not a question. Pride expanded inside him that she trusted him again, and saw his fundamental truth.

"No. But the law still calls what I did and do illegal."

"The right thing to do isn't always legal. And as long as no innocents were harmed, as long as you help them like when you crush those corrupt people to save helpless children, then *I* call what you do heroic." She sighed wistfully. "Sometimes I wish I could do the same, but I don't have enough power. I'm only thankful someone like you who does exists, and that you use your power this way."

Was it possible that once he destroyed her father—if she ever realized it was him who did it and she found out the reasons why—she'd find his actions heroic? At least, excusable and understandable?

"You can't imagine how helpless I feel most of the time." Her pain made him want to go out destroying everything that had ever made her feel this way. "I try to reach out to as many children as I can—to provide them with someone who cares, who's there to listen to their problems and ideas, to take part in their activities, to encourage their interests and talents. But no matter how hard I try, I always feel nothing I do is enough. Thank God for people like the sisters who do far more. But someone like you? You can do the most."

His throat tightened. "What you do will make a difference in those children's psyches. I just throw my money and weight around, but I never made a child's day better in person. Truth is, I never even interacted with one, until Diego today."

"But without your 'money and weight,' we wouldn't have the places and projects to offer any children anything."

"So we complement each other." She snuggled deeper into his chest, nodded. "We already knew that, just not how completely we do."

Raising her face, her smile and gaze caressed him. "But you must now know everything about me since I sprouted my first baby teeth. And I know nothing about you."

He rose on one elbow. "What do you need to know?"

"Tell me about your family."

He'd been prepared with a fabricated history. But he couldn't bear more lies between them than necessary. He'd tell her the truth—a carefully edited version of it.

"My parents divorced when I was ten. My mother re-married two years later and had three more children, two girls and a boy. My father remarried much later, and had two children, a girl and a boy. I exited their lives early and never reentered it. I sort of watch them from afar, keep my distance."

"Is this what you want?"

"With my kind of life, with what I've been involved in, they were better off with me as far away as possible. When it became feasible for me to approach again, I still felt it wasn't in their best interests for me to disrupt their lives."

"How can you say that? I'm certain they'd love to have you be an integral part of their lives."

He tickled her, trying to inject lightness into what was suddenly oppressively serious. "Who's being biased?"

She grinned impishly, then turned back to seriousness

at once. "But I really do imagine they would choose to be as close as possible to you if you gave them the choice."

The talons in his throat sank a little deeper at her conviction. "It's a bit more complicated than that."

He expected her to probe this vagueness, but she only exhaled. "As long as you're sure that it's for the best. But even if it is, I still hate to think you've exiled yourself from your family. That you've chosen to be alone."

"I'm not alone. I'm part of a…brotherhood, if you will."

"One of them is that terror you have for a partner, huh?"

He guffawed at her wary-feline expression. "He was an addition to our brotherhood. He used to be my mentor."

"He thinks he's your father. Or your 'Big Brother.'"

He laughed harder as she made the quotes gesture. "You're uncanny. You analyze everything with such absolute accuracy."

"He didn't need analysis. He knocked me over the head with his 'shining qualities.'" Another quote gesture.

"I assure you he hasn't gotten *and* won't get away with it. But speaking of family…I insulted your father almost as much as Richard did you."

"Oh, no, there's just no comparison. My father almost didn't notice you, as anxious as he was about me."

"I would still like to apologize. Will you please set up a proper meeting?"

A still look came into her eyes. "You want to meet him… as my father or as a potential partner?"

"Can't I meet him as both?"

She grimaced. "You know where I stand on this issue."

"Why don't you let me handle this?"

"I've never been as miserable as I was last night, and I don't want to risk something like that happening again."

"It won't. I promise."

The troubled look that gripped her face almost made him

tell her to forget it. But before he could say anything, she nodded, then nestled back into him.

As he received her into his embrace, that trust he craved, which she was bestowing on him in full again, weighed on him. It didn't feel like a privilege anymore but a responsibility.

One he ultimately had to betray.

Seven

The meeting with Ferreira took place the very next afternoon. During lunch hour so it would be brief, at Eliana's request.

Rafael picked Casa de Feijoada, a busy spot in the posh beachside Ipanema district, a mile away from Eliana's place, and Ferreira's offices, for their convenience. The restaurant was cozy, with a tropical, rattan-walled look and family-style table service. He came a bit early to arrange a table on the beach and order the lunch courses in advance so no unnecessary delays would occur during their hour-long meeting. They arrived at one o'clock sharp, and Eliana greeted him with the same ardent kiss with which she'd said goodbye when he'd left her apartment at 2:00 a.m.

Though she'd confided that she'd told her father everything, so he must have an idea how things stood between them, he glimpsed a spurt of anxiety in Ferreira's eyes as he witnessed that intimacy. But like the gentleman everyone believed him to be, the impeccably dressed and behaved

Ferreira made no comment. Not on that nor on Rafael's offensive behavior during the last ball, nor his no-shows in the previous ones.

From then on, they settled down to the smooth flowing lunch courses. Apart from the effort Rafael expended to sit across from Ferreira—the man he'd once loved as an uncle and who'd betrayed him in the most unspeakable way—pretending this was their first real meeting, nothing of note happened.

Ironically, the man who'd been trying to meet him for the past two months didn't seem to care that Rafael possibly held his professional future in his hands, only that he might affect his daughter's adversely. Ferreira spent the entire lunch watching them interact, saying little. He never once broached the subject of the partnership. The only questions her father asked him were when Eliana went to the ladies' room: oblique ones probing his intentions and warning him against toying with her. In turn, Rafael as indirectly let Ferreira know that where Eliana was concerned, they were on the same page. She came first to him, too.

That seemed to disturb Ferreira instead of reassure him. He considered Rafael's statement an exaggeration, since the sum total of their liaison had taken place over three days. But when Rafael told him that the power of their connection had dispensed with the usual stages needed to reach their current level of involvement, Ferreira finally relaxed. Though he'd evidently never thought Rafael was capable of forging such a connection, from what he'd heard about him, he confessed that he knew how it could be that way from intimate experience. It had been the same between him and Eliana's mother. They'd married a week after meeting and had lived ecstatically ever after—until aggressive pancreatic cancer had taken her from him.

On Eliana's return, the conversation turned to anecdotes about Eliana's mother, and her half brothers and their mother. Ferreira had had two extreme opposites in the marriage department. The first one when his father had arranged his marriage to his partner's daughter and the battlefield that marriage had turned into. Then the marriage to the love of his life, which had started with love at first sight and had ended with him living in her memory and for their daughter.

The lunch ran thirty minutes longer than the agreed on hour before Ferreira rose to leave. As Rafael shook his hand, the man gave him a pointed look. *Don't hurt my daughter* was the gist of the volumes it spoke. His answering look said *I would* never *hurt her.* He hoped the *but I'll hurt you... bad* part went unsaid.

The moment her father disappeared, Eliana dragged Rafael by his tie and planted a hot kiss on his lips.

Starving for her already, he moved to deepen it, and she pulled away, chuckling, eyes heavy with hunger. "I shouldn't be kissing you after I just binged on that *feijoada*. Rinsing my mouth can't begin to counteract its garlicky goodness."

Brazil's national dish was indeed an antisocial stew. This restaurant that proclaimed itself the meal's house was lauded by Cariocas, Rio's residents, as serving the best *feijoada* in Rio. Even after he'd ordered their best meal, he hadn't expected the giant pot of meats swimming in saucy black beans they'd gotten. The tureen had been piled high with smoked and peppery sausages, *carne seca* ham and an assortment of other pork cuts. He was glad he remembered to tell them not to serve the pig's ears, tail and tongue.

He pulled her back against him, claiming her lips. "Having binged on the same pungent bomb, all I taste is your sweetness." Another savoring kiss. "And the tartness of acai and *maracuja* and dragon fruit from that Amazonian fruit smoothie."

She suddenly yelped, pulling back once again. "You always scorch me, but now you literally do. Those deadly *malagueta* peppers you gobbled are still lacing your lips and tongue." Licking the burning away, she smiled. "Thank you."

He pressed his lips as if to secure her kisses there. "What for?"

"For being so nice to my father."

"He's a nice man."

He didn't even have to lie. Apart from the sadness he glimpsed in Ferreira's eyes—which Eliana said had been there since her mother's death—and his wariness of how the power Rafael wielded would affect his daughter's well-being, Ferreira was apparently the kind and agreeable man he remembered. The evil he'd committed against him had carved no visible telltale signs on his visage.

Eliana sighed. "I actually think you didn't like him much, but you were still extremely nice to him. So thank you."

Deus. Those instincts of hers continued to prove sharper than he'd even thought. He'd thought he'd been seamless.

Before he could say something to alleviate her suspicion, she added, "But it's expected on a first meeting with my wary father hen. He spent lunch watching your every move. And you're a man who suffers no monitoring or judgment."

Relieved she'd found a benign reason for the hostility she'd felt from him, he exhaled. "It's only natural he'd be worried about how fast things developed between us. I think I ended up allaying his anxiety."

"I know." She smiled up at the waitress, who put the bill before him. "Why do you think I went to the ladies' room?"

"And there I thought you didn't have a wily bone in your body." He grinned as he got out his credit card.

She chuckled. "No wiliness involved, I assure you. I was instructed to do so. On the way, Daddy begged me to give him any chance to be alone with you. He claimed there was no way he could 'read' you as long as I was around. He also begged me not to be my shockingly candid self while he's around." She shot him a devilish look. "I did manage not to say things like, 'Don't worry about Rafael seducing me, Daddy. I spent a whole night slithering all over him and begging him to have sex with me, and he was the one who held back and reprimanded me about my language, too!'"

Rafael threw his head back on a guffaw. "It's a good thing you exercised some self-control. You would have given him a heart attack."

Her laugh tinkled like crystal. "I did give him a minor one with that kiss when we first came in. The poor man always bragged he was the only man he knew whose daughter never gave him any nightmares about boyfriends, since I never had any. Then I go and get all mixed up with someone who's as much trouble as ten thousand men put together."

"So I'm all his postponed nightmares come all at once."

And she didn't know how literally true that was.

"Exactly." She laughed, her gemlike eyes radiating mischief and joy in Rio's midday sun. Entranced as he gazed into them, he threw some bills down, and she giggled harder. "That tip could make you a partner in this restaurant."

"The food and service were impeccable. They earned it."

"It *was* lovely. But then it didn't have to be. Just being with you would make anything wonderful."

He knew she meant every word. She was the first woman, the first person, who'd ever told him everything she felt, no games. And it was intoxicating.

"I also want to thank you for not talking business."

"I want to discuss a few things with you before I bring up anything with him. I have reports, but I want what only an insider would know."

"Let it go altogether, okay? Even my father didn't bring up business. Now that he saw us together, I believe he won't."

"I know he has big problems, Eliana."

Dismay flooded her eyes. "I guess it was too much to hope that you of all people wouldn't find out. But we're working on a resolution, and I'm hopeful we'll soon have it."

"I know a partnership with me would help resurrect his business. Even if I don't give it to him, I still want to help." He did intend to save her father's business, for her, to preserve her legacy. He'd seen Ferreira's will, and she was his only beneficiary. No matter what he felt about her father, he wouldn't let her inherit an ailing enterprise. He buried his lips in her palm. "Let me help."

She caressed his cheek, hand trembling as it was singed by his passion, her gaze softening with gratitude. "It doesn't matter if you can help, it's enough you want to."

"I can do anything, remember?"

"Oh, yes, you can." Her smile was tenderness itself. Then suddenly she pushed her chair back and stood up.

He rose at once. "Where are you going?"

"Back to work. Then to the orphanage." She grinned as she reached for her coat. "As you already know."

He helped her on with the coat that matched the deep royal-blue dress he'd spent much of the lunch hour fantasizing about ripping off her.

She hooked her purse across her body. "See you at my place later? Or would you rather I come to yours?"

"I'll come to you. And I don't want you driving on that road alone again, so whenever you want to come to my place, I'll pick you up. Eight o'clock?"

"Make it nine." Her smile lit up the whole world as she walked into his arms and met him halfway in a kiss that had the whole restaurant watching.

After she left, some men gave him the thumbs-up. One was giving him two.

Mock bowing to them, he walked out into the hubbub of Rio's midday congestion. Cariocas filled the streets as they did every hour of the day. Anyone coming to Rio came for its laid-back beach culture as much as its breathtaking landscapes and abundant tourist attractions. And everyone got the impression the Cariocas were on perpetual vacation.

He breathed deep of the ocean breeze and the unique scents of this city he'd spent his formative years in. It was strange how alien he felt here. His kidnapping had truly cut all the ties he had with his past, with the being he'd been.

But Rio was still the place he'd been taken from, and it was where he'd returned to enact the vengeance he'd waited for almost a quarter of a century. Three quarters of his life.

Then in three days, Eliana had turned his world upside down and shifted his priorities.

But his plans were only postponed, not cancelled. He would still punish her father.

Just not before he secured her.

At eight o'clock sharp, that Amazonian parrot she had for a bell burst into song.

Ellie flew to the door, heart soaring as she snatched it open, expecting to see Rafael. He was there. Only not alone.

"Please meet my boor of a partner, Richard Graves."

Her heart plummeted as she leveled her eyes on that menace, before turning her scowl on Rafael. "You shouldn't be walking around with him so blithely. Without a leash, too."

Rafael laughed. "I promise you I have him well in hand. Invite us in, *querida*."

"No."

Rafael's smile tried to coax her. "Not even now that he got what he deserves?" He shoved Graves forward.

Graves rolled his eyes, moved into the light of her foyer and showed her the right side of his face. It was a swollen deep purple beneath the beard he now sported. After he'd given her a good look, he stepped back, resettled that harsh gaze on her.

She blinked dazedly up at Rafael. "You hit him?"

"You think I'd do anything less once I found out what he'd done? What he'd said to you?"

She turned her gaze to Graves. "You told him about propositioning me, huh?"

"Of course."

Suddenly, a realization hit her, made her turn anxiously back to Rafael. "Is that how you hurt your hand?"

Rafael nodded. "You think anything less than his concrete jaw can break my bones?"

She gaped at him. "Your hand is really broken?"

"I do have fissures in two metacarpal bones."

She dragged him inside, heart squeezing as she feathered anxious touches over his splint. "God—and I made fun of your injury! I thought it was a sprain or something and you were only teasing me."

"No teasing." Graves walked in without invitation and closed the door behind him. "Under your thrall, he went and broke his hand. After I spent years teaching him how to fight without ever injuring himself. Terrible student." A mirthless laugh. "And he didn't even get his boo-boo kissed for his trouble."

She took Rafael down on the couch with her and glared up at Graves. "Oh, he will now. And then he'll get everything kissed. Anything that hasn't already been, that is."

At Graves's raised eyebrows, Rafael turned to him with a triumphant smile. "For the record, I didn't employ your generously imparted techniques because I just wanted to hurt you. And myself. I was the one who gave you the impression you can be rude to Eliana when I walked away from her."

"Is he always that vicious to women he thinks you're done with? Or is he that brutal by default? Which wouldn't surprise me. He doesn't feel quite human to me."

Graves turned his gaze to Rafael. "Very astute, this one. Foolishly outspoken, too. You may have to keep her."

Rafael's eyes ate her up. "Oh, I am keeping her."

She mock scowled at him. "How kind of you both. But I've been known to keep myself, thank you. So why don't you unstoppable forces of nature just run along and go exude charisma and testosterone all over someone else?"

Graves's lips spread. "It really looks like you'll have to keep her."

Rafael gave an exaggerated sigh. "If only *she* keeps *me*."

Graves tsked. "I trained you better than that, Numbers."

"Seems all your efforts went down the drain, Cobra."

She gaped at them. "Numbers? Cobra? You have code names in that brotherhood of yours?"

Graves raised one eyebrow at Rafael. Seemed he was surprised Rafael had told her about that. Not that Rafael had told her much. Rafael gave him a "deal with it" shrug.

"Numbers…" she mused. "I don't really see why you got named that. But Cobra is definitely apt. Though a more accurate name would be the raw material of deadliness. Like Venom."

This time Graves guffawed. "You're definitely keeping her."

Rafael's smile widened before it faded gradually. "Now, apologize to Eliana or I'll break my other hand and your jaw this time."

Ignoring him, Graves fixed his gaze on her, his British accent deepening. "He talks big, even when he knows he's in one piece because I have this inexplicable fondness for him. That said, and knowing that I'm doing this out of my deeply buried gentlemanly tendencies, I do apologize. If only for…"

She raised both hands. "Stop. Quit while you're ahead."

Rafael gathered her to him. "Is he forgiven?"

A harrumph. "On probation."

He chuckled and devoured her lips. She smiled against his lips at Graves's vocal disgust.

After Rafael released her reluctantly, she kissed his splint, then each finger. "No more breaking anything for me, okay?"

His head shake was adamant. "No promises."

Sighing her frustration at his terminal machismo, she looked between him and Graves. "At least no more fights between you two because of me, hear?"

Richard bowed in mock deference. "I'll do whatever it takes to keep your boy toy in optimum working condition."

And she laughed. That daunting dude had a sense of humor after all. She might even end up liking him.

Jumping up, she looked between the two men. "If you're good tycoons, I'll invite you to eat my magical seafood medley. You even get to help prepare it."

Rafael sprang to his feet. "I'm very, very good."

"I'm very, very nauseous" was Graves's contribution.

She and Rafael laughed, then headed to her kitchen. Muttering what sounded like paint-peeling expletives, Graves followed.

The evening turned out to be an unqualified success.

Eliana was the perfect hostess. She orchestrated all the details with ease and efficiency and handled them, men the world bowed to, with utmost confidence and grace. Richard miraculously kept his snark to a minimum, even followed her lead as she made them her sous-chefs while preparing the seafood medley, which did turn out to be magical.

Time flowed over and after dinner as they cleaned up then adjourned to her living room to drink hot *yerba maté*, eat *cocadas*—a traditional coconut confection—chat and verbally duel. Eliana held her own with Richard like no one he'd ever seen. Then, nestling into him on the couch, she started yawning.

Kissing her forehead, he gestured to Richard, who rose to his feet at once.

As he made to follow, she clung to him. "Stay."

His blood hurtled through his veins with temptation. "You need to sleep."

She rubbed her sleepy face into his neck, burning him wherever she touched. "I need to sleep with you."

"Tomorrow. I'll come alone."

She looked across at Richard. "You can go home on your own, right, Graves?"

"It's Rafael who can't. I have to tuck him in."

"Should have known you'd be no help." She clung to Rafael's neck. "At least carry me to bed."

"You, my enchantress, *are* wily."

"I just want you."

"And I want nothing but you." He kissed her pout as he rose and her arms fell off his shoulders like petals. "Lock up after us."

He rushed Richard out before he succumbed. They strode to the elevator with him already suffering withdrawal.

"What are you going to do with her?"

At Richard's quiet question, he exhaled. "None of your business, Cobra. Your role here is done."

Richard pressed the elevator button. "One piece of advice. A warning, really. This woman will turn you inside out."

"Don't you believe she already has?"

"I thought so. But now that I've been exposed to her, to this…live thing between you, I know I've been optimistic in my evaluation. This?" He made a gesture at all of him. "What you're feeling now? Is nothing to what you will feel a week from now. In a month's time, you'll be totally lost in her."

He cocked an eyebrow as they entered the elevator. "So you like her now?"

"I don't like anyone. But her? She's lethal."

He frowned. "You still think she's her father's accomplice? That her orphanage work has sinister motivations? You think I'd look the other way if I suspected such a thing?"

Richard shook his head. "I actually believe your verdict

of her benevolence. And that's what makes her deadly. She's for real. You'll have no defenses against her."

"Who says I want any?"

Richard fell silent as the elevator crowded with more and more people in this city that didn't sleep. Once out on the street, and before they went their separate ways, he said, "Are you giving up your revenge?"

His heart fisted. "I will never do that."

"Then do you have any idea how to have it and have her, too?"

"I'll figure out a way."

Richard only gave him a "sure you will" scowl before turning and walking away.

He watched Richard recede, his mind in an uproar.

He *would* destroy her father. He had to. But if she ever suspected he was the one who had done it, he could lose her. He couldn't even contemplate that.

This meant that his plan to let Ferreira know it was him who destroyed him was out of the question. He'd have to burn every bit of evidence leading back to him so she'd never know.

The one way this wouldn't be necessary was if in a month's time he cooled toward her. He could strike at her father and not fear the fallout to their relationship.

But he didn't need time to know it would only intensify, this all-consuming passion he felt for her.

And that was his verdict as the man who was never wrong.

They stumbled all the way from the mansion's doors to Rafael's master suite, snatching at each other with wrenching lips, straining against each other as if they'd merge.

It took a while to get there, as Rafael's suite spanned the whole fourth level. At least he'd made sure the mansion was empty before he got her here, after everyone who worked there had managed to walk in on them during the past three weeks.

He threw her down on his extra-large king-size bed and she slid over the satin sheets to its middle as he launched himself over her. She bowed up to intensify his impact, loving his weight and ferocity as he bore down on her.

His lips mashed against hers, his tongue plunging inside her while his hips rammed between her splayed thighs through their clothes.

He rose to snatch her top over her head, bunching her skirt to her waist then tearing her panties off her hips. As her legs fell wide apart for him, his hands, big enough to span her waist, raised her against the headboard. Then he buried his face in her confined breasts.

The sight of the dark majesty of his head against her made her keen, pressing his head harder to her aching flesh.

He muttered something deep and driven, the sound spearing her heart as his hands went to her back, releasing breasts now peaked and swollen for his ownership.

Imprisoning her hands above her head in his good one, he drew back to gaze at her. His eyes crackled with lust at how she must look. Like she had that first night, almost naked, the image of pure wanton abandon.

Growling, he let go of her hands to greedily take her breasts in his hands. She arched off the bed in the shock of pleasure, making a fuller offering of her flesh. He kneaded her, pinched her nipples, had her writhing…begging.

He tore his shirt off, exposing the body she'd told him made Greek gods seem like weaklings. Her awed hands shook over his burnished, sculpted perfection. His growls roughened as he rubbed his chest against her breasts until she thrashed.

"Querida…" He bent and opened his mouth fully over her breasts as if he'd devour her. Pleasure jackknifed through her with each hard draw of his lips, each hot swirl

of his tongue, until she was shuddering all over, her readiness flowing down her thighs.

She lay powerless under the avalanche of need as his hand glided over her, taking every liberty before settling between her thighs. His strong, sensitive fingers slid to her intimate flesh, now throbbing its demand for his touch. As his lips clamped hers, his fingers opened the lips of her femininity, slid between her folds, soaking in her arousal.

It took only a few strokes of those virtuoso fingers to spill her over the edge. She convulsed with pleasure, screeching it into his mouth.

His stroking fingers completed her pleasure, circling her nub soothingly. Desire seared through her again instead, that emptiness that gnawed her all the time now unbearable.

She drummed her feet against the bed in a fit of frustration. *"Just take me."*

He cupped her core, gathered her still trembling body to his, shushing her. And she knew he still wouldn't take her.

She turned her face into his chest, sobbed. "You once said you didn't want my heart pounding or me agitated. My heart is hammering, and I'm far beyond agitated...*all the time.*"

"You're just aroused."

She glared up at him. "Gee...I didn't realize that!"

His face was a mask of savage hunger even as he smiled at her. "I mean you're too aroused to think straight. Three weeks ago you didn't want to see me again."

"Three weeks ago I asked you to take me. Just like I've been doing every day ever since."

"You were trying to get rid of me then."

"Maybe I just couldn't wait to have you. Just like I can't now. Didn't you think of that?"

"I want us to have this first, *querida,* the courting, the anticipation, all the routes to pleasure but the ultimate one. When I join our bodies I want you certain that you want me inside you, not just the release I'll bring you."

Her fingers twisted in his hair, eyes pleading. "I *am* certain. I've been certain since the moment I saw you."

"But when you were thinking straight, you knew what was best for you, for us, wanted me to slow down."

"Not to *this* extent."

"You sound as if I've been tormenting you for months."

"It feels like *years*."

His smile devoured her brimming with pure male satisfaction. "I love you on fire for me like that."

She almost blurted out "I love *you*" but bit it back at the last moment.

She had no illusions about the nature of his involvement, didn't want her far different and more intense feelings to alarm him or put him off. There was no way a man like him would be hers except transiently. And she felt as if the more time that passed, the shorter the time she'd have him in full intimacy.

And now he was going away. He was traveling with one of his "brothers" to Japan. Even though he promised it would be only for a few days, it felt as if it would curtail her time with him further.

All troubled thoughts came to an end as he spread her thighs wide and slid down her trembling body.

Then he spoke against her molten feminine lips. "Let me ease the burning in your blood, *querida*."

He had been doing so in every way but the one she craved.

She tried to close her legs, needing him, not release. "What about the burn in your blood?"

"You can ease that if you wish."

"Oh, I wish, I so wish."

It was what ameliorated the gnawing, when he let her worship him. Getting intimate with the daunting beauty and massive proportions of him sent a frisson of danger through her as she wondered if it was possible he'd fit inside her.

But she couldn't wait until he did, yearned for the pain she knew he had to inflict. She wanted it to hurt at first, needed him to brand her with agony as his.

But though the intimacy gave him release, it only drove her madder with hunger, and left him harder and more on edge.

"Then you shall have your wish. Right after I have mine."

And he took her core in a hot, tongue-thrusting kiss and the world vanished in a whiteout of sensation....

"Can you please turn the anxious vibes down? They're drilling holes in the hull."

Rafael's head snapped up at the sarcastic tone. He watched its owner blankly as Raiden sat down in his private jet's plush seat, facing him.

As Raiden buckled his seat belt with a bedeviling look in his slanting eyes, Rafael's aggravation shot to maximum again.

"I would," he snarled, "if your damn pilot picked a route where I got cellular coverage."

Raiden aka Lightning had asked him to accompany him to Tokyo five days ago. He'd had the biggest lead yet in his quest to establish his bloodline and needed him to examine records that couldn't be moved out of their institutes and temples and to come up with a pattern. He had. And Raiden had finally uncovered his legacy.

Rafael had only uncovered the meaning of agony.

Richard's prediction about time worsening his condition had come to pass. But then, hadn't it always been that bad? It was now a full month since he'd met Eliana, and he *was* fully submerged.

Since he'd left her side, he'd called her a dozen times per day. Given the opportunity, he would have had her on speakerphone all day. Would have had her on webcam all night.

Then came the torture of the twenty-four hour flights

from and back to Rio. For twelve of those, cellular transmission was cut. Being unable to call her for that long frayed his nerves. On the outbound flight, he'd managed to rein in his discomfort. Now, he was going ballistic.

Raiden had remained respectful of his agitation at first. But now he was outright making fun of his condition.

"My pilot says there should be transmission any time now." Raiden smoothed back the hair he'd cut short for the first time in his life, in preparation for entering the conservative upper crust of Japanese society. "But you still can't turn on your phone, since we're starting our descent."

Rafael hurled at him an infuriated glance. "Why are you talking when you don't have something useful to say?"

"Whoa, Numbers." Raiden grinned, stretching his long legs, the eyes he knew froze people in their tracks twinkling with mischief. "You were the last one, after Richard and Numair, that I thought I'd ever see in this state over a woman."

"And in this state, I'm liable to do things the Numbers you know wouldn't. So shut *up,* Lightning."

Raiden didn't shut up. Not until Rafael hurled state-of-the-art headphones at his thick skull. He outright guffawed then.

Caring nothing about their descent, Rafael had his phone out and turned on. Hands shaking with inexplicable and all-encompassing anxiety, he accessed his voice mail. There was one from Eliana.

Then the message began.

"Rafael…I—I've been in an accident…. They're taking me to Copa D'or Hospital. Oh, God…where are you?"

A loud clattering noise followed, as if she'd dropped the phone.

Then there was nothing more.

Eight

Rafael lost his mind.

With every heartbeat, he lost it again and again.

Eliana's phone was out of service. She wasn't in Copa D'Or, the hospital that was flooded with casualties in the aftermath of the accident.

A dump truck exceeding the allowed height had smashed into a pedestrian bridge, which had collapsed onto dozens of cars in the morning rush hour. Four people were killed. Dozens had injuries ranging from minor to critical. He turned the place upside down looking for her, questioned everyone. No one could report on Eliana's condition. Or where she'd gone.

Richard believed this meant she was well enough to walk out on her own. But the only thing that mattered to Rafael was that he couldn't reach her, couldn't protect her. His men and Richard's were combing the streets and had already looked in all the places she could be. She wasn't at her apartment or at her father's villa in Copacabana or his offices. Neither was her father, who Rafael belatedly remembered was back in San Francisco. And the damn man's phone was out of service, too.

Long past his wits' end, he charged over to the last place he could think of. His mansion.

Of her usual haunts, it was the farthest away from the hospital, more than a two-hour drive in this traffic. And there was no reason she should go there with him out of town and with her own apartment only twenty minutes away. But he had nowhere else to try.

Feeling the world crumbling around him, he arrived at his mansion just after dusk. The guards said no cars had come near the gates. And the mansion was empty since he'd given everyone time off while he was away.

He still tore through the mansion roaring for her. Then he exploded into his bedroom...and almost keeled over.

She was on his bed.

Curled on her side with her back to the door, her hair was a wild mass of loose curls rioting across his pillow. Her pastel green skirt suit was ripped in places and smudged in soot and blood.

And she wasn't moving.

Feeling like he had when he'd had too many brutal punches to the head, he staggered toward her, heartbeats shredding his arteries.

He crashed to his knees beside the bed, terror razing through him.

He couldn't touch her. He couldn't discover that she... she...

No. She was all right. She'd come all the way here. She must just be exhausted from the ordeal....

But she was so still. As if she wasn't breathing.

Throat sealing shut with panic, his tongue swelled, twisted on butchered pleas. "*Eu imploro, por favor, meu amor*...Eliana, I beg you please...wake up."

Nothing happened. No response. And he knew.

If she didn't wake up, he didn't want to live.

With the new certainty, knowing he wouldn't suffer long without her if she weren't with him anymore, he finally had the strength to reach out and touch her.

His shaking hand closed over her neck. And before a heartbeat could reanimate him, her heat devastated him.

Warm, hot, and she…she…

She opened her eyes.

"Rafael…"

That tremolo was a thousand volts to his heart, reanimating it after it had shriveled. And he was all over her, his hands everywhere, exposing her flesh, gliding over every inch, making sure all of her was intact, was functioning… was there.

A maddened beast rumbled in his gut at every bruise and graze he found. It dismantled his mind all over again that he'd been unable to prevent her injuries and was now unable to erase them. His lips documented each and every one, tried to soothe and seal them, pouring litanies of regret all over her for failing to do so.

All he could do was have her skin to skin, no barriers for the first time, exposing himself totally for her to take of his power, and for him to absorb her ordeal into himself.

As if he was succeeding, her enervated arms started to cling, her limp body to strain against him until he felt they'd merge. Then her feverish sobs started to make sense.

"My…my driver…was crushed. I—I tried to get him out…but I—I couldn't…then I was facedown on the ground and they were taking me away…. And I only thought of you…had to reach you…but got only your voice mail… then my phone died…"

His body convulsed around hers, holding her tight as weeping overpowered her, his lips drinking her tears, pledging over and over, "I'm here now. I'll never leave you again."

Her hacking sobs became words again. "I—I lost my purse, had only my phone…gave it to the taxi driver as fare. But he said coming all the way here would take him another hour out of his way in the opposite direction, so he dropped me on the main road…."

And he finally found something he could put right. "I'm going to find that driver, and I'm going to make him regret every contemptible act he's committed in his life."

Her tears suddenly stopped, her eyes widening with dismay. "No, no…it doesn't matter…."

"Don't try to stay my hand, Eliana. This sorry excuse for a man not only took your phone—your only method of communication—in lieu of fare, instead of getting you a charger, but then he left you stranded miles away from your destination, injured and alone. He *will* pay."

The next second he wanted to bludgeon himself at the way she seemed to shrivel at his aggression, even when it was on her behalf. She was so shaken, felt so fragile, as if she was…

Dread swept him all over again. What if she was hurt internally, something that would manifest gradually…?

"*Deus, meu amor*…I have to take you back to the hospital."

She resisted when he scooped her up. "There's nothing wrong with me."

"You can't know that. Some injuries, like concussions, become symptomatic later. You need to be monitored…."

"But nothing even came near me. The half of the car I was in was totally untouched."

"But the scratches and bruises all over you…?"

"I got those as I tried to get my driver out."

"But you said you found yourself facedown when they came to take you. You could have lost consciousness."

"It was just a reaction to the horrific sight of my driver's injuries, the flood of adrenaline as I tried to extricate him, then when…when he died right before my eyes."

Helplessness pummeled him again because he knew that he couldn't rewind those terrible moments, wipe away their memories.

But he could do something else. "Still, a couple of nights in hospital are a must."

"They aren't. Apart from my self-inflicted bruises, they gave me a clean bill of health. But even though I miraculously escaped without a scratch, I was just…distraught thinking how I could have died or worse." Her eyes welled as she clung to him. "I needed to be where I can feel you. Then I found a damaged part of the wall around the estate and entered through it, as the gate was too far and I just had to get to your bed…."

Groaning with raw, gut-wrenching emotion, he pressed her to his heart. "I'm here now, *preciosa*. I found you and I'm never letting you out of my sight again. I'll keep you safe from now on. *Always.*"

"You can't stop fate." Before he could swear he would, she went on, hands trembling over his burning flesh. "When that bridge was collapsing and I thought I'd die, I had only one regret…that I was never with you completely."

The insupportable thought that her life could have been snuffed out in seconds, that he could have lost her, ravaged him again.

Then she sobbed. "You can't stop fate, Rafael, but you can have *now.* Let me have you now, all of you. Take all of me and show me how alive you are. Show me how alive I am, *meu amor.*"

Meu amor. She'd called him my love.

And everything inside him snapped.

He bore down on her, felt her heart beat to the same insane rhythm beneath his, knew she couldn't bear preliminaries or gentleness, needed him to reaffirm her life ferociously.

Hand bunching in her locks, tethering her head down to the mattress, his eyes captured her streaming ones as he rose between her splayed thighs and pressed his crown to her molten entrance. Then he lunged.

He felt her flesh trying to ward off his invasion, tearing around his advance. Her shriek boomed inside his head as he pummeled through her barrier. Her body bowed beneath him, a deep arch of agony, but her nod was frantic. She wanted him to give her a ravishing, a full possession. He'd give her everything he had.

He withdrew through the clinging ring that clamped him like a vise, then thrust back harder, tore through the rest of her innocence, felt the scald of her blood and submission gush around him, coating his shaft.

Her cries became pain mixed with exultation, ripping through him. They became whimpers of loss as he withdrew until only the head of his erection remained caught in her flesh. Then he powered his unbearably hard length back into her mind-blowing tightness and heat, forging a new path inside her. His alone. His only home.

Bending, he sealed her lips with his, swallowed her gusting breaths and tortured keens as her flesh began to yield to his shaft, sucking him into an inferno of sensation.

The carnality, the reality, the *meaning* of being inside her... It was too much. He needed to give his all to her, to lose himself inside her, to pierce her essence and consume her.

He glided out of her tightness, pummeled back just as she pumped up, impaling herself further on his erection. Pleasure detonated, almost blew out his arteries.

"Eliana—there can't be pleasure like this, there can't be. Take it all, Eliana, give it all to me...."

"Yes...Rafael...*yes*."

She crushed herself against him, catapulting him into a frenzy. He pounded into her now, building in force and cadence, had her voluptuous breasts jiggling beneath him, her trembling legs spreading wider as her core poured more welcome over him.

The heat, the friction escalated until he sensed the heart thundering beneath his might burst with need for release.

Tilting her hips, he angled himself, still unable to sink inside her to the root through the tightness of her untried body. But he adjusted his position, seeking her inner triggers to ignite her release. Until he did.

Shrieking, she shattered around him, her flesh wringing his shaft with convulsions, the flood of her release razing him, its current snapping his sanity.

He detonated inside her, streams of ecstasy scalding through his length, pouring into her womb, his seed mixing with her pleasure in jet after jet of pure culmination.

Everything started to vanish. Only Eliana remained, her being and flesh melting into his....

Rafael came to with a gasp.

As his senses flickered back, he realized he'd lost consciousness...for the first time in his life. The discharge of fright and craving had been that brutal. It hadn't been a sudden blackout, but a descent into a realm where he'd merged with Eliana on every fundamental level there was.

He lifted his weight from her cushioning softness on shaking arms. She came to only when he moved, her core involuntarily clutching the hardness that hadn't subsided a bit, dragging a groan of pleasure from his depths.

Her eyes fluttered open and he saw how red and puffy they were, and the memory of her ordeal twisted his gut.

But when her lips spread into such a smile, as if she'd discovered an exclusive secret, her eyes growing heavy with such fulfillment, it made him feel like thumping his chest.

The next second, the bite of shame at the ferocity with which he'd initiated her doused his self-satisfaction.

She whimpered as he began to pull out. "Stay inside me."

He stilled. "You must be sore."

"Oh, I am…magnificently so." Her silky legs caressed his sides, her heels digging into his buttocks, driving him back inside her. "If I knew just how incredible it would be to be ravished by you, I would have found a way to make you do it to me before. As it was, it took a near-fatal accident to break your resolve." Her eyes darkened before she made an effort to brighten them. "Being an overachiever in everything, you went and knocked me out with too much pleasure."

Heart quivering with the enormity of everything that had happened in the past several hours, he said, "You knocked me out, too, and I don't even have your excuse of being a novice."

Her eyes widened. "I did?"

"Indeed. I blinked out for the very first time in my life. I never have, even when I got punched square in the face. Richard used to say I have something in my head that doesn't cut out. It took you to KO me."

Her look of delight and smugness was worthy of a hundred portraits. It had a chuckle bursting on his lips as his heart expanded with gratitude. That she existed, was whole, and was his—in every way now.

Debilitated with relief, he rolled onto his back, taking her with him, staying inside her as she'd demanded. She enveloped him in intimacy, her hair gleaming waves of silk strewn over his chest.

He traced the exquisite profile pressed over his heart, the velvet limbs entangled with his. Dismay surged again at her bruises, at how much worse it could have been.

He exhaled the excess fright, the mounting guilt. "And to think I once asked if you were a virgin so I'd adjust my approach. Then I realize you are one and I still take your virginity with all the finesse of a plundering marauder."

She raised his head, eyes urgent. "I needed you, too. I couldn't bear any more gentleness. I needed you to take me with all your strength, to give me the full ferocity of your life and mine, no holds barred. The pain only made the pleasure almost too much to bear. I think I did die for a while with it."

His arms convulsed around her. "You will always *live* with it. Live and thrive and be your vivacious, bursting-with-life delight of a self, do you understand?"

She nodded, eyes growing dreamy. "And I want to live every possible second with you inside me."

"The hard part for me would be *not* being inside you." He thrust deeper inside her hot tightness.

Throwing her head back with a cry, her eyes filled again.

As he cursed himself and tried to withdraw from her depths, she tightened her inner grip on him, her heat and tightness becoming unbearable.

"I need you again, Rafael."

"It would hurt more, with you already so sore."

"I want it to hurt."

Holding her now-feverish eyes, he read her need. He'd always do whatever it took to fulfill each and every one.

Sweeping her to her back, he spread her beneath him and lay down on top of her. She needed more proof that she'd survived, and only something as intense as pain-mixed pleasure could make her feel truly alive now.

She writhed beneath him, her desire flowing, arousal blazing in her eyes. She needed him to ride her and dominate her and wring her of every spark of sensation. Make her live to the fullest.

As he started moving inside her again, trying to work up the heart to give her the ferocity she needed, knowing it would hurt her, the belated realization dawned on him.

He'd taken her without protection. He was doing so again. But there was no thought of consequences. In fact, he welcomed them. He wanted—*needed*—her pregnant with his child.

This woman he loved with everything in him. This woman he'd die for; he'd no longer wanted to live when he'd thought he'd lost her. He wanted her bound to him by every shackle.

He already had those of desire and ecstasy. But now he had to make sure he had the most binding ones of all. Love. And a child.

That would be how he'd brand her as his forever, in every way, so when he finally struck her father down, and if she ever found out, he wouldn't lose her.

Ellie spread her legs wider for Rafael, her nails sinking into his back and buttocks, urging him on. It hurt having him inside her, but she felt she'd implode if he withdrew. She needed his flesh filling her this way, to hold her together.

Her whole being was still in shock. Revolting at the horrors she'd witnessed, petrified at the brush with death.

When he hadn't answered her, she'd lost her mind. The need for any part of him had been what had driven her. She would have walked here just to be where his feel and scent were.

Then he was here and enveloping her in his passion and protection and the world righted itself. It was frightening how dependent she was on him, but it was also exhilarating. To know that he existed, the only one to make her truly alive.

Now anything she'd *thought* she'd known about intimacy had been decimated. From the moment he'd invaded her, joined their bodies, taken her to the very limits of her mortality. It had been beyond description, transfiguring. She was now a totally different person. A woman. *His woman.* At last.

Aware of what pleasure was now—profound, pervasive,

overpowering pleasure, she was maddened for more. For the proof of his life and hers. The pain only intensified their union, confirmed his absolute domination and her utter surrender.

Rafael now loomed above her, the struggle to control his power blazing on his face. He withdrew, then in one burning plunge pierced her to her recesses.

The shock to her system was total.

Paralyzed with too much sensation, she stared up at him. This sublime suffering *was* more intense than the first time. The scream that ripped from her throat was the sum total of her every cell shrieking with life.

He rested within her, stretching her beyond capacity, seemingly as incapacitated as she was at her captivation. Pride played on her lips as blackness frothed from the periphery of her vision, a storm front of pleasure advancing from her core.

It was he who broke the panting silence, his voice feral. "Eliana, the pleasure of you...*Deus*..."

He rose on his palms, withdrawing again, dragging a shriek of loss from her. She clung blindly, crazed for his branding pain and pleasure. He gave them to her, driving back inside her.

On his next withdrawal, she lost what was left of her mind. She thrust her hips up, seeking his impalement. He bunched her hair in his fist, tugged her down to the bed, exposing her throat, latching his teeth into her flesh.

"Yes, Rafael," she cried out. "Eat me up...finish me."

"I will. I always will."

He plowed back into her, showed her that the first time he'd taken her, her inexperienced flesh had impeded his advance. This time, those first plunges had just been preparations. Now he fed her core more with every pounding thrust, causing an unbelievable, almost unbearable expansion within her, until she felt him hit the epicenter of her very essence and unleashed everything inside her.

Ecstasy rent her with its intensity, had her shrieking, convulsing, clinging to him in her tumult. All through, her swimming vision clung to his magnificent face as he focused on completing her release until she saw it seize, tension shooting up in his eyes, as if unsure when to let go.

And she begged for him, for everything. "Give me—give me…"

And he gave. She felt each throb and surge of his climax inside her. The hot jets hit her intimate, swollen flesh, had her thrashing, weeping, unable to endure the spikes in pleasure as everything dimmed, faded….

Awareness trickled between cottony layers of fulfillment. Then Ellie realized what had roused her. Rafael was rising off her, leaving her body.

Before she could whimper with his loss, she moaned her contentment. More bliss settled into her bones as he swept her around, draped her over his expansive body, stayed inside her, mingling their sweat and satisfaction.

Closing her eyes, she let the moment integrate into her cells. She'd need these precious memories to tide her over for the rest of her life.

When one day this ended.

But it wasn't over yet. And she'd cherish every moment with him. Celebrate being alive and desired by him for any length of time.

"If I'd known how it would be between us…" his voice rumbled beneath her ear. "That it would far exceed even my perfectionist fantasies, I *would* have taken you weeks ago."

She raised a wobbling head, marveled anew at his beauty, and at how incredible their bodies looked entwined.

"See? Next time just give in to my demands."

His lips curved. "I certainly will. But then I think we

needed this past month, of deepening our knowledge and appreciation of each other and suffering denial, to reach this unprecedented level of intimacy and ecstasy."

"If you say so."

"I do." He tugged her hair, turning her face to where he was pointing. "See this?"

"Your jacket?"

"Yes. The jacket full of protection I didn't use."

She rose on trembling arms, palms on his sculpted chest, dismay surging. She hadn't even thought of protection. Again.

Or had she…?

In a heartbeat, she saw a whole realm of possibility, a life revolving around a baby with raven hair and silver eyes.

She sat up, feeling his seed inside her, transforming her from girl to woman, a woman who'd give anything for it to take root in her womb.

But that was her. He wouldn't feel the same.

"You could be already pregnant."

She looked away. "You don't need to worry about it."

His finger beneath her chin turned her face back to his, but she kept her eyes averted. She didn't want to see anxiety in his eyes, and the beginning of the end.

"Look at me, *meu coração*."

The way he said that—*my heart*—dragged her eyes back to his. And what she saw in them had now-familiar hot tears crowding behind hers.

"Though I hope you're not, just because I would like us to have more time to ourselves before we become parents—there's nothing I want more than for you to eventually carry my child."

Her throat closed, emotions a burning coal. "Rafael…"

"*Eu te amo,* Eliana, my answer to my every prayer."

She stared at him. Had he really said *I love you?*

"I believe I loved you at first sight, and even before that. I believe I've been waiting for you my whole life, recognized you even before I saw you. Now I know I can't live without you. Literally." He sighed deeply. "Today, when I thought I might lose you, I no longer wanted to live. I want you with me forever, *meu amor*. And I want our forever to start now." A touch that was worship itself cupped her trembling face. "Tell me you want me forever, too. Tell me you love me."

She tried to obey his command, blurt out all that was in her heart. But she couldn't breathe. His words, his confessions… As usual, he was too much.

"You don't love me?" He rose beneath her, scowling. Then a look of absolute arrogance gripped his face. "You might not love me yet, but you will. I will make you love me."

That made her splutter, "Are you kidding? Wasn't it the most blatant thing in existence that I loved you from the first moment, too?" She cupped his face, hands trembling in wonder. "I love you so much it's been a constant pain and dread."

His frown was back full scale. "Why pain and dread?"

"Because I thought you'd never feel the same. Because I thought you'd one day walk away and I'd never see you again."

His scowl deepened. "How could you think such nonsense? Haven't I been showing you in every minute and in every way how much I feel for you? And I'm never, ever, walking away."

Knowing it would take her a while, maybe forever, to come to terms with the idea that he felt all that for her, she exhaled raggedly. "Now I have one regret."

"I can't have you feeling any such thing."

"Oh, it's a benign one. I now wish I didn't tell you I love you totally. I would have loved to see what lengths you'd go to 'to make me love you.'"

"No need to wonder or imagine. I will go to all those lengths anyway. To that end, I'll need to make you my wife."

She gaped at him.

He dragged her to him, possessed her lips in a kiss that almost extracted her soul before he withdrew, his voice a deep, ragged entreaty. "Marry me, Eliana."

Nine

Ellie bent to taste the powerful pulse in Rafael's neck.

Dragging her teeth down his shoulder and chest, she whispered hot, explicit words of desire into his flesh.

Then she came to the scar that was the one thing marring his perfection. It snaked from his back over his left kidney around to his abdomen below his ribs. He'd only told her it was an emergency surgery when he was much younger, and wouldn't go into specifics. It hurt her, terribly, every time she saw it or touched it. But it didn't seem to hurt him. And when she touched it, like now, especially with her lips and tongue, it sent him berserk. As she traced it now with both, his great body shuddered beneath her on a long groan of torment.

Feeling all-powerful eliciting such desire from him, she squeezed his steel buttocks as she slid her leg between his muscled, hair-roughened ones, her knee pressing an erection that felt harder and more daunting than ever before.

It never ceased to amaze her, the constantly renewable

need they shared. They were both on fire again and it had been only an hour since they'd last made love.

Like always with him, time warped. It had been six weeks already since he'd asked her to marry him. Since she'd said an inordinate number of yeses. And those six weeks felt at once like six hours and six years. So much had happened since. So many experiences, so much delight. So much love.

Love. She still couldn't believe it sometimes. Rafael loved her. As much as she loved him. Though being the supreme alpha male who had to be superior in everything, he insisted he loved her more. *Way* more, according to him. She'd only said she had a lifetime to prove him wrong on that front.

She'd moved in with him that same day. Or rather, she'd stayed where she was. He'd assigned her a PA who'd gone to her place to pack everything in meticulously sorted boxes and to get her out of her lease. He wasn't about to let her keep a place a two-hour drive away, and if he had his way, she wouldn't drive again. Or be in a car again. He actually assigned her a helicopter to take her to and from her father's offices.

She let him shower her with extravagances. For now. He was too rattled by her accident and was overreacting. She would gradually pull him back from the extremes he now went to—to protect and pamper her—to a more rational level.

Though in one arena, she really hoped he'd never stop being excessive. In bed. Those unusual demands he'd said he'd make on her that first night? That had been an understatement.

If anyone had told her in her oblivious inexperience that she'd meet the insatiable demands of a sex god like Rafael, she would have scoffed. What they had together shouldn't even be possible. But it was better than possible. It was real. And it was beyond description.

What made their intimacies even more incendiary was that they continued to be just as incredible together out of bed. Rafael was getting more and more embroiled in her work with her father, as well as her work at the orphanage. And he was letting her into his world, introducing her to his "brothers" and involving her in his work.

And that was where she'd discovered the level of his sheer, mind-boggling *genius*.

She now realized that his Numbers pseudonym was apt. He was a literal genius in that regard—and the ramifications of his ability were almost endless. Not that he appreciated it when she used that classification. He'd made it clear she shouldn't repeat it to *anyone,* because he never wanted anyone to know the true extent of his capabilities. It was very helpful for him to be underestimated.

Realizing "anyone" included her father, she made it clear that anything about him, or between them, would never be divulged to anyone else.

It remained the only dim area in the glittering wonderland that was her life with Rafael. That the man she loved was taking longer than expected to warm up to his future father-in-law. And that was when her father, seeing how magnificent Rafael was to her, now thought him an answer to his prayers, too.

Not that Rafael did anything to indicate he disliked her father. It was just…a feeling. Overtly, he went to every length to be attentive and welcoming, and he was taking serious interest in her father's business woes. He even had her providing him with all the details so he could come up with solutions. She had no doubt he would. After all, he *could* do anything.

Another thing she was gladly letting him orchestrate was their wedding.

She still could barely believe that in two weeks' time, she'd be Senhora Moreno Salazar. Or, as she'd told him while laughing until she cried, she'd be Eliana Larsen Ferreira Moreno Salazar.

Rafael had put the world at her disposal in preparing their wedding. But she'd insisted he do it instead, on the caveat that he made it a *very* simple ceremony. Just them, her father and half brothers and his brothers, right here on the mansion grounds.

She wasn't widening the circle to friends and colleagues because it would only detract from the real purpose of the ceremony. Their union. All she wanted was his ring on her finger, and to profess their vows in front of their nearest and dearest before rushing off to resume "plunging deeper into passion."

Yeah, that had turned out to be the only accurate way to describe what they had.

She now couldn't wait to tumble into that abyss once more.

Painting his body with her fingertips, trailing patterns over him with her hair, she chuckled when his whole body vibrated.

"I hope you know what you're inviting with this act of extreme provocation."

"Which act are you referring to?" She nipped his nipples, pouring fuel on his reignited passion, her own raging.

And it was his fault. In their last hour-long lovemaking session, he'd upgraded her experience from multiple to continuous orgasms. He'd sure created a monster. At least, a bigger monster than the one he had spawned from the start.

He grabbed her around the waist, lifting her as if her one hundred and forty pounds were minus the hundred, making her straddle him, scorching lust flaring in his eyes. "I have a list. Each with a consequence all its own."

She rocked against him, sliding the lips of her core up and

down his incredible length and girth and hardness, bathing him in her flowing arousal and their combined pleasure.

"Terrible consequences, I hope."

"Unspeakable." He dragged her down at the same moment he thrust upward, impaling her to her core.

Eyes rolling back, his name tore out of her, body and mind unraveling at the excruciating expansion and pleasure.

Then he was showing her the consequences of teasing him, his full force behind every ram, sparking orgasms from the trigger he hit over and over in her depths until all existence converged on him and what he was doing to her.

It soon became too much, and she shrieked for that final explosion that would finish her. As always, knowing just when to give it to her, he quickened his thrusts to a jackhammering rhythm until her body gushed molten agony. Just as ecstasy became a constant current, he roared and lodged into her womb, jetting his seed, filling her to overflowing.

She jerked with every hot wave of pleasure, her insides quivering, overloading—then blackness....

Reluctant to exit that realm of bliss but eager to rejoin Rafael, Ellie's eyelids drifted open. Slowly adjusting to the light, she saw he was now at the end of his expansive bedroom, theirs now, putting the last touches on his immaculateness in front of the full-length gilded mirror.

He met her gaze in the mirror at once, his nostrils flaring with that all-out passion she'd become addicted to and that now formed the foundation of her world.

"I didn't want to wake you. You looked so peaceful. All I wanted, of course, was to disrupt that peace and corrupt that apparent innocence, but regretfully, I have an appointment."

She kicked off the duvet he'd covered her with, stretching luxuriously, jutting her delightfully sore breasts at him. "One that couldn't be postponed for a mere half hour?"

"Temptress. I'll take it all out on you when I come back."

He strode back to her in all black, looking every inch the ruthless, unstoppable god of finance. "But for now, I'll have one for the road." Sitting down beside her, he pulled her into his arms, lips soothing her nipples, hands caressing her all over until she twisted in his arms, her breath hitching.

"Shh, let me take care of you, *meu alma*."

Her thighs fell apart for him, and his fingers sought her core knowingly, tenderly, as they plunged inside. Pumping into her while his thumb ground her bud in circles, in the exact pressure and speed to spill her into a hot, sharp climax almost at once.

Melting in his embrace, she sighed. "Even when pressed for time, my fiancé knows how to give me a sample of delights to come, to ensure he leaves me burning for more."

"It *is* my evil plan." Suddenly his lust-hooded gaze turned serious. "Speaking of plans…I wanted to talk to you about something."

She struggled to sit up, feeling this was big. "What is it?"

"It's about Diego, and the bond we share. I want to offer him more than visits and sponsoring. I want to discuss the possibility of fostering him or even adopting him. I know he's a little old to be your son, but maybe a younger brother…"

She leaped into his arms, clinging around his neck frantically. "*Yes.* Oh, God, yes, Rafael. Whatever you wish, whatever works. Diego is an angel and he loves you so completely. Oh, God, *I* love you so completely it *hurts*."

His eyes and lips filled with such tenderness. "As long as the hurt is a good one."

Burying her lips in his neck, she trembled with emotion. "The absolute best."

Pulling back, he caressed her flushed cheek. "I shouldn't have broached this huge subject when I have to run. But mull it over. Think practicalities and logistics. I realize it's a lot to take on, but I want us to do it. For Diego, and for us."

She nodded, a galaxy full of stars in her eyes as he kissed her and stood to leave.

Cupping her cheek, he pledged, "*Eu te amo, minha* Eliana, my answered prayers. The prayers I never even prayed."

She went back to sleep as soon as Rafael left, dreaming such wonderful dreams. All vague and unconnected to their reality or the new possibilities with Diego. But she woke up soaring. And almost certain about something.

An hour later, after calling one of those pharmacies that delivered, the "almost" part was gone.

She *was* pregnant.

Sitting down, heart pounding, she held the strip with the vivid pink lines in her hand.

This was…too much. Everything was too perfect. Too incredible. Rafael on his own was already all that. But his love, a future with him, with Diego joining their family… and now a baby already?

She was certain she'd conceived that first time he'd taken her. He'd claimed her so completely, and she'd surrendered so totally that night, needing him to put his mark on her. And he had. His seed had taken root inside her and was growing into a precious, little miracle.

She couldn't wait to tell him. Though he might be a bit disappointed he'd have to compete with his child so soon for her love and attention, it was up to her to show him he never had to worry. Her love for their baby would never interfere with hers for him. Never.

Jumping up, she dressed in a hurry, intending to surprise him. As he now no longer went to his offices on weekends, he was having his meeting in a hotel nearby. He never brought work and work-related people home. The only ones exempt from being considered work were his brothers.

Stopping, she groaned. She'd *forgotten*. He'd invited three of those intimidating Black Castle men for dinner.

After meeting the other two who were coming tonight, Raiden Kuroshiro and Numair Al Aswad, she considered Graves the lesser evil.

Rushing downstairs, she called Rafael's driver, and Daniel told her Rafael had finished his meeting and was already back home.

Joy swept her as she rushed to find him. It was 6:00 p.m. and his brothers should arrive around eight. She had time to tell him the news. And maybe for one more lovemaking session.

Approaching his study—"their place"—she heard him talking. Slowing down, she debated whether to walk in or wait until he finished his call. Then she heard another voice. Then another. His brothers were already here.

Dammit. What were they doing here so early?

As she stood undecided about what to do, one of them said something. It was Numair. She'd recognize his arctic voice anywhere. And what he'd said hit her between the eyes like an icicle.

He'd said, "We put our bigger plans on hold so you could come to Brazil and get close to Ferreira. We did only because you wanted the satisfaction of looking him in the eye as you destroyed him."

Before she could muster an explanation for those words, Rafael spoke and ended her fumbling efforts.

"Destroying him anonymously will do, as well."

"Stick with your original plan, Numbers." That was Raiden. Deceptively suave and even more deadly for it. "Once that guy is rotting in prison, you can walk up to him and tell him it was you who put him there. He wouldn't be able to do anything about it or say anything to anyone."

"Actually, your original plan is nothing compared to your new one," Numair said. "Landing his daughter, making her spill his secrets, is your best weapon yet. Right after the wedding, you can use it to strike him down and be done with it."

"Then you can tell him," Raiden added. "With his daughter in your bed and at your mercy, he'd keep silent forever."

Graves cracked a harsh laugh. "You, my boys, have no idea what kind of land mine you've just tripped over here."

Their voices kept coming closer. It was only when she found herself on the threshold of the room where her life had once changed forever that she realized she'd walked in on them.

They all rose as one. Dismay was the one thing she saw in their eyes. Something made her seek Rafael's last. Dread that she'd find confirmation in them. And that was exactly what she found.

"You want to destroy my father?" The voice that croaked out of her didn't sound like hers anymore. "You 'landed' me to bring down my father? That's why you've been milking me for information? Why you're marrying me?"

"Eliana, no…" He stopped, swung toward the others. "What are you waiting for? Get the hell out."

Raiden and Numair looked at him as if he'd gone mad. Then, with no trace of their earlier dismay, they regarded her stonily as they passed her on their way out. It was only Graves who looked almost as apologetic as he did.

Once alone, Rafael neared with the caution he'd use to approach a frightened gazelle. "I'm sorry you heard that."

Numbness spread. "That's all you have to say?"

His lips thinned, his jaw hardened more. "I would have given anything for you to never know that. Especially now."

"*Now?* That's your only problem? That I heard it before your plans come to fruition? That's the only reason you're upset? Because now that I've heard them, they won't?"

"I didn't want to upset *you.*"

"You want to send my father to prison, but you don't want to upset me?"

His eyes, the eyes of the man she'd loved with every fiber of her being till minutes ago, sparked with danger. "Your father deserves whatever I will do to him. But I wanted to spare you as much as I could."

And it registered at last. The blow of realization. What rewrote the past ten weeks, explained them far better than what had seemed too good to be true. Because it was.

This was the truth.

The ice that encased her started cracking. "Everything we've had...from the first moment...it was all a plot. A lie."

"No." He hauled her to him. "That first night was all true. I didn't realize who you were until I saw you with him."

She tore out of his embrace. Unable to go far, she slumped to the ground by the couch where they'd shared their first intimacy.

Swearing harshly, Rafael swooped over her, swept her up into his arms and sat down on the couch with her on his lap. Unable to push away again, she lay limply against him, tremors racking her body.

"That's why you walked away," she choked. "Then you realized you could use me...and came back as soon as you had another plan in place. Everything ever since...a lie. *Everything.*"

His arms convulsed around her. "No, Eliana. Everything between us was real. *Is* real."

Her head rolled weakly over his shoulder, her eyes refusing to meet his, tears beginning to fall. "I can see it all now. Everything that didn't register at the time. I always sensed something in you—a calculation—but I couldn't find any reason you'd be playing me. I would have never been paranoid enough to imagine it was never me you wanted, but just a weapon to use against my father."

"It was *always* you I wanted." Gripping her head, he tried to make her look at him. She finally did and tears flowed thicker. He looked exactly like the man she loved. That man who didn't exist. "I *never* intended to use you against him. And the only calculation you felt targeted your father."

"Now it all makes sense. The...viciousness I felt from you toward him. And I kept rationalizing it so I could be with you. And I ended up giving you everything you needed... to destroy my father." The first sob tore out of her. "All an act..."

He squeezed her tighter. "I *never* acted with you."

"I don't believe...anything you say...anymore."

"You have to. *Eu te amo,* Eliana—I love you and that's the only truth. And when you remember everything we had..."

"I do...remember." Her every word now got hacked in two, the pain unbearable. "Every touch...and word...and look. And they're all tainted with...what I now know."

His hands roamed her face and body, as if he'd wipe away what she now knew. "That's shock talking. You're just angry."

Sobs caught in her lungs, almost tore them apart. "I'm not...angry...I'm...destroyed. You...destroyed *me*...Rafael."

"No... *Deus,* Eliana, don't say that. I would never hurt you. I only care about you, about us."

"There is...no...us."

"There is nothing *but* us. My plans for your father have nothing to do with us. *Nothing.* And after our wedding..."

It finally hurt enough. It made her lurch out of his arms, tumble onto the couch, pushing against him as if he burned her. "You...think I'll go ahead with the wedding...as if nothing happened? As if you're still the man I loved?"

He burst to his feet, his frustration pummeling her. "If this had happened a month after the wedding, I would have already secured you, us."

This made tears and sobs stop abruptly. "If we'd been married ten years, it would have still ended things between us."

Stabbing his fingers through his hair, he exhaled heavily.

"I can see I'm not talking you down but just making it all worse. But I swear to you, Eliana, we have nothing to do with anything I ever planned for your father. I never lied to you about my feelings, and I never wanted to hurt you."

"Then prove it. Don't hurt *him*."

The fire went out in his eyes, that terrible, terrifying ice impaling her. "Your father has to pay."

And she wailed, *"Pay for what?"*

His face became an opaque mask. "It's nothing to do with us, Eliana. Nothing to do with you."

"It has *everything* to do with me. He's the most important person in my world."

His eyes flared again. "I thought that was me."

"I don't even know *who you* are anymore. But I know who he is. He's the man who's been there for me every single hour since I was born. He's my *father*."

She pulled at her finger in a frenzy, almost pulling it out of its socket. By the time she yanked his ring off, she was panting, weeping, shaking all over.

"Put my ring back on your finger, Eliana. *Now*."

Holding his volcanic gaze, she let the ring drop to the pristinely polished hardwood floor.

For one last moment, she looked up at him—the most incredible dream of her life, who'd turned out to be its most devastating nightmare. And said goodbye.

"If you're my father's enemy, you're my enemy, too."

Staggering around, she stumbled out of the room. Out of his mansion. Out of his life.

Where she'd never truly been.

Ten

Crumpled on a bed in some hotel, Ellie lay like something broken and discarded, the storm of misery buffeting her.

She hadn't been exaggerating when she'd told Rafael he'd destroyed her. He'd crushed something inside her. Her belief in her judgment, which balanced her, which she depended on to guide her through life. He'd done so once before only to heal it, then boost it to no end. Now he'd crushed it again, irrevocably this time, along with everything beautiful and hopeful inside her.

Just hours ago she'd been on top of the world, secure in the love of the man she adored, pregnant with his baby, and a couple of weeks away from marrying him. Now everything lay in ruins at the bottom of the hollow shell she'd become.

Everything had been a lie.

But how had she ever believed it had been real? The more she thought back, the more she remembered how he'd made her give him every detail of her father's work, the clearer it became that she'd always been a means to an end to him.

And *this* made sense. That she'd been just an instrument to him. How had she ever believed a man like him could love her like she loved him? Hadn't she already known that he was too much for her?

Then the avalanche began again.

Every second from the moment she'd laid eyes on him, every memory, so brutal in clarity, so heartrending in beauty, blasted holes in her heart. The cascade strengthened with every snippet of remembrance, decimating her self-worth, submerging her in humiliation. Every word she'd uttered, admiring and believing in him; every glance that hungered for him and adored him; every liberty she'd begged him to take with her body, with her being; every surrender and trust she'd bestowed on him, certain he'd treasure it.

The damage would only spread, deepen, until there was nothing left of her but ashes. And it had all been for nothing. She'd been nothing to him. Worse than nothing. She'd been the knife he'd been honing to stab her father with.

She could only be thankful he'd broken that knife before he had a chance to use it.

Suddenly, she bolted upright before slumping back, faint with the hours of soul-tearing weeping…and with true terror.

For her father.

Rafael was too powerful, could be—*was*—ruthless. Whether he wielded her as a weapon or not, there was no stopping him.

If only she could find out the reason for Rafael's enmity, she might find a way out. But she'd seen it in his eyes. He was never telling her why.

There was only one other possible source of info.

"Are you sure it's only a stomach bug?"

That was the fifth time her father had asked her that question inside five minutes. That had been the one thing she could think of to explain how horrible she looked.

Ellie nodded. "The worst of it is over."

Her reassurance did nothing to allay his anxiety. After her mother had complained of what they'd thought digestive troubles, which had turned out to be terminal cancer, her father had been a full-blown, worst-case-scenario worrywart. All her life, he'd been obsessed with her health.

"Daddy, please answer me."

She'd asked if he'd ever committed any serious indiscretion. He'd thought she was asking because she didn't believe untimely decisions were the only reason for the trouble his business was in. He really had no clue Rafael was after him or why he would be. At least this reassured her she wouldn't discover she didn't know her father, either.

Her father sagged down beside her on the couch, his unseeing eyes scanning the expansive living room, which was furnished in warm earth colors and had perfect panoramic views of the Atlantic.

He'd given this villa to her mother as a wedding present. She'd been the one to decorate it, and he hadn't changed a thing since. He'd been loath to come back for years after her death. Now it seemed it was where he found his only comfort.

"I'm sorry I never worked up the nerve to tell you, Ellie. I didn't want to lose your respect."

Heart pounding painfully, she squeezed his hand. "I'll never love you any less, Daddy. Just tell me."

A ragged exhalation. "After those losses hit me hard, I did some tax evasion to compensate, and everything got twisted out of all proportions. Now it's gone from bad to worse and I might declare bankruptcy soon." He dropped his head in his palms. "Oh, my little darling, I'm so sorry, but I have to confess something else. I was actually feeling desperate enough to ask Rafael for help. I know you don't want to ever mix your marriage with business, but I was thinking it would be child's play for Rafael to solve all my problems."

While tax evasion was bad, it didn't warrant Rafael's cold-blooded plan of revenge. She didn't believe her father *could* do anything to warrant it. But this was clearly a dead end.

Rising to her feet, she bent to kiss him. "Next time, promise you'll tell me everything so I can help before things snowball into a huge mess, okay?"

After her father promised, and she reassured him that they'd see this through, he saw her to the door, totally oblivious to the danger he was in and the devastation in Ellie's life.

Back at the hotel, she fell into bed, her mind churning as exhaustion dragged her under into tumultuous darkness.

She had to seek Rafael again. It was all in his hands. Everything was.

Her world, her being…her destruction.

Rafael. Always Rafael…

Warm power rejuvenated her drained body; delicious fire roamed her aching flesh. Sighing softly, she drove deeper into the solace, a moan of longing on her lips.

"Rafael…"

"*Si, meu amor, si*…I'm here, I'm yours."

The pledge felt like a resurrection, after the death her spirit had suffered.

Her eyes fluttered open. The phantasm had Rafael's face, his body, his hunger…and it—he…

He was really here!

Suddenly drowning, her body violently lurched against his, as if kicking up to a surface that didn't exit.

"Don't push me away, *meu alma*…"

And they overtook her, every agony and bitterness and

desperation, burning from her depths and gushing from her lips on racking, uncontrollable heaves.

Lost in the tumult, she felt Rafael carrying her to the bathroom, securing her in his infinite strength as the misery overpowered her. He held her, kissing and soothing her. Finally collapsing against him, empty and depleted, he stretched her in his arms on the floor, kneading the muscles that had almost torn with the violence of her retching. Then ridding her of her soiled clothes, stripping himself, he took her into the shower.

He held her up beneath the warm cascade, caressing and coddling her with such gentleness and patience. At last, he took her down on the floor of the shower, and the potency that had planted the miraculous seed of life inside scorched a furrow in her buttocks. He made no sensual overtures, his touch bolstering, not arousing, his body pressed to hers only to transfer his vitality into her. Yet the unwilling bliss she felt at his ministrations caught fire. Her insides cramped, clamoring for his occupation.

As always, in tune with the slightest nuance of her needs, he adjusted her position over his lap, pressing the wide crown of his erection against her opening. Her body melted, inside and out, her thighs splayed wider in submission.

Holding her eyes, hunger and entreaty and determination mingled in his. Reading her capitulation, he flattened her breasts to his chest, flexed his hips and forged inside her. Her flesh fluttered around his hardness, delight searing from every inch he stretched beyond its limits. Once buried inside her, he stilled at the gate of her womb. Twisting his long-healed hand in her wet hair, he withdrew so agonizingly slowly.

He whispered as he thrust back, his voice the deepest, darkest spell it had ever been.

"You're mine, Eliana. Mine to pleasure. Mine to protect. Mine to love." He nudged her very heart. *"Mine."*

That was all it took. Her core spasmed over his hardness in the exquisite scalding of release. Baring his teeth, a harsh hiss flayed her cheek as he unleashed his pleasure inside her, marking her, mastering her, intensifying her orgasm. She shook against him, eyes clinging to his as he finished her.

Long after she lay in his arms quivering, body replete, heart shattered, he gently withdrew from her depths, then finished cleaning her. Taking her out of the shower, he dried her off and carried her to bed.

Gathering her in his arms under the covers, he kissed her all over her face, his caressing hand moving down to her belly. "You're carrying my child."

She huffed weakly. "Whatever tipped you off?"

His gorgeous lips twitched. "The morning sickness fest just confirmed it…but I've been noticing changes in your body." He tasted her nipples, sent pleasure forking through her to lodge in her womb. "Those delights are becoming thicker, darker, and they give you even more pleasure when I do this." He suckled each hotly, had her arching helplessly, surrendering her flesh to his mastery. "You're also more responsive, when I thought that impossible, igniting into a conflagration much more quickly."

"That's just your overachiever self. You taught my body to expect more pleasure each time, until you had it perpetually ready to go off at a touch."

Her confession was rewarded by a look of supreme male satisfaction before he rose off the bed, knowing what the sight of his arousal would do to her.

Striding into the bathroom, she heard him rustling around. Then he rejoined her, took her hand and slipped his ring again on her finger.

Looking down at her, he pressed her hand to his heart. "You'll never take my ring off, never leave my side again. I let you go only so you could calm down, but I won't let you do this to yourself. Take your anguish out on me, never on yourself." At her miserable silence, he gritted his teeth. "Weren't you going to tell me about the baby?"

"Don't you know me at all?" she countered.

His eyes softened with such…adoration. It still felt like the most genuine thing she'd ever known.

"I know all of you. It's why you have all of me." Pain entered his gaze. "You must have found out yesterday, must have been coming to tell me when you overheard us."

As always, he just knew. It had been how he'd manipulated her so seamlessly. "Yeah, I arrived just in time to hear them congratulating you on the adjustment of your plan."

"If you'd waited you would have heard me blasting them for refusing to believe you were never part of my plan and forbidding them to ever mention you again. Richard is the only one who knows what we have together, and he knew they'd stepped on forbidden territory." She did remember Graves saying something to that effect. "But I don't care what they think. I only care about you. I'm here to take you home, *meu amor*."

"I can't…I can't be with you anymore."

"You were just with me now. And you'll always be with me."

"You know what this was. I'm unable to resist you, but it will kill me to be with you now."

"Don't ever say things like that. I'll give you time to come to terms with all this on the condition you never shut me out again."

"I'm more valuable now that I'm a dual-purpose instrument, right? A weapon in your revenge, and a vessel for you heir." Before he voiced his thunderous disapproval of her interpretation, a terrible idea sparked in her mind. A bargain. "But I will do everything you wish, Rafael…if you let your plan to destroy my father go. Whatever that would cost you, I will compensate you."

He sat up, the animosity she'd always felt and he'd hidden so well on full blast now. "There's no compensating me for what your father did. And don't ask what that was. I already told you it has nothing to do with you. And it will remain so."

Giving up, she left the bed on shaking legs and went to retrieve her clothes. Once she'd pulled on the clean layers, she exited the bathroom to find him blocking her way.

Circumventing him, she stopped at the door. "I can't stop you, Rafael. But I can stop myself."

He prowled toward her. "You can't. You will never stop loving me, just as I will never stop loving you till the day I die."

"Even if I never do, it makes no difference. What we had, whatever that was, is over."

"It will never be over between us, Eliana. You'll always be mine to protect and cherish every second of my life. And I will be there for every second of your pregnancy, and our child will be born with us long married."

His conviction overwhelmed her. Warding off another wave of nausea, she staggered past him.

She was at the door when he said something else, so calm and final, it made her stumble the rest of the away out of the hotel.

Once outside, she found Daniel there, waiting. In no condition to refuse his services, she entered the luxurious, perfectly air-conditioned limo, slumped in her seat and closed her eyes, Rafael's last words looping in her mind, deepening her desperation.

He'd said, "Our wedding will take place on time."

Knowing it was pointless to keep running from Rafael, that he'd only keep coming after her, Ellie returned to the mansion. But she drew the line at sharing his bed.

He let her choose where she'd stay. She chose the suite as far away from him as possible on ground level, and she was relieved he didn't try to invade it once she sought its refuge. He was apparently giving her time to "come to terms," as he'd called it.

But there was no doing that while she mistrusted his motives, didn't know the secret behind his enmity and expected a catastrophe to befall her father at any moment.

After another day in hell, longing for him and knowing it was a futile effort to again demand he tell her everything, realization descended on her like a hammer.

She knew who could tell her the truth.

His brothers.

For all their ruthlessness, Ellie was certain Graves, Raiden and Numair loved Rafael.

At least to the extent that those men *could* love. She bet, whatever they felt, they wouldn't further jeopardize his plans if they could at all help it.

So she demanded to meet them, threatening that if they told Rafael, it would be on their heads when she left him standing at the altar.

Since Raiden and Numair didn't think much of her, they couldn't risk her carrying out her threat and complied. Graves didn't believe her for a second, but followed suit anyway.

After resorting to elaborate maneuvers to throw Rafael's surveillance off, she now sat in Graves's ocean-facing penthouse suite at the Copacabana Palace Hotel. Looking at those three Olympians who sat across from her like some ancient tribunal that would decide her fate, she wondered again how they had so much in common with Rafael.

It felt as if they'd been forged in the same merciless crucible, molded into the same brand of lethal weapon.

Raiden was coolly assessing her, as if deciding on an attack strategy. She had no doubt that when he struck, he did so out of nowhere and turned his opponents to ashes, as his code name, Lightning, suggested.

Numair—Phantom—was every bit his code name, too, chilling, elusive and impossible to fathom. With him no one knew where they stood, and she had a feeling that made him the deadliest of all.

Graves was looking at her with the tolerance someone would have for a posturing cat that didn't realize it wasn't so much intimidating as endearing.

She finally sat forward. "Got enough of sizing me up?" When the men just continued staring at her, she blew out a breath. "To business, then. As you so kindly shattered my illusions the other night, you now must finish your task and tell me what Rafael won't."

Graves shook his head. "Let it go. Knowing the truth would only hurt you."

"Is there more hurt than knowing the man I love— the father of my baby—is using me to send my father to prison?"

The men looked at each other. The baby was news to them. So Rafael did consider her forbidden territory he shared with no one. But she felt a baby somehow changed everything to them. The shift in their attitude was almost palpable.

"There is always more hurt, Ms. Ferreira," Numair said in that hair-raising sereneness. "Some snake pits are better left closed forever."

She gave a mirthless huff. "Well, this one is wide-open, and serpents have been slithering out all over me. I know you're here because you'd rather spare Rafael further trouble with me. But if he thinks this is hurting me less, I'm telling you he's wrong. I can't live with not knowing."

Another eloquent glance passed between the men before Graves finally sat forward. It seemed they'd elected him to be their spokesman.

Holding her breath, knowing what she was about to hear

would change everything, she hung on to his every word as he started talking.

And she finally understood what they'd meant by saying there was always more hurt. This was a level beyond her worst nightmares.

What happened to Rafael, to all of them, the suffering they'd had to endure… It was beyond her worst nightmares.

Numbness spread in her every cell, an attempt to ward off the horror, to protect her psyche from being torn apart. Imagining Rafael as a child, taken and imprisoned, abused and broken…it was…it was… No way to describe, to take in, to bear…

Ellie's eyes fluttered open.

Jackknifing to a sitting position, the whole world heaved around her, making her collapse back. On a bed. It had to be Graves's hotel bed.

"Dammit," she moaned as she struggled to sit up. Hands on both sides helped her. Raiden's and Numair's. "I've never even felt dizzy all my life, and now I faint every weekday."

"You must promise *you'll* never tell Rafael of this." Graves's intimidating face came into wavering focus as he stood at the foot of the bed. "He can't find out you were in my bed, under any circumstances. I'm fond of certain anatomical parts."

She looked up at him, at the other two, and tears gushed from her depths.

The men's consternation rose as sobs almost tore her apart before their eyes. These men who'd vanquished the world's evils had no way of dealing with a woman's tears. As they fidgeted and exchanged anxious glances, it was clear they would have rather been dealing with a ticking bomb.

But she couldn't help it. The more she imagined the atrocities that had befallen Rafael all those years ago, the more violent her weeping became.

Her distress soon overpowered the men's ability to withstand it, and they took refuge in action. Swarming around her, she found herself propped by pillows from all sides, and they were blotting her tears, bathing her burning face in cold compresses, warming her freezing hands in heated ones and offering her every comfort food and drink that existed in Rio.

Limp with anguish, she surrendered to their ministrations, all but the dietary one. At the first warning heave, they rushed to take ingestible stuff away. She had a feeling they would rather get shot than deal with *that*.

It felt like hours before she was finally drained of all her tears, and lay there barely managing the in-out motions of breathing. The men seemed just as depleted, sitting around the bed as if they'd been through a thirty-round fight with a gorilla.

"Please tell us you're done crying," Raiden groaned.

Her breath hitched. As they all tensed again, she only nodded. There was nothing more in her. For now.

Exhaling in relief, Graves said, "How is it possible a woman your size has all that water in her?"

"Speaking of water." Raiden grimaced at the memory as he fetched a carafe. "You need to replace the rivers you lost."

Contradictorily the one who looked most rattled by her weeping storm, Numair warned, "Sip it slowly. Otherwise, you might choke. Or throw up. Or both. Or do some other catastrophic thing. Like burst into another crying jag."

As she did as instructed, Numair regarded her heavily. "That was for Rafael. You can't bear imagining what he's been through."

Her breath hitched again. "And that I can't do anything about it."

Numair exchanged a look with Raiden. Then he shook his head. "You *do* love him."

She looked at both men through almost swollen-shut lids. "You figured this out on your own?"

And she saw what she'd thought impossible. A semblance of a smile on Numair's cruel lips. "It was a long-shot deduction."

Suddenly, it all crashed into place. "Rafael thinks my father had a hand in his abduction!"

Exchanging another of those glances, and making another decision, Numair was the one who told her the details.

This time there were no tears. Just conviction. It made her sit up steady. "No way my father did that!"

Raiden shrugged. "Rafael has evidence."

Slumping back with this new blow, she felt her world churning.

Graves, who'd been silent for a while, came forward, checking her temperature.

She clung to his hand. "I need to know more."

Another shared glance between the men, then Graves asked, "What do you need to know?"

"These aren't your real names."

He shook his head. "They are our names now."

"How did Rafael pick his name?"

"He was wounded on a mission. Bones, our medical expert, performed a desperate field surgery on him, removed his kidney and spleen to stem his internal bleeding, thinking he'd die anyway. But he recovered fully as if by an act of God."

"Rafael. *God has healed...*"

At Graves's nod, another sob tore her. That scar. She'd felt it resonate with such...pain, such...loss. She'd been right. Oh, God, Rafael...all he'd lost, all he'd survived...

"He picked Moreno Salazar," Raiden said. "*Dark old house,* just as I chose Kuroshiro, which means *black castle* in Japanese, as a sort of twisted tribute to our being the product of this ancient, sinister place where we were imprisoned and created."

"Before you told me all that," she whispered, "I was thinking you did feel as if you've been forged in the same hell."

"I'm beginning to see why Rafael fell for you," Raiden said, that assessment in his eyes tinged with approval.

"He didn't. He was just using me."

Graves waved her words away as if they were rubbish. "He fell for you. All the way. I was there that first night he did. I can't begin to explain how it happened, but it certainly did." At her mournful disbelief, he growled, "Bloody hell, the man went prematurely gray with fright over you. What more proof do you need?"

Silver *had* appeared in his temples after her accident. Rafael had waved the coincidence away, but she'd believed it just the same…until she'd overheard that fateful conversation. Believing it again, believing he loved her, made things worse not better.

Shying away from the implications, she sought a diversion. "If Rafael is Brazilian by birth, why didn't he make Brazil his base of operations all along?"

"His homeland was always the one place he didn't want to be," Numair explained. "He's one of only three of us who know their family, but when we first escaped, he couldn't contact his, fearing the Organization might be keeping them under surveillance in case he returned to them. Then he found that his parents got divorced after his abduction, remarried and had more children. But even when we established our new identities, he didn't want to disrupt their lives all over again."

That was also what he'd told her, just without the compelling reasons that had stopped him from seeking his family again. It hadn't been a choice but a necessity that had been forced on him.

"He thought he'd become someone totally different from the boy they'd lost," Graves said. "He still believes they're better off not knowing the man he's become. For years, he watched them from afar, but I guess I wore him down because he finally reentered their lives a couple of years ago. Though the stubborn boy only did so with his new identity and remains a peripheral acquaintance."

Even when he'd finally sought his family, he settled for the comfort of seeing them up close…as a stranger.

"But he's in Brazil now as some sort of poetic justice," Raiden interjected. "Because this was where he was taken, where it started, and it's where he wants to exact his revenge, where he wants it to end."

That fist perpetually wringing her heart tightened.

This was all beyond comprehension, beyond endurance. Even if he'd manipulated her, he had an overwhelming reason for it. What had been done to him had been monstrous, unforgiveable, irreparable.

But it couldn't have been her father who'd done it.

It couldn't.

"Rafael…"

He could swear he'd felt Eliana the moment she'd thought of seeking him. But he'd curbed the urge to stampede toward her. If she didn't give herself voluntarily, it would mean nothing.

But she was seeking him now, standing there on his threshold looking as if she was in deep mourning.

"I know everything."

He rose slowly to his feet, gritting his teeth on the surge of dismay. "I'll skin them alive."

She approached, and it took all the self-restraint he had not to obliterate the distance and crush her in his arms.

"I insisted I wouldn't go through with the wedding if they didn't tell me." She stopped two feet away, red-rimmed eyes filled with a world of pain, reproach and...empathy? "You were wrong to hide the truth from me."

"I'd rather you hate me than your father." Surprise flitted across her pale, haggard face. Apparently, that motive hadn't even occurred to her. "I thought I'd manage to break through your resentment in time, but I didn't want the world you've built on your belief in your father to come crashing down. Even when I punished him, I wanted you to continue thinking of me as the villain, not him."

She surged forward, gripped his arms. Even though her touch was distraught, it felt like sustenance when he was starving.

"But you have to be wrong, Rafael. My father isn't a villain. And he would die before he harmed a child."

Her butchered protest told him if he insisted to the contrary, he risked sundering what remained of their tenuous emotional bond.

Everything inside her had been damaged; everything between them hung by a thread. She was still unable to stop loving or wanting him, but it was still possible he'd exacerbate her injuries, making them incurable, and end up losing her altogether.

He'd die before he did.

There was only one venue open to him now.

He took it. "I'm open to giving your father every benefit of the doubt, and to uncovering new evidence. However long it may take to find it. Is that acceptable to you?"

And this being who was everything to him looked at him with those eyes that were his world and nodded.

He crushed her in his arms at last, her feel reclaiming him from the wasteland of separation.

"Will you marry me now?"

Eleven

Eliana had agreed to resume their wedding plans.

But it seemed her faith in his feelings was still damaged, or at least hadn't recovered yet. There had been no return to intimacy between them.

Rafael couldn't push. Not when everything inside her felt doused, no matter how passionate and attentive he was. All he could think was that she still thought everything he did for her was self-serving, that she continued to think herself an instrument to serve his purposes. First vengeance and now the child he couldn't wait to have, a child to give the life he'd been deprived of.

There was nothing he could do but continue to love her and hope time would prove to her what pledges never could.

Ellie rushed through Rafael's expansive, exquisite mansion, inspecting the guest suites for readiness.

The wedding was tomorrow. And her half brothers were flying in from the States, while all of Rafael's brothers were coming over for the wedding rehearsal. They'd all be spending the night in the mansion.

Rafael had left it up to her to distribute their guests. He continued to give her carte blanche with everything. Not that this made her feel anywhere near the lady of the mansion. While before she'd felt at least at home here, she now felt like a trespasser, and wondered if that feeling would ever go away.

For now she had to focus on making sure everything was ready for their families' arrival. She'd assigned the poolside suites to them. Some of the suites had panoramic views of the ocean, gardens, waterfalls and the hillside plunging deeply into Ferradura Bay. Others were tucked away, opened to the lush botanical gardens, sparkling lagoons and cascading waterfalls.

But none had the stunning three-hundred-and-sixty-degree views, open-air shower, sundeck and spa of Rafael's master suite. What used to be *theirs,* and would be so again starting tomorrow night.

But how could she share his personal space and bed again? Although he'd said he'd consider new evidence, how could she possibly find any? And even with him putting his revenge plans on hold, what kind of life would they have with all of this between them? His initial duplicity, his unresolved animosity toward her father, her unabated fear he'd act on it?

Unable to think any further than today, she went about the mind-emptying chores of stocking all the suites with Rafael's legion of hired help.

Starting tomorrow night, the rest of her life as Rafael's wife and the mother of his child would begin. And the idea struck her at once with joy…and despondence.

In the southern gardens overlooking the Atlantic, Rafael stood watching Eliana as she walked toward him down the aisle with her father, the man who'd sentenced him to hell.

It was only a rehearsal. Only the people who had a role in the ceremony were there. Others, like her half brothers and Ferreira's PA, Isabella Da Costa, would be coming tomorrow. But everything with her always felt like the real thing. The only thing that mattered.

And as she approached him in her flowing pistachio dress, her hair swept up in that ponytail it had become one of his life's keenest pleasures to undo, he felt his being well up with love for her.

Her eyes embraced his all the way, so much emotion filling them. He was beside himself being unable to read it all. Then she was a breath away, and that man he'd hated for so long, even before he'd known his identity, was giving him her hand.

He looked at Ferreira for a long moment...and suddenly realized.

He was no longer angry.

He no longer cared about anything. Nothing mattered to him anymore. Nothing but her.

Though this rehearsal was about going through the motions, getting the sequence flowing smoothly, and he wouldn't be saying his actual vows until tomorrow, he couldn't wait until then to share his epiphany with her.

So he took her hands to his lips, to his heart. "Eliana, my every answer to my every prayer...I'm letting go of everything, my heart. I cling only to your love, want nothing but your happiness and peace of mind, *meu coração*."

Rafael's pledge had been the last thing Ellie had expected from him. It had been reverberating inside her ever since, knocking down every barrier, ending every uncertainty.

Unable to wait to be alone with him, she gazed at him as the rehearsal came to an end, her heart shedding its sluggish despondence, back to the hammering of anticipation.

As he hugged another three men, the rest of his brothers—

minus one all were loath to talk about—she couldn't really see anything but him.

Dressed in all black, he'd lost weight in the past two weeks. It only made him seem taller, his shoulders and chest even wider in comparison to the sparser waist and hips. His face was hewn to sharper planes and angles, his skin a darker, silkier copper, intensifying the luminescence of his eyes. The discreet silver in his luxurious raven hair, that testament to his absolute love, added the last touch of allure.

Then she was swept up in his arms among his brothers' hoots and hollers that he was disgracing them by anticipating the wedding night. Not in a condition to be embarrassed, she clung to him all the way to their quarters.

But the moment he placed her on the bed and came down beside her, her disquiet returned.

Twisting her ponytail around his wrist, harnessing her by it, ferocity barely leashed by gentleness, he tilted up her face. "No more distance, *minha vida,* ever again."

"That's not it…I just—just… Oh, God, please, Rafael, show me your evidence against my father."

His face settled in adamant lines. "I *have* given this up. I consider anything I've been through the path to finding you. You remember when you said you'd compensate me? Finding you is more compensation than I've ever dreamed I could have."

"But what you have against him is airtight, right?"

"This is what I was afraid of, for your faith in him to be irrevocably damaged, causing you this much pain."

Her chest ached, her eyes burned. "Everything in me rebels against believing any such thing of my father, but it isn't why I'm in agony. It's for you. What you suffered was unthinkable."

"It's in the past."

"But this is the present and future. How can I share my life and body and baby with you if there's even the slightest possibility my father committed such an unforgivable crime against you? Even if he had done so under unspeakable duress? Throwing you in hell while he lavished his love on me?" She released a shuddering breath. "Even if you've decided to look the other way for my sake and that of our lives together, *I* can't. I can't live believing one of the two people my life has been built around did the other such unimaginable injury, for whatever reason."

After a long moment, he said, "Do you believe in your heart your father didn't do it—or at least was forced to do it somehow?"

She nodded. "But I can't even begin to think how this could have happened."

"Then that's it. I'm now ready to disbelieve anything but the verdict of your heart. It's never wrong. That heart saw through the hatred cloaking mine, blew away my bitterness and anger, made me experience what I never thought I was capable of—a love without bounds. I trust your heart, and only your heart."

She gaped at him, unable to take that much love.

He had more to give. "I'll do anything to find new evidence in your father's favor. To that end, if you permit, I want to face him. He's the only one who might provide missing information needed to paint a truer picture."

It terrified her that a confrontation might provide definitive proof that her father's reasons hadn't been overwhelming enough. But knowing this must be resolved, she consented. But on one condition.

"If it turns out my father did what you think he did and had no acceptable reason for his actions, I want you to deal with him as you see fit, to make no more allowances for his being my father. You have to have justice…and closure."

Not intending to ever fulfill that condition, Rafael escorted Eliana to her father's suite.

The man, who'd already gone to bed, seemed to think he wasn't quite awake when Rafael told him who he really was.

His expression changed from blank, to flabbergasted— then he shot up and pounced on Rafael.

He pulled back, tears in his eyes. "*Deus,* could it really be you? Oh, *meu caro*...your disappearance hit me almost as hard as it hit your parents. The indescribable loss brought me back to your father's side after we had our stupid falling out and I was idiotically sulking. He clung to my support during the search for you, but then your case was closed. We turned the world upside down looking for you on our own, but once your father became certain you were lost to him, he pulled away from everyone." Deep sorrow creased his face. "It was why he and your mother divorced. They dealt with their grief in different ways and couldn't find their way back to one another. I tried to keep in touch with him, but he couldn't bear knowing anyone from the life that had you in it."

From Ferreira's reaction, Rafael no longer doubted he'd had *anything* to do with his abduction. Which left only one explanation. The real culprit had left the threads of evidence that would lead to Ferreira, clues that had been so ingenious, the police had missed all of them, and only he with his abilities and reach had found them twenty-four years later.

Eliana told her father Rafael had thought he was the one who'd orchestrated his abduction, and Ferreira's dumb-founded reaction solidified his belief in the man's innocence.

Looking relieved beyond measure, she sought his confirmation, and he rushed to give it to her. "It wasn't him, *meu amor.* As always, your heart is my compass."

After a clinging, tearful kiss, she turned to her father. "Do you have any idea who could have framed you, Daddy?"

Ferreira looked dazedly from his daughter to Rafael, obviously struggling to readjust to everything he thought he knew of the past months since Rafael had entered their lives.

Then Ferreira burst out in belated affront, "You're telling me all this time you thought it was me? You came here to punish me? That's why you went after Ellie?"

"I wasn't part of his plan, Daddy."

Relief and pride spread though Rafael. Her faith in him had been healed, and was back to the purity he now depended on.

"Eliana is why everything was put right," he said gruffly. "Her love pulled me back from the path of destruction and into a life I never thought I'd have. But I need you to think. Anything you can remember around that time would help. It had to be someone who was close to you. Think, Ferreira."

The man blinked numbly. Then he said, "You used to call me Tio Teo."

"I used to love you almost as much as I loved my father." He tried to smile through the pain stabbing in his chest. "But I don't think I can call you that now."

Eliana kissed his shoulder. "How about only Teo?"

Looking down at her, his heart in his eyes, he pledged, "Whatever you wish, *minha alma*."

Suddenly, Teo grabbed his arm. "There's something. When I first met Ellie's mother, she had a stalker. I hired a security specialist to deal with the situation until that stalker was caught. I can't think of anyone else in my whole life who had the kind of skills and underground connections needed to do something like…like…"

Ferreira fell silent, eyes feverish as he chased new realizations, connected seemingly unconnected events.

Then he focused back on Rafael. "He must have realized through me that you were just what that organization was looking for, and he'd had all the access to me he needed to doctor evidence to incriminate me."

"Give me his name."

After Ferreira did so, Rafael rose to his feet and bent to kiss Eliana. "I'll initiate a targeted investigation at once."

"Thank you, *meu amor*," she whispered against his lips.

"Anything and everything for you, *minha vida*. Always."

In an hour, Rafael walked back into his father-in-law's suite. He stopped at the door, savoring the sight of the love of his life curled into her father, with his arm around her and their heads nestled against each other.

Overpowering emotions swept him. And not only for Eliana. But for her father, too. He was again the uncle he'd loved, but now far more, the man whose adoration for his wife had given him Eliana, a being made of total love.

Blinking back the burn behind his eyes, he walked in. And, oh…the welcome, the warmth, he saw on both their faces! He felt any lingering pain and bitterness and rage just drain away.

He came down on his haunches before them, delighting in how Eliana surged forward and took him in her arms, pressing his head to her heart.

"Thank you for believing Daddy, *meu amor*. Even if you can't find proof, it's enough you want to."

"Found anything?" Teo asked anxiously.

Rafael pulled back from her embrace to look at him. "Once I had a name and a connection to you, everything fell…or rather crashed into place. I traced the man's every move and contact and bank account transaction since the day I was abducted. And there's no doubt. It *was* him."

Eliana's choking cry shook his heartstrings as she pulled them both to her, buried her face in their chests in turn and soaked them in her tears of relief.

His own relief was even fiercer, and all for her, that she didn't have to live with something this horrible standing between the two people she loved most, that she wouldn't feel guilty about his ordeals anymore.

After they both kissed and soothed her, he reached for Teo's hand, squeezed it. "I beg your forgiveness, Teo, for believing in your guilt once my investigations led to you. I didn't want it to be you, but when I dug again and again to make sure, I kept finding the same trails."

Teo squeezed his hand back. "It was impossible for you to realize that man's involvement. Anita was so scared of the whole thing, I couldn't tell anyone, even your father." He sighed in regret. "Ironically, it was the massive expenses of hiring that man, and which I couldn't account for, that led to your father dissolving our partnership. And then I lost her, then your father…and that man disappeared from my memory."

His viciousness now targeted the man who'd cost him so much, and who'd almost made him destroy innocent lives. "You don't need to ever think of him again. He's already… being taken care of."

Teo's eyes widened. "You mean you…?"

Eliana clutched her father's arm, cold fire arcing from her eyes. "Rafael will make sure he never hurts anyone else. And that he gets what he deserves."

Teo's surprise at the blade in Eliana's tone was nothing compared to Rafael's. Delight soared as he pulled her closer.

"So my made-for-and-from-love flower can be deadly when defending and avenging the innocent."

The flames in her eyes licked his every nerve. "You bet."

He cocked an eyebrow at her, wanting to see how far she'd go. "So you condone anything I choose to do to that man?"

Her lush lips hardened. "He's no man. He's a monster. And you and your brothers are monster slayers. I know whatever you choose to do to him will be the right thing to do."

Joy swelled inside him as he pulled her closer again. "Have you told Teo our news?"

Her eyes drained of righteous wrath, flooded with shyness. "I didn't ask if you wanted to let anyone know."

Throwing his head back, he guffawed. "'Anyone' didn't

include those six huge pains who've been teasing the hell out of me all day with parenting jokes, huh?"

A fiery flush spread across her exquisite cheekbones. "I sort of let it slip to your trio of terror while I was milking them for info." She mumbled something about poking his blabbing brothers with sharp objects when next she saw them. "And they ran with the news to the rest of the roster!"

"You're pregnant?"

Teo's explosive exclamation snapped their eyes to him, and he threw an arm around each of them, exalting, "I'm going to be a grandfather!"

Eliana kissed him soundly. "I know you've given up on the others and think I'm your only chance at grandbabies. But you're not going to have only one grandchild, but two."

Surprise was now Teo's only expression. "You're having twins? Is it even possible to know that early?"

Eliana got Rafael's silent consent before turning to her father. "We're going to adopt Diego."

Teo slumped back. "Any more monumental, life-changing surprises? Just pour them down on me all at once."

Rafael chuckled again. "That's enough for now."

"More than enough for a lifetime." Teo's eyes filled. "If I die right this moment, I'll be the happiest man on earth."

Rafael gave him a mock-stern look. "Now, Teo, let's not restart our relationship on the wrong foot. The happiest man on earth is me. Got that?"

"If you say so." Teo gave the acquiescing sigh of a man who was letting a younger man think he had his way.

Laughing outright this time, Rafael swept his hugely grinning, teary-eyed bride up in his arms. "I do. Oh, how I do."

"I certainly don't!"

Ellie laughed as her eldest half brother, Leonardo, vehemently denied that he liked having those seminaked photos of him leaked online. They'd gone viral with half the globe's females drooling over him and captioning them no end.

"All those straining muscles and the pouring sweat and provocative poses?" Santiago winked at them. Her middle half brother relished how his looks affected anything that moved, not like Leonardo, the scientist who wanted his brains to be his prominent feature. "No way those masterpieces were without your consent."

"I was exercising," Leonardo growled. "And since when are chest flies, squats and one-armed push-ups provocative poses?"

"*Have* you seen the photos, Leo?" Ellie giggled.

Leonardo harrumphed. "Phones with cameras and the internet will bring civilization to an end."

"Just enjoy the notoriety, Leonardo. It's harmless." Rafael's lips twisted. "I hope."

Leonardo looked at him gratefully. "*Thank you* for recognizing the world is full of nuts."

Suddenly worried, Ellie caught Leonardo's forearm. "Did anyone do anything nutty?"

Leonardo rolled his eyes. "Apart from walking into the lecture hall and finding hearts and chocolate all over the counter or the collection of panties spirited into my briefcase with photos and phone numbers stuck on them? No."

As they all laughed, Carlos, her youngest half brother, and her closest sibling slapped him on the back. "And you didn't share your crop of panties with your brothers?"

Leonardo scowled at him. "Shouldn't you be exporting panties, given the way women throw themselves at you?"

Carlos shuddered. "Not when I've perfected the art of dodging feminine missiles. Unlike you, I don't stand still long enough for them to stuff panties in my personal effects."

As everyone laughed again, Ellie felt euphoric.

After treating the news of Rafael's real identity and his

history with due gravity, her half brothers had proceeded to seamlessly treat him as an old childhood friend, and their very welcome new brother-in-law.

Suddenly, she felt Rafael tense. After looking at his phone, he made their excuses to her brothers.

Heart thudding, she turned away with him and crossed the garden overlooking the ocean where they would have their ceremony. As they rushed, she was again thankful for her both functional and pretty wedding dress—white as snow, embroidered in pearls and sequins, chiffon and satin with a strapless, pleated bodice and a flowing, easy-to-run-in skirt.

Not that *she* could run. "Easy, *amor*."

At her wince, Rafael slowed down at once. They'd ended the previous night by going to bed. After the two weeks of turmoil and alienation, the discharge of passion had been cataclysmic. She was deliciously sore after he'd ravished her again and again, as she'd pleaded for him to, and had spent the day struggling to walk straight.

They reentered the mansion from its western entrance, and her pulse raced with anticipation as they neared the man and woman who stood rooted in the middle of the foyer.

His parents.

She'd begged him to contact them, to let them know that the son they thought they'd lost was alive and well and incredibly happy. She couldn't bear knowing they existed, had that permanent scar of his loss and would not be given the choice to reconnect with him. He'd finally succumbed to her wishes and called them.

His parents, especially his father, had been distraught.

Asking them not to tell anyone until they figured out a safe way to introduce him to his siblings, he'd asked them to attend their wedding. Both he and Numair had sent their private jets to fetch them from their homes in Fortaleza and

Belém. They'd postponed the ceremony to around sunset until his parents could arrive.

Now Rafael was face-to-face with them. Though they'd both known Rafael for the past two years, they'd only known him as his new persona. Now they saw him as their long-lost son come back to life.

It felt surreal to Ellie, meeting his father, Andrés Ríos Navarro, who was also her father's once-best friend. Bianca Franco Molena, his mother, had once been her mother's friend, too.

"I'm so sorry…" Andrés blurted out, swallowed, then he burst into tears. Rafael's mother followed suit.

Rafael pulled his father into a fierce hug. "I'm the one who's sorry I didn't tell you before." He dragged his mother into the hug, and let them weep for all the years of helplessness, dread and heartache as he enclosed them in his power and protection.

When their emotional storm abated, Rafael reached out to Ellie. She rushed to join them in his all-encompassing embrace.

Kissing them all, he smiled gently at his parents, and adoringly at her. "You owe my coming to my senses to my bride, the one who put everything in my life right."

And Ellie found herself in his parents' arms, squeezed and kissed and thanked for the miracle of having their son back.

"It's me who thanks you for giving me the only man I'll ever love," she choked out. "But has he told you my full name?"

Both blinked at her uncomprehendingly. After she told them, they gaped. Then they burst out talking at once.

"Teo's daughter?"

"How is that even possible?"

"Where is Teo?"

"Is he here?"

She hooked her arm into theirs and steered them out to the garden. "He is here, and he's been waiting all my life to see you again."

Their ceremony went without a hitch, and sort of felt like an afterthought. Apart from Rafael's parents meeting her father, and Rafael pulling her father into his embrace as he gave him her hand, and her father finally exchanging his first kiss with Isabella in jubilation after her and Rafael's "I dos," all the monumental stuff had already happened during and after the rehearsal yesterday.

Everyone had retired to their suites after long hours of celebration, and she was in Rafael's arms again. And she couldn't hold her tears back again.

"*Deus, coração,* I can't see your tears even if they're ones of joy…." Then he exclaimed, "Those aren't tears of joy!"

"I'm sorry, *meu amor,* but I don't know if I'll ever finish weeping for the boy you were, for what you lost."

"With what I've gained—you, our coming baby, Diego and even more brothers—I am now obscenely blessed. I even got back everything I lost—my parents, with their new broods sure to follow them. And Teo." He pulled her with him to a reclining position and she burrowed deeper into his chest. "And together we will give our baby and Diego everything I was deprived of, and what even you didn't have, both a mother and father." Suddenly he squeezed her tight. "Who won't let them out of their sights!"

Laughing through the tears, she spluttered, "Don't you go smothering our baby and Diego with love!"

His lips twisted. "Any complaints yourself?"

"Hmm, you've got a point." She pulled him on top of her. "Smother me some more."

"Sorceress." His chuckle poured into her lips.

But as he started making love to her, lightness drained as her hand feathered his scar.

"I wish I had real magic, *meu amor*. I would have erased this scar, its memory and all the memories of your suffering."

"You already have. You found me, *saw* me for what I am. You made me yours and healed all my wounds and erased all my scars." He joined their bodies, swallowed her cry. "Now you'll love me forever. You don't only have magic. You *are* magic."

She wrapped herself around him, inside and out, took him to the very heart of her, and whispered, "Look who's talking…."

* * * * *

MILLS & BOON®

Want to get more from Mills & Boon?

Here's what's available to you if you join the exclusive **Mills & Boon eBook Club** today:

- ✦ *Convenience – choose your books each month*
- ✦ *Exclusive – receive your books a month before anywhere else*
- ✦ *Flexibility – change your subscription at any time*
- ✦ *Variety – gain access to eBook-only series*
- ✦ *Value – subscriptions from just £1.99 a month*

So visit **www.millsandboon.co.uk/esubs** today to be a part of this exclusive eBook Club!